THE
*E*NDLING

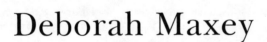

Deborah Maxey

FIREFLY
SOUTHERN FICTION
imprint of Iron Stream Media

Firefly Southern Fiction is an imprint of LPCBooks
a division of Iron Stream Media
100 Missionary Ridge, Birmingham, AL 35242
ShopLPC.com

Cover design by Hannah Linder Designs

Iron Stream Media serves its authors as they express their views, which may not express the views of the publisher.

This is a work of fiction. Names, characters, and incidents are all products of the author's imagination or are used for fictional purposes. Any mentioned brand names, places, and trademarks remain the property of their respective owners, bear no association with the author or the publisher, and are used for fictional purposes only.

Library of Congress Control Number: 2021934269

ISBN-13: 978-1-64526-264-0
EBook ISBN: 978-1-64526-329-6

PRAISE FOR *THE ENDLING*

In *The Endling*, Deborah Maxey grabs you with her first line and takes you on a high octane adventure through mountains and cities. Readers will be flipping pages as fast as possible to see if Maxey's character can find a way to defeat the odds stacked against her by using her Native American background and training. An engrossing read.

~**Ann H. Gabhart**
Bestselling author of *An Appalachian Summer*

Dive into a world of enchanting characters from the small Virginia mountain town of Colony Row. You'll fall in love with Emerson Grace as she unravels the last secret her grandfather left for her to solve. The mystery twists into powerful suspense that leads Emerson back to herself and gives her the wit and strength to stop the sinister plot to her own murder. Powerful.

~**Linda Evans Shepherd**
Bestselling author of *The Potluck Club*

Make room on your bookshelf, because once you've read it, you'll want to keep *The Endling* by Deborah Maxey. With a compelling plot, an element of suspense, memorable characters, and lush descriptions, she's written a page-turner that will draw you into her story. I loved this book!

~**Michelle Cox**
Bestselling author of *Our Daily Biscuit: Devotions with a Drawl*,
Just 18 Summers, and the *When God Calls the Heart* series

The Endling kept me glued to every page. I simply had to have more. *More* of the mountain mysteries. *More* of the compelling characters. And *more* of Emerson, whose quiet dependency on holy guidance gleaned from her ancestors makes for the reader "good medicine." My highest recommendation for a beautifully memorable read!

~**Debora M. Coty**
Award-winning author of over 40 books,
including the *Too Blessed to be Stressed* series

As someone with deep roots in a Native American tribe and in colonial Virginia, I found my attention held page after page to the very end. From the heights of Easterbrook Mountain to the streets of New York City, a lot of research and knowledge went into this story's writing. Highly recommended.

~**Debra DuPree Williams**
Author of *Grave Consequences*

DEDICATION

To Mack. I am the most blessed person
I know to always have your love and support.

ACKNOWLEDGMENTS

Thank you. Yes, *you*! Since my first inkling of an idea for this book, I've wanted to write a story worthy of your time and imagination. Books have touched, changed, inspired, excited, and motivated me my whole life. Characters, dialogue, and plots dance in and out of my memory and consciousness as freely as reality. I am humbled that you are giving me an opportunity to be a part of that for you.

The book you are reading would never have come to fruition if not for my beloved husband Mack. There are truly not enough words to describe the depth of his love and support.

Huge thanks go to Jessica R. Everson, Eagle Eye Editor Extraordinaire. Under her guidance, rough stones became multi-faceted and polished jewels. I'm grateful to everyone at Firefly Southern Fiction for believing in this book.

And, Eva Marie Everson, thank you. I wonder if you knew that voluntarily editing a chapter for a stranger at a writers conference would launch her into this incredible world of her dreams.

The Alpha and Omega of all acknowledgments is to You, Father. You continue to show me that when I leave everything in Your hands, I see You in everything.

You will go out in joy
and be led forth in peace;
the mountains and hills
will burst into song before you,
and all the trees of the field
will clap their hands.
(Isaiah 55:12)

Ask the Lord your God for a sign,
whether in the deepest depths or in the highest heights.
(Isaiah 7:11)

And he answered and said unto them, I tell you that,
if these should hold their peace,
the stones would immediately cry out.
(Luke 19:40 KJV)

CHAPTER ONE

I knew my mountains were full of mysteries, but it had not occurred to me there might be a secret inside the cabin.

I sat back on my heels and closed my eyes. When I opened them, the lines were still there. Deep crevices forming a rectangle in the planks under Grandfather's old oriental rug. This meant that since my first steps—for my whole life, in fact—I had walked over a trap door. Over a secret Grandfather kept from me. I could not remember him ever having done that.

The stone cabin atop Easterbrook Mountain had been my home since birth. When I was two, my mother and grandmother died in a car accident, making Grandfather my legal guardian. Since that time, he had made it his life's mission to teach me everything he knew. There had been no secrets. If his knowledge was to be handed down, it would have to be through me. I was an endling. The last of my tribe.

So why had he kept the trap door from me?

Tears caused the dark lines to wave and then blur. I blinked to clear my vision. I had no chance now of him telling me why he had not shared such a big secret.

Grandfather had loved surprises. He delighted in teaching major life lessons through what he called "mystery hunts." They always began the same way. I would stumble upon a tin box in an obscure place—beneath a roosting hen, deep in the hollow of a tree, hidden in a bale of hay—then turn and find Grandfather standing nearby. He would smile, his eyes closed, and nod twice—his signature of approval. Inside the box, I would find instructions to begin unraveling the mystery.

If I turned now, would I see his spirit standing nearby? Would I catch the morning light reflecting from his long, gray hair? Would he be wearing the white buckskins he was buried in or one of the plaid flannel shirts he so loved to wear? To turn and not see him would only stir the hot ashes of my grief into a flame. So I did not turn. I closed my eyes instead to imagine that he was there, my mind's eye revealing his joy when I found his hidden treasures.

I drew my thoughts back to the wood pattern in the hundred-year-old oak floor as I pulled the band down my long brown ponytail and rewrapped it in a bun. I crawled my way around the dark lines to the edge that held the hinges. It was a bit wider than the others. There was no doubt about it—this was a trap door.

I rested back on my knees, pressed my palms flat to my thighs. Why on earth would we have a trap door in the cabin? My ancestors had lived here since before the Civil War. Was it that old?

I allowed my fingertips to examine the depth of the crevices in the wood, as though it were braille, and stuck the thick nail of my thumb into one of the cracks. A fingernail would not be enough. I would need a tool. A screwdriver would work.

My moccasins were silent against the great room hardwood, and again when I reached the kitchen's shiny greenstone floor on the other side of the fireplace. The large L-shaped island and its dark gray slate top were cluttered with the groceries I had brought in when I arrived late the night before, too tired to unpack them. The jumbled top contrasted greatly with the rest of my orderly kitchen, bare countertops and no appliances other than a coffee maker. A must.

I opened the pantry door and swung my hand like a blind ninja to find the pull string. The bulb in the tiny windowless room blinked but stayed on, allowing me to find the toolboxes on the middle shelf, directly in front of the door. Grandfather's gray toolbox was rusted around the edges and showed years of use. My small red box still had a shiny coat.

As if their size and color were not enough to distinguish them, the Christmas I received mine, he had allowed me to paint our names on them. I had started with his box. I painted *Edward Two Eagles* across the center. When I got to mine, I did not account for its smaller size and wrote my first name—*Emerson*—too large. The result was that my middle and last name—*Grace Coffee*—were written so tightly, the letters were barely legible. But Grandfather had only nodded his approval. "We will surely know one from the other now, Little Bit." A tight knot formed in my throat. If only I could hear him call me that once more.

I reached into Grandfather's box and grabbed the largest flathead screwdriver, then walked back to the great room. Sunlight slanted through the skylights in the tin roof, illuminating the warm reds and browns of the cedar-covered walls and ceiling. Light splattered across the beige sectional leather couch that sat in attendance, waiting for the accompaniment of a roaring fire in the massive greenstone fireplace.

I squatted on the side of the door opposite the hinges, facing the fireplace. Sure enough, a small indention showed me where a fulcrum had been used to open the door. I put the edge of the tool into the black line and began to push down on the handle, but the frantic sound of crows, unusually loud, drew my attention.

Caw, caw, caw!

Crows are sentinels. They band together and cry when their sanctity is disturbed, scolding the offender in loud, repetitive tones. Beneath the rising volume of their calls, I could hear heavy engine sounds. An automobile coming up the mountain. Fast. No one who knew Easterbrook Mountain would drive that way. And no one would come up by accident. Our driveway was hidden, and the cabin was the only destination.

Caw, caw, caw!

I flew into protective mode. No one could know what I had found. I still did not know what it was myself. I hurried to roll the rug back over the trap door. It more than covered the lines. No wonder I had never noticed them.

I stilled to listen for the vehicle, scolding myself for not staying aware, for not hearing the sounds sooner. I had been totally preoccupied.

Caw, caw, caw!

With giant steps I reached the open screen door and listened. Someone was coming up the mountain swiftly, about two minutes away. I shoved the heavy oak front door shut and locked it, bracing my stiffened arms against the wood, calculating the time I had left. I could not remember ever having locked the door when I was at home before.

I stepped back to look through the windows that ran the length of the front of the cabin. Something was not right. My scalp crawled, my spider senses alerting me.

If Madeline or Aunt Hattie were coming, they would call. Nothing good came up the mountain without notice. The only times were to bring bad news or the two times people came to start a "raid on Injuns." Men with lit torches had piled in the back of pickup trucks, and waved guns in the air as they shouted their demands, threatening to return with the Ku Klux Klan if we did not get out of Rockcliff County. Both times, Grandfather and I had stayed behind the front door and waited until the local sheriff's department came up, sirens blaring, threatening arrests.

But, as Grandfather predicted, there were never any arrests.

The engine sounds became louder as the vehicle approached. Whoever it was, they were almost here. I laid my hand over my chest and tried to take a deep breath. Was I overreacting? I rubbed at the hairs rising on my arms. No. This was real.

Caw, caw, caw!

I watched until a four-door black SUV pulled up toward the veranda, its windows dark with tint. As it approached, I was able to make out government plates. It stopped several yards back from the veranda's wide steps, and the front doors on either side opened simultaneously.

Beneath each door, a pair of polished shoes fell to the ground in a synchronized move. The men stepped out and into view. Both wore black dress suits and dark sunglasses. The driver was tall and thin. The passenger much shorter, stockier, his forehead high from balding. I moved behind the door and pressed my back against it.

Footfall on the steps told me that the men were of equal weight and walked with determination. They were sure of themselves. Thought they had every right to come up my private driveway and walk so purposefully onto my veranda.

The door vibrated against my back with their knocks. Hard. Loud. Insistent.

I waited, my breath shallow.

They knocked again. Harder this time. I did not have a plan, other than knowing I would not open the door. Maybe they had come to the wrong place. If I did not answer would they leave?

"Ms. Coffee?" one of them shouted through the door.

I froze. Their arrival was not a mistake.

"Ms. Coffee?" The voice was louder.

They knew my name. They looked like government officials of some sort, and I could sense their entitlement with the determination of their steps and knocks. My knees wobbled. "Yes," I replied in a flat tone.

"We are with the US Marshals Office. I'm Marshal Davidson, and I'm here with Marshal Stinnett. We need to speak with you."

Me? What in the world could US marshals want with me? How did they even find me? I had only come back home from New York City last night. Not to mention, there was no mailbox along Colony Row. We used a post office box.

As though they could read my mind, the other man spoke boldly through the door. "Madeline Matthews said she texted you."

They had talked to Madeline. I was close to only two people on earth, and these men had invaded that tiny circle. Punctured my privacy. Anger flew through me.

My fingers fumbled with the denim flap covering the back pocket of my jeans as I struggled to pull my phone free. My index finger trembling, I punched the home button and pulled up the screen. Sure enough, there it was. A text from Madeline: *US Marshals on the way up.*

Your Aunt Hattie and I are worried. Please call ASAP.

I had not heard the vehicle or the text. It had taken a murder of crows to get my attention.

I turned toward the door and looked through the peephole. Both men had removed their sunglasses. They must have noticed me peeking out because both lifted their badges. I smoothed my hair back, then opened the door about a foot. I stared at their badges and then at them. The taller one was Davidson.

They put their badges away. Davidson spoke first.

"Ms. Coffee, we hate to disturb you."

"You have come at a bad time. What is this about?"

"Ma'am, can we come in and speak with you?"

"You will need to tell me what this is about." I looked from one man to the next, hoping to read something in their faces.

Stinnett, the shorter one, spat his words with impatience. "I expect you'd better speak with us."

I looked him in the eyes to make it clear I was not someone he could intimidate. What I saw in Stinnett's expression settled me in a strange way. I had seen the look before. Always with those who held disdain for Natives. His prejudice would not affect me. Bigotry was not new. This I could handle. This, Grandfather had prepared me for. A steely resolve gave me oppositional strength, curiosity, and determination to face them.

But what came next sent a charge of electricity up my spine.

"Ms. Coffee, your life is in danger."

CHAPTER TWO

I went numb for a moment, then the reality of Stinnett's words found my center, wrapping itself tightly around my chest like a bandage, squeezing the air out of me. I reminded myself to focus on keeping a neutral appearance. I might be anxious, but I would fight like a grizzly to keep them from seeing it.

I pushed the door open. Both men moved back, and I stepped outside.

Davidson gestured to a sitting area on the veranda. I walked to the porch swing on the west side and took a seat in the middle. The men each pulled a wooden rocking chair around to face me, then sat.

A light breeze flowed across the mountaintops and fanned the fine hair around my face. Their hair moved in a mass. Both men used hairspray. I detected two different versions of aftershave.

Davidson spoke first. "We apologize if we've come at a bad time." He eyed me with scrutiny as though he were comparing me to my driver's license photo. "I need to begin with some preliminary questions."

I gave him a quick nod of agreement.

With his right hand, he reached into his inner-left suit pocket and pulled out a small leather-bound notebook with a slim sliver pen attached, then opened to a blank page. "You are Emerson Grace Coffee."

He had made a statement. He had not posed a question.

"Ms. Coffee, it is our understanding that until just a few days ago you legally resided on Fourth Avenue in New York City. You moved there in September of last year to begin a residency as a researcher for Information Station Publishing."

I nodded.

"You have owned Crawl, Crow, and Easterbrook Mountains since your grandmother and mother died in a car accident when you were two. Your grandfather, Edward Two Eagles Coffee, raised you, homeschooling you most of your life."

The matrilineal nature of my tribe was common knowledge. Women own the property, homes, and children. I, not Grandfather, inherited the mountains. As a researcher, I knew the information he taunted me with was simple to find. But what reason did they have for researching my life?

Again, I nodded.

"Your father is unknown."

Now he was treading where he should not.

My stomach knotted. He had obviously seen my birth certificate, but I could not fathom how this was necessary. Why was my life suddenly transparent? How was this not an invasion of my privacy? A violation? My hands trembled. I placed them under my thighs to still them and keep them out of sight. My movement put the swing into slight motion, causing the chain to creak.

If they knew so much, they might also know my mother had been severely injured at thirteen when a group of Native and Caucasian boys got drunk on moonshine, then raped her. She had suffered near death to carry and deliver me. I never learned the identity of the other person whose DNA I shared. "Unknown father" was listed on my birth certificate. But none of this was information I spoke about. Ever. Of course, that never stopped bullies. Growing up, I had not escaped the cruelty of being tormented for the violent act that created me.

"Is that correct as well, Ms. Coffee?"

"Why are you here?"

Davidson looked over at Stinnett. He had passed the baton. Stinnett took a deep breath and straightened his shoulders. He appeared happy to oblige.

"Four weeks ago, in New York, you had dinner with your friend Sasha Waring. She was your coworker until July when she left to open a gift shop in Soho called A Little Bit of Heaven." He paused and looked at Davidson, lowering his voice as though he was speaking only to his partner when he said, "She sells angels." His disrespect for Sasha's inventory was obvious.

Stinnett tilted his head slightly and shook it just a bit. He wanted me to know he found the whole conversation obnoxious. Not once did he make eye contact with me. It was clear he thought he was smarter. And better.

Or, more likely, smarter and better than Natives.

Davidson leaned forward, offering a Mona Lisa smile. Their good cop, bad cop routine needed work.

"Ms. Coffee, we're not your enemies. We're here because we want to protect you. We're trying to show you that even though your lifestyle has always been extremely, let's say, reclusive, it's still very possible to know a lot about you. And you weren't difficult to find."

Good cop sat back and stared at me. A long moment passed.

He leaned forward again and lowered his voice. "We are not the only ones looking for you."

Stinnett interjected, his voice like a stabbing knife. "You're being hunted, Ms. Coffee."

I could not seem to gather my thoughts. None of what they said made any sense. Why were they talking about Sasha? Why would anyone hunt *me*? What was the connection?

Davidson took a deep breath and licked the edge of his bottom lip. "We have surveillance video from four weeks ago when you and Sasha Waring were in Greenwich Village. Do you recall a man barging out of a black limousine in front of the East West Café, just after you and Ms. Waring locked up her storefront?"

Sasha and I had gone to dinner. Memorable because it was only one of two times I had ever gone to a restaurant in New York during my residency. And I did recall the incident.

I looked to Davidson and nodded.

Davidson drew a deep breath. The muscles in his face appeared to relax. He looked down and held the pen in his right hand, kept it poised over the blank page. "Can you tell us everything that happened?" he asked as he clicked his pen.

"I remember stepping back for a man in a limousine to get out of the car. There was a taxi's horn blowing from the street. The driver was angry that someone was taking so long to park. The people in the back of the cab were not paying attention to any of it."

I looked from one man to the other. They were both quiet, signaling me to go on. I shrugged. I did not know what else they wanted to hear.

Davidson cleared his throat. "Ms. Coffee, please tell us everything you can remember about the man who exited that limousine."

I looked down a few moments to gather my thoughts. I shrugged again and shook my head.

Davidson leaned forward. His eyes had softened, and he wore a frown. "Ma'am, we have surveillance video from the bank across the street that shows you and Ms. Waring were both looking at the man as he exited the limo. Please try. Tell us anything you can remember."

I looked over at the black SUV sitting in my driveway and focused on the cluster of trees reflected in its freshly waxed paint. I had not wanted to go out to dinner that night. I had ignored my instincts.

"I remember the smell of garlic and freshly baked bread."

"What did you *see*, Ms. Coffee?" Stinnett said.

I looked at him defiantly and answered in a steady monotone stream. "Sasha and I were walking close to the curb to avoid the tables near the street. I was in front of Sasha. The cab driver blew his horn. I looked at the driver and the people in the back of the cab. I paid no attention to the man."

Stinnett's nostrils flared as he growled his next words. "The man that almost knocked you down was Anthony Enaldo, an assassin. A hired killer. He went straight into the cafe and planted a *bullet* between another man's eyes. And you, Ms. Coffee are on a video that shows you looking at him." Stinnett's chin jutted out with his last words. He let it hang there, like a physical exclamation point, while he glared at me.

I looked out at the blue of the mountains to gather my thoughts. A casual dinner with a friend had resulted in a target on my back. And Sasha's. I had encountered evil before, but never a murderer. Had I really come close enough to touch a killer and had no awareness, no intuitive feeling?

I looked up at both men. Their expressions had not changed.

"Do you recall hearing about the shooting on the news?" Davidson asked.

"No. I do not watch the news."

Davidson shifted forward in his seat, planted his elbows on his knees, and looked down at the veranda floor for a moment, then back at me. "The wrong people have a copy of that video, and they know that we have it too. They'll expect us to look for you. They've already identified Ms. Waring. Our inside sources say they're close to identifying you." He paused and his eyebrows drew together in a frown. "When was the last time you spoke to Ms. Waring?"

"Not since that night."

"So, you aren't close?"

"Sasha was a coworker. She was kind to me when Grandfather died last March. She knew my residency was almost over in New York and called to invite me to see her shop before I left the city. So I went. But no, we are not close."

They both frowned, then waited for my next move.

"Who are these *wrong* people who have the video?"

Davidson leaned back. The rocker squeaked. "They're the mob, Ms. Coffee."

Cold chills swept over me.

Their story sounded like a movie. A bad movie. But if what they said was true, this evil was real. I wanted to rub the gooseflesh from my arms, but I would not let them see how they had affected me. A vague notion of pain shooting through my flesh brought me back. I willed my fingernails to let go of the underside of my thighs and my body to relax against the swing, then struggled to ask my next question with normal volume and inflection.

"Is Sasha okay?"

Davidson shook his head. " I'm sorry, no. She's deceased."

I unconsciously sucked in a quick gulp of air. "How did she die?"

Davidson hesitated. I noted the light changing in his eyes when he looked left before responding. My research in neuro-linguistic programming taught me that when right-handed people are lying or imagining, they sometimes look left before they speak. Davidson was hiding something.

"Unknown causes."

Both men allowed silence. It had become obvious that they were quiet whenever they wanted me to react. I remained quiet too. Eventually, Davidson continued.

"We have experts on staff and a lot of tools. We have psychologists, hypnotists, forensic artists, and any number of techniques that can help you remember. We can help you recall what you saw so that you can identify him. You can help us get this guy off the streets. There is no telling how many more times he will kill if we don't."

But I had not looked at the man. No memory could occur.

"We can guarantee you will be safe. Much safer than you would be isolated up here. If you agree to testify in federal court, we can take you into protective custody and assure your safety. You'll be assigned agents that will be your roommates at an undisclosed location until the court date, then you'll be reassigned to another location to live. You'll have a new identity and a handler available to help you whenever you need it."

My first thought was of Grandfather, who had spent his life teaching me to be self-sufficient on these mountains. They were proposing that I abandon everything and allow the government into my life. That I rely on the government to protect me until the day I die. The same government that had waged genocide on Natives. The idea seemed ludicrous. But Sasha was dead, all because we were in the wrong place at the wrong time. And I was next. I swallowed to loosen a knot that was growing in my throat.

Davidson continued. "Ms. Coffee, I know this is a lot to take in, but I assure you we are not wrong. You *are* in danger. Even with Anthony Enaldo incarcerated right now, we are gravely concerned about his boss Ginnova Giovanni. These men are ruthless. You need our protection."

My heart pounded hard against my chest. They wanted to protect me now because they wanted my testimony. But what would happen when their experts came back with the truth? That I had no testimony. That I saw nothing. I would be on my own. "And I never return home?" I hated that my voice rose almost an octave asking a question I already knew the answer to.

Davidson nodded. "Yes, ma'am. We'll help you get established somewhere else."

I was taught that everything in nature speaks the will of God. To use nature to settle me, trust it to give me guidance if I focused on my surroundings. That, if necessary, even the rocks would cry out.

I turned to look out over the Blue Ridge mountaintops scalloped against the sky for as far as I could see. I moved my eyes to the sheer rock face of Crawl Mountain across from us, where my ancestors hid in caves during the Indian Removal of 1830. My family had found safety there and later offered that same protection to slaves and runaway soldiers during the Civil War. These mountains were my roots. My sanctuary. The same view that spoke to me now had greeted my ancestors at the start of each day. Nothing had changed. Grandfather and I had always been determined to keep it that way. How could I leave and not defend it? How could I let all he and others had sacrificed be worthlessly tossed away?

I looked at the men. "And if I left, what would happen to the mountains?"

"The government would take ownership to help pay for your relocation."

Certainly they realized how insulting the proposition of giving up land was to a Native.

"You will be instrumental in helping us bring this man to justice," Davidson added, as though it were his winning argument.

Justice? These men invade my life and now they have the nerve to speak to me, a Native woman, about justice?

The hairs on my arms stood tall in what Grandfather called "an anointing"—a divine plan flowing through my body. I pulled my hands from beneath my thighs and laid them in my lap. I looked from one man to the next and spoke with the resolve of all my ancestors, echoing back centuries.

"I will never leave my mountains."

CHAPTER THREE

The sound of the marshals' SUV waxed and waned as it made its way down Easterbrook, taking the curves far faster than caution would warn. As though there were nothing else to consider, I sat listening, testing myself on which curve they had entered or exited. The bend to the right with the giant hickory tree where ice formed every winter and never melted. The small dip near the oak grove where heavy spring rains collected and left puddles for days.

A strange sense of suspended animation stopped me cold and held me down on the swing. Only my eyes and chest seemed able to move. Like a stunned bird that flies into a window then lies in the grass until some internal process takes over, I was frozen. When the SUV revved its engine on Colony Row below my mountain, I shifted my focus.

There was something familiar about being frozen. What memory was it jogging? Something long packed away, out of reach of my conscious mind's grasp. Suddenly, just as the sun breaks through on a cloudy day, the recall emerged. Third grade. At home after what would be my last day of public school. Grandfather's devastation at my utter brokenness. At my desk, paralyzed, ruggedly shorn by dull scissors, two feet of hair braid cut off and stretched in front of me.

When he saw the depths of my inability to cope, he concentrated his life on building my defenses. Overcoming fear, being powerful not powerless, action not re-action, facing not avoiding fear. For these and many other skills he would devise ways of teaching me.

One lesson he used was "counting coup." In his version, my goal was to stealthily enter a difficult place without him noticing and leave a feather or stone to signal that I had been there. My first big success came when he found me one morning, stretched out his hand, and showed me the stone I had left on his bedside table while he slept. He closed his eyes, smiled, and nodded twice.

My courage built enough with each trial that, eventually, I waded through bees to leave an arrowhead near the hive where he would find it when he harvested honey.

Gradually, my lessons became more challenging as I learned the skills of tracking bears and eventually leading Grandfather to them. Soon, nothing on our mountains caused me to back down or away. In so many ways, he taught me to be brave. And I thought I was. But now, that kind of bravery seemed like child's play.

Thoughts and memories continued to swirl, but none would stay seated long enough to be examined. I looked out to the blue of the mountains and inhaled the cold morning air until it seemed I had moved back into myself. I had no doubts about my decision to avoid witness protection. There was no vacillation on my part. But duty reminded me that major decisions should involve the wisdom of my elders.

Though neither was blood kin, both Aunt Hattie and Madeline had served as surrogate mothers since my own mother had entered the Spirit World. My grandmother, Pale Whispering Moon, had been the one to honor Hattie, her best friend since childhood, with the title of "Aunt." They had been closer than sisters. Madeline had grown up next door and was always like an adopted daughter to Aunt Hattie. Now that Grandfather was part of the Spirit World, these two women were the only constants left in my life.

I entered the cabin and paused in front of the oriental rug and the trap door that lay hidden beneath. Whatever was below the floor would have to wait. I grabbed my keys and checked the locks on the back door and windows. The beginning of a new normal.

Driving down Easterbrook, my foot alternated between the brake and gas. I shook my head to clear other thoughts; lack of concentration could be perilous, no matter how many times I had driven down the mountainous curves. Despite my efforts to focus on steering, thoughts fired repeatedly, as though a concealed sniper sat in my head, jolting me with adrenaline and demanding my attention.

What if Aunt Hattie and Madeline said I should enter witness protection? I had always accepted their counsel. If I did not this time, would they still love me? Trust me? Feel valued and respected? l was taught their decision was as valuable as Grandfather's. Were elders always right? Should I rate their guidance over my instincts again? I had done exactly that when both mothers and Grandfather advised that I take the internship in New York, suggesting that at twenty-two years old with no experience and an online degree, the opportunity would fit me. As a researcher for magazines and universities, I would be able to work from the cabin. And all three believed that leaving the remoteness of Easterbrook to live in the city would catapult me past my demand for isolation. Grandfather had said being brave and living around millions in New York would make small towns, small talk, and communicating with strangers easy, "like adapting to a vast ocean then returning to a bathtub."

Gravel popped beneath my tires, unusually loud. I jumped in reflex and overcorrected, my right front tire leaving the gravel for the hard-packed dark mountain dirt in a slight ditch. Within moments of returning to the familiar ruts in the driveway, avoiding small holes, an occasional tree branch my SUV would easily drive over, the knots of worry returned with strength. My instincts were clearly warning me.

I was being hunted. My life was at stake, every plan for my future unraveled. All because I went somewhere I did not want to be, did something I did not want to do, and denied the strong instincts that cried out from every cell in my body not to go. If I had listened to those instincts, I would never have left Easterbrook. If I had been less interested in pleasing others, I would never have gone out with Sasha. And if I had not gone to New York, I would have been home to take care of Grandfather. I would have known he was ill. Would have been there when he transitioned to the Spirit World.

And I would not be in danger.

No one would want to kill me.

I drove out of my driveway and into the clearing at Stopping Place, where Easterbrook Spring empties from a natural crevice in the rocks, and people pull off of Colony Row to stop and fill containers with fresh mineral water. Something within me settled into an old rhythm of my former self, of trusting child to loving parent. Looking straight across Colony Row, down Aunt Hattie's driveway and toward her porch, I knew I would be met with a scene as old as myself, as predictable as daybreak. Aunt Hattie, who rarely missed any action near her home, always came out on her porch, no matter the weather, to await me. Madeline was usually with her.

I sat for a moment in the clearing large enough for three parked cars and waited. I wanted to encode the memory of seeing them keep an unspoken promise to wait for me. Within moments, Aunt Hattie's front door opened, and there they stood. Loving sentinels. Anticipating the sight of me. How could I resent any guidance they had ever given out of their best intentions for me?

Even from a distance, Aunt Hattie's tiny eighty-something frame seemed smaller and more bent than just seven months before when Grandfather died. Her gray cap of curls shimmered in the sunshine. She bobbed her head as if to say, "Here she comes."

Never without a bib apron, Aunt Hattie wore a flower-patterned one now, which covered most of her calf-length floral dress. Her patterns never matched, nor was that ever a concern to her. Using both hands, she smoothed the apron over her small stomach, an act I had witnessed hundreds of times before.

Madeline, in her sixties, towering three heads over Aunt Hattie, looked toward Stopping Place as well. Looked for me. As always, a silk scarf was tied around her head to cover the ravaging nodules of neurofibromatosis that had created hair loss many years ago. Today the scarf was cobalt blue.

I crossed Colony Row, drove six hundred feet up Aunt Hattie's driveway, and came to a stop in front of the sidewalk. Madeline reached over and gave Aunt Hattie's shoulder a squeeze, and my eldest mother looked up and nodded. Neither smiled. A rare occurrence. Their concern was clear.

For a little while, I could let them nurture me with their care. Allow myself to accept and surrender to their sanctuary. The tightness in my chest began to loosen, and I could breathe deeply. I was not alone.

They watched as I walked up the sidewalk to the front porch steps. Aunt Hattie gathered me into a wordless hug. Madeline did the same, then Aunt Hattie looped an arm through mine. "Let's get in the watchin' room."

The three of us stepped through the heavy walnut door of her white clapboard farmhouse.

"I seen them marshals flying up that mountain like their pants was on fire. Didn't waste no time a-tall getting back down neither," Aunt Hattie said.

She steered us to the sunroom Uncle Bill had built on the front of the house before he passed eleven years ago. Even on the darkest of days, the glass walls made everything brighter.

Over the years, the room's décor had been modified to accommodate Aunt Hattie's comfort, much like a pair of old shoes. Family pictures, books, and devotionals sat neatly on cherry tables. With no matching style or color theme, Aunt Hattie's crocheted afghans and pillow tops created a riot of color and warmth. But the room's main function sat dead center. The watching chair—a forest-green recliner with overstuffed upholstery. And within arm's reach, binoculars laid in wait, ready to take in the view of Colony Row, Stopping Place, and my mountaintops that stretched out for miles in front of her.

"I told Madeline, you watch. Our girl is gon' tell us what they wanted as soon as she can get herself down Easterbrook. And sure enough, here you are."

Madeline nodded. "She did, hun."

I took a seat in my usual spot, a brown wingback on the other side of Aunt Hattie's watching chair, and looked out at the familiar view. Aunt Hattie sighed as she dropped into her chair. She smoothed her apron over her lap and straightened. Madeline sat on Aunt Hattie's other side in a wingback chair that matched mine.

"All right, Emerson," Aunt Hattie said. "We are ready whenever you are."

I avoided their loving faces, knowing emotions would likely spill out of me. So, I studied my hands. Once I began, the words came in a rush. Within minutes, I had filled them in on what Davidson and Stinnett had said, eventually giving me the strength to look at them and determine their reactions. Both frowned and took in my words silently.

I took care to share the marshals' exact words, without inflection, recounting every detail that I could recall. Grandfather had trained me not to share my thoughts, beliefs, or emotions when asking for guidance. As I spoke, both of my mothers seemed to press their backs into their chairs, as if my words pushed them. Aunt Hattie's mouth dropped open. Madeline shook her head slowly.

"I ask you both for your counsel. What do you think I should do?"

I wanted them to instantly tell me it was unthinkable for me to consider leaving the mountains. I wanted them, without a moment's hesitation, to be irate at the very idea. Aunt Hattie was usually so openly passionate and outspoken about things. Clearly, this decision would not be spontaneous.

Aunt Hattie drew a deep breath, turned her head, and looked for a long moment at Madeline before turning back to me. "Well, that right there is a mouthful. Might be the biggest decision I ever knew anybody to have to make." She stilled for a moment and looked out the window, then shook her head before looking back at me. "It sounds to me like them marshals was trying to scare you into signing up."

I did not confirm or deny that I agreed. I looked to Madeline. Her eyebrows were pinched in concern. As usual, she was silent, waiting for her elder to take the lead.

Aunt Hattie took a deep breath and straightened in her chair. Her face was stern. Her jaw set. My stomach flipped. I waited on full alert for her to continue.

I looked down at my hands folded in my lap. They were calm. Not shaking as I expected. How deceitful hands can be. When I looked up, Madeline tilted her head to the side, her eyes softening. Seeing the concern in their faces as they studied me brought me up suddenly. How selfish of me. I was not the only one affected by what the marshals had said. I had come counting on them to hand me the solution. But my news affected them too. No wonder they did not answer right away. They couldn't help me. At their age, it was my turn to take care of them. Why had I not realized that?

They had changed so much in the seven months since Grandfather's funeral. Madeline's neurofibromatosis was a bit more obvious now. Since she was a teen, the disease had migrated from café-au-lait spots on her shoulders to hard knots on her torso. In the last ten years, the landscape of her disease began encroaching on her forehead, neck, and toward her face, exposing hard lumps and bumps where clothing could no longer conceal them. Now the fibrous skin bubbles were creeping up over the edges of her jawbone.

Madeline nodded and poked out her bottom lip in an obvious pout. "We hate seeing our girl suffer." The corners of her blue eyes crinkled with a smile when she caught my eye. She had seen me looking at her jaw, but what she offered in return was only love. She had lived her whole life with curious stares and ridicule, yet it never appeared to affect her.

I looked at Aunt Hattie. So tiny. There were more creases on her face. Her skin was thinner and bluer and sprinkled with brown age spots. An urgent need to cherish every moment with these two women engulfed me. I had not anticipated Grandfather's death. I could not repeat that mistake. I could not leave them now when they needed me most.

The sound of gravel crunching beneath a vehicle on Colony Row drew our attention. A black pickup rolled into view.

"That new artist, Jons," Aunt Hattie announced. "Madeline, the other night I seen Miah, that little girl of his, walking around holding Maestro. I think she's done kidnapped your cat."

"Not to worry, honey. Maestro comes home to eat."

The truck passed, and the silence in the watching room was deafening. Aunt Hattie sat for what seemed like an eternity with her eyes closed. Finally, she leaned forward to pat my knee, then looked down at her gnarled hand on my jeans. When she raised her eyes, I saw tears forming in them, and the muscles in my shoulders, neck, and jaw tightened. She did not like what she had decided.

I placed my tanned fingers over hers.

When she spoke, her voice quivered. "I'm scared, Emerson. My insides are just a-shaking. And I ain't got no right in this world to speak into a decision like this. That's the plain truth of it. If losing you to witness protection means you get to lead a long life and be happy somewhere else, how can I tell you to stay? You're my girl. You've always been my girl. This is like asking me to tell my own child to do something that could get her killed."

The bitter taste of bile worked its way up to my mouth. I swallowed hard to keep it down.

Aunt Hattie looked down at my hand over hers and squeezed my knee. "You know, I was praying to the good Lord above just now, and I'm rightly scared to tell you what I think He said. And I don't usually worry none after I hear Him." She looked at me, her eyes soft with hurt. "But this here decision . . . this one don't bring me no kind of peace."

CHAPTER FOUR

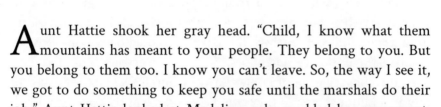

Aunt Hattie shook her gray head. "Child, I know what them mountains has meant to your people. They belong to you. But you belong to them too. I know you can't leave. So, the way I see it, we got to do something to keep you safe until the marshals do their job." Aunt Hattie looked at Madeline, who nodded her agreement. As though a backpack full of mountain rocks had been lifted off my shoulders, my muscles softened.

Aunt Hattie pulled her hand free and patted my arm. "Emerson, you've never been one to pretend to be somebody you ain't. And there's no telling what them marshals might do to get you to remember something. They might plant some idea in your head to suit themselves, or shock your brain, or . . . well, no telling. If you ask me, if you was supposed to remember that man Enaldo, *God* would have had you remember him." She sat back in her watching chair. "And it don't matter a whit to me if they ain't never lost nobody in that program. You ain't gone be the first."

She pointed out the window. "Now, you looky here, Emerson Grace Coffee." Aunt Hattie made a sweep with her hand to the landscape beyond the glass wall. "Ain't nothing getting past me. I'm gon' be your lookout." She sat up straighter and looked over at Madeline. "We can come up with a plan. I guarantee it."

Madeline again nodded her agreement. Aunt Hattie took the bottom of her apron, shook it, smoothed it over her stomach, and spread it flat over her knees. She had said her piece.

When Madeline looked my way, I raised my eyebrows and lowered my chin, inviting her to speak.

"Well, honey, if you ask me," she began, "you are in a no-win situation. I agree with the marshals. You certainly can't contact the folks you work for in New York. It's too risky. Even if Enaldo doesn't make bail, you still have his boss Giovanni looking for you. So maybe you should go somewhere else for a while. Or you could stay with me at Maple Grove. You know it's built like Fort Knox."

Madeline's estate was surrounded by a ten-foot-high stone wall with two twelve-foot iron gates. Her father had made billions investing in railroads and coal, buying all the land he could on Colony Row to "control for unsavory neighbors." To him, everyone was unsavory, even the congregation of Poplar Grove Church. When they asked to buy an additional acre so they could expand, he purchased the church instead.

"And, honey," she continued. "Did the marshals tell you that Sheriff Rick Martin is your liaison?"

I nodded. Once the men understood that nothing was going to change my mind, they had given me a rundown of some details and what I could expect.

"Did they mention he's your neighbor?"

I shook my head.

"Well, he built an A-frame on the land his family owned and moved in about three months ago. And of course your Aunt Hattie has already spoiled him rotten. He certainly hasn't gone hungry. Sheriff Martin will take a personal interest, I feel sure."

"You are so right, Madeline Olivia Matthews," Aunt Hattie said, smacking her leg for emphasis. "That right there is what we need. We need us a sheriff, not a marshal."

Their anxiety had lifted a little with the thought of the sheriff. Of course, he would look out for the two of them and perhaps me, but lead weights lined my stomach when I thought about Enaldo or Giovanni anywhere nearby. Surely the sheriff couldn't quit his job to stake out the area. And innocent people might be caught up in the mob's web. I took a deep breath. "One more thing. The marshals said Enaldo's MO is to take out his target only. But I am still worried about . . . collateral damage. Who else is on Colony Row?"

Aunt Hattie spoke. "Good question. Let's see. Other than the artists . . . well, Sheriff Martin for one. There's the Crocker farm on the south end. It's been empty since they moved to Maryland, but they still own that trailer across the street that they rent out. Two little girls been living there with their Aunt Stella since last spring. Their mama's in jail for life 'cause she killed a man in a bar fight, but that Stella ain't much better. She's rough as a cob. Rick's gone down there many a-time to bust up a party, but them little sisters ain't never there."

Aunt Hattie turned to Madeline. "I won't be nary bit surprised to hear you done bought both the farm *and* the trailer from the Crockers. All you'd need then is my house and Rick's and you'd own everything on Colony Row. Of course, you gon' get this one soon as I make my big exit."

Madeline smiled. "You'd better not exit anytime soon, Hattie Mae. You can't leave me here alone with nothing but eccentric artists."

Aunt Hattie threw her head back laughing. "You're right as rain. I have to say, we've had us some strange art people over the years. But *this* year you've got yourself a batch of strange ones in a whole different way. This here group is the most self-centered, disconnected bunch I ever did see."

Madeline nodded. "I agree. The weekly potlucks don't seem to help draw them together either."

"But don't let that worry you none, Emerson. I know with all my heart," Aunt Hattie said, her voice louder and stronger when she turned to me, "that this is the exact right bunch of people to be here in case you need 'em. God don't make no mistakes."

"Emerson," Madeline began, "we want you to come to a potluck to meet them all. But you raise a good question, and the more I think about it, we do have to let the artists know what the marshals said and give them a chance to decide if they want to finish their residencies."

My stomach flipped. I knew she was right, but the warning Davidson had given just before he left my veranda repeated in my head: *Two people can keep a secret as long as one of them is dead.* Telling all of Colony Row about Enaldo might be the right thing to do, but it might also get me killed.

Aunt Hattie looked at me; her voice lowered. "Now you listen here, Emerson Grace. One thing you ain't got to doubt nary bit. I'll be your watch out. You tell me everything you hear about that man and I'll file it in the big file." She pointed to her curly gray hair. "I lose a few things ever now and again, but I ain't losing a thing that will keep my girl safe." Placing both hands firmly on the arms of her chair, she pushed to standing. "Now. You get on in there and wash up while we get lunch on the table. I'm so hungry, my stomach thinks my throat's been cut."

Chapter Five

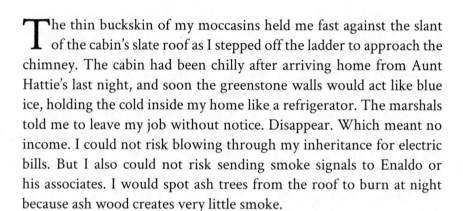

The thin buckskin of my moccasins held me fast against the slant of the cabin's slate roof as I stepped off the ladder to approach the chimney. The cabin had been chilly after arriving home from Aunt Hattie's last night, and soon the greenstone walls would act like blue ice, holding the cold inside my home like a refrigerator. The marshals told me to leave my job without notice. Disappear. Which meant no income. I could not risk blowing through my inheritance for electric bills. But I also could not risk sending smoke signals to Enaldo or his associates. I would spot ash trees from the roof to burn at night because ash wood creates very little smoke.

It took a moment to get my balance on the slant. Lack of sleep was taking its toll. I had researched Anthony Enaldo and his boss, Ginnova Giovanni, until sunrise. Despite zero sleep, I would have to use the daylight to make things secure. Although everything in me wanted to dive into the mystery of the trap door. And hopefully find a tin box.

The only thoughts that lightened my spirit all night had revolved around Grandfather's mystery hunts. He hid the tins with the hunts in strange places. Each time I opened one, the first thing that greeted me was a drawing of two eagles touching wings in flight, representing his name, Two Eagles. Then life became exhilarating. With hunts, I learned to track animals, divine for water, navigate by the stars, and, in many ways, live off the land. Each hunt included incentives, rewards, and challenges designed to teach me some of life's most important lessons. Grandfather's aim was to instruct me on how to approach all challenges as a mystery, knowing the solutions and rewards would follow.

Just yesterday I had sensed his presence when I was standing near the trap door. What if one more hunt was hidden there? One final tin that held the chance to connect with him. Even if it were posthumously, I would come to know his presence in a new way, not just as memories. And his secret would have a purpose.

The rustling of dried leaves below drew my attention. In the woods, at the edge of the last curve in my driveway, a mother skunk was shepherding six kits. I sat down with my back to the chimney and wrapped my arms around my knees to observe. Mother skunk led her young to the far end of a downed log. She stood aside a small hole, and we both waited for all six kits to scurry in one at a time. Then Mother followed.

Grandfather taught that when we see skunks, their message— their "medicine"—from God is to remind us to contemplate our own self-protection. No coincidence. And since kits cannot leave the nest until they have manufactured musk, these babies were armed and dangerous. I would not be taking a shortcut through the woods on that S-curve any time soon.

The morning air carried the musky smell of damp leaves and fertile earth. Looking out over the Blue Ridge Mountains, I watched the early morning sunlight peak mountain crests to light the fall foliage, section by section. The mountains glowed orange, red, and yellow, contrasting the dark evergreens. On the roof, I was a tiny puzzle piece of a huge rolling landscape.

This was my second year checking the chimney alone. On a call from New York last year, I told Grandfather I had to work the day after Thanksgiving and urged him to check for debris without me. He insisted he would wait until I got home. When I arrived the week of Christmas, he stated it was time for me to climb to the roof alone. "You are ready," he declared with confidence. A phrase he always used at a rite of passage. My heart sank. I had cherished our time on the roof together.

Grandfather stood in the driveway that morning as I went up by myself. When I stepped out onto the slate, I looked below at him. My heart rose in my throat. He seemed so small. So frail. It is a trick of the eyes, I told myself. It is only because I am seeing him from this height. Then a southern breeze blew from behind Grandfather, lifting his long gray hair out and around him on both sides, forming the shape of angel wings. A deep thud in the pit of my stomach threatened nausea. Was this a vision? A prophecy? My knees became weak. My legs trembled.

I searched his face. He studied me as well. We held each other's gaze. It was only for a moment, but it seemed like forever.

"Have you become frightened, Little Bit?"

"No, Grandfather," I managed. "It is just . . . strange doing this alone." I would not scare him with the image I had seen.

"You will check the chimney alone many times. You are ready." His expression did not change, and climbing to the roof by myself no longer seemed like a proud rite of passage but a necessary one.

A thousand questions rushed through my mind that I could not find my voice to ask. A moment later, he flashed a smile. His face lit up, causing his smooth, tanned skin to wrinkle at his eyes. Surely what I had seen was just a reflection of my fear. Nothing could happen to Grandfather. He was "tough as nails," as Aunt Hattie advised. He held my gaze, giving my thoughts time to settle. Was he allowing this moment between us so that I would realize what was happening? I wanted to climb back down the ladder and beg him to tell me he would be okay.

Behind him, a cardinal called "birdie, birdie, birdie" in quick succession. The bright red bird, named for the clothing of church cardinals, reminds us to contemplate our spirituality. Grandfather did not fear death. He believed his Christian death would mean a change of location, closer to God. He taught that death is a challenge for the living and a promotion for the departed.

The red bird sounded again, and Grandfather closed his eyes for a moment. He bobbed his head two times. I returned the gesture.

But my spirit remained unsettled.

While he stood watch that morning, I found the tin for the last hunt we would solve together hidden under the chimney cap. I looked down to see Grandfather again close his eyes and nod. I told myself that all was well. I allowed myself to discount my vision and believe that the tin box had been his reason for me to climb alone.

Now, the driveway was empty. But it was as though out of the gravel arose a hologram of him with wings, and the image sent pulses of grief that I breathed in.

A purring noise came from behind me in the northern sky. Within seconds, I recognized the sound of helicopter blades. Looking over my shoulder, the chimney blocked my view of the aircraft. It approached quickly, then suddenly slowed. The hair on my neck stood with a warning. Instinctively, I drew my knees up close to my chest so that I was hidden by the chimney.

I could not remember a helicopter ever hovering over Easterbrook. Ever. My pulse raced. There was only one reason I could imagine.

I was being hunted.

To stay hidden, I would have to remain on the opposite end of the compass from the helicopter, back flush against the chimney, knees tight under my chin. The image of Sasha's obituary on the internet flashed in my mind.

Keeping my knees as close to my chin as possible, I used my hands to push myself up the slant of the roof so that I was facing west while the helicopter was on the east side.

The sound came closer to the cabin. Right behind the chimney. Hovering.

I flattened my back against the greenstone. Prayed that it would not go directly over the cabin, or I would be seen.

Helicopters sometimes hovered and small planes buzzed over Madeline's estate, the verdigris of her copper-domed mansion and her expansive grounds being landmarks. But never over Easterbrook. From their height, the entrance to my driveway at Stopping Place would be visible. And my SUV was parked so that my tags were visible from that angle. At least the ladder was well covered by a canopy of trees.

My mouth went dry. My chest hurt, and I realized I held my breath. I forced air into my lungs. Perhaps lack of sleep and the continuous internet search had made me paranoid.

I tried to reassure myself. Anthony Enaldo was incarcerated. But there was no peace in that thought as my ears filled with the sound of the helicopter hovering. Because Ginnova Giovanni was not.

Sasha's obituary said she had died five days ago. I was likely their next target. By now, they would be looking for me.

The sound of the helicopter blades became deafening, just yards from where I sat. Tree limbs clattered around me, protesting the wind they created. Sweat broke out on my upper lip, my pulse pounded in my temples. Every nerve in my body was supercharged. I held my knees so tightly to my chest it seemed they would break through my rib cage. Time stood still while thousands of thoughts flew with breathtaking speed. What were they waiting for? Why would they hover so long?

Suddenly, it became clear, and electricity pulsed across my scalp with the realization. They were waiting for me to step out of the cabin. They were waiting to engage a sniper.

The helicopter moved again, south. I scooted around to the broader north side of the chimney. The sound was between Easterbrook and Crawl Mountain now. Clearly in the middle of my mountains. Hovering for what seemed like an eternity. As I closed my eyes and listened closely, it sounded as though the aircraft backed up some and hovered, moved forward and hovered again. No mistaking this. There was nothing to see on Crawl Mountain. The target was Easterbrook.

The helicopter moved west.

I scooted until I faced east.

Suddenly, the sound changed again. Faster. Moving north, back to where it originated.

I scooted back down to where I was sitting when I first heard the sound, looking south, and listened until the sound was so faint, I could no longer hear it.

I unfolded my legs. My knees shook. I placed the palms of my cold hands against the roof to warm them by the sun, but my nails created a rattle as they tapped the slate. So I placed them under my arms instead.

New plan. If ever again I heard a helicopter coming from any direction, I would go inside as fast as possible. And I would need to get rid of my vehicle. Park it in Madeline's garage. Change nothing else outside.

I searched my mind for other things that would help make the cabin look deserted but came up blank. I knew Grandfather would tell me to settle. *No immediate action. Look around. Is God sending a message through nature?* I would have to follow his guidance and calm before I could trust my legs to get me off the roof.

I looked to my right to follow the outline of Crow Mountain, a curvaceous woman lying on her side. I squinted to make out the almost imperceptible line of an old trail for wagon trains. How many times had Grandfather told me the story?

Sitting on the roof beside me, Grandfather would point to the landmarks as he talked. He would tell me about when settlers moved west. How the Blue Ridge was the first mountain range they encountered, and they had chosen the dip at her waistline on Crow Mountain to blaze a trail.

My breath came more easily now, but my legs and hands still shook.

When the trail was complete, the wagons that had been camped around Stopping Place pulled up stakes and began their ascent over. One family had an upright piano and china, as well as essentials, like a coop with chickens for homesteading. While the other wagons moved up and over the top ridge, this family's horses would not move farther than halfway. The piano was too heavy. The wife became furious when her husband told her they would have to leave it behind. She insisted the horses should do their job. He got out of the wagon to lighten the load and lead the horses forward. It was not enough. So she got out and yelled at them. The horses reared, sending the contents of the wagon spilling out of the back. The piano, the crates, and the coop went tumbling back down the trail while the horses took off, up and over the mountain, the man and woman running after them. The wife demanded that her husband go back and see if anything could be saved. He returned empty-handed and told her that the piano and china were all in pieces.

At this point in the story, Grandfather would stop and let me say the punch line: "And the chickens had flown the coop." Then he would say, "Story is that if you listen close, you might hear that ole rooster's kinfolk still a-crowing." To play along, we would both act as though we were listening for the sound.

Grandfather would then say, "The mountains are teachers. Those folks learned that sometimes we have to leave things behind to move ahead."

I felt my eyes widen. The hair on my arms stood at the thought of all I would have to leave behind. My job as remote researcher. Income. Transportation. Freedom.

The sun was higher in the sky now, and the temperature rising. I again placed my palms against the warmed slate. My nails did not tap.

My eyes searched for ash wood in the small valley that separated Easterbrook from Crawl Mountain then suddenly were drawn to movement at the top of Crawl. At the crest, on a large flat rock, a mountain lion stood with his head hanging, his huge tail sweeping out behind him. He would be the only male in the area. King of the mountain.

I watched as the cat moved his head, surveying his kingdom, and found me. Even at a great distance, we acknowledged one another. I wondered what a fearless mountain lion would think of a woman who had just scooted on her butt around a chimney, hiding.

He studied me for long moments, then turned his head sharply to look down the east side of Easterbrook. He had spotted something. Moving my eyes to the spot that he watched, I saw a flock of starlings rise above the tree line in a disorganized pattern. They had been startled. Something was coming up my driveway. The lion watched his target. His head moved slowly in concert with where I knew the bends and turns of the drive to be. Faint sounds of a vehicle approaching grew stronger. It was not Madeline. The marshals said they would not return unless I invited them. The lion looked toward me, backed up a step, and turned to saunter away.

My heart quickened. Should I get off the roof? But if the helicopter had signaled to someone on the ground that my vehicle was in the driveway, they could be coming to storm the cabin. I would be better off on the roof.

Until they discovered the ladder on the west side.

I scooted to the west side of the chimney; the vehicle approached from the east. Once I heard it enter the last S-curve, I would peek around the corner of the chimney. If they were hostiles, I would slide down the northern backside of the roof, with the chimney blocking me from view, drop, and run to the old ancestors' trail behind the cabin that winds its way down Easterbrook.

The trail had not been used since the Civilian Conservation Corp built the driveway on the southeastern slope during the Great Depression. But Grandfather and I had traveled it on foot many times. Taking that path, I would end up in the ancestors' cemetery, near one of the artist's residences. From there I could run to Aunt Hattie's. And my moccasins would ensure that I could do it quietly.

I worked at taking deep breaths for energy to drop and run.

I would be ready.

CHAPTER SIX

When the sound of an engine entered the last clearing, I peeked around the chimney. A white cruiser topped with a row of blue lights came through the last curve. ROCKCLIFF COUNTY SHERIFF and a large brown star were emblazoned on the door.

I lowered my shoulders and wiggled them to release tension and tried to regulate my breathing after the flood of adrenaline and subsequent crash that had come from seeing the helicopter and it speeding off. I left my hiding spot next to the chimney and slid down the roof enough to be seen when they arrived, hoping to look as casual as a woman might look sitting on a roof.

The vehicle stopped short of my veranda steps, and two officers exited. The driver, the taller of the two, with a muscular physique, looked up and spotted me on the roof. He tipped his hat. The corners of his mouth turned up into a ghost of a smile. The shorter, stocky man looked in the opposite direction at the rolling view of the Blue Ridge Mountains. The driver was my neighbor, Sheriff Rick Martin. Aunt Hattie and Madeline had described him well. Black hair and eyebrows, chiseled face with a dark complexion and a tall, powerful frame. He moved with a natural sense of grace and confidence. Or as Aunt Hattie's called it, "movie star handsome."

"Hello, Emerson. I'm Sheriff Rick Martin."

His voice was deep.

When he spoke, the second officer followed his line of vision and found me on the roof. His head jerked back sharply in surprise.

"We'd like to talk with you. Would you like us to come up there?" He sounded sincere. I shook my head, then before I could speak, he added, "Because I'm guessing that's some view."

I nodded my agreement. "I will come down." I could only imagine what my elders would say about me talking with them from the roof, let alone on it.

I stood tall and straight, looked out over the blue ridges one more time, and held my head even higher as I took in the mountain air around me. Grandfather always said, when you need strength, stand strong, remember you are the sum of all your ancestors, and claim your power. I was about to meet two strangers—law enforcement at that—to talk about the mob hitman hunting me. I was ready.

I turned to complete my task of checking the chimney. A double win. My heart lifted at the memory of Grandfather humorously instructing, "If you can't fix a problem, flaunt it." The action would make my roof-sitting look purposeful.

I peeked inside the opening. The chimney was clear. Satisfied and having saved at least a little face, I moved toward the ladder on the opposite side of the house, then made my descent.

As I rounded the corner of the veranda, Sheriff Martin stepped forward and extended his hand. "I'm Rick Martin. This is Deputy Al Lewis."

Lewis nodded.

I waved toward the veranda. "Please."

The sheriff extended his hand as though to say, "You first."

I led the men onto the veranda and, again, sat in the middle of the swing. The rockers the marshals had sat in were still pointed in my direction. Sheriff Martin and Deputy Lewis took their seats in them. Just one day before, in this very spot, my world had been turned upside down. Some of the shock rushed back, as though emotional energy were attached to the chairs.

"It's nice to meet you." The sheriff's voice was deep enough to vibrate the floorboards.

I nodded.

"The US Marshal's office has been in touch with me. I also had a long conversation with your Aunt Hattie last night." He squinted his brown eyes just a bit as he talked, then his head tilted left. He was waiting for me to speak. I gave him time to tell me why he had come. The smell of clean clothes and soap lingered in the air between us.

He cleared his throat and began again, this time with a softened tone. "The marshals told me you could still change your mind and enter WITSEC. I know you've only had one night to sleep on it, but have you changed your mind? Or do you still want to ride this out on Easterbrook?"

I had not slept, but sleep would not have changed my mind. "I am confident. I will not enter their program."

"Well, your Aunt Hattie told me you were positive. So, I'm here because it's our job to protect the citizens of Rockcliff County. Not to mention, you're a neighbor."

"I am afraid I am a risky neighbor to have."

Sheriff Martin blinked and looked down with my words, then nodded slightly. Honesty. When he looked back at me, he wore a slight frown. "We'll make some plans," he said. His voice was firm and resolute. "Lower the risk. In fact, I came up this morning to get moving on some ideas. You know, if anything happened to you on my watch, your Aunt Hattie and Madeline would have my head."

A cell phone buzzed in Deputy Lewis's pocket. "Excuse me," he said, looking up at me, then stood and accepted his call as he walked off the veranda.

I leaned forward and lowered my voice. "My elders told me I can trust you. And I will try. But I know nothing about Deputy Lewis. I mean no offense, Sheriff Martin, but . . ."

The sheriff nodded his head. "Please. Call me Rick. And I understand." He looked over his shoulder at Deputy Lewis sitting in the passenger seat of the cruiser on his phone, then at Crow Mountain behind me. He was silent for a few moments. His dark eyes moved up to the rafters over our heads. Was he thinking what an impossible task it would be to work with a stubborn Native who trusted almost no one? He turned his eyes to me, his long, black lashes sweeping when he blinked. Fine, untanned lines around his eyes bore proof of a history of smiles. Could a person tell by smile lines if another is trustworthy?

"Emerson, you should know that Enaldo's attorneys filed a motion late yesterday evening to lower his bail. As of now, his bail is set at four million. We suspect they will try and get that cut at least by half. They wouldn't file the motion if they weren't prepared to pay. His hearing will be next week. If they're successful, he could be out on bail that day."

I nodded. I had seen a motion to reduce bond petition online.

"Is there anything I can help you with?"

I opened my mouth to speak and then shut it, changing my mind. My thoughts swirled. At least half of them were warning me not to trust the sheriff, the other half reminding me that he had access to databanks I did not. I would need to know what he knew. In order to do that, I would need to form an exchange of information.

My instincts propelled me, despite the risk. "Yes. There was a helicopter hovering over Easterbrook about ten minutes before you got here."

Rick straightened in his chair. "Did they see you?"

His quick response meant he too must think there was cause for alarm. I squared my shoulders. "I managed to stay out of sight." I saw no reason to confess how. "I have never known a helicopter to hover over Easterbrook before. But I cannot give you a description."

Rick nodded, frowning. "I'll look into it and get back to you if I learn anything."

"Thank you. I will make sure the driveway is empty. I will not create daytime smoke or change anything outside. I will not gather leaves or move things around."

Rick nodded. "Good thinking. You'll be pretty isolated up here with no vehicle."

"I can get off the mountain if I need to." I stopped. But a nagging feeling urged me to be more forthcoming. "I ask that we keep this between us. My ancestors' trail is behind the cabin. It is not well worn, so it is not likely to be visible from the air. If I took it, I would end up down at the old cemetery on my land, the burial site shared by several tribes. It borders an artist's residence. But I do not want anyone else to know about it."

"I understand. It goes no further unless you are in jeopardy."

"Also, I would like your opinion. The marshals told me that Enaldo takes great pride in taking out only his target. They think others are at minimal risk. From what you know or have been told, do you agree?"

Rick considered my question for a moment, then poked out his bottom lip just a bit and frowned as he nodded agreement. "This kind of guy takes pride in hitting the bull's-eye every time, not the rings around it."

I flinched.

"Sorry about that."

"That is okay." I would not tell him I had read every crime report on Enaldo's alleged assassinations, even the hype and fake news, along with the court records on his proceedings. I also knew about his boss, Giovanni.

Rick cleared his throat before he spoke. "Even if the helicopter wasn't the mob, they could use a drone. You'll need to destroy your cell phone. Get a burner. Don't move any money around in banks. If you need to, make one large withdrawal or, better yet, close your accounts. It might look like you ran. The mob is connected in a lot of ways. Will you be okay without a salary?"

His thoughtfulness seemed protective. I nodded my head yes. Since Grandfather became ill, Madeline had been getting my mail from the post office. Once he died, she began paying the bills. I always repaid her, but now she insisted I accept her gift instead of using my inheritance. "I may have to run the heat pump some, so the electricity bill will jump. That is the only thing that should show a change."

Rick nodded as I spoke. "Good thinking. Your power usage might be at the bottom of their list of things to check. But I like your attention to detail. You have to stay warm and it would take a pretty long extension cord to hook you up to Hattie Mae."

"I can be gone during the day and use a lot of quilts at night. I will be okay."

"That's a tough way to live, but something tells me you're tough."

I nodded.

Rick leaned forward slightly; his voice lowered. "I'll come back later, and we can talk about protection you can have on hand—a gun, a Taser, Kevlar, alarm systems, security lights. Things like that. Every little bit helps."

I closed my eyes and nodded twice. He seemed sincere, and I did not know what he knew. But he did not know what I knew when he suggested a Kevlar vest.

Enaldo's target was between the eyes.

CHAPTER SEVEN

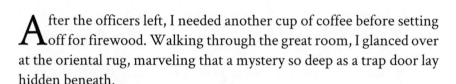

After the officers left, I needed another cup of coffee before setting off for firewood. Walking through the great room, I glanced over at the oriental rug, marveling that a mystery so deep as a trap door lay hidden beneath.

In the kitchen, I pulled a mug from the cabinet, poured the rich brew, and held it close, allowing the warmth of the steam to spread upward on my face as I began an internal pro and con list for opening the trap door before scouting for wood.

No. I should concentrate on survival first.

But what if there was a hunt waiting beneath the door? What if it contained just the wisdom I needed at the moment?

As I turned the cup for the perfect angle to drink, I froze. The logo on the cup read "Just do it."

I could hear Grandfather's voice. *There are no accidents. You are ready.*

Energy flew through me as I set the cup down on the drain, walked to the great room, and flung back the rug. I centered myself, feet directly below my shoulders, inserted the screwdriver, and pressed down on the handle. I slipped the fingers of my free hand into the space and grunted to lift the heavy hardwood square.

The trap door squeaked as it moved up, my arms trembling under the weight. I shoved the thick wood panel to rest against the stone hearth. A rope used to close the door from below swung back and forth like a metronome.

A southern breeze from the screen door caught the dust below and created zillions of rainbow reflections that swirled in the sunlight streaming through the skylights above. Looking down, I could see a rudimentary ladder built against the shorter side of the opening to my right. An earthen smell told me there was a dirt floor.

Giddy as a child dashing to the Christmas tree, I rushed to the pantry to retrieve the flashlight, grabbed it off the shelf, returned, and pressed the button.

Nothing.

I shook the light, beat it against my palm. Of course not. I could not remember the last time I had used it. I would have to find another way.

I walked to the other small end of the opening. Maybe there was a pull chain. I bent to look.

No pull chain.

I dropped to my knees and leaned forward, steadying my weight on my palms to look deeper into the hole. Something rested on a dirt ledge behind the third step. It looked metallic, a dull shine. I bent at my elbows to lean farther forward and squinted, trying to make it out. When my eyes adjusted, the object's lines became clear.

A tin box.

I stood and backed away from the hole in one seamless motion, my hand rising to my mouth, gooseflesh on my arms. The temptation to look around, as though I would see Grandfather nodding his approval, was great. But I was getting ahead of myself. It could be a random tin box. This could be where he stashed the boxes for the hunts and this one was left over.

Flashlight or not, I would retrieve the box.

I tested the ladder by bouncing a bit on the first wooden step. I could not afford to end up in a heap, alone on a mountaintop. I edged farther down until I could reach the ledge behind the steps. Holding on to the floor above me with my left hand, my right hand found the box, and my fingers firmly gripped the small metal handle on top. I shook it to make sure the latch was secure. The box was light. There was a clunk when I placed it on the floor above. The sound filled me with hope.

I climbed up, then carried the tin box to the kitchen island. It looked old and tarnished in contrast to the shiny slate countertop. The box for every hunt had pictures on top that Grandfather hand selected to symbolize some aspect of the mysteries. This one had a scratched picture of eastern bluebirds on a limb, their ruby chest and bright blue bodies contrasting with white dogwood blooms. Their medicine: joy and happiness. I remembered this box from a former hunt, one that had been designed to teach me to identify birds by sight and calls. Inside, it held a mini recorder, and I had solved the hunt for the prize of a bird book, binoculars, and a camera with a photo lens.

I brushed the top of the box with my hand to swipe off a layer of dust, then placed my thumb on the little lever to open it. What if there were no drawing inside? No eagles on a page. Just a box of odds and ends. Was I prepared to face another heartbreak?

The lever caught when I pushed it. Fine, red rust scattered in a pile beneath the latch, but the box did not open. I used the heel of my palm to push down on the front of the box, then the top sprang up, and there it was. On a thick piece of sketch pad paper, in pencil, was a drawing of two eagles in flight, the tips of their wings touching.

I was transfixed, scarcely able to breathe. My hand flew to my mouth. How could I have dared hope or dream of having yet another chance to learn from him? Surely my insides were lighter than air. Could a person float away if they were any happier? I had within my hands another hunt.

With a surgeon's caution, I removed the drawing. Beneath it was an envelope marked with Grandfather's scrawling cursive. The familiar swirls caused a lump of longing to rise in my throat. *Read the letter first*, it read.

I pulled the letter out, noting the two items wrapped in notebook paper under it, the numbers "One" and "Two" written on them. My hands trembled as I unfolded the letter with the same care one would show ancient papyrus.

> *All of life is a mystery, Little Bit. We solve one at a time until we become*
> *part of the greatest mystery of all. When you read this, I will be a part*
> *of that mystery.*
> *Open the object marked "One."*

I picked up the lightweight object and slid my nail under the tape. Inside the layers of paper, I found a delicate gold chain with a pendant cut from deep purple amethyst shaped into a cross. I held the stone up so that the light from the kitchen window caught its facets. Like every piece of jewelry Grandfather had made for me, this stone would be from Mineral Springs on Easterbrook.

I placed the shiny cross and chain on the counter, admiring its beauty against the dark stone. Picking up his note, I found my place and continued.

> *Your task is to solve the mystery of the Wild Woman. When you do,*
> *you will find an identical cross. Your Aunt Hattie and Madeline will*
> *guide you.*

I laid the letter down and gripped the cool edge of the counter with my hands, my mind reeling. I had not thought of the Wild Woman in years. The tiny woman was a legend in Rockcliff County.

I had been six and sitting on the veranda steps with Grandfather when I first heard her storied howl reverberate between our mountains. "What was that?" I asked him. After a long moment, he spoke, his voice holding an echo of sadness. "That is the sound of a heart breaking."

On Halloween, many children in Rockcliff County dressed up like her, imitating her sound. Folks who attended Poplar Grove Church on Colony Row, before it was decommissioned and became one of Madeline's art houses, commonly reported seeing her. They described her as a tiny woman with bushy, flaming-red hair, who wore a red quilt for a skirt. Her howl would alert them to her location, but when she caught sight of them, she would disappear.

I only saw her once while riding behind Grandfather on the tractor. She seemed to appear out of nowhere, at the edge of the woods near Crawl Mountain. I pulled on Grandfather's sleeve and pointed, but he never looked. When we stopped for lunch, I told him I had seen her. Grandfather shook his head and said, "Let the little woman be."

The last time I asked him about her was a few months later, when I went with him to leave her supplies at the same spot where I had seen her that day. Again, he admonished me, "Let the little woman be." I never asked again.

I picked up the letter and found the next line.

Open the object marked "Two."

My fingertips sensed through the paper that this bundle held an object the size of a silver dollar. From the paper cocoon slid a white circular disc with a carving of four eagles, two soaring on the top and two along the bottom. In the middle was the face of a bear. At the top, a gold chain was threaded through a small hole in the disc. The piece was exquisite. I ran my finger over its edges. Carved bone. In all my years I had never seen anything like it.

I returned to the letter.

The totem is circular and white to honor your Grandmother, Pale Whispering Moon. It is carved of bear bone, and the bear in the middle represents your mother, Standing Bear.

I ran my index finger over the fine carving of the bear's face. My mother became Standing Bear at the age of thirteen, after the rape. Doctors advised her to abort me. They warned that she was too small and too damaged from the trauma and would not be able to carry or deliver me. She would likely hemorrhage, they said, and die if she tried. But she stood firm. She defended her cub.

The two eagles at the bottom represent me. One day, when you have completed a Spirit Warrior Woman's mission, defending others, the four eagles together will represent you. You will be called Four Eagles because you will not have family as I did. You must be twice as brave and courageous.

I felt sick to my stomach, my face hot with shame thinking of my panic as I slid around the slate roof, so scared I could hardly breathe. I was not brave *or* courageous. I was scared to death. I did not know if I could defend myself, much less others. My mother was a Spirit Warrior Woman. I could not compare myself to her in any way.

I am sorry I could not be here for your transition. It is not meant to be. You will face these and many other mysteries alone. When the time comes, you are ready.
Remember that you are loved, Little Bit.
Grandfather

I could almost hear him saying the last line. He had said it so many times. With each good-bye, each bedtime, each moment of encouragement, it had been the same. His deep voice would echo within me long after the words "Remember that you are loved, Little Bit" were spoken.

I closed my eyes. Warm tears slid down my cheeks, leaving a trace of saltiness in my mouth and landing on the letter below. One dropped with a large splat in the middle of the word "loved," and I watched as the ink swelled and distorted, growing disproportionally larger than the others. My heart lifted.

There are no coincidences. Grandfather would have surely smiled, closed his eyes, and nodded twice.

• • •

Every mystery hunt Grandfather designed had always included my mothers. This time would be no different. And Sunday dinner at Aunt

Hattie's was the perfect time to let them know I had found the tin.

Both women greeted me on Aunt Hattie's doorstep. The anticipation of telling them I had found the hunt made me grin foolishly as I approached them.

"Now looky there," Aunt Hattie said after a round of hugs. "First smile I've seen in many a day. Emerson Grace, you look like the cat that swallowed the canary, if you was to ask me."

"You do look happy, hun. We are so glad to see it," Madeline said.

Aunt Hattie steered me directly to the kitchen table, and both women set about taking platters of food from the oven. "The menu is 'Preacher's Dinner.' That's what my Mama always called it. We got fried chicken, mashed taters, milk gravy, lima beans, spoon bread, and corn pudding. I figure we need a feast to celebrate whatever it is you going to tell us. I suspect you've done found something up there in that cabin, and I want to hear about it after the blessing."

When my mothers were seated, Aunt Hattie reached for both of our hands and gave her thanks for the food as well as having me home on Easterbrook. We uncoupled our hands and Aunt Hattie sat back with a grin. "Now spill it."

"Grandfather left another hunt. I found it beneath a secret trap door in the great room."

Both women looked at each other and smiled. Then Aunt Hattie turned to me, patted my hand and chuckled. "We was wondering when you were ever gon' get 'round to deep cleaning under that rug."

"We had already decided," Madeline began, "that if you didn't come tell us you found it pretty soon, we were going to suggest you air out the orientals."

"So, you both knew about the trap door?"

Both mothers nodded. No wonder they had not looked astounded when I told them. Madeline leaned toward me. "Not only that, I insisted I would be the one to put the box behind the third step. I didn't want him going down that old ladder.

"He told me and your Uncle Bill about that door way back yonder. He was saving it for hunts when you got older. Even older than you are now. I expect he wanted you to have a little life experience before you found it. This hunt you found is right special, I reckon, seeing as how it got him through those last months when he was suffering something terrible."

A hot rush burned my face. Talking about him suffering was almost too much to bear. I looked down at my plate, but tears began to pool, so I looked up at the ceiling and blinked hard to hold them back.

"Hun," Madeine began, her voice soft. "Creating that hunt gave him a positive focus those last few months. He loved imagining everything about it. Every time we went up there, and you know we went six and seven times a week there at the end, he perked up when we all envisioned what you would do and how you would react. It filled his last days."

A knot of hurt in my soul began to unravel. The confusion lifted; I now understood. He had kept the secret to create a surprise. All along he had been thinking of me.

Both mothers were silent while I collected my thoughts.

"It makes sense now why Grandfather always chose the great room when we divided chores. And why he cleaned it when I was not home."

Both women smiled.

Conversation began to revolve around the food as we passed dishes to one another for serving, but as we ate, my mind wrestled with questions I had no answers for. I chewed and swallowed but could not move my attention from the mystery.

"I just don't know why we have a trap door. Did he tell either of you?"

Aunt Hattie took my hand for a moment and squeezed it. "You always did want to know everything right away. The whole point of them hunts was to teach you everything in its own time. I expect there's a history to that room under the cabin, and you'll find out what it is one of these days."

I nodded my understanding. "As you know then, Grandfather's instructions are that the two of you will guide me in solving the mystery of the Wild Woman."

"That's right. I declare. I think the day he told us I took him a Preacher's Dinner. Ain't that right, Madeline?" Aunt Hattie let go of my hand, used her napkin, and placed it beside her plate.

"Yes. It was this same meal," Madeline said.

Their conspiracy only served to remind me that, despite my concerns when I talked with Grandfather on the phone, he had not told me that he was dying from pancreatic cancer. But he had allowed my elders to know and be there for him. I thought he was closer to me than anyone on earth. But he had shared the biggest secret of his life with them instead. An emptiness engulfed me. Who had I really been to him? Why had he not confided in me? What inability or lack had he seen in me that he drew a circle that left me out?

Aunt Hattie read my look. "I know you're still all crumbled up inside that he didn't tell you about his ailments. But, Emerson, he told us that was the way of your people sometimes to die alone. He was mighty afraid if you came home, you'd never go back and finish that internship."

"We believed he was right, hun," Madeline added. "And it wasn't our call."

I nodded.

"Emerson Grace, him planning that hunt was a way of him being with you even when he isn't."

I forced a smile, my stomach muscles relaxing slightly with the thought that finding and opening the tin had awakened me to a sensation of his presence. Exactly what he must have intended.

"I know you wish you could have been here," Madeline said, her voice soft. "But I think he believed the last thing he could do for you was to support you getting that job and help you see that there is life outside of your mountains."

I nodded out of respect, but of course I knew it had all been for nothing. Now I had lost the job and, following the marshals' advice, had not even given notice. Nothing good had come from leaving the mountains. I should have been with him.

"And, Emerson, it just might be that he didn't want you to see him vulnerable like that."

The long legs of ice-cold spiders walked up the back of my neck. I reached up and rubbed my skin. Her words bore truth. He had always been stronger, wiser, more capable. My elder was right. I looked at her as she leaned across the table to touch my hand.

"Thank you, Madeline."

She gave my hand a squeeze.

"Well now," Aunt Hattie chortled. She stood and smoothed her cotton apron and adjusted its wide shoulder straps as though she were suiting herself up with armor. "He told me my job was instructions, and I've got 'em in my bedside table. We might as well do this now and eat after. Hang on." She shoved her chair away from the table and headed to the back of the house. When she returned, she held a folded piece of notebook paper.

Before Aunt Hattie took her seat, I cleared my throat and hesitated, but asked them anyway. "Given everything with Enaldo, do you both think now is a good time to start this hunt, since I . . . since the mob is after me?"

Aunt Hattie looked to Madeline. They both nodded.

"Ain't never no bad time for wisdom." Aunt Hattie reached down and touched the side of my face, her huge brown eyes soft with care. "That's what your granddaddy was all about now, won't it, Emerson? Wanting wisdom for you. I expect, considering what's going on, he'd want you to have it *now*. He'd know you need it."

Madeline nodded.

But what if I couldn't concentrate? What if I went about solving the hunt and lost touch with the feelings that he was still with me? I would waste the last opportunity to sense him in daily life. And what if it distracted me from outrunning a mob hitman? How would I find a time to just let go of every concern? The raw grief of losing him was as thick in my heart as it had ever been. Returning to Easterbrook had only increased that. If I jumped into the hunt, would it intensify even more? How could I run that risk, knowing I would be distracted from signs that the mob was closing in?

I leaned back in my chair as Aunt Hattie sat down and began to open the folded notebook paper. "Okay, Emerson," Aunt Hattie began, wearing a look of mischief, and I had to wonder what else she knew that I did not. "I've got something to say before I hand you this. You know that granddaddy of yours always made me and Madeline part of these hunts."

I nodded.

"Well, this time ain't no different."

Aunt Hattie handed me the folded paper.

Emerson,
Everyone you meet has wisdom. Your first task is to meet all the artists
at the next potluck.
Grandfather

When I looked up, both women were watching me. Never in my life had Grandfather asked me to meet one artist, let alone all of them. Or to attend a potluck. My stomach knotted with the prospect of all those strangers who knew each other, but who I did not. A potluck. A room full of people I have nothing in common with. All of them expecting small talk.

"My job is to solve the mystery of the Wild Woman, and this is how I start?"

Aunt Hattie smoothed her apron over her stomach. "There always was a lot of steps that seemed disconnected in them other hunts. You'll see. After the potluck, you come back here, and I can give you the next instructions. This time you gone be coming back after every step."

"And, hun, the potlucks are still every Tuesday night."

"I'll cook you up something to take, Emerson. You ain't gotta worry about none of that."

My mind spun. In addition to Enaldo, I now had a whole new set of things to think about. Perhaps exactly what Grandfather would have wanted.

My mothers waited for me to speak.

"Aunt Hattie, one thing is still confusing. I always thought you were the only person who knew the story of the Wild Woman. So how am I to solve her mystery?"

Aunt Hattie smiled as she shook her curly head. "That's part of the mystery, and you ain't getting one more word out of me, Emerson Grace." She shook her apron and smoothed it over her knees. "Not nary bit of it till you come back here after the potluck. My lips is sealed. Now, time for dessert."

CHAPTER EIGHT

——— ••• ——— ❋ ——— ••• ———

As Madeline drove me home from the bank the next morning, her mood was light and her voice full of energy. We spent the ride discussing my plans, and she offered me ideas to help outsmart Giovanni and his men.

She steered her SUV off the state road onto the southern entrance of Colony Row, a half-moon-shaped road that curved past artists' residences, Stopping Place, the ancestors' graveyard and the private homes of Rick, Aunt Hattie, and Madeline. "Thank you for being so supportive, Madeline. The teller did not even blink when I closed my accounts and transferred the funds to your deposit slip. Perhaps that happens more often than I imagined. But it helped knowing you were on the lookout for strangers while I did."

"I was glad to do it, hun. You can't be too careful. Of course it sure would help if we knew what these men looked like."

Madeline pushed on her brakes. Ahead in the road, a squirrel started to scamper across, paused, then returned to his original side. Madeline laughed. "I name every squirrel that does that Midway." She glanced over at me. "Emerson, you are making some smart moves. Like leaving your vehicle parked in my barn. But I do hope you'll consider taking my little four-wheeler back up Easterbrook when you go. You could hide it in the woods, I would think."

"I am sure I could, and thank you. I might consider it later. Right now I want to be sure I can manage the terrain physically. With you getting my supplies today, I think I am set to be a hermit for a while."

Madeline navigated the first curve of Colony Row. On the left, steep banks with thick forest came almost to the road. On the right, the terrain was flatter, with pastures and fields.

As we climbed in elevation, I pointed to an older trailer at the top of a steep driveway on the left, wedged among tall oaks and nearly hidden, if not for the leading line of blue gravel driveway connecting it to Colony Row. "Is that where the little girls live?"

"Yes. That's the one the Crockers rent to Stella." She pointed to my right at a large, white farmhouse surrounded by fields with a barn towering behind, no cars, trucks in the yard, no items on the veranda. "That's the Crocker farm. We are negotiating. But Colony Arts Trust *will* buy it." Madeline smiled and winked. "You know, this is a great time for me to give you the residents tour before the potluck tomorrow night."

I nodded my agreement.

She pointed to the next house on the left, built up into the mountains, "That's the old Pierce log cabin. No artist right now. And across the street"—she pointed across me, directly right—"is the old barn we converted into a residence."

"I remember when you did that."

"It's still beautiful, and the artist-in-residence is Leena Rose, a watercolorist and a former nun who left the sisterhood to care for her aging parents. She never went back."

Pointing up the hill to the left, she said, "And of course, right up there you can see the spires of Pleasant Grove Church. Even after it was decommissioned and remodeled, I didn't have the heart to remove what made it look like a church. The cinderblock recreation center in the back is still where we have all our meetings and potluck dinners. The current artist-in-residence is Stewie, a comedian. And he tries to be funny. All. The. Time." Madeline looked over and raised an eyebrow. "You've been warned."

Memories flashed as we drove by the church. Sunday School, Vacation Bible School, and hundreds of dinners on the grounds with long picnic tables set up, covered in cotton cloth and laden with excellent homecooked food. Coming up the hill, I got a glimpse of my favorite stained-glass window on the south wall, a huge angel hovering over two little children crossing a rickety bridge. Over the front door, a rose window, facing east, was filled with late-morning sun and would be casting a warm, pink glow inside. I could not imagine the church as a residence, but I could relate to the idea of being surrounded by the ambiance the tall ceilings and multicolored windows would create.

Two hundred feet later, to my right, a six-foot-high stone wall marked the lines of Madeline's estate.

Madeline pointed to her left again, "There's Rick Martin's A-frame. His grandparents had that land back when I was a child and wouldn't sell to my father. Rick built there last summer."

I took in the large modern house nestled into the side of the mountain. Somehow it seemed to fit exactly the man I had met—current, up to date, conforming to the environment, and attractive.

Madeline slowed as we topped the hill and the fort-like entrance to Maple Grove came into view. "Of course, you know the house between mine and your Aunt Hattie's is where Jans, the metal sculptor, lives with his little ballerina daughter. Her name is Miah. Your Aunt Hattie can see her playing in the yard with Maestro from her watching window." Madeline stopped her SUV on Colony Row just before entering her driveway and pointed up ahead. "Emerson, look up there at Stopping Place. The little sisters."

I turned my focus from Madeline's huge iron gates to the small roadside pull-off across and a half block down the road. Two small girls with unkempt hair, shabby coats, dirty sneakers, and no socks were bent over Easterbrook spring, poking at something with sticks. Both children turned to look in our direction and instantly dropped their sticks as though they had been holding hot pokers. My stomach plummeted at the sight of them. They looked like street urchins. Children of the homeless in New York City had looked the same or better.

"They act as though they are in trouble, Madeline."

Before she pressed the remote on her visor to open the gates, Madeline turned to me, her voice solemn. "Your Aunt Hattie and I believe they're in trouble for almost everything at home. Every now and then they will say a little about it. They told us their Aunt Stella tells them they have ruined her life and she's sorry they were ever born. They've only lived with her for four months, and already things seem to be getting worse."

"What are they doing out of school?"

"Today is a teacher workday. I told them I would be back before noon and we'd all have lunch with your Aunt Hattie. She likes to get at least one meal a day in them, and I seem to be the ticket to make that happen. Well, me and Beau. They love my dog."

She drew a deep breath. "Let me finish telling you what's left on the residents tour, since I don't think you are getting back in a car any time soon." She rested her arm on the top of the steering wheel and pointed left through the windshield. "Just past your Aunt Hattie's is the house with two separate studios where the newlyweds Gideon and Megan live. They aren't getting along so well, I'm afraid. Next to them is the A-frame where Dr. Goff, the former-pathologist-turned-screenwriter, lives. He writes those *About to Kill* movies."

I nodded. I had heard of the series.

"And across the street from him is the latest coup de grâce for the trust, I suppose. The house that went viral on social media last year. The artist-in-residence at the time asked the trust if he could paint a mural on the old farmhouse. I figured, why not. Well, I found out why not. He painted a woodland scene with fairies in the au naturel. Your Aunt Hattie led the charge." Madeline chuckled. "She told him he had to make them 'decent,' and he said it would destroy the integrity of his work. She told him unless he could show her a picture of a living fairy, there was no integrity. Put some clothes on them. Of course, Colony Arts Trust backed her up. That's the house that is right next to your family cemetery. Agnes Mendell lives there. She asked specifically for that house. Here's another warning. She is extremely grumpy, to say the very least. Your Aunt Hattie told me she secretly thinks of her as

'Snarla.' Strangest part is, Agnes is a famous humorist."

"That's quite a collection I'm about to meet."

"I've just never had such an odd mix. They seem to repel each other. Even the married couple."

Madeline pushed the remote, and her twelve-foot iron gates opened. She pulled her vehicle into the circular drive and stopped in front of the huge columns that lined the west-facing portico as the gates closed behind us.

"Rick has asked me and your Aunt Hattie to keep an eye out for the sisters. He worries about them too." She pushed the gear shift into park, then turned in her seat to face me. "In addition to them, little Miah worries us as well. She's eight years old but looks about five. Or younger. At any rate, she's way too skinny and tiny for her age. Of course, your Aunt Hattie wants to find a way to feed her too. You know, hun, having three little girls on Colony Row has given your Aunt Hattie and me a mission we haven't had in a long time."

"Since I was small?"

Madeline smiled. Her eyes lit up with the thought. "Yes. What joy you brought us. Anyway. I invited all three girls to this week's potluck tomorrow night. I'm going to do my best to matchmake a friendship out of them. Plus, your Aunt Hattie and I really want you to meet them." She pushed the button to kill the engine, then looked at me again. "It's odd, you know. We both feel like that's really important somehow."

I declined Madeline's invitation to go inside as she got Beau, and instead proceeded to her smaller walker's gate next to the larger one for automobiles, pressed the security code and passed through. The small hum of the gate motor announced that the sensor had detected my crossing it's threshold and the gate shut behind me. As I crested the hill on Colony Row at Stopping Place, I paused before reaching the clearing to observe the sisters. They looked like children in Little Orphan Annie urchin costumes. Most little girls their age would still delight in having bows in their hair, princess outfits, light-up shoes, or clothes that sparkle with rhinestones. But the ragged, well-worn clothing these children wore bespoke secondhand shops. Their unkempt hair and unbathed condition did not depict poverty but neglect. Extreme neglect. Like odd puzzle pieces placed in the wrong box, they did not fit in an environment of eccentric artists with illustrious careers. The knuckle of my right hand hurt, and I pulled it from where I had unconsciously put it in my mouth and bitten down hard as I observed them. A strange sort of energy flew through me. How could their Aunt Stella allow such a travesty? Had they ever been read a bedtime story or been tucked in? I could not imagine any such loving acts, considering their appearance.

The girls did not hear my moccasins as I approached until I got within three hundred feet of them. They turned suddenly to look at me, standing at attention as though they had again been caught in a misdeed, then their heads dropped, and both stared at their feet.

"Hello," I said, careful to keep my voice soft.

The younger one looked at the older, her eyebrows pinched, summoning her sister to take the lead.

The oldest one looked at me. "We ain't trespassing or nothing. Miss Madeline said we could wait here for her."

"Of course." I stepped closer to introduce myself.

She took a step back.

"My name is Emerson."

The smaller one looked from me to her sister but did not reply. The older girl reached out and held her little sister's arm and pulled her close to her side. "I'm Deetsy and this here is my little sister, Bunny. She's six."

"My Aunt Hattie Mae and Madeline have told me nice things about both of you." I smiled.

Bunny returned a weak smile. Deetsy did not. Her eyes examined me as most people would a snake. I could not recall ever having someone more anxious to meet me than I was to meet them.

"You live up there on top-a Easterbrook, don't ya?" Bunny asked.

"Yes."

"Miss Hattie told us you was coming home," Bunny said, then

leaned her head against her big sister's arm. "Is it all right if we play in the spring? Miss Madeline said it was, but this being your land and all—"

Deetsy, still grasping Bunny's arm, shook it slightly, a signal to stop talking.

"I give you permission to be here anytime you like."

Bunny's eyes widened, despite her sister's warning. "Anytime?"

"Yes," I answered, unable to imagine why the idea of anytime was so exciting.

Over their head, high in a tree, a barred owl screeched. Both girls jumped.

"It is just a barred owl," I said casually. "If he calls again, you will hear him say, 'Who cooks for you?'" I pointed up to the top of the oak. "See him there? He is alerting others that we are here. Have you heard him before?"

Both girls nodded. "He's done scared us a whole lotta times," Bunny said.

"Then I would bet he has a nest nearby. He's standing watch."

The sound of a Carolina wren began.

"Can you hear that?" I asked.

They nodded.

"That is a wren saying, 'tea kettle, tea kettle, tea kettle.' They are small, chubby, and brown. Really cute little birds."

The bird repeated its song.

"I can hear it," Bunny squealed with excitement. A huge smile spread across her face, causing her nose to crinkle. "Now I wanna see it too."

Deetsy frowned, but then the bird sounded again, and her frown lifted. "I can hear it too." She released Bunny's arm.

I pointed to a bird swooping in Aunt Hattie's driveway across the street. "That is a blue jay. When he cries, he says his name. 'Jay, Jay, Jay.'"

The girls looked eagerly past my finger, but the bird was silent.

"You're a Injun like Pocahontas, ain't you?" Bunny asked.

"I am."

"I can tell 'cause you wear Injun shoes and all," Bunny added.

I smiled at her.

"Who taught you all that stuff about birds? A Injun chief?" Bunny asked, and Deetsy used her elbow to poke her little sister on the shoulder.

I squatted to be eye level. Both little girls looked at me eagerly. "Grandfather taught me. He taught me a lot about the mountains. How to tell one tree from another, how to predict the weather, which birds are which, and how to survive if I had to live outside."

At this, both girls' eyes widened. Bunny looked to Deetsy, who then shook her head, but Bunny leaned close to her sister so she could whisper in her ear. "You think he would teach us?" I heard her ask.

"Grandfather passed away last winter. But he taught me almost everything he knew."

"Can you teach us?" Bunny blurted.

Deetsy's eyes shot toward me, then back at Bunny with a scowl.

"I would love to teach you." I pointed to my ear. "Do you hear it? The jay?"

Both girls listened and nodded yes. Bunny giggled. "I done heard a jay say its name. Ain't that something?" She looked at her sister, smiling so hard her nose crinkled again.

Hearing Beau's excited grunts, we all three looked to see Madeline coming up the road. Beau led the way, his leash taut as he pulled Madeline along.

"You gotta dog, Miss Emerson?" Bunny asked. Her bright blue eyes glistened from her tiny, dirty face. It seemed her excitement made her freckles even more prominent, giving her a devilish look.

"No. Do you?"

"No, ma'am. Aint Stella says she ain't studying on no more mouths to feed. But we get to play with Beau nearly 'bout every day."

The tiny Yorkshire Terrier strained at the leash to get to the girls. About a hundred feet away, Madeline let go of her end, and Beau bounded to them, his tail wagging furiously. The girls crouched down and allowed him to lick their faces while Bunny giggled. Little sounds of excitement escaped from him as he licked them, his tail wagging so fast it became a blur.

"Beau loves these girls," Madeline said as she reached us.

"I can tell."

"And Maestro has taken up with Miah. I guess I'll have to get myself a hamster."

At this, both girls looked up at Madeline.

"I'm just kidding, sweethearts. Emerson, now that you've met Deetsy and Bunny, you need to meet Miah." Madeline winked at me, then turned to the girls. "Girls, do you know Miah?"

Obviously comfortable with Madeline, Deetsy stood up, faced her, and answered with eye contact. "Well, kinda. She's one of them art kids. We ain't never really met her, but she rides our bus." She bent to pet Beau, who rewarded her with a hand lick.

"Everybody at school calls her Skinny Girl 'cause she's so skinny," Bunny added.

Deetsy jabbed her sister with her elbow, and Bunny looked at her with curiosity.

"Well she is. And they do," Bunny defended.

"Is she bullied about it?" I asked.

Deetsy nodded. "And 'cause she's a ballerina. She told the teacher first day of school they was art people and she's a ballerina. From New. York. City," she said, as though the city was extraordinary.

I had addressed an issue that Deetsy was willing to talk with me about. I could understand why the sisters were bullied and why children from a rural area might be intimidated by the truth of Miah's life. The three girls had harsh treatment at school in common.

"But she wants to play with us," Bunny said.

Deetsy looked sharply at her little sister. "Why do you say that?"

"'Cause she waves to me when she gets off the bus. And 'cause you can see it in her eyes," Bunny said, defending her intuition.

"Well," Madeline said, placing her hands on her hips, "I mailed special invitations last week for the potluck tomorrow, and I hope all three of you will be there. It is going to be a welcome party for Emerson." Madeline looked at me and grinned, then looked back at the girls. "Miah will be there with her father. I hope you girls can come too. I'll be glad to talk with your Aunt Stella if you want me to."

Bunny reached out and pulled the sleeve of Deetsy's coat. "Can we go, Deetsy? Please?"

Deetsy stood stoically as though she were considering a life-or-death decision.

"I'm going to get a big cake to welcome Emerson. What kind of cake do you girls like?"

Bunny's eyes lit up with unmasked enthusiasm. "*Frosting* cake."

Deetsy again used her elbow to jab her little sister.

"You'll have to tell me what frosting cake is so I can be sure, sweetheart."

"You know," Bunny began, her voice now slightly diminished for having spoken out. "It's that kinda cake with roses on it."

Madeline was nodding as the child talked. "Oh my, yes. It is going to be frosting cake. There are going to be tons of roses on this cake. What color roses do you girls like?"

Bunny looked to Deetsy, awaiting her older sister's nod to offer her choice, which she gave. "I like red ones. And the blue ones. Oh, and the yeller ones," she said enthusiastically.

"And how about you, hun?" Madeline raised her eyebrows and looked toward Deetsy.

Deetsy shrugged as though she didn't care, but said, "I like the red ones too." She bent to pick up Beau, holding him to her chest as though she needed his companionship after being vulnerable and stating her wishes.

Madeline looked over at me, her eyes softened by the exchange. "Well, Emerson, that is exactly the kind of cake we have for you tomorrow night. What a coincidence."

I grinned in return.

"And I will make sure that Jons brings Miah," Madeline added. "You three can sit together, and I will bring some puzzles and games for you to play while the adults have the business meeting."

"She was coming anyways," Bunny said.

Madeline's eyebrows furrowed. "How do you know, sweetheart?

"'Cause she had one of them little invitations with the cat on it. I saw her pull it out of her pocket on the bus."

"You all got one too, didn't you?" Madeline asked the girls.

Bunny pulled a postcard from her coat pocket. The white card had the image of Maestro on the front—the exact design of the signs that Madeline puts in front of each artist's house before they arrive so they'll know which art house belongs to them.

Bunny looked adoringly at her card. "Is this cat gone be there tomorrow too?"

"No, hun, Maestro won't be there. But do you girls know why the cat is on the cards?"

"'Causing it says cat right here on the card," Bunny blurted, which earned her another jab from Deetsy. "Well, it does!" she returned defiantly.

"You are right, sweetheart. This way 'cat' can mean two things. CAT stands for Colony Arts Trust, the name of our art community, and it stands for Maestro too." Madeline looked at me and grinned. Turning to the girls, she reminded them, "The party is at five o'clock in the recreation hall behind the old church. We'll have a big dinner before the cake. I can pick you up in my car if you want."

Frowning, Deetsy tucked and re-tucked her hair behind her right ear while Bunny pulled at her coat sleeve. "Please, Deetsy. Pretty please. I wanna play with Skinny Girl and I want some frosting cake. Please."

Deetsy shook her arm to free herself of Bunny. "Aint Stella," Deetsy firmly half whispered to Bunny.

"Aint Stella works at '3P' tomorrow. I saw it on the 'frigerator."

Deetsy's frown loosened a bit with Bunny's words. "If Aint Stella don't go to work we have to stay there. But if we can, we'll walk."

"Okay. No worries, sweetheart. And I will save you some frosting cake no matter what. Emerson, we are headed to lunch at Aunt Hattie's. Why don't you come along with us?"

The girls bobbed their heads hard in agreement.

"I need to go home. But give Aunt Hattie my love."

Bunny dropped the invitation and squatted to pick it up. Still in the squatted position, she put the card in her coat pocket and used her fingers to pry a stone from the driveway. Turning it this way and that, she stood and showed it to her sister. "Look here. I done found me a diamond."

Deetsy nodded without emotion, and Bunny turned to me. She stretched her hand with the stone in her tiny palm. "Here. It's for you, Miss Emerson. Cause you done taught us 'bout them birds."

I held out my hand and accepted the gift, then examined it as carefully as Bunny had, turning it in different directions. The multiple facets in the stone caught the sun and reflected light back to me. In places, the rock was clear like diamond. "Thank you, Bunny. This is beautiful. I have always collected rocks. I am pretty sure it is not a diamond, but something called quartz. And it is an exceptionally pretty piece of quartz too. I am going to put it in my kitchen window."

"Quartz. Now I done learned me a rock name too," she said, her body wiggling. "I'm gon' know me some stuff 'cause Miss Emerson's gon' teach me."

Madeline looked at me for a long moment and nodded. She turned back to the girls. "Emerson is an incredible teacher. Just like her grandfather."

• • •

As I walked up the mountain drive, I contemplated the sweet-and-sour experience of meeting two orphans eager to learn. I wanted to teach them. Bunny's enthusiasm and Deetsy beginning to come out of her shell around me had tempted me to go to Aunt Hattie's with them. But what good would it do to become more involved? If they became attached to me and Enaldo or his associates found me and murdered me, they might be scarred for life.

A sudden movement up ahead in my driveway caught my eyes. A flash. Something had dashed behind a thick stand of mountain laurel. I immediately scolded myself for having let my guard down. I had been walking up the middle of the drive. There was an unobstructed view of me.

I ducked and scurried off the gravel, diving behind the trunk of a huge oak, holding my breath to hear better. Whatever was behind me had gone silent. My eyes searched the woods and the portion of driveway I had walked up. Nothing moved, nothing unusual. My heart pounded. I leaned hard against the oak so that I could remain rock steady, concentrating on every sound. Birds, wind in the top of the trees. But I had seen movement at ground level. I was trained to wait until my intuition was clear. And there was no need to take a risk. Who or whatever was out there would have to make the first move. I could outwait anything or anyone.

About three minutes later, fifty feet or so up the mountain, I heard the slightest sound of leaves rustling. A step or two by something heavier than a small woodland animal.

Then, silence.

As I waited for something to move, the same something waited for me. My heart had the hard, steady rhythm of a percussion instrument.

After a minute or two, leaves rustled again in the same spot.

I did not move. Whatever it was did not have the patience Grandfather taught me to have. I could wait a very long time if I was prey. At the thought, my legs trembled. I leaned harder against the tree.

Another series of leaves, and a twig snapped. This time closer, moving down the mountain.

My heart leapt to my throat. If something continued to advance toward me, I would be forced to move. My eyes scouted the path I would take, zigzagging back through the woods, down Easterbrook, toward Madeline's. If they shot at me, I would be hard to hit darting between trees. Heading to Stopping Place would be far too easy for my predator; they would likely have come that way. Avoiding Colony Row, the path through the forest to Maple Grove would be unknown to almost anyone but me.

Suddenly a loud snort resounded up the driveway behind me. A male deer had sounded a signal to his herd. I had alarmed him, perhaps as much as he had alarmed me. I straightened against the tree, my legs regaining their strength.

He snorted again. I turned to watch a large buck dart through the trees. Eight points. He would be at least three years old.

Before Enaldo, I would have felt joyous seeing the buck. He had been here when Grandfather was alive. But what I felt instead was glad that Deetsy and Bunny had not witnessed me hiding behind the tree. And what I felt was shame.

CHAPTER NINE

I sat on the wooden back steps of the former Pleasant Grove church. As a child, I had attended the small white country church, sang hymns sitting on hand-hewn pews in the cedar-lined sanctuary, and marveled at the beautiful stained-glass windows. And I had also sat in this very spot on the back steps of the church hundreds of times, waiting for adults to finish talking, waiting for children to gather for a game of tag, or watching as the grownups prepared the covered dish meals for picnics on the grounds or gatherings in the cinderblock fellowship hall less than a hundred yards in front of me.

With climate control, the fellowship hall usually won out over outdoor dinners on the grounds. Most occasions included food; holidays, birthdays, and even wakes. The huge front window of the rec hall that faced the back steps of the church allowed me to watch as a couple of the artists, under Madeline's direction, hung a welcome banner inside the front window.

Behind me, Stewie, the comedy writer, whose residence was the old church, had left a security note on the back door. *Joe. The python is loose in the house again. He's too big for one man. Wait till I get home.*

Gravel sprayed as a black pickup turned a sharp corner and rounded the south side of the church, coming to an abrupt halt in the parking lot in front of me and to my left, its bumper landing well over the sidewalk between the church's back steps and the fellowship hall. The fast entrance created a ghostly cloud of blue-gray dust. A tall blond man stepped out from the driver's side and slammed his door. The top of a tiny blond head was just visible above the passenger side window. The man retrieved two grocery bags from the bed of his truck. With just a few hurried strides, he reached the sidewalk and began walking toward the fellowship hall, then turned to look back at his vehicle.

"Whaddaya doing? You coming or not?"

The top of the small blond head bobbed affirmatively from the passenger seat. Then a tiny hand held up an index finger just above the level of the dashboard as though to say, "One second."

"Okay, then," Jons shouted back in a gruff voice. With more long strides, he walked toward the fellowship hall and continued without turning. "Have it your way. You always do. I want you in there in just a few minutes though. Don't make me come back out here."

I wrestled with guilt for having watched this private interchange. Madeline had warned me that she believed Jons was a widower caught up in his art at the expense of his daughter's needs. In less than two minutes, I had witnessed an example of just that.

Miah had told Madeline that if you are light, you get picked for the ballet dances with lifts. Madeline reasoned this was why Beau regularly found breakfast Pop-Tarts thrown in the woods where Miah waited for the bus. Aunt Hattie had mentioned that almost every night, Miah was outside in the cold, carrying Maestro around, talking and singing to the cat. "Her daddy is all tied up in that studio till late at night, and most times she's alone till after midnight. That right there ain't no fittin' childhood." So it seemed both Miah and her father used artistic goals to overcome the mother's loss.

The pickup's passenger door opened, and Miah emerged, then shut the door carefully, as though she was concerned about making noise. I should have been prepared, given the descriptions of Miah, but I was not. Her hair, tied back in a ponytail, fell midway down her back. Dressed in a pale pink sweater with the sleeves pushed up to her elbows, pink tennis shoes, and skinny denim jeans, she looked closer to five, certainly not eight. She was painfully thin, her bones jutting out in sharp angles along her collar bones and wrists.

She stood at the truck's door and looked down, first at her feet, then toward the sidewalk. She bobbed her head up and down as though counting a beat: *one . . . two . . . three . . . four . . .* but instead of a dance step, like a toy soldier with a strange marching style, she stepped toward the concrete with wooden knees. When she reached the sidewalk, she turned her upper body and looked back at the truck door, then back toward the fellowship hall, and again bobbed her head. Her shoulders slumped. Looking back at the truck again, she frowned and slid the index and middle finger of her right hand into her mouth.

She was scared. Her father had mistaken her stalling for opposition, but she had been estimating or . . . counting her steps. Guessing how many it would take from one point to another. Perhaps miscounting the number from truck to sidewalk. She was grasping for some sense of control.

Miah's chest rose sharply as she forced a few deep breaths. Taking her fingers out of her mouth, she bent to brush off her jeans. Then her tiny fingers appeared to be picking something off of her jeans from her waist to her ankles, one pinch at a time. Like a tiny pretzel, she curved herself around her leg and froze when she caught sight of me watching her. She straightened immediately and stiffened, eyes wide.

"You must be Miah," I said, hoping to put her at ease.

She nodded yes. Her tiny blond eyebrows were furrowed over bright blue eyes in a perfect oval face. As I stood and moved toward her, she backed up slightly like a cornered animal. This marked the second time in as many days that I had met someone more anxious than I was.

"I am Emerson," I said, hoping to reassure her. "That is my name on the welcome sign in there. I was just watching them hang it." I pointed in the direction of the rec hall; her eyes followed my finger to the large window where the banner had been hung from inside. "Madeline said they had a party here for you and your dad not long ago."

Miah nodded, her neck stiff.

I stood and walked toward her as I spoke, "I have been sitting out here because I am nervous about going inside. Were you nervous about your welcome party too?"

At my admission, Miah's shoulders relaxed slightly. "Yes," she replied. Her luminous eyes fringed with dark lashes contrasted with her peaches-and-cream complexion.

"Can I ask you some questions about these parties?"

"Okay."

I squatted to be eye level. "Do the adults talk about art?"

"Yes." Her head bobbed; her ponytail swayed.

"Do they play games?"

"Not since I've been coming."

"Then what do we do if we are not artists?"

"Eat and talk and stuff."

"Adult stuff?"

Miah nodded.

"That must not be a lot of fun."

Miah paused. "It's okay."

"So, what is the best part?"

"Going home." Miah startled, her head going back slightly as she frowned. "I didn't mean to be rude. It just popped out."

"You were not rude. You were honest. I respect that."

Her face relaxed.

"Actually, Miah, this party may turn out to be fun. Do you know Deetsy and Bunny that ride your bus? They get on right down the road from you." Miah nodded.

"They are invited tonight. Madeline thought you three girls might like to get to know one another."

Miah looked down and kicked at a piece of gravel on the sidewalk with her tennis shoe. Clearly, I had increased, not reduced, her anxiety. I lowered my voice further. "Is that a bad idea?"

"No," she started, tentatively. "It's just that . . ." She continued to move the stone an inch one way and then the other. "I bet the oldest one doesn't like me."

"Why do you think that?"

"Well, the little one waves to me. But her sister . . . her sister is in the class where the kids call me . . . bad names." She looked up to gauge my reaction.

"I too was called bad names when I was your age, Miah. It really hurt."

Miah looked down and watched her foot move the rock as though it were acting independently.

"I was bullied at school. Do you get bullied?"

Miah shook her head hard enough for her ponytail to sway from shoulder to shoulder. "No. They whisper it so I can hear it, but the teacher doesn't."

I paused, unsure if I should tell her that she was being bullied even though the teacher could not hear it.

"Do the sisters down the road call you names?" I asked, my heart in my throat.

Miah looked back at me and shook her head no.

Tension released in me. Thank goodness. "I know when I was bullied it made me very lonely. Have you made any friends?" Miah shook her head, less aggressively this time.

"Bunny and Deetsy were very excited about coming tonight because they wanted to meet you. They seem lonely too. I am guessing that people make fun of them as well."

Miah nodded. "I hope that after the three of you meet tonight you can be friends."

She nodded without enthusiasm still watching her foot.

"Will you help me keep an eye out for them and let me know if you see them? They may be a little afraid to go into the party like we are. You and I can come out and get them when they come."

She looked up at me. "Okay."

"It looks as though you have been around a cat or a dog," I said, pointing to the ankles of her jeans. "I will bet that it is a cat because cats like ankles."

She looked down at her ankles, then looked up and behind me, her eyes darting.

"Sometimes it is really nice to hold a cat or a dog. They are soft and warm and furry." I bent at the waist and brushed the hair from her ankles. "Have you been holding a pet?"

She paused for a moment, took a deep breath, and half whispered, "A cat."

"There," I said, straightening. "You are all clear now." I set my hands on my hips and pulled my shoulders back. "I guess it is time for us to go to the party."

I walked toward the rec hall, Miah behind me. Steps before reaching the door, Miah tugged at the bottom edge of my sweater. I looked down. She was looking at me with a frown, her index and middle finger in her mouth.

"What is it, Miah?"

She pulled her fingers out and asked so softly I could barely hear, "Do you . . . do you know what angels look like?" Her tiny brows squeezed in a frown, her eyes probing mine.

"No. I do not know. But the Bible tells us that we often interact with angels and are not even aware of it. So, I believe God can make an angel with any sort of appearance."

Miah nodded, her eyes never wavering from mine as she considered my words.

"Why, Miah? Do you see angels?"

She looked down at her feet. When she looked back up, she whispered. "I have an angel kitty." Her bright blue eyes filled with tears that spilled down her cheeks. She brushed them off with the back of her hand. "He . . . he came up to me." Miah put her head down, swiping once more at her flawless complexion.

I squatted beside her. "Miah, I would love to hear more."

"My . . . my . . . my mom sent him to me from heaven. That's where she lives."

"I am so sorry your mom is not here with you. Every girl needs her mother." Numbness washed over me as I recognized that I repeated to Miah the words Grandfather had said to me many times. But he would have scooped me up and held me when I needed her. A desire to comfort Miah the way he had comforted me flooded through me. I could not imagine Jons consoling Miah, but I also knew that I could not.

Miah's bottom lip began to tremble. She swiped at tears as she said, "My mom . . . she made sure I would know the kitty was from her. It says Mom on her collar."

MOM. Madeline Olivia Matthews. Miah looked up at me and scanned my face for a response.

I wished something in my research had taught me the right words to say to a hurting child. I resorted to how I thought Grandfather would respond. "I am so glad, Miah, that an angel kitty came up to you."

Her eyebrows furrowed as she looked at me with pleading eyes. "Can . . . can this be our secret? Please?"

"Yes, Miah. You have my word."

Just as I was about to ask Miah what she called the cat, the rec hall door opened. From above where I squatted, her father loomed over us. He was frowning, his lips tightly shut in a grimace as he stared at his truck so intensely that he failed to see the two people crouched within inches of the door. He jumped back with a start when he did, then clumsily collected himself, his demeanor shifting in a moment. "There you are. I was just coming to look for you." He forced a smile. "Who's your friend, Miah?"

I rose, my jaws clenched. I could not muster the obligatory smile that should have been offered in return. His anger had been palpable. I wanted to defend the child that already had enough on her plate without her oblivious father's high expectations. But Miah was watching me.

I offered my hand for him to shake. "I am Emerson."

"Has Miah been bothering you?"

Heat rose in me. I turned to look at the small waif beside me. Her eyes were huge, her frown begging me for help. I turned to Jons. "No. In fact, meeting Miah is one of the best things that has happened to me in a long time."

Looking back at Miah I smiled and continued. "Miah and I have a lot in common."

Her frown disappeared.

"Well, just tell her to back off if she bothers you."

So many responses passed through my mind. None that I would give air to. I met his eyes squarely. "I do not think that will ever happen."

"Good." Jons turned and walked into the rec hall.

I looked back at Miah and squatted beside her again.

"Miah, I have loved meeting you."

"He's mad because I didn't come in . . . and because he didn't see me."

She was correct in ways she could not comprehend. Her father was oblivious. And I was overwhelmed with love for Grandfather. What a difference it made in my life that he had seen me.

CHAPTER TEN

The artists were milling about the inside of the recreation hall making small talk when I entered the room with Miah. The sound of chatter stopped, and from the sound system, only the strains of Pachelbel's *Canon in D* could be heard in the background. A mixture of food smells like fried chicken, chili, and the aroma of coffee filled the air. Madeline came forward and said she would take me around to meet each of the artists individually.

There was a lot to take in. The plain gray cinderblock walls outside were in stark contrast to the museum atmosphere inside. Artists of great renown who had once been in residence with CAT had left behind contributions of their signature works. In addition to introducing me to the artists in residence, Madeline gave me a brief tour of the framed paintings, famous photography, prints, and various sculptures around the perimeter of the ivory-colored walls. The collection, individually lit from ceiling tracks, provided an exquisite ambiance that matched the long, hand-hewn oak table against the back wall with twenty ornate chairs, also a gift from a former resident. Creating a more casual ambiance, the abstract, brightly colored tablecloth was paper, as well as the place settings.

While polite, most of the artists were formal in their greetings as Madeline introduced us, with the exception of Stewie, a short balding man with a Santa Claus belly. When Madeline introduced me to him, Stewie stepped back and looked me up and down critically, as though

I were modeling a fashion he had designed. He put his hands in front of his chest, acting as though he were holding up a rating card. "Ten. You score a perfect ten." With that, he swept his right arm out to the side and gave a steep bow, the light from the windows reflecting on his bald head. "Welcome Emerson Grace Coffee. We have sorely needed your company. You may be a foot taller than I, but I'm up for the challenge."

Madeline looked over to me, her eyebrows raised as if to ask if I was okay with his humor.

"Thank you just the same, Stewie, but I will not be challenging you."

Stewie shook his head slowly. In a softer voice he said, "Oh, but my dear Emerson, you must be prepared. Once you encounter the force of my charm, you will find yourself effortlessly pulled into my magnetic field. It's like a black hole." He hunched his eyebrows and threw his arms to the sides, and with a joyous voice he proclaimed, "It just happens." Stewie looked at Madeline, "It's a numbers game. The odds are in my favor. Right, Madeline?" Stewie chortled and his belly bounced. Then he wiggled his eyebrows and moved off to speak with a tall, distinguished man with an expertly clipped gray beard, wearing a tweed jacket.

I looked to Madeline who smiled and shook her head. "That's Stewie. I'm pretty sure he's harmless. He hasn't realized yet he enjoys himself more than others seem to enjoy him."

The two of us watched Stewie's exuberance in stark contrast to the older man in his expertly tossed Burberry scarf, who stone-facedly observed Stewie like a scientist watching a petri dish. "Dr. Goff," Madeline offered. "Former medical examiner from California. He's the one that writes all of those *Time to Kill* movies."

When my introductions were complete, Madeline, refusing my help, left me to bring the dishes from the kitchen to an intricately carved oak buffet table between the kitchen and the great room. I moved to the table and sat in the chair Madeline suggested, next to her at the head nearest the kitchen. I had gravitated to my default setting, observing instead of interacting. Something else Miah and I apparently had in common. She had isolated herself as well, positioned in a wingback chair facing the large window under the welcome banner. An oversized book on birds was open on her lap, but she glanced up every few seconds to keep an eye on the back of the old church and the driveway where Deetsy and Bunny were due to make their appearance.

The talk among the artists drifted toward me. It centered on deadlines and an upcoming community art show. But when I switched my focus to the emotions in the room, there was no sense of joy or warmth among friends. Just a drone of chatter. The room, it seemed, was filled with introverts. Stewie was the only artist intent on making rounds. He did not move from a conversation until he laughed at least once.

Madeline called everyone to the table as she stood at the end. "Go ahead and take your seats." She waited while everyone found a seat, and sat last. "I am calling the meeting to order. First of all, Emerson, I talked with everyone this morning and filled them in. CAT gave each artist an opportunity to leave and come back another time for a residency. Or they could decide to stay. They all decided to stay."

The artists were quiet and did not appear too interested in the topic. Except for Agnes Mendell. Her head was bent so deeply over a composition book as she wrote furiously that her pageboy-styled black hair and long, thick, blunt bangs hid her face.

Madeline looked down the silent table. "Emerson's grandfather, Edward Two Eagles, was fond of saying, 'The wisdom of others are the arrows in our quiver.'" She looked at me and winked. No mistake, this was part of the mystery hunt. "Tonight's icebreaker will be each of you sharing with us an especially important lesson that you've learned. A bit of your wisdom. I'll go first.

"I learned very young that my neurofibromatosis was a powerful tool capable of revealing the true character of another. People could hurt me by calling it Elephant Man's Disease or they could look past my disfigurement and truly see me. If they saw me instead of my deformities, I began to trust them. So my most important lesson would be that if someone can accept the worst in you, you can trust that they will accept the rest." She looked around. Although they had listened, only Dr. Goff and Leena Rose acknowledged that they had heard and understood with head nods. "Okay, who will go next?"

After a moment, Leena Rose cleared her voice to speak. A petite, plainly dressed woman who looked to be in her early sixties, she wore her graying brown hair short with wisps that curled near a face that held deep wrinkles around the eyes, the gift of many smiles. "I will. As most of you know, I'm a former cloistered nun. I left the convent after twenty years to care for my ailing parents. When I took up art as a stress reliever, I became a revelation artist, using no pictures or models. I allow God to reveal himself through my work. Which leads to what I learned. When I don't know what to do, I have to remind myself that I am only an instrument. I have to trust that God will reveal what he wants through me. So I wait."

"Thank you," Madeline said.

After a pause Dr. Goff spoke up, leaning forward over the table toward Madeline, looking somewhere over her head. His voice was stern, and his words clipped as though he were a professor instructing. "Self-disclosure here will be vital in order for all of you to understand the wisdom I intend to share. I carry a diagnosis of Asperger's Disorder, which aptly explains my idiosyncrasies. While some may view it as a condition, I see my eccentricities as advantages. They give me a penchant for super focus and singleness of purpose, making me extremely prolific. I left the field of medicine as a medical director to write scripts and exhaust my imagination. However, that depletion point has become a Quixote mirage. At present, I am writing the sixth in the series of About to Kill movies. The nature of my current script is a serial killer living in mountainous terrain. Ergo, I sought out a residency with Colony Arts Trust to gain the ambiance that I would need for a successful portrayal of such a psychopath."

There seemed to be a shift in the energy at the table. Everyone stilled as they listened.

"The muse visits me most commonly at night. This is quite fortuitous, or perhaps one should say opportunistic, for me, as I am an insomniac. The dark of night creates a setting that is quite unsettling for most because the unknown abounds. I, however, derive advantage from that situation. I nocturnally exploit my own anxiety by writing at night."

He straightened slightly, holding his head back, chin out. "Perhaps now my best advice will be relatable. Early on, I was a starter of imaginative quests and not a finisher. Until I applied a principle I learned as medical examiner, I would become impatient when I did not get the results I wanted and prematurely abandoned projects that I now believe could have become successful. When I was a medical examiner, however, police detectives would harass me to hurry up and report to them on the results of toxicology and other cultures. But no matter how anxious they might have been, no matter how much they might have pushed for me to rush things, I could not hasten the chemicals in the cultures. Each procedure required a specific amount of a significant ingredient—time. Ergo, you can apply this to any application. As an artist, I might hit a block. But I must not quit at that point. I must allow for time. Mysteriously it appears, time creates an energy that resolves blocks. Be advised, once the wheels are in motion and you have nothing else you can do, time is the ingredient that works with you and for you. Or, as I told the detectives and police officials, 'You have to give the chemicals a chance to work.' Thank you."

Dr. Goff sat back. He blinked hard a couple of times and then rested both hands in his lap. He tilted his chin up and looked at the ceiling.

Silence filled the room.

"My name is Jons." He was sitting next to me and did not look toward anyone but Dr. Goff, who appeared to be studying the beams in the ceiling. "I am a metal sculptor. And I'm working on the biggest installation of my career, a piece commissioned by a museum in Minnesota. Oddly, my best advice is don't listen to advice." Jons chuckled a bit. "See, everyone told me I'd be crazy to give up my job as a welder. They said, 'Don't move to New York. Get serious. Grow up.' My wife had died; Miah was small." He was oblivious to Miah next to him, who looked up at the sound of her name. "But I realized the people telling me that were scared for me. I learned you can't listen to people who are afraid. You have to take a chance, even if you don't have any support."

"Thank you, Jons," Madeline said.

"I'll go next. I'm Stewie, and even though I'm round, like I've been eating too much stew"—he patted his stomach—"Stewie is short for Stewart. And it pretty much describes my life. I'm, like, always in a stew." He laughed, his belly shaking. "Not a former nun, and no diagnosis for this guy." He pointed both thumbs at his chest. "Other than maybe Looney Tunes. Not that anyone has officially labeled me that. But then I've been told that I'm 'off label' anyway.

"Up until a few years ago, I was a head writer for a late-night comedy king. But he got himself into a twist with the network, and I got pitched out on the street." Stewie threw out his right arm to demonstrate. "So, my agent said why not write a sitcom? So, I did, and darned if it didn't sell. It's in its fourth season now.

"Last spring, I got the first advance on a movie script. But I kept finding reasons not to sit at the computer. You know, places to go, people to see. So, my agent said I needed to do the art colony gig so I would be forced to write. She wants me to stay put so I don't get sidetracked." He shook his head as he gave account. "You know, with, like, coffee here, dinner there, or 'let's do lunch.' On Colony Row, that's no problemo. Since I'm on my own, surprise, surprise, I can finally crank it out." With this, he looked at Gideon to his left and Agnes to his right. "I've been here a month, and already I'm, like, talking to the church mice." At this he chuckled out loud. "Emerson, you're probably the only one that doesn't know. That's because I'm in the old church. Obviously CAT has a sense of humor too." Stewie chuckled, his belly keeping time. No one joined him.

Madeline smiled.

"Okay, so, my advice . . . I figured out a long time ago, the only jokes that people remember are the ones that make them feel something. So I've learned, by process of . . . well, a lot of misses and a few hits, that if you want to be successful, you have got to make people feel something . . . *anything*." Stewie shook his head and threw up his hands in a gesture of surrender. Then, attempting to replicate Porky Pig's voice, he said, "The-uh-the-uh-th—That's all, folks." He chuckled and rested his hands on the table in front of him.

Again, no one laughed with Stewie. I found myself smiling, and Madeline had worn a grin as well.

As the others gave advice, I noticed the lack of interaction between all of them. Most did not even appear to be listening. Except for Leena Rose, who kept her eyes on each speaker. Agnes must have been writing every word spoken in her journal, and Dr. Goff appeared to listen while attending to the ceiling tiles.

I agreed with what Aunt Hattie and Madeline had told me. This group was disconnected.

The moment Madeline adjourned the meeting, suggesting a ten-minute break before dinner, Agnes slammed the cover of her notebook shut and growled toward me. "Emerson, am I to understand that the old graveyard that borders my side yard is part of your mountains?"

Dr. Goff looked my way. Obviously, the question was of interest to him as well, his residence being an A-frame across the street from Agnes.

Megan stopped in her tracks beside her chair and looked at me for my answer. She and Gideon could see Agnes's house from theirs.

"Yes. That is correct." I said.

"Well, I'd appreciate it if you would kindly tell your kinfolk to stop leaving their newspapers on the graves. The dead can't read. The wind scatters them, then I'm the one who must pick them up." She clicked her pen hard, opened the spiral notebook, and shoved it in.

Dr. Goff chimed in. "I too have had my share of newsprint to contend with on the lawn. Technically, however, it's a cemetery because it is not connected to a church. But, nonetheless, it is annoying to find their litter."

"I apologize," I said. "I am not sure what you mean."

"I would think if you own that graveyard"—Agnes looked over at Dr. Goff with a scowl, then back at me—"excuse me . . . cemetery, and if these visitors are part of your tribe, you would know what's happening. Every single Monday it's the same. They roll up in an old gray pickup with a blue hood. Three of them pile out and take their huge Sunday newspapers to the graves, stay a few minutes, and then leave. I don't care if they visit the dead, I just don't want them leaving the newspapers. That's all. Is that too much to ask?"

I nodded, although I had no idea where to start.

As the rest of the artists moved about during the break, Miah walked up to the table and stood across from me. Her eyes glistened, her little eyebrows rose in excitement. "They're here," she said with a smile.

I stood and walked with her to the big front window. Miah pointed to the little sisters standing in the middle of the driveway near the side of the old church. They were within a foot of each other. Deetsy pushed her hair back behind her ears repeatedly while Bunny plead with her big sister about something, her hands in a begging clasp beneath her chin.

I bent down near Miah's ear. "Why don't we go out and get them."

Miah looked up at me and nodded agreement as the index and middle finger of her right hand found her mouth. We opened the door, and the girls looked our way. I waved and smiled. Following my lead, Miah offered a tiny wave with her left hand. The two sisters spoke to one another. Bunny had her head down, and Deetsy appeared to be commanding her to do something by pointing to Bunny's shoes.

Deetsy looked at her feet as we approached. Bunny watched us.

"Hi, Deetsy. Hi, Bunny. We have been watching for you." I stepped sideways to reveal Miah, who had walked directly behind me. "Miah saw you first. Right, Miah?"

Miah nodded agreement, then looked at her own feet.

Bunny eyed us as though we were snakes coiled to strike.

"I am glad to introduce you to each other." I smiled as I pointed to each of them. "Deetsy, Bunny, and Miah."

Miah offered a small smile, Bunny grinned, and Deetsy nodded her head.

"Guess what. There is a big frosting cake in there for dessert. Right, Miah?"

Miah frowned.

"The whole top of this frosting cake is full of roses made of creamy delicious frosting so that we can have all the roses we want."

Miah bobbed her head in understanding.

"But first, everyone has to eat some dinner. Is that a deal?" Bunny and Deetsy both nodded. I looked down at Miah and she nodded as well.

Deetsy faltered a bit as she spoke. "Miss Emerson . . . we're sorry we're late . . . Aint Stella didn't leave at her right time, and she told us we had to clean up and stay put till she was gone." I squatted down to be at eye level with the group. "Deetsy, it is okay. We will always understand."

Deetsy's shoulders softened, and Bunny grinned and elbowed her sister as if to say, "Told you."

"We are just glad you came. Do you agree, Miah?" I asked conspiratorially.

She nodded with a slight smile.

"Come on, girls. They need us inside to get this party started. And we have some roses to eat." I stood, then turned on my heel and walked. Like little ducklings, all three children followed behind me. My heart lifted with the faint sound of little girl giggles.

CHAPTER ELEVEN

---·•••·——✻——·•••·———

In a half sleep, I pulled one of Aunt Hattie's handmade Shoofly quilts over my mouth and nose. Then I was fully awakened by a smell and sat up.

Skunk.

The odor pervaded the bedroom.

I hugged the warm quilts around me and listened for the sound of tiny feet on the veranda, or a larger predator that may have chased a skunk up the steps. Although I could not fathom skunks using steps as an escape route. I heard nothing. Something must have disturbed Mama Skunk and her kits.

Lying back down, I pulled the covers over my head to block the smell. But sleep would not come. There were too many reasons to be awake.

Once again, I sat up. The clock on my antique dresser read 3:20 a.m.

I left the warmth of the quilts, my feet hitting the cold floor, and slid one foot around on the hardwood to find my moccasins just beneath the edge of the bed. If an intruder of the human sort were outside, I would not want them to see my light. I felt my way to my bedroom door and grabbed the heavy bathrobe I had left hanging on a hook. I tied the belt and reached in the right-front pocket to make sure my flashlight was still there. It was.

I moved in the dark to the cedar chest under the window and

slipped my fingers behind the outer edge of the heavy blackout curtains, then pried a small opening in the slats of the venetian blinds and looked out.

Darkness. Heavy cloud cover muted the moonlight. The wind had lain down. The smell of skunk was so pervasive I could almost taste it. I pulled the neck of my gown up through the opening in my robe so that it covered my mouth and nose.

Something had aroused the skunks, and I would not be able to figure out what from upstairs. The creak when I opened my bedroom door echoed through the cabin.

I crept to every window in the great room to look out. Each footstep seemed to find a squeak in the floor, and I froze to listen after each. The lack of wind had created a sinister silence. It felt as though someone were listening. Why was I so anxious?

From every direction, what little I could see in the dimmed moonlight yielded only the natural view of my landscape. The smell was definitely stronger near the front of the house. For long moments I stood behind my oak front door, looking through the peephole. This view also yielded nothing out of the ordinary. When I realized I could not imagine a scenario of a gangster using a skunk to bait me, I unlatched the lock, mentally filing for future reference that the sound was loud, and pulled the door open enough to exit.

I surveyed the darkness. Nothing stirred.

While scouting for movement, I slowly pushed on the screen door. The bottom hit something, and it made a scraping sound as it moved over the porch floor. I quickly shut the screen and oak doors and latched the latter behind me. Had something fallen in front of the door? But what? I could think of nothing on the veranda small enough to only hit the bottom of the door.

Grateful for the quieting of the wind, I tiptoed around the great room, stopping to listen at each window. Once again, I lifted a thin blind slat to peek out, and once again nothing moved. The clock on the kitchen stove read 3:40. Twenty minutes I had wandered the house on high alert. I moved back to the front of the cabin. Perhaps the wind had blown a tree limb against the door. Although that had never happened before, and I couldn't imagine how it would have, I could think of nothing else. Whatever I had hit had not been heavy.

I determined to open the door again because sleep would be impossible until I found out what was on my porch. The click of the oak door latch was resolute. It had never occurred to me how decisive that sound could be. Locked or unlocked. No in-between.

I opened the door and this time looked down to the other side of the screen door.

A shoebox.

I froze. There was no way a shoebox had blown up onto my veranda. Stepping back inside, I closed the door and locked it, grateful now for the decisive sound. My head cleared instantly as though I had drunk a full pot of coffee. Even with the new discovery, I had more questions than answers. But I was certain someone had been on my veranda.

The day after I met him, Rick had insisted on burying four vehicle alarms under the gravel along the driveway. Were someone to drive up the mountain, the first alarm, at the base of the mountain, would have sounded a single long, shrill note through a speaker in the cabin. Halfway up the drive, two long shrill notes, and two-thirds of the way up, three. Finally, at the S-curve where the skunks lived, an approaching vehicle would have set off four very long, very loud notes. Had someone driven up in the night, a series of alarms would have alerted me, so whoever left the box could not have come up the driveway by car.

I also had not heard footfall on my steps or the veranda floor. But someone had been on Easterbrook last night. So close to me, and I had slept through it. How could that have been possible? I could not gather my thoughts to make sense of things. My brain grasped for logic.

Then, the story laid out instantly in my mind.

Someone had walked up Easterbrook. Had taken a shortcut. They had used the S-curve to avoid crunching over the gravel near the cabin and had been sprayed on the way up, carrying a heavy load of musk with them when they approached the veranda. If the box were heavy, it could have been a dirty bomb of some sort, but it had moved easily when I opened the screen and had not detonated with the disturbance. And whoever had left the box would likely be long gone by now.

I unlocked the door, then shoved the box even farther with the screen door, concentrating on the probable weight of it. Just ounces.

It did not shake or wiggle when I moved it. Rather than open it outside where an intruder might see me if they waited, I determined to grab it quickly and bring it inside for examination. I took a deep breath and moved as quickly as I could to open the door, grab the box, place it inside the house, then shut and latch the oak door.

Using the flashlight I kept behind the door, I pointed a beam at the shoe box. I squatted and could see that the original contents had been men's Dr. Martens, size ten and a half. The retail sticker read, *Mister Shoes, Soho, NYC.* A box from New York. Was the location meant to scare me?

I did not want to be close to the box when I opened it in case something waited to jump out, although I had not detected movement. I walked to the fireplace and grabbed a poker. When I returned, I stood as far as I could from the box, pulled my heavy robe over my nose and mouth in case there was a powder inside, like anthrax, and using my right hand, pried the top up with the hooked edge of the poker. The top flipped open.

I directed the flashlight's beam into the box. The light reflected a dull glow off of a plastic toy with a long tail. A gray rat.

CHAPTER TWELVE

The smell of Aunt Hattie's kitchen reminded me of the best bakeries in New York. Only, whatever she had created would taste even better.

Aunt Hattie poured Madeline and me a cup of coffee. "Ta da," she said as she uncovered a platter. "Fresh homemade cinnamon rolls for *this* here occasion."

I smiled and reached for a roll, then wiped the warm icing from my fingers with a napkin.

"You look tired, Emerson. I guess you aren't sleeping well," Madeline said.

I nodded and pulled a strip of the sticky pastry from the roll, then let its warmth fill my mouth. I would not worry them with the plastic rat. Aunt Hattie would lose sleep watching Colony Row even harder than she already was. Having to call Rick earlier in the morning to tell him had been hard enough. He had instructed me to leave the shoebox on the veranda for him to collect while I met my mothers for Wednesday morning breakfast to review the completion of the first leg of Grandfather's instructions, the potluck.

"Your Aunt Hattie and I have been looking forward to this hunt since your grandfather roped us into it. I'm so glad he has you coming back to see us after every step."

"That's right," Aunt Hattie chimed in. "He wanted to make dang sure you didn't come home to Easterbrook and hibernate."

"I told Hattie Mae all about the potluck before you got here. Your grandfather had a stroke of genius wanting the artists to share their best advice. I'm going to use that as an ice breaker again in the future. I think everyone learned from it."

I nodded. As I sipped my coffee and delighted in yeasty, cinnamon pleasures, I realized my stubborn resistance to meeting the artists had been childish. I *had* learned a lot. Agnes surprised me the most. When Madeline called on her, she looked up from her composition book, her eyebrows set in a deep frown, and thought for a moment. "Never underestimate people. Everyone has a heart. You just have to find it. It's usually a soft spot," she said, then picked up her pen, bowed her head over her notebook, and returned to her writing. Was she advertising that *she* had a heart? I wondered if anyone had tried to find it.

My mothers watched me think. I knew what their soft spot was. Me.

"I am ready when you are," I told them.

Madeline reached in her pocket and drew out a folded sheet of notebook paper, then handed it to me with a smile. "These are the instructions your grandfather wanted me to give you after the potluck."

I unfolded the paper. His handwriting created a warm glow inside of me, a loving feeling, and for the first time, the love came without crushing grief. My sorrow had steadily lifted since I found the hunt. I read the note.

Emerson,

Continue to seek the wisdom of others. You will always need new arrows in your quiver.

Go back to what you know about the Wild Woman. You will know the next steps when you find them. Then you must come back and let Hattie tell you her story. After that, you must take a neighbor with you.

Grandfather.

The room was quiet. I looked up to see Madeline and Aunt Hattie watching me expectantly. I looked back down at Grandfather's instructions. "My next step is to go back to what I know about the Wild Woman." I shook my head. "That's almost nothing."

Aunt Hattie smiled. "Your granddaddy knew what you do *know.*"

"Well then, as Dr. Goff would say, I suppose I need to give the chemicals in my brain a chance to work."

Aunt Hattie smacked the table lightly with her hand. "There's our girl. Already got her hand in her quiver, just like her granddaddy figured she would."

• • •

As I walked up Easterbrook, scanning my environment for signs of intrusion, I re-examined what I knew about the Wild Woman. First, she created a haunting howl. I had heard it. Grandfather said it was the sound of a heart breaking. I could believe that.

Second, I had seen her at the foot of Crawl Mountain, near the fence post where Grandfather left things for her. She had briefly stepped out of the woods, then retreated when she saw us.

My arm hair rose in anointing. I needed to go to the foot of Crawl Mountain.

The next day, I got up early to find the fence post where I had spotted her with Grandfather so many years ago. I readied myself with a burner phone for emergencies and a Taser that clipped on my waistband. Rick had insisted I always carry both.

The morning was turning out warm with a light breeze. My moccasins were snug from the thick wool socks I had chosen. They afforded extra cushion as I stepped out onto the gravel drive. As I approached the S-curve, there was still a slight smell of skunk musk, faintly lighter than yesterday. But still there. The turned-up leaves near Mother Skunk's log showed disturbance. The kind of pattern seen when a human drags their feet in thick leaves, the spacing between disturbances a normal width for adult legs. Beyond that, the autumn floor was chaotic. Leaves overturned and scattered, like a scuffle had ensued at the end of the log where I had seen the mother shepherd her kits. The smell was strongest there. I looked for scat, signs that another animal had been close, but I knew there would be none. Skunks were not prey for other animals. The animal that had accidently stumbled on Mother Skunk's home was human.

I continued my walk down the mountain, my feet registering the changes beneath me like tactile GPS. In New York, I had missed the sensation of heavy moss, dried leaves, and pine needles beneath me. Textures of the earth. My feet sent signals to my heart. This was home. My native environment. Peace, where I knew I was a perfect fit. As much as any animal or plant on the mountains, I was a part of my natural habitat.

When I arrived at the gate that led to the pasture between Stopping Place and Crawl Mountain, my spirit sagged. Undergrowth and small cedar trees had taken root. When Grandfather was healthy, nothing ever looked this unkempt. If I ever managed to find safety again or felt confident in the open, where a drone might see me, I would make it my mission to pick up where he had left off.

I stood at the gate and looked around for clues, allowing the memories to move in and play a re-enactment in my mind. The day I saw the Wild Woman, I had hopped down from behind Grandfather's tractor seat to open the farm gate, then waited for him to pull the tractor through. When I shut the gate behind us, I ran and climbed up on the tractor to sit behind him again. We were halfway through the pasture when I looked around him and spotted her.

She was tiny, with a head full of bushy, flaming-red hair, and wore a flowing skirt that looked like it had been made from a red patchwork quilt.

Following what I remembered from that day, I opened the heavy gate and shut it behind me. This time out of tradition, not necessity.

Walking to the middle of the field, I saw the clump of cedar trees where I had caught sight of her. She had been standing behind the fence post with a wooden box attached to its top. It was still there. The box's tin lid was no longer shiny, but the box was intact. I made my way to it.

For years, Grandfather and Uncle Bill had left supplies for her inside the box. It had not been used in years. I swept a few moss-covered twigs from the box's lid, then opened it. The top squeaked, but the rusty hinges held. I leaned forward to peek inside. Empty. I searched at the bottom of the post. The tall grasses were not disturbed. Nothing had been near the box in years.

Four lines of barbed wire prevented me from getting a view of what the Wild Woman had seen from behind the box. I looked around me but saw no large branches or sticks on the pasture side to use as a prop. I would have to hold each strand from above and below to get through. After a couple of trials, I squeezed through. When I unfolded myself on the other side, I rubbed my aching hands on my jeans, then opened them palms up. Bright red stripes marked each one.

I moved behind the post and turned to see what her view would have been. I was only six when I saw her here. Six and small. She would not have seen me behind Grandfather until I peeked around him, just as I had not seen her until I did. She must have stepped out from the cedar grove after I ran and jumped back on the seat behind Grandfather. Maybe she had heard his tractor and come to see if he was leaving something in her box.

I walked into the line of cedars and turned again to look. I could not see the gate from where I stood.

There was nothing of interest in the grove. No large rocks piled for shelter. No old lean-to. No remnants of a refuge of any kind.

Where would she have come from?

It had been many years since she was last seen. If there had been a shelter, there would still be remnants of it. Old barns stand for hundreds of years. Without housing, how would she have survived the winters?

As I reached the end of the cedar grove, the rock base of Crawl Mountain came into view. I stood at the foot of the mountain and allowed my eyes to search in quadrants for any unnatural pilings of stone. What I saw halfway up the bank that led to the steep north face of Crawl Mountain made me gasp. As if binoculars had been focused, a pattern of rocks suddenly became clear. Crude steps led from the bottom of Crawl to the topmost cliff facing Easterbrook. My heart danced when I realized the last step led to a small ledge that ran along the front of the cliff.

And then I understood.

You will know the next steps when you find them.

CHAPTER THIRTEEN

Everything in me wanted to ascend. But Grandfather had anticipated this and had instructed me accordingly. I would have to take a neighbor with me. And, first, I would need to hear Aunt Hattie's story. Still, it could not hurt to get a better look before I left.

I stood at the base of Crawl and looked up. Because of the tall trees between the base of Crawl and Colony Row, the only possible view of the steps themselves would be from where I was standing at the start of the rock base. Or from Aunt Hattie's house, set far enough back from the road. And I had little doubt she knew of these steps. No wonder she had her watching chair.

My eyes charted the course. Some of the steps had crumbled, or perhaps had never existed. The legends of the caves seemed real now. I knew for certain my ancestors had lived and hidden out in them, and perhaps all the other legends were true as well.

Energy surged within me. I had not felt such excitement for a long time. Rather than return to the cabin, I walked the fence line to check for downed barbed wire or rotting posts, hoping life would soon resume normalcy and I could make repairs. There was overgrowth in my way, but the early frosts had killed back much of what would have made the path more difficult. As I came to the south end of the pasture, I turned east toward Colony Row and began to walk the fence line that separated the pasture from the side property line of Pleasant Grove. Ahead and to the right, I could see the back of the rec hall and the old church where Stewie lived. As I continued to walk the fence, a faint odor stopped me. Skunk musk.

There were downed trees and other places where a den could be. I placed each foot meticulously in the dried leaf beds, but as I got closer to the buildings, the smell grew stronger. I slipped between the fence slats to investigate. Within feet of the rec hall, I realized the smell was coming from the area around two trash cans that had been moved to the side of the rec hall from their usual spot near Stewie's. I did not see him at his windows or outside, so I walked closer to the cans.

The smell was heaviest at the cans.

I walked between the rec hall and the back of Stewie's and turned left onto the sidewalk that ran to the back of the old church building. Before I reached Stewie's back steps, where I had watched Miah and her father, I stepped into the gravel parking lot, then turned left to continue down the driveway to Colony Row. Out of a lifetime of habit, I paused along the south wall of the church and looked up at the stained-glass rendition of the hovering angel. A squeak from the back door drew my attention. I turned and walked back around the church. Stewie had stepped out on his back stoop.

"What is it with that window?" he asked. "It attracts more females than a leading man."

"I am sorry. I do not understand."

"Those little sisters. They come around to stare at it too. Only they do it at night."

I frowned with curiosity.

"I've caught them a couple of times, but they're squirrely about it. They get up real close."

"Can you show me how they do it?"

"Ah . . . okay."

Stewie walked out to the corner of the building as I walked to the window. I stood in front of it and looked to him for guidance.

"Well, they are closer to it than you are, but yeah."

I stood within three or four feet of the stained glass, then turned to look at him.

"Yeah. About like that," he said.

I squatted for their perspective and watched as the angel grew until she appeared to watch over me too. I straightened. "Then where do they go?"

He pointed down the driveway past the rec hall.

"Have you seen where they end up?"

"No. It's dark out here. There's a sensor light on the rec hall, but it only comes on if you're on the sidewalk. They walk along the other side of the driveway. Probably don't want to get in trouble for trespassing."

No, they did not want to trigger the light.

"So how do you see them at night, and how did you see me just now?"

"Oh, that's simple. I have superpowers." Stewie laughed, and when I did not join in, he added, "I do have superpowers, but, in this case, if someone walks by the windows in the daytime, I get a shadow inside. And when the girls come at night, I hear the gravel and them whispering."

I nodded without expression, as though I did not really care. If the girls had not wanted to be seen, I would not divulge any of my thoughts to Stewie.

"I am scouting around for wild medicinal herbs. I have always stopped to admire this window. Will it disturb you if I walk down in the field behind the fellowship hall?" Although the intent of my walk had not been herbs, if I had seen any, I would have been pleased.

"Help yourself. And if you want something real wild, come on back." He chuckled slightly.

As I turned to walk back down the driveway and past the rec hall, Stewie turned abruptly and walked toward his back door, as though a force field shoved him away from me. Although I hardly knew him, his quick departure without additional snappy repartee seemed out of character.

I crossed to the far side of the drive and walked the path the girls had taken, parallel with the sidewalk between Stewie's and the rec hall front door. When I reached the end of the driveway, I had a better look at the field of grass that ran thirty yards or so to the edge of the woods alongside and behind the cinderblock building. I saw nothing of note, besides a fresh blanket of autumn leaves. Along the south-facing side of the rec hall, the blinds were drawn, as usual, over the kitchen sink area. When I turned the corner to move behind the rec hall, I was about ten feet from the concrete pad that housed a three-sided lean-to built on rollers and pushed against the cinderblock, which formed the fourth wall. For as long as I could remember, it had housed the nativity scene that goes in front of the old church every Christmas.

I walked to the back of the building and placed my fingers between the cinderblock wall and the wooden frame of the lean-to. The unit moved easily, its wheels squeaking over the concrete. Inside lay the plastic Holy Family and the rest of the manger scene lay. The jumble of life-size figures stood like Chinese clay soldiers, never meant to be exposed by the light. Without the context of their proper placement around the manger, the plastic statues appeared chaotic, shambolic, superficial, old, and faded. My eyes were drawn to the contrast of brighter colors beneath them. A collection of old blankets laying in a heap on the concrete floor.

As I looked closer, it became clear that there were two piles of blankets. One pile was close to the edge of the cinderblock wall. The other was in a small hollow in the middle of the statues, as though a nest had been made. I leaned forward to look. In the center of the blankets, a plastic figure of the baby Jesus lay dressed in a child's pink sweater with a baby doll bottle tucked to his side.

Numbness spread throughout my body. Deetsy and Bunny had chosen this dark, cold storage space over home. How could they comfort themselves here? Even if their body heat managed to warm the lean-to the smallest bit, the concrete would be cold and unyielding, despite the old blankets. And the same children that had startled with the owl would find so many noises to scare them here, so near to the mountains, at night.

Were they ever afraid they would be found? Did anyone ever come looking for them?

I pushed the lean-to back into place, rounded the rec hall, and walked briskly up the driveway before anyone could realize my discovery. I had invaded the girls' sanctuary. I did not want Stewie to do the same.

Chapter Fourteen

"Sheriff Martin." Rick's deep voice was businesslike as he answered the phone.

I leaned back, causing the rocking chair on my veranda to move slightly. I had not anticipated needing his help again so soon after finding the rat. But all the way back up Easterbrook after my encounter with Stewie at the window, I had debated with myself and finally realized I had to ask. "Hello, Rick. This is Emerson. Do you have a moment?"

"Of course," he said, his tone changing to warm and inviting.

"Do you need a search warrant in Rockcliff County to check someone's trash cans?"

Rick hesitated. "Well, Emerson, there are two answers to that. If the trash can is in a place where trash collectors pick it up, it is considered abandoned and can be searched or collected by anyone. If the can is in someone's yard, then looking in it or taking something from it is illegal search or seizure. Why do you ask?"

Rick sounded upbeat. Hopefully he was not thinking this was the exact sort of question one might get from a woman he first met sitting on top of a roof. "Is someone going through your trash?"

"No. I take my trash to Madeline's."

"So do you want to tell me what's up, or should I keep asking questions?" Rick asked, his voice lighthearted.

"If I am wrong, you may think I am foolish. If I am right, my suspicions may still prove to be nothing."

"Well, now I'm really curious."

"Okay. Today I was . . . I was walking the fence line. I crossed over to the driveway at the rec hall. That is where I noticed Stewie's trash cans were in the wrong place, and there was a heavy smell of skunk musk coming from them."

"Okay."

"You collected the shoe box from my veranda with the rat. It did not smell like skunk. But I mentioned the thing that awakened me was a heavy smell of skunk."

"You did."

"I believe the person who left it walked up Easterbrook Mountain using the driveway. After they put the box on my veranda, they likely cut through the last curve near the cabin as they headed back down. I had seen a skunk den there. I believe it may have been Stewie. He was likely sprayed. I think he may have thrown his clothing in the trash can."

"You want a job?"

"Excuse me?"

"No kidding. You'd make a great detective. If it *was* Stewie, the prints we lifted from the shoe box and the rat won't get a hit. Madeline thoroughly vets these folks, so I doubt he's in the system. But your theory makes sense."

"I cannot say if I am right without going into the cans."

"Okay, when is the trash collected?"

"On Friday mornings."

"Tomorrow. I'm on it."

• • •

The next day, the cloth bag over my shoulder held the weight of my morning treasures—perhaps a pound of wild edible mushrooms. The exertion of climbing the steep terrain around the cabin had left me breathless. Although I walked everywhere in the city, it was nothing like climbing mountains. I had grown softer in New York than I liked to admit.

On my way up the west side of Easterbrook, just as I was about to crest the edge of the woods near the side of the cabin, I heard the low groan of an engine coming up my driveway. It was not an engine sound I recognized. As though my ears were connected to my energy level, I was suddenly wide awake and felt as though I could run up the highest mountain. I quickly slipped behind a huge oak tree and waited for the vehicle to round the S-curve and come into sight, my pulse pounding in my temples. When the groaning of the motor was close enough, I peeked around the trunk to look through a small clearing.

A black SUV with dark tinted windows.

I jerked my head back behind the tree. My stomach cramped. I wanted to slide down the tree and make myself as small as possible, but I had to stay erect to be ready. My best plan would be to run behind the cabin to the springhouse and descend the ancestors' trail.

When the vehicle entered the last curve of my driveway, I darted from the tree to a large stand of evergreen mountain laurel and froze. I concentrated on breathing deeply in case I had to run. Either my nerves or the cold made me tremble. Probably both. I peeked through the evergreen as the SUV pulled in front of the veranda. I strained as best as I could, but the angle made it impossible to see what state was represented on the license plate. Whoever it was, they were fearless. Enaldo's men would be.

My stomach cramped harder. I hugged my middle to apply pressure. When I heard the car door open, I peeked through the laurel leaves. Rick, dressed in uniform, stepped out onto the gravel.

I straightened slowly and took some deep breaths trying to regain my composure. I walked toward the cabin, coming into the clearing just as Rick reached the top step of my veranda.

"Are you looking for me?"

Rick turned, caught sight of me, and flashed a huge smile. "Yes, ma'am." He took off his black cap with SHERIFF written across the front in gold and waited as I walked toward him.

"You sure can sneak up on a person in those moccasins. I might need to make them part of the county uniforms."

I nodded.

"So I can tell, being the trained observer that I am, that you've been collecting mushrooms." Rick smiled again, crinkling the skin around his eyes.

"You are correct. Would you like to sit down? It is chilly out. We will be warmer out here than in the cabin,"

Rick nodded.

"I did not recognize your SUV," I said as I climbed the veranda steps.

"Oh, that's our unmarked patrol car."

Rick sat heavily in a rocker that now faced the southern view of the mountaintops. I sat in an identical chair to his right.

"I'm here because I have some good news and bad news. First, the helicopter you saw that morning was state police. The guys from Richmond were checking out the terrain in case they have to send in a tactical unit. I suppose that might make you feel a little safer."

"It does." I did not think I needed to tell him it also made me feel foolish.

Rick removed his cap and clasped it between his hands. He leaned forward and rested his forearms on his knees, then began twisting his cap in his hands. My chest tightened. Whatever the bad news was, it was very bad.

He watched the brim of his cap bend together under his strength then straighten as he released it. "There's no easy way to say this, Emerson. Enaldo walked out on bond this morning."

The news was not unexpected. Still, my heart dropped into my stomach.

Rick continued to lean on his elbows. His hands were still now. He contemplated his shoes as he moved the toes of his right foot up, then down, and then did the same to the left. When he did not move or speak, I opened the door for his words. "And there is something more."

He nodded. "The worse news is that he has already slipped the net." Rick looked up at me, his head tilted as though to ask, "What do you think of that?"

I must have previously been experiencing some level of felt safety, because I recognized now that it was gone. My body tensed, then became flooded with a need to spring up and run. My body reacted as though Enaldo was hiding behind the cabin at that very moment. And he could have been. What chance did I have of authorities keeping me safe when he had eluded them just hours after release? We sat in silence, Rick studying his cap, turning it around again.

"There are agents on it. Lots of them. But for now . . . he's in the wind. You might want to consider staying at Madeline's or taking a little vacation." He looked up at me, then straightened his back against the rocker and placed his cap in his lap. "Just a matter of time before we get him. Too many men on it."

But Rick's face betrayed him. His brow was deeply furrowed.

My thoughts were disorganized. I had been anxious enough thinking Enaldo's associates were hunting me. But now the professional hitman with a real investment in killing me was out and loose. Maybe I should climb Crawl Mountain, find a cave, and hide in it.

"But . . . the same men that let him slip the net are the ones looking for him. Is that correct?"

Rick's head lowered toward his chest as he nodded. "Yes." He turned his head sideways and looked at me, then spoke slowly, as though from deep thought. "I would think they are all embarrassed by this. They probably called in more agents and officers. We can hope for that."

Every muscle in my body demanded I move. I suppressed the need to stand up. To walk away. Or run. I twisted in my chair and looked out over the mountains. If ever I had needed ancestral guidance, it was now. Looking up at Crawl mountain, I thought maybe I could build a structure there, deep in the mountains. Abandon the cabin. Or find a cave. Grandfather had trained me to survive in the wild. Or perhaps I could go and find Annie, the goat woman on the other side of Crow, and ask to live with her and her twin daughters. I hadn't thought of her in ages, but I knew she existed. Grandfather visited her several times a year to bring back herbs, salves, and ointments that the three women made for healing. However, none of these ideas created a sense that I was on the right track.

"This is bizarre. I could not identify Enaldo if I had to. He might track me down and kill me, and it would be for nothing."

"I know that, you know that, but the mob would never believe that. I've seen the video. It does look like you looked at him. The mob is convinced, and that's all that really matters."

Rick put his cap on his right knee near me and turned his body toward mine. "Emerson, I have to warn you." He caught his cap before it slid off of his knee, squeezed the brim, then placed it back on his knee. "When I talked to the marshals this morning, they said Giovanni has everyone in New York looking for you. All over the city. They want no witnesses. Intel reports they are camped out at your old job, the train and bus stations, and the airport."

I had no words. No longer pumped with adrenaline, I now felt frozen to my chair.

"The marshal's office said the FBI has a huge team on this."

But was it the same team that had lost Enaldo?

I was propelled into a world of thought that swirled like water circling down a drain, taking hope and energy with it.

"Do you want the second piece of good news?"

My mind still stunned, I looked at him and nodded. Would I be able to concentrate on what he said? Would I understand it as good news when the bad was so all-encompassing?

"Well, you deserve an honorary spot in the department for figuring out the mystery of the rat. I checked Stewie's trash can yesterday. Sure enough, there were jeans, socks, and a pair of trainers covered in skunk musk. I asked him about it, and he confessed right away. Said he thought it would be a funny prank and figured you would know it was a joke if the rat was plastic. He told me he wanted to find a plastic horse head, like the one in *The Godfather*, but couldn't. He also said he wanted to confess to you yesterday when you were there, but his legs smelled like skunk. Actually, I was downwind of the guy when we spoke, and he still smells like skunk."

"I expect he was hit by the whole skunk family."

Rick gave a small laugh. "That explains it."

I sat back to think, taking a deep breath. The alleviation about the rat was such a small relief.

"The guy thinks he was being funny, but if you want to press charges, you could."

I shook my head. I had spent too much precious time on it already. I had allowed a plastic rat to steal my serenity and my sleep. And figuring it out was a hollow victory. Stewie's prank had reflected back to me exactly who I had become—a woman defending herself with a fireplace poker against a shoebox and a toy rat. A woman darting behind trees and hiding behind laurel leaves.

"I would not press charges on a resident of Madeline's. I am sure, between you and the skunks, he has learned a lesson. Thank you, Rick."

"You're formidable, Emerson. But that doesn't mean I can't help. I hope you'll trust me."

There had only been three people in my life I could trust. But I was trying. "I take the burner phone and Taser with me everywhere, and I will leave the house if I hear the second alarm on the driveway, just in case an animal trips the first one. All of that is a level of trust."

Rick nodded and looked down at his shoes. "Good. I worry that because you're so skilled, your confidence will put you in danger. In police work, we have backup. We ask for help."

I paused to wonder if this were the right moment, then considered perhaps I could no longer afford to be choosy about moments. Rick had opened a door that Grandfather's hunt insisted I walk through. I had to ask for help.

"Okay then. As if maintaining my safety is not enough, I have a mystery I could use your help with. And because Enaldo is out, I think I need your help as soon as possible."

"You've got it," Rick said, straightening in his chair.

"Have you heard of the Wild Woman?"

"Of course. I've lived in this county all my life."

"Grandfather left me a mystery hunt to solve, and she is the basis of it. I have found a set of steps going up Crawl Mountain. I believe she lived in one of the caves in the mountain, but Grandfather's instructions are that I must take a neighbor with me. Would you be willing?"

"Of course." His voice was energized. "When are we going?"

"I am meeting with Aunt Hattie and Madeline for dinner tonight. Before we go, Aunt Hattie is to tell me and whoever will help me what she knows about the Wild Woman. Then we can take the next steps. We could do that tonight if you are available."

Rick nodded. "Count me in."

"I will tell her we are coming." I pointed to Crawl Mountain. "It will be quite a hike."

Rick followed my finger with his eyes and took a deep breath, pushing his chest out in an overly dramatic fashion. "Well, they didn't name it Crawl for nothing. But I think I can handle it. I climb a bit now and again. And any plan that starts with a dinner at Hattie Mae's is a plus."

"I realize this is asking for a lot, but do you think we might try going up tomorrow?" I did not say it, but everything in me echoed the wish—I wanted to solve Grandfather's last mystery before Enaldo found me.

"I think we'd better. I expect if we don't, you'll hoof it up there alone. Or, worse yet, ask Stewie."

I tried to image Stewie climbing up Crawl Mountain. It wouldn't come.

CHAPTER FIFTEEN

———— ••• —— ✳ —— ••• ————

Aunt Hattie took off her pink-flowered apron and hung it beside the dishtowels on the rack near her kitchen sink. "I done always heard many hands make light work, and I guess it's true 'cause I ain't never cleared a table that fast before. Thank you." She turned toward the three of us sitting again at the kitchen table. "I'll run that dishwasher after we talk. It's as noisy as a restless mule in a tin barn." She leaned her back against the kitchen counter. "We could go to the watchin' room, but I hope ya'll don't mind, I think I might need me the table to lean on. I ain't a'tall sure I'm strong enough to do what I've got to do next."

She pushed away from the counter, walked to the table where only coffee mugs and a pot remained, and pulled out her chair. After she sat, she looked at us quietly for a moment, then closed her eyes, her lips moving slightly in prayer. I had seen her do this many times throughout my life. When she was done, she opened her eyes and looked at me.

"Emerson, I'm going to tell you, Madeline, and Rick what your granddaddy told me to tell ya'll now." She looked down at her gnarled hands in her lap, twisting them around themselves. I had never seen her so at a loss for words. When she looked back up at us, she shook her head, then warned in a low voice, "This here is a mighty sad story, and ain't a soul on earth left that knows it except for me."

Aunt Hattie looked down at her lap again as she inhaled deeply.

When she looked up, something in her eyes had visibly shifted. I braced myself for what was coming.

"When I was a young wife to Bill," she began, "with four children of my own, I was a midwife like my mama before me. There weren't a baby born in this part of the country that we didn't attend to. Now, back then, phone companies didn't run no lines up these mountains, and the hospital was so far way, many a-baby were born on the way to getting there. So sometimes of a night, kinfolk would come and bang on our door, needing a midwife. Most folks was usually scared half outta their wits. And rightly so. Anytime a baby is coming, that mama's got one foot on this earth and one in the grave.

"Well, one night, somebody bout knocked the door off the hinges. A mama was out there, and she told me her daughter was having a baby and something wasn't right. She and her family were passing through, and they were renting that old house up in Snake Holler, next to Booker's store. Well, I got dressed and followed her, and when I got there, her husband let me know straight out that he didn't want me there. He told his wife she had defied him taking his truck to come get me and told me to go back where I come from. I told him to let me find out my own self, and if they didn't need me, I'd leave. I knew if I had to, I'd get the sheriff to come back with me, but I had to stand up to him because there was a mother suffering on the other side of his door.

"Well, he pointed at his wife and said she was going to pay, and I believed him. She led me to the bedroom where a little girl no more than twelve years old was on the bed, just writhing in pain. Tiny little thing looked like a toothpick with a pea on it. Her cheeks and arms were black and blue with bruises, and she had long, red, bushy hair soaked with sweat. The way she was breathing, I knew she'd been at it for a while.

"When I walked in, her eyes were shut, and her little face was all screwed up with hurting. I spoke to her, but she still didn't open her eyes. Then, when she did, them eyes of hers got huge. I started telling her who I was and why I'd come, but her daddy was at the end of the bed saying it weren't no use to talk to her. She couldn't hear nothing and couldn't say nothing neither. I told him to leave so I could examine her, and when he said he weren't leaving, I told him no man—and especially not no daddy—was gon' be in a room when I exposed her lady parts."

Aunt Hattie's face became very stern then. "I meant business, and he could tell it," she said, then sharply dipped her chin to punctuate the point, and I could immediately picture her doing the same that day.

"The girl's ma sat in a corner the whole time. I knew that was strange. What kind of mama don't at least hold her daughter's hand? I'll tell you what kind, the kind that's scared to death. So, I told her to get me a pan of cool water and a washrag. When she got back, I asked her how long the girl had been in labor. She said for two days. Oh, I was worried when I heard that, but I didn't say nothing. That woman had enough miseries."

Aunt Hattie stopped to look down, then swallowed hard and slow as she brought her hands to the table's edge in front of her and gripped it. "I asked her what the child's name was, and she *whispered* it to me. 'Lenore Lee,' she said, and then her head dipped down like saying that girl's name was a shameful thing." Aunt Hattie pursed her lips to keep from crying, but they quivered still. "I had me a notion why."

After a few moments of silence, Aunt Hattie sat up straighter and began again. "I asked her if Lenore Lee's water done broke yet. She told me the water broke just before the pains started a couple days before. I knew right then that baby won't going to be born alive." Aunt Hattie placed her hands back in her lap, looking at them for a moment before glancing up and slowly taking in all three of us, but she had a far-away look, as though instead of us, she was seeing the scene that night in Snake Holler. "Then I asked if she could motion to her daughter that it was okay for me to look and see if the baby was coming, and she did. When I looked, I saw what was wrong. That baby was breech, and I was gon' have to turn it or that little girl was gon' die.

"Now this whole time, Lenore Lee's daddy was out in the hall bellowing like a bull for me to get out of his house. He said to stop talking and start getting the baby out or leave. And let me just tell you, his wife shook and cowered every time he yelled. I thought then about how Bill didn't like it nary bit when I left the house and he didn't know the people, and I knew he had been right to feel that-a way. I hadn't been scared nary time up until that day, and when it was all said and done, Lenore Lee's daddy was the only man that ever did scare me.

"Anyway, that baby was wedged tight. It took some doing, but I turned it. And Lenore Lee never made a sound. Not a moan or a groan. I couldn't understand that." Aunt Hattie slowly shook her head when she paused. "I could tell by her face she felt the pain. But then I put it together that was how her little face and arms got bruised black and blue. He had hit her whenever she'd cried. Boy was I fired up then. But I had bigger fish to fry. That child was going to die if I didn't help, and if I crossed him, I had a feeling he could kill us all." Aunt Hattie watched as each of us at the table silently nodded our agreement, completely mesmerized by her story.

"I don't know where the courage to stand up to him come from, other than from the good Lord. That little red-headed child needed me. I balled up both of my fists, gritted my teeth, and pretended like I was pushing, then I motioned for her to do the same. And it worked. She pushed once, and I started nodding my head big time. She pushed even harder then. It took some doing, especially as tired as she must have been, but she pushed that baby out without a peep. In all the time I'd been there, I'd not heard one single sound from that poor little girl."

Aunt Hattie gripped the table's edge again. "When the baby come, you could tell it had been dead for some time. Its color was all wrong. Lenore Lee struggled up on her elbows to see. When she looked, she knew it too. She let out the most mournful howl I ever did hear. The same howl we heard all over the mountains for as long as she lived. Her daddy come busting through that door, took one look, then turned on his heels and left. Lenore Lee's mama just stood there while Lenore Lee howled her little heart out. Her own mama didn't reach to comfort her. Not so much as to pat her hand."

Shaking her head, Aunt Hattie pursed her lips, making loose fists with her hands as she laid them on the table. "After a minute, the daddy come back in with newspaper while I was cutting the cord and trying to stop his daughter from bleeding to death. 'Give it here,' he said. So, I looked at him like he had two heads and told him, 'This baby ain't no *it* and this baby ain't going *nowhere*. Your daughter done carried him and fought like crazy to deliver him, and now she's gotta hold her little boy. Just a little if nothing else.' She was in mourning, and she wasn't going to understand if she didn't. But he grabbed that baby from between her legs and wrapped him in the newspaper like yesterday's fish. I can't tell you how scary it all was. I was knee-deep trying to save Lenore Lee's life, worried she was leaving this world on the heels of her little one, and Lenore Lee was just a-wailing. It was breaking my heart."

She relaxed her arms and returned her hands to her lap, looking at each of us for a moment as she spoke. "I had to think fast. I'd seen how mean that man was, and I knew he could do something to me too. I wasn't about to accuse him of nothing right then and right there, but I figured by the way that child balled up in a knot whenever her daddy came in the room, he had been the one to get her in the family way to start with and then he'd beat her for it. And I knew that mama wasn't much better off. I was trying to think of how to help the both of them.

"But God was with me. When that man came back in, he told me to leave. That's when I knew I had to lie. I told him that it was the law in these parts that if a mother lost her baby or was in labor too long that they had to go to a hospital or they had to come home and be nursed by me. I knew he'd never let her go to no hospital. I told him that I had special stuff at my house. I said since she couldn't neither talk nor hear, I needed one of them to come to my house with us to tell me about her because she couldn't tell me nothing. I was sowing the seed that if she came with me, his secrets was safe. I told him my husband always came to the houses where I delivered babies to see if I needed anything, and Bill would be there any minute and would help me load his daughter into my car or he could help me right then. His choice.

"When I said all that, Lenore Lee's mother almost fell in the floor. She walked over and grabbed onto Lenore Lee's bed, gripping it hard to hold herself up. I think she knew right then she won't likely to ever see her little girl again. Well, I didn't wait for him to make no decision. I told him to help me load her because time was a-wasting and she needed what I had at home. I told him I needed her mother to come with me to help nurse her, because I wanted to get her out of there too. But he said no with the most curse words you ever heard all strung together. Ain't no sailor ever talked that bad. He said that Lenore Lee's mother was not leaving under no circumstances and turned and walked out of that room. Lenore Lee's mama looked like she'd seen a ghost.

"I put the sheets round Lenore Lee best I could and picked her up. I got me some of that supernatural strength you hear about when people lift trucks off their loved ones, because I lifted her like she was light as a feather and carried her to my car. She was too weak to fight me. Her mama followed me out, and I told her to come with me right then. When she shook her head no, I told her to come to my house after he went to sleep, and I'd make sure they were both safe and we could sort it all out.

"When I got home, it was a long night. That girl 'bout died. Whenever she'd come to, she'd howl like a wounded animal. The next day, Bill went back up the holler to their house with the sheriff, but they were gone."

Aunt Hattie sat back and took a deep breath. She leaned forward and filled her favorite yellow mug full of coffee from the pot on the table. Looking up, she held it in front of us as if to ask if we wanted some. We all shook our heads. She leaned back in her chair, then took a sip and set the cup down before continuing.

"I didn't have nothing but Lenore Lee's name. Didn't even have no last name. The sheriff tried for a while to find 'em, but eventually, he gave up."

Rick shifted in his seat. "You did some fast thinking to get yourself out of there alive, Hattie."

"One thing about me has always been true: the more scared I am, the more clear-headed I get. 'Specially if I know I'm right," Hattie said. "Anyways, over the next couple of weeks, Lenore Lee got stronger, but just any old time, she'd get to thinking about that baby boy and let out that mournful howl. Bill and me did what we could for her. We kept her. We couldn't send her off nowhere. She turned into one of ours.

"She loved to cook with me, and when she saw me sewing on my grandma's old treadle machine, she wanted to give it a go. So, I took her down to the mill and let her pick out a pretty feed sack to make an apron." Hattie smiled at the memory and took another sip of coffee. She set the mug down, and her fingers traced the curve of the handle for a moment. "She was smart as a whip, just never had no way to learn. Couldn't read nor write and didn't pay no attention to any of that. But if you showed her how to do something, she could follow. Over time, we learned how to make little hand signals to each other, and we figured out to turn lights on and off to get her attention."

Aunt Hattie adjusted the peach-colored tablecloth in front of her, pulling it down by the hem, then smoothing out the wrinkles where her plate had been.

"Makes me some kind of happy remembering how she loved going out and swinging with our children or sitting on the back porch watchin' 'em." Her head dipped and she shook it slowly. "But she never played. I gave her a little kewpie doll about the size of my hand. You know, the little necked plastic baby dolls with the big heads and a curl on top. But she didn't know how to play with nothing, so she just kept it hid under her pillow. I reckon it was some sort of treasure to her. Might've made her think of her own little one. I don't know.

"She never got over being afraid of men. If she saw Bill or Two Eagles coming, she'd cower down. Eventually we kept finding her in Estelle's room, standing at the window, looking out at your mountains, Emerson. So we moved Estelle out and put Lenore Lee in it so she could see the mountains anytime she wanted."

Aunt Hattie smiled and looked around the table. We each mustered some sort of return smile to support her. My heart ached with the sadness of it all and how hard Aunt Hattie had struggled to help.

"All in all, she did real good. We had plans for someone to come and teach all of us sign language and everything. But one day, 'bout six months after she came here, she must have looked out that winder long enough to see those steps going up Crawl Mountain." She looked from one of us to the other and took a deep breath. "So, she just up and took off walking. Weren't no use in this world calling her. She couldn't hear. And if you took off after her, she'd run like the wind. It would scare her to death. So for a while, she'd leave and come back, leave and come back. Then she got to staying away longer and taking things when she went. Blankets, a cup, a fork. Things like that.

"We weren't a-tall sure where she was going. But we figured she'd found a way to feel safe, somewhere up in them mountains. Two Eagles didn't see no movement from his cabin, and we couldn't see where she was going either, though we sure tried. We figured it was up in them caves on Crawl, or maybe she'd done took up with Annie the goat woman and them twin daughters of hers that live behind Crow. There weren't no telling.

"We took to leaving her things in a box that Two Eagles nailed to a fence post down under Crawl. That's where we saw her most. We'd leave things, and sometimes she'd leave us things too, like a robin's egg, an arrowhead, or some pretty rock she'd found. That's when Bill put me a room on the front and made me a watchin' winder to look for her. He bought me a strong pair of binoculars so I could look even harder and sit 'em by a chair so I could watch her close if I was to see her.

"She got things out of her box right regular for years. But then about the time you were nine or so, Emerson, Two Eagles let me know she hadn't got things out of her box for weeks. That wasn't like her. Then the weeks turned into months. I musta looked out the watchin' winder a million times, holding my breath, hopin' I'd see her. But I never did." Aunt Hattie looked around the table. Madeline poked her bottom lip out in a sympathetic gesture. Tears welled in Aunt Hattie's eyes. Watching her sadness, I felt the same building behind mine.

"Then it was too long. I couldn't have told you how long. I was a wreck. We got us a search party together. The church folk all helped us look. Some of them was young enough to go up those steps and tramp around them mountains. But nobody found her. I can't rightly say they went all the way to the other side of Crow 'cause they might-a been scared to go that far and tangle with Annie. She was known to set all kinds of traps so people couldn't get to her. Well, nobody but Two Eagles. But I figured if she found her way to the goat woman and that's where she was, she was safe enough."

She looked at us and shook her curly head. "Never did find her though. Don't know what happened to her. Might never know. And if we don't, I won't never have no real peace. She deserves proper burial."

My head swirled trying to put the puzzle pieces together. The haunted look on Grandfather's face when we heard her howl. How angry he had been when teenagers dressed up like her at Halloween and howled. Aunt Hattie and Grandfather's reverential silence about her. I knew now why Grandfather never told me her story. But I also understood his satisfaction when he saw that she had taken the things he left her and his joy when he the found treasures she left in return. And later, the pained look on his face when he opened the box week after week without adding anything new. The growing knowledge that she was gone had shown in the stoop of his shoulders on each return to the tractor.

Aunt Hattie, too, had lost someone she cared deeply about. Almost like her own child. Somehow, in talking about Lenore Lee, Aunt Hattie looked older, her head more bowed, her frown so deep. Even the lines in her pale skin seemed more pronounced. Losing Lenore Lee had cost Aunt Hattie. Finding her might make a big difference.

"Aunt Hattie, if we do find some signs of her or . . . or her remains, what would you want to happen?" I asked.

Aunt Hattie sat motionless, not answering. Madeline broke the silence.

"We can bury her at Maple Grove. It would be very private. You could visit her there. No matter what, I'll pay for the arrangements."

Aunt Hattie looked at Madeline. "That's mighty kind of you," she said, then pressed the fingers of her gnarled right hand against her mouth for several seconds before speaking again.

"Emerson, I told your granddaddy it's always felt like I wasn't finished with what I was supposed to do until she's laid to rest proper. Because she was in my care. So I was mighty proud that day your granddaddy called me up that mountain and told me what he had in mind with this here hunt. It was his way of helping three of us with what we needed. Me finding Lenore Lee, you learning what he wants you to learn, and your granddaddy having something to give him joy, right up to the end." Aunt Hattie smoothed her apron over her knees with both hands, then began tracing her finger over the floral pattern in the fabric as though she had never seen it before.

"Aunt Hattie, it will be up to you where she is buried. You are her next of kin. But you could also bury her on Easterbrook since she loved the mountains. Perhaps near Echo Rock. From there you can see miles of the Blue Ridge. Or perhaps in the ancestors' cemetery. You could visit her grave in either place."

Aunt Hattie continued looking at her lap. "I think if she coulda talked, she woulda asked to stay on them mountains," she said, then looked up at the three of us. Tears spilled over and ran rivulets down her withered cheeks. None of us said a word.

"If you find her, we'll bury her on Easterbrook. That's what we'll do."

CHAPTER SIXTEEN

As our steps edged closer to the top of Crawl Mountain, Rick stopped on a flat spot and turned, holding out a hand to assist me. The last step up to where he stood was at least two feet tall. I accepted his help.

"This is some climb, Emerson. I wanted to look out over the vistas, but there hasn't been any place to catch a breath until now."

I nodded. My thigh muscles burned from the continuous climb. When I stood fully upright for the first time in over an hour, my back told me I had been in an awkward position far too long. I looked out over the valley between Crawl and Easterbrook then up toward the cabin. I had been successful. It looked abandoned.

"You're tough," Rick said. His eyes danced as he smiled down at me. "I didn't do anything much tougher than this when I was at Parris Island. You could consider joining the Marines if boot camp was ever a deterrent."

"Good to know." I looked at him with a grin. "Maybe then I would be in good shape to outrun Enaldo since he is middle aged."

Rick smiled.

"But that would only work if it came down to hand-to-hand combat."

Rick gave an exaggerated surprise expression with his eyebrows. "My money would definitely be on you if that were the case."

He looked out over the valley, Easterbrook in front of us and

Crow Mountain to our left. "It's certainly worth the climb. The view is incredible. The North Ridge behind your cabin rolls like a serpent covered in blue. And the air up here is cooler but even more clean and crisp."

I nodded, then pointed to our right. From a great height over the trees we could see Aunt Hattie's house and a few yards of her front lawn. "So this is how Aunt Hattie watched for her."

Rick nodded. "And we have no doubt she did. Just think, Emerson. Lenore Lee would have smelled this same fresh air, seen those hawks riding the currents"—he pointed to two large birds high in the clouds above us—"and seen all those beautiful shades of blue in the mountains too. Maybe she couldn't hear or speak, but they say that makes the other senses stronger. Imagine."

Grandfather would say it showed character that Rick thought of the deceased that way, showing reverence for those gone before.

Rick pointed to a layer of rock to our left. "I'm going to go first and make sure this little ledge can support our weight. She was pretty small, so she must have been light." He moved slowly, hanging onto the rock wall, and after each step, bounced a bit before taking the next step. After twenty feet, he turned and motioned for me to follow. I sidestepped my way to him, holding onto the rock as I had seen him do.

With both of us stopped again, I looked around. I understood now why I could not see caves from my cabin. There was a deep recess and steep curves like little alcoves in the rock face. From a distance, they would not be apparent.

Rick adjusted his backpack. "She had to be part mountain goat if she lived up here. No wonder she didn't come up and down very often. So, you think she's on Crawl and not Crow?"

"Grandfather suspected that. I suppose it is possible that she made it to the other side of Crow. But I do not imagine that she went up Crawl Mountain to get to Crow. I expect she would have just walked through the valley."

"I thought the same thing. Have you ever been on the other side?

Met the goat woman?"

"No. But Grandfather knew her. He told me about her and her twins, Annie and Fannie. The three of them can treat almost any illness with herbs, but they only allowed Grandfather to visit them for medicine. That is why there are traps that whisk people up into the trees. They shoot slingshots too."

"I thought the mother's name was Annie."

"It is. She named her first twin after her."

"Glad you told me. I wouldn't have guessed that." Rick shook his head. "These mountains are full of mysteries."

"Grandfather would love that you said that. Those were his words exactly. Many times." He also would have liked you, I thought, then shook my head to clear it. I could not risk allowing thoughts that were not mission centered. I had to focus. I had needed to ask for Rick's help to solve the mystery. And to survive Giovanni's men. He was law enforcement and had to be involved at a dangerous level. But I could not fathom dragging anyone more deeply into my life than need be, escalating their risk.

Rick pulled out a water bottle and handed it to me. "Here. Be sure and stay hydrated. This could take a while."

At the top of the mountain, the ledge became flatter and wider with crevices here and there and large rocks protruding as if shoved out of the mountain from the inside. As we walked, we veered off course regularly to examine holes that could lead to caves. After nearly an hour of searching, Rick called out to me. "Hey. I think I found something here."

I scurried over the rocks as he pushed aside a pile of scree, loose rock that had shifted from above and piled up in front of a hole in the stone face. Rick took off his backpack, unzipped it, pulled out a folding shovel, and began to move the rock. Eventually the opening was big enough, and he lay on his stomach and stretched his arm into the gap, shining his flashlight around while I waited, wishing I were the one looking into the hole. He wiggled on the earth until his head and shoulders were in the opening, then began to scoot backward.

"No luck," he said as he stood and brushed dirt and small pebbles off his clothing. "But I'm betting that when the search teams came up the mountain, they didn't account for rockslide. Something could have shifted and covered her entrance if she lived in a cave. We'll have to keep an eye open for that. It probably won't look fresh like this slide though."

"So, essentially, we poke every pile of scree?"

"Yep." He turned and swept his arm in front of us down a quarter mile of rock face. "And we've got a lot of poking to do."

"Did you see a cave in there?"

"Yes, ma'am," he said with a grin. "But I didn't see anything to make me think a human had been there. I guess there could be something farther in, but it's not worth our effort right now. Let's eliminate some other spots first."

We searched in parallel rows, poking sticks into the rocks, moving small piles of scree or peeking into openings with our flashlights. The quiet of the mountains made the bird calls seem louder. As I poked, my mind registered red-winged blackbirds, cardinals, mockingbirds, blue jays, dark-eyed juncos. When we reached the ridge of Crawl facing Crow on the other side of the valley formed by the three mountains, a breeze blew. But as we were surrounded by rock, only the loose hair around my face moved. Without coordinating it, both of us turned and doubled back in parallel rows, again headed back eastward toward the steps. We walked at a snail's pace, poking and prodding to find a place where a cave might be.

After what seemed like hours, I developed a system: poke the stick into various places in scree as far as it would go and shove hard to dislocate small rocks. Just as I began to think my arms would not hold out much longer, my eyes were drawn upward to the near crest of Crawl Mountain where two huge rocks, the size of small cars, faced each other. If I moved even a few steps I would not be able to see through the crack between them. With my head just so, I could see through the crevice. There appeared to be a C-shaped formation because daylight was reflecting through the small crevice onto scree that was likely in an alcove.

I walked up a steep incline to examine it. A natural recess was formed by the rocks inside the almost closed C shape. I took off my backpack and laid it on the ground. The small opening between the two large rocks was just large enough for me to squeeze into if I turned sideways. There was little more than three-foot square of foot room inside. The opening to the C faced Easterbrook. If the scree was hiding a cave, there was no mystery why Grandfather would never have seen it. Had I not looked up the hillside at precisely the right angle, I would not have spotted it.

The scree that resulted from the pile of rocks on the back side of the C was about at my stomach's height. I poked it with my stick. A strange sound registered back. I moved it a bit to the right and shoved again. The same odd noise. Unlike what I had heard at any other pile. I pulled the stick out to try again a few inches farther over. The sound was clearer there. Metallic.

"Rick." I called loudly, waving my stick above the level of the large rocks in case he didn't see my head or my backpack lying near the entrance. In just moments he was behind me peeking through the crack.

"Wow. Amazing you even saw this." He put his arm through the opening between the large rocks. "I won't get in this way even if I hold my breath." He moved around the large rocks and hoisted himself up on top of the rock facing Crow Mountain. I turned to look as he smiled and crouched down to talk with me. "Only thin people like you and Lenore Lee would be able to get through that opening. That's actually a pretty good safety feature. And boy is this well hidden. If this is where she lived."

"Listen to the sound before you climb down in here." I demonstrated, pulling the stick out and pushing it in, and looked back at him when I heard the sound.

"That's metal."

I nodded.

"One more time, Emerson, and move it around a little to see if it scrapes."

I did, and the sound was very much like my stick was hitting a metal pan of some sort.

Rick stood atop the rock, took off his backpack and handed it down to me. "Okay. You back out and let me hop down."

I eased out and stood in front of the opening where I could watch. He jumped into the alcove. At first, he used his hands to pull off the bigger rocks, then he grabbed the shovel out of his backpack and began to dig, throwing the rocks over his shoulder to his left. "It's metal all right. I think you have something, Emerson," he called over his shoulder. "I can't imagine any reason why metal would be up here."

I wanted to dig. Or pace. But all I could do was watch as he moved the rocks.

The scraping sounds became more intense as his shovel seemed to be moving mostly small rocks away from the metal. He stopped, turned around, and looked at me with a smile. We both nodded, then he turned and dug even faster. My heart danced with joy. I was more excited than a child running to a Christmas tree. I strained forward so that I could watch over his shoulders and saw that he was unearthing something with a round edge and dull, chipped, white paint. As he continued to dig, the faint outline of a red star along with black lettering that read "Texaco" emerged on a rusted sign.

"Whoa. Would you look at that," Rick said as he took the top of the sign and worked to pull it toward him. "This is one of your mountain mysteries for sure," he said between grunts. "There was never a gas station on Colony Row." He stopped, caught his breath, and looked back at me. "I would bet money Lenore Lee found this somewhere and rolled it up the mountain…" He pointed to the crevice I was standing in front of, "and through that crack so that she could use it as a door."

When the metal was clear, Rick pulled it back at the top an inch or so and retrieved his flashlight from his pocket, sending a beam behind the sign. "You might want to stand even further back. I'm not sure what we might find. Or what might run out."

I wondered what he would do in that small space, surrounded by huge rocks since he would be trapped in the tiny alcove.

As he struggled to free the sign, I considered why he felt the need to protect me. Was it because he did not realize I had been reared to survive on these mountains? Although Grandfather knew I was capable of handling dangerous situations and he was sure I knew how to take care of myself, he too had assumed the lead, explaining to me that it is nature's way for the male to face the fiercest challenge first or forge the path. I backed up and watched, settling myself with the Milton quote Grandfather used to say to me: *They also serve who only stand and wait.*

When Rick pulled the sign free he leaned it against the larger rock to his right. He had exposed a hole in the formation of larger rocks that was about four feet high and three feet wide. He directed his flashlight inside the opening. "Emerson, we have it. That sign *was* her door. The rocks must've slid and covered it. Wait here. I'm going in." Rick bent down and maneuvered into the opening.

Surely this was her home. And if it wasn't, what in the world was behind the sign? If it was, Aunt Hattie would finally have peace. But if the cave was empty . . . No. I could not allow my hopes to get too high. Long, quiet moments passed with only the sounds of birds overhead.

Rick's voice echoed from the cave opening. "This is it, Emerson. We found her."

My spirit was filled with a sense of reverence. We had uncovered her tomb. Lenore Lee, a loner by choice, hunted by the people she did not understand. Just like me. She had found solace and sanctuary in the mountains just as I had. She had limited human connections, just like I did. I blinked away tears, my body's witness to how much I had in common with the tiny woman who had stood on the edge of the cedars that day. Who ran from the sight of me. And from Grandfather. People who would have protected, nurtured, and loved her. Oh how I wished I could have befriended her.

Rick's voice projected from the opening. "Her remains are here . . . under an old quilt . . . No vermin scatter . . . everything is orderly. It looks like she died peacefully."

I took a deep breath. Aunt Hattie would have peace.

Eventually, Rick reappeared at the mouth of the cave. "I covered her up. Do you want to come in?"

I nodded, picked up my backpack, and held it at arm's length to go before me through the crevice, then I squeezed through the rocks and laid it at the opening to the cave. Only two steps through the alcove and I would be inside the cave where Lenore Lee had lived. My heart was beating so hard I could feel it pounding in my ears as I bent to enter the hole. Then I waited for my eyes to adjust. The light from the opening illuminated the first few feet of the cave. Just inside the mouth, rocks were stacked to create a fire ring. Beside it sat a coffee pot, mug, and a large Mason jar that still held water. Decaying wood was stacked nearby, next to the cave door. On the other side, Lenore Lee had built a pallet out of quilts. That is where she lay now, a faded red quilt covering her, a shock of dulled red hair peeking out from its edge. I recognized the quilt as one of Aunt Hattie's favorite designs, wedding ring.

"She had it good up here," Rick said. "There are people who choose to live in caves for reasons other than hers. Good temperature modulation for sure. Safe in storms. Some of them are pretty upscale. Her life truly may not have been so bad."

I nodded. Perhaps Rick had seen the expression on my face when he emerged and thought her living conditions were what concerned me. The idea of living in a cave had never caused me worry. Many of my ancestors had lived in them. Maybe even this cave.

As I looked around, it became clear—Lenore Lee had created a home. In places, the limestone was level, and Lenore Lee had used the flat edge as a shelf, placing various rocks and minerals on display, decorating her home with her finds. On the side of the cave opposite her bed, dishes and various cast iron pots and pans sat in an orderly fashion. Cans of food, their labels yellowing, were stacked against the wall along with lots of mason jars. The clear glass showed some of them were filled with flour or meal. Jars filled with water sat near the back of the cave, their tops covered in dust. A large family could have survived on the contents for a very long time. Aunt Hattie would be glad to know that Lenore Lee had not died of thirst or starvation.

Rick extended his hand toward me, his voice soft. "This was around her neck."

I reached forward, and he released something into my open palm. We held eye contact for a moment as I closed my fist around the shape of the amethyst cross. It felt the same as the cross from the tin.

Rick turned around to continue his search. I closed my eyes to imagine Grandfather beside me, smiling and nodding. Grandfather had made identical crosses for the two of us. I was holding a treasure he promised I would find. He would have been proud.

I opened my eyes and fingers. Even in the low light of the cave, the facets glimmered a bit as I moved my palm. It had been precious to her. I believed she had worn it proudly in life and until long after her death. The matching crosses bonded us in a way I had not predicted. We were both Grandfather's girls. My heart ached with a loss I did not know how to recognize or catalog. I was lonely for someone I had never met, someone I could have been a sister to. Grandfather had known this as well.

"Thank you." I put my hand in my inside jacket pocket and slowly opened my palm to release the amethyst. I would soon release it again to the woman that had been Lenore Lee's surrogate mother, just as she had been mine. "I will give it to Aunt Hattie." I zipped the pocket closed for safety.

Rick scanned the cave ledges. "I think it's best to leave her remains intact now. I have a good friend who is a semi-retired medical examiner. He can help affix a death certificate and he and I will bring her down the mountain. But you have a look around, and if there's something else you want to take, I suggest you go ahead and take it."

His words jarred me. I believed that Grandfather meant for the necklace to be retrieved. But, taking more? This had been Lenore Lee's sanctuary. Somehow that seemed selfish, vulturous. One thing I would take with me, however, was the peace I gained from seeing that she was a survivor. The assurance that I could live as she had lived. In fact, I could live in her very space if the need arose. That knowledge quieted my spirit. Perhaps it would Aunt Hattie's as well. Rick stood silently as I considered his suggestion. I pulled out my phone and snapped as many pictures as I could to show Aunt Hattie that Lenore Lee had lived well. I would describe for her the cool but comfortable temperature and the deep undisturbed silence of the cave that matched the quiet of her world. I would tell her about the felt sense of safety, protection by the massive limestone rock, the very earth itself. The light from the door illuminated her space well, and Aunt Hattie would be glad to know she had numerous unused candles to light the darkness whenever she shut her door.

A few stones seemed to be in prominent places on a small ledge by her door, the place of greatest light. Surely, these were among her favorites, as they caught the most refraction. I picked up a large piece of light-brown topaz as big as my thumb and a dark-burgundy piece of garnet the size of my index fingernail. I had found such treasures myself along Mineral Springs on Easterbrook. I examined them while imagining Lenore Lee squatted by the rock bed there, her small figure crouched at the sparkling water's edge, her red quilt skirt behind her, her tiny hands sifting through the cold mountain water for the gems. Perhaps she would want us to see their beauty and be reminded of her life, her journey on this earth, and her love of the mountains. I unzipped the inside pocket of my jacket and placed the two stones there, then zipped the pocket closed.

When I was finished, I nodded to Rick. Then, as though a strong internal brake was pressed, I froze. "Wait," I said, then turned and walked the perimeter of the cave again. I could see nothing that called out to me. But I had an overwhelming sense that I was forgetting something. The same feeling I might have if I had left a candle burning or something electrical turned on.

Seeing nothing, I turned back around to leave, but again felt overpowered with the nagging sense that I was missing something. I squatted and looked from a lower angle. Nothing. I turned completely around, scanning from all directions.

"You're certainly thorough," Rick said, watching me.

I stood in silence. There was still no sensation of closure within me. Then, as though a late messenger had arrived, the memory emerged. "Aunt Hattie said she hid the kewpie doll."

"Do you think she hid it even up here?"

"I do not know." I moved to the back of the cave, pulling my flashlight out of my coat pocket. "But hiding things is as much about keeping them sacred as it is secret." I began to move the larger mason jars.

"Do you want some help?" Rick asked.

"Yes, please."

I continued to look between the jars and the cave wall and shined my beam into each jar, holding the flashlight with one hand and moving the jars with the other. Rick started at the opposite end of the cave wall, working toward me as he did the same, checking the contents of each jar then moving them to look around them.

As I directed my flashlight into a half-gallon, cobalt-blue mason jar, a giddy feeling flew through me. "Wait," I said. I pocketed my flashlight and lifted the jar. It was lightweight.

Rick walked over and directed the powerful beam of his flashlight into the jar.

"Cloth," I said and looked up at him. We both smiled. "I think this is it."

"Will you look at that. I wonder if she knew or sensed somehow that this old blue mason jar is a treasure on its own. It's an antique. The only place I've ever seen one is in the Rockcliff Museum."

"Aunt Hattie probably gave it to her because it was so pretty. And, the color of the mountains."

He moved his flashlight around the side of the jar. "It looks like the cloth is wrapped around things."

I shook the jar lightly, and faint noises came from inside. "I will save it for Aunt Hattie to open." I walked to the mouth of the cave, retrieved my backpack and opened it, placing the jar inside.

"You know, Emerson, I have thoroughly enjoyed this. And there may be other caves up here. I've heard the legends in Rockcliff County all my life about bank robbers holing up in a cave on this mountain. If you ever want to use that intuition of yours to find out if the tales are true, I'm game."

"I have enjoyed this as well. Especially since we found Lenore Lee's home." Having never explored with anyone other than Grandfather, I had been tense all day and concerned that Rick's manner as a policeman would be intrusive or demanding. But he had been respectful and thoughtful.

"If the bank robbers really did leave treasure up here, we might find it," he said with a lilt in his voice.

"Or we might just find more skeletons."

• • •

Aunt Hattie sat back in her watching chair. On the table beside her, Lenore Lee's necklace caught the light from the window as her soft pale fingers reached over to touch it. Madeline and I, sitting on opposite sides of her, shared a smile.

"You done something I can't thank you enough for," Aunt Hattie said as she picked up the necklace and clasped it in her hand. She looked over at me, and a slow smile spread across her face. "And your granddaddy would be so proud."

"I think it's a miracle you two were able to find her cave. It must have been well hidden," Madeline added.

I nodded. "Every single pile of rock looked the same up there."

"And the two of you did it all in time to get back down the mountain for Sunday dinner," Aunt Hattie added.

"Only because you did not mind us sitting at your table in our dirty rock-climbing clothes."

"Emerson Grace, after what the two of you did, you could have been up to your chest in mud and you would have been putting those feet under that table." Aunt Hattie smoothed her apron over her lap. "You know, Emerson, I got to thinking on that Texaco sign after you and Rick left yesterday. Ed Roberts had him a Texaco gas station in town back in the day. Around that time, the well at the church kept giving us trouble, so they were always working on the pump. Ed brought his old sign to cover the well until they could get it straight. When they built a proper well house, they must have rolled that sign off in the woods. That's probably where Lenore Lee found it. I can't even imagine what it must have took for her to roll it up that mountain though. She might've been small, but she was strong as a ox."

Madeline and I nodded.

Aunt Hattie pulled a note from her apron pocket. "Okay. Well, you've done earned the next step from your granddaddy for sure."

Madeline looked at me and smiled as Aunt Hattie reached in her apron pocket and handed me the note. My hands trembled slightly as I unfolded it. Another encounter with Grandfather. I read this one aloud.

Emerson,

 Always add arrows to your quiver and your treasure will never end. Tell Hattie and Madeline what you have learned.

I refolded the note and placed it in my lap. Both women looked at me expectantly. Perhaps they had already discussed the answers I might give when they planned the hunt with Grandfather.

"My first thought is that seeing the peace Aunt Hattie has is treasure enough," I said. "I have learned how valuable peace—and closure—can be."

"I've got to say, I have peace all right. That little thing was lost up there a long time," Aunt Hattie said.

Madeline smiled and nodded. "It is a good feeling, closure."

I could tell there was more as they both sat waiting for me to speak.

"Another gain is that I realized that I could live in that cave if I needed to. But of course Grandfather would not have known what a treasure that could turn out to be."

"I can't even think about what your granddaddy would have thought on Enaldo. But you're right, that's a plus too," Aunt Hattie said.

"I hope it doesn't come to that," Madeline said.

Again, both women waited for me to continue, as if there was a particular answer they were expecting.

I looked down at my lap, uncurling the fingers of my right hand to see my palm, envisioning Lenore Lee's cross in it. I could teach others about the mountains and what Grandfather taught. But could I do justice to such a tender moment in a dark cave?

When I looked up, my mothers remained motionless and quiet, accustomed to my own silence and pauses. "Perhaps he knew . . . perhaps he knew there would be a moment when I would realize he had created two identical necklaces for two little girls . . ." I cleared my throat to push back the tears that made my voice quiver. ". . . that had a lot in common. Two little girls his heart wanted to rescue."

Both mothers nodded.

"And it would have made us like sisters, or cousins, had things been different."

"He did everything he knew to do." Aunt Hattie reached over to the arm of Madeline's wingback where her hand rested and patted it. "We all did."

How many times had the two of them sat in the cabin with Grandfather and processed this? He had always been one to want a lot of mileage out of every hunt with a lot of wisdom included.

"Well," I continued. "Rick feels sure she died of natural causes . . . and she was young. He said it was probably something simple, like a cold or pneumonia that got complicated. So . . . I learned to take a simple illness seriously."

My mothers offered no response.

"Grandfather had me coming up and down the mountain to meet with both of you for every step." And he never involved any action in a hunt that didn't have meaning. Since the day he began homeschooling me, he had actively created social situations for me too. Left to my own devices, I always chose solitary activities. "Perhaps that goes with Lenore Lee not choosing to be social even with people that she could trust." I looked up to my mothers. "When she stopped coming . . ."

Both women nodded their heads now. I was on the right track. I had connected the weight of our similarities in her cave. I had a kinship with her, her vulnerability, her limited relationships, her isolation.

When Grandfather insisted I be social, that I take the internship and come off the mountain, I had viewed it as a lack of freedom to make my own decisions. Now, as if a fog had cleared to reveal a sunny day, I knew why Lenore Lee was a part of the hunt. The hunt, hidden under the trap door, there the whole time without my knowing. Just as she had been hidden in the cave within sight of Easterbrook, without anyone knowing. Chill bumps rose on my arms.

Sadness came as suddenly as the chills had. I was deeply remorseful for having been angry with Grandfather for not allowing me the freedom to choose isolation. With the hunt, he had wanted me to understand the inevitability of Lenore Lee's destiny by that same choice. I looked up and met my mothers' loving eyes.

"When Lenore Lee got a taste of freedom, she used it to hide out and excluded everyone," I said. My eyes fell back to my lap. Back to the hands that had held her stones, moved her jars, picked up her treasures. They trembled now. The depth of Grandfather's wisdom touched my core. "Whenever I've been given freedom, I have always chosen as she did. To isolate. If she had . . . if she had come to Aunt Hattie for help, she may have survived. She may have lived a good life." Electricity ran up my spine and neck, and it was as though I could feel every tiny hair rise in anointing. I looked up and into Aunt Hattie's eyes. "Grandfather wanted me to learn to ask for help and . . . he wanted me to use my freedom to make the right choices, even when those choices are not what I want."

They both nodded.

I looked back down at my hands, opening both of them, palms up, in my lap. Ready to receive. "And now I need to learn what Lenore Lee never did—how to let others in. To be a person around other people."

When I looked up, Aunt Hattie nodded. "He was 'bout the smartest man that ever did live, Emerson Grace. This here lesson might be the one that saves you."

I imagined him behind us, eyes shut, nodding twice, smiling. My heart was filled with love as I looked at both Madeline and Aunt Hattie. I smiled broadly, closed my eyes and nodded twice.

CHAPTER SEVENTEEN

The next few weeks, life seemed to settle into routines of looking for wood during the day, tracking animals to better understand the inhabitants that shared my mountains, and mind mapping any hazards, fallen trees, stumps, or gullies I could stumble over if I had to run from the cabin at night.

Sunday dinners at Aunt Hattie's with Madeline were joined now by the three girls. Those dinners became a light at the end of the tunnel each week. The companionship brought laughter over their innocence and their delight at the smallest things, giggles during games after eating, and a sense of purpose for me when they asked questions about nature, birds, and animals.

After the last Sunday dinner, Madeline volunteered to drive me home. But, since it was not cold, I asked the girls if they would like me to walk them home and perhaps we would hear the call of night birds. They enthusiastically agreed.

Miah, who lived next door to Aunt Hattie, was the first to leave the pack. After our goodnights, Deetsy, Bunny, and I continued to walk down the steep hill to the long, dark driveway leading up the side of the mountain to their trailer. I offered to walk them the rest of the way, but both insisted I stay on Colony Row, that I had come far enough. I questioned their reluctance but said nothing. These were children who hid in a lean-to in the dark of night. They likely had their reasons.

Bunny turned to me and asked for a hug good-bye. As I bent and she put her arms around my neck and squeezed, I registered that I had never hugged a child.

"Night, night," she said.

I straightened and looked to Deetsy, but she quickly averted her eyes and walked up the drive with Bunny following behind. I waited until I saw the trailer door open, them enter, and the door close behind them.

The walk home became a standard ping pong match of pros and cons about whether it was wise—or safe—to allow myself to emotionally connect with the children. Every encounter between the four of us, I struggled with the same choice, always deciding to allow it.

That night, the heavy meal at Aunt Hattie's brought deep sleep until, suddenly, I sat bolt upright in bed at the sounding of an alarm. The first one, at the base of Easterbrook. Besides the day Rick spent installing and testing them, this was the first time that any had gone off.

Shocked and fully awake, I felt every muscle in my body ready to pounce from beneath the warm covers and investigate. But better to wait. My mind went through the possibilities. Perhaps the first was a false alarm.

The clock on the bedside table read 2:14 a.m.

I knew I would not go back to sleep, even if no other alarm sounded. I got up in the darkness and grabbed jeans from a drawer, hopping across the room as I pulled them on. Without looking, I slid on my moccasins while peering vainly out my front bedroom windows that overlooked the veranda and my driveway. I might as well have been blindfolded for all I could see. With little moonlight, darkness was a thick blanket cast down, enclosing the cabin. I finished dressing. My feet froze to the floor at the sound of the second alarm. Two long and shrill tones. This was no malfunction. Someone was halfway up Easterbrook.

I couldn't stay frozen. I had to do something. I needed to be prepared. My hands shook as I reached under my pillow for the Taser. Rick had taught me how to point the little red dot and shoot, telling me I could aim from twenty feet away, administer the world's worst total body Charlie horse, then drop it and run or use it like a stun gun until help arrived. I hoped I would be able to drop it and run to the ancestors' trail. I had to coax myself out of my frozen position and into fight or flight.

Move. Now. Follow the plan.

My moccasins were silent as I ran through the great room and grabbed my jacket from the hook by the front door. I checked its pocket for my flashlight. Opened the small door under the marble-top credenza beneath the coat hooks, pulled out my wallet with my identification. By the time I put on my coat and pulled a dark hat over my head, the third alarm went off, so penetrating it could wake the dead. Was this actually happening?

How crazy that now, when the alarm was real, my instinct was to cry. To find a place to hide and cry. This must be bad. This time it was someone dangerous. Someone who embraced danger.

My chest tightened, making it hard to breathe. I grabbed my keys from the marble top table and made my way quickly through the great room into the kitchen, unplugging my burner phone on the counter and zipping it into my jacket pocket. I had rehearsed the plan a hundred times in my head. There was nothing else on my mental checklist to cross off. I raced to the back door, only to pause when I got there. Should I start down the ancestors' trail now or wait and peek out the front windows to see who was coming? What if something had happened to Aunt Hattie or Madeline? What if it were Rick coming to get me?

My eagle-shaped key fob bit hard into the flesh of my palm. I relaxed my grip and reminded myself to stay calm and breathe.

Think, Emerson. Stop and think.

The fourth and last alarm pierced the silence of the cabin, splitting my ears. My heart rate went nuclear. Whoever it was, this was record speed. I could not imagine Rick driving that fast up the curves. Enaldo. It had to be.

I slid through the back door and dashed around the west side of the cabin. From there I could make a quick retreat behind the line of mountain laurel if the need arose. Other than Rick, I was the only living soul that knew if I moved through the laurel and around the springhouse, I would find the entrance to the ancestors' trail behind it. My feet knew the path by heart.

Stationing myself against the side of the cabin, I got into position to peek around the veranda. My chest ached from shortness of breath, but my mind was alert. All systems go.

I detected the rattling sound of an older vehicle. There was a miss in the motor, and a clunking sound, as though part of the frame was loose. A heavier vehicle. Maybe a pickup with extra weight in its truck bed. If men swarmed in different directions from the back of the truck, I could still avoid them, shielded by the laurel and the darkness.

Under the moonlight, a battered gray pickup rounded the last curve in the driveway and made a fast approach to the front of the cabin. Within feet of the veranda, the truck braked so abruptly its body rocked forward, back, then forward again before coming to rest. The moon's light reflected dimly over its mismatched blue hood.

After a moment, the door opened, and a tall, thin male stumbled out, narrowly regained his footing, then slammed the door. He staggered to the veranda steps and began pulling himself up with the banister, then stopped on the second step and swooned backward, teetering on his heels. He grabbed the banister with his free hand, swayed backward once more, but eventually caught his balance and continued.

He went to the door and tried to open it, cursing when he found it locked. His fingers searched above the door then cursed again. No missing his intent. He wanted to break in. My stomach knotted. Anger rose within me, and heat tingled across my face.

The man stumbled over to the windows of the sitting room, which he tried unsuccessfully to lift. More cursing. His voice was familiar.

He felt above the window ledges. Moved to the opposite side of the front door and repeated the process. When he turned west, I ducked below his line of vision. He staggered to the swing just feet from where I crouched and plopped down heavily, causing the chains to groan. His back was so close to me I could have touched him. He sat for a moment, then wobbled and pitched over sideways onto the swing. A few moments later, the swing squeaked again as he pulled his knees up in a fetal position.

I shuffled through memories, trying to recall his voice. It was someone I did not like. Someone that evoked in me fear and anger. I took a deep breath and rose slowly, in case he could sense movement. I let my mind flip through mental records, but I could not place the voice. Perhaps he was from my childhood. He would be older now. His voice changed. Or maybe he sounded different because he was drunk.

I waited until I heard the soft, even breath of sleep and then a snore, and moved silently around to the veranda steps, placing my feet close to the edge where my footfall could avoid the squeak of old wood. With my Taser uncapped, I approached the swing to look at the sleeping intruder in what little moonlight there was. Long hair covered his face. The moon was not bright enough under the veranda roof for me to identify him.

He had not been holding a weapon, nor could I see one on him, but I suspected, like so many rough men in the area that might try to break into a private home, he had at least a few knives stashed in his belt or boots. I crept closer. My nerves had settled a lot, and I had a sense of confidence about what to do. If I awakened him now, I would have the upper hand. But if he were a mean drunk, he would be stronger and even crazier when intoxicated. Better to wait and hope a hangover would leave him vulnerable in the morning.

I slowly opened the screen door and used my key to unlock the wooden door, grimacing when the lock tumbled. I turned to check, but he slumbered on undisturbed. I tiptoed through the dark cabin and grabbed a quilt. I would rather he slept through the night than be awakened by the cold.

When I bent to cover him, he stirred, and his hair fell from his face. The angle of his cheekbones was sharp. Native. My stomach tightened with an unclear memory. I had to get a grip. No need for panic. Not yet anyway. I took a seat in a rocker by the front door and listened to my intruder snore, thinking back on what seemed familiar. The cheekbones. Something about his voice . . .

The hair on the back of my neck stood as a memory resurfaced. Third grade. I was riding the bus home when three boys approached me from the seat behind. Before I knew what was happening, two of them held my shoulders down while the other cut my waist-length braid at the nape of my neck. With a dull knife.

Suddenly, I remembered how the boy's hands felt pressing down on me. My panic and rapid breathing as I struggled to get free of them. The pull on my scalp and the sound the knife made as it slowly sawed through my hair. The voice in the background, cutting through the chaos, encouraging the assault. Joey Horseshoe's voice. The same that had cursed my front door just minutes ago.

Joey wiggled and the swing creaked. I waited until his snoring became heavy again, then crept inside to make coffee, put on warmer clothing, and grab my tablet before returning to the rocker to wait. Going back to sleep was not an option.

• • •

When morning light began to break, I was ready to awaken him, absolutely certain that I was ready for an encounter with my first violent nemesis. He would turn to find me sitting in a rocking chair seven feet away, poised and ready to demonstrate his unwelcome status. Determination flew through me as, shifting sideways to face him, I uncapped my Taser and pointed the red light at his back.

"Wake up," I said, forcefully.

Joey grumbled and pulled the quilt up around his shoulders.

"Wake up. You are trespassing," I said, louder this time.

He began to stir, then his body went rigid.

"Make one wrong move and you will be in serious trouble."

"Hang on . . . Emerson?" He propped himself up slowly on one elbow, then raised his free hand in the air. "Is that you? It's me. Joey Horseshoe."

He made an effort to sound playful, as though I would be happy to see him. What I felt instead was energy coiling up from the pit of my stomach. Pent-up rage from years of his bullying and the havoc it had created in our lives. I tightened my grip on the Taser.

"You would be wise to turn around slowly and keep your hands where I can see them."

"Holy smokes." He grumbled as he turned and faced me. "What's got you so riled up? I didn't even know you were up here."

"Why are you here, Mr. Horseshoe?"

Joey sat up and looked at the red Taser penlight pointed at his chest. "Good grief. I've got a splitting headache. Can you put that thing down?"

I did not move.

"Is this how you welcome another Native?"

"This is how I greet trespassers."

"You can put it down. I'm unarmed."

"You will be. Pull your knives out slowly and place them on the floor, then take your foot and slide them to me."

"Geez. Are you kidding me, Emerson?"

"*Now.*"

Joey shook his head but reached obediently into his jacket pocket. He pulled out a large bowie knife and tossed it to the floor.

"Use your foot to slide it toward me."

He grumbled but obeyed.

"And the rest. The one in your other pocket. The one in your boot."

"You got X-ray vision?" He pulled a knife from his other pocket and slid it across the floor to me, then raised his jeans leg to pull a knife from the cuff of his cowboy boot and slid it as well.

Picking up the knives, I laid them on the rocker next to me, away from Joey. "You are trespassing, drunk, and unwelcome. Explain or I call the police."

"No, no. Don't call the police. I'll explain," he said, his voice now more highly energized than before.

I leaned against the back of my seat, never breaking eye contact. "Now."

"All right, all right. Give me a minute, okay?" He placed his hands on either side of his head and pressed. "I had a lot to drink last night."

My eyes narrowed, silently daring him to test my patience.

Joey sighed. "Okay, okay. You see, my girlfriend, Portia . . . well . . . she got mad at me . . ."

I turned and looked straight ahead, watching the baby pinks and blues of early sunrise caress the top of Crawl Mountain. I could still see him in my periphery.

". . . so, I came up here because she kicked me out."

I did not stir.

"I didn't think anyone was up here. I figured the cottage was empty since Two Eagles died. Geez, where's your car?"

The blue jays began to call as the sun illuminated the edges of the trees. I picked up my cell phone.

"What are you doing?"

I cued up my camera and took his picture. "And now I am going to call the police."

"No, wait. Emerson, wait. Don't do that. Geez, you play hardball."

"Then you have one more chance to tell me the *real* story." I put the cell phone on the arm of my chair and looked at my watch.

"Good grief. Okay. Okay. I borrowed money from Portia's dad and her brothers. They wanted it back, but . . . I kind of lost it. Gambling. I was at the Dew Drop Inn having a few when they came to find me. I went out the bathroom window and my buddies held them off long enough for me to drive away. I couldn't go home. Mama's mad at me. Grandma won't let me come anywhere near her since . . . well, anyway, I needed somewhere to crash. I don't even remember laying down on the swing. I just needed somewhere to go."

I did not look at him.

"Good grief, Emerson. I thought maybe I could just stay here until I figured out my next move."

"You want me to believe that you came up with this plan while drunk? I do not think so."

"No. I had it planned if I ever needed it. I didn't figure anyone would mind. After all, nobody lives here anymore, and it's basically tribal land anyway."

I glowered at him. "That is where you are mistaken. This is *my* land. And I am just as firm as Grandfather. Easterbrook will never be yours and it will never be a casino."

"Come on, Emerson. I just mean this land is tribal land, sort of. I figured it would be okay. You know, one tribe to another? Native to Native? Like family."

"You have never treated me like part of a tribe, let alone family, and you are trespassing."

"Geez, we were just kids. Can't we put that behind us?"

I looked at him. His face was puffy from the alcohol. He looked years older than his age. I had no sympathy.

"Don't be so hard, Emerson. Can't a brother stay here until I get this sorted out? I just need to lay low for a while."

"And what is your problem with the law?"

"Huh?"

"You are in trouble with the law, Mr. Horseshoe. You can tell me or I can call Sheriff Martin."

"Good grief." Joey shook his head and rubbed his mouth and chin. "You are still impossible."

"I am also correct." Why else would he panic at the idea of police?

Joey sighed heavily. "Okay. Yes. I'm in a little trouble. There are some outstanding warrants, I'm on parole, and there's a gun in my truck. If you called the police I would go straight back to jail, no questions asked."

I looked back out over Crawl. The whole sky was turning fuchsia. A bright fiery morning.

"Look, Emerson, I'm sorry, okay? I'm sorry I picked on you. Give me the list of things you want an apology for. I'll say it."

"That list should come from you, not me."

"Okay. I know I was mean, and I got my buddies to go along with me. But I was a kid. We all were."

"I do not want to hear your rationalizations. They nullify your apology. So spare me your reasons."

"Good grief, what are you, an apology professor? Okay, okay." Joey sat up straighter and took an exaggerated deep breath, then as if reading from a checklist, he recited: "I'm sorry we called you Half Breed and Injun Wannabe. And I might have—no, I *was* the one that made sure you got beat up that time. And . . . and I started the rumors that you were pregnant when you didn't come back to school. Okay? And I'm sorry we threatened to rape you. And that we cut off your braid. Okay?"

Every muscle in my body froze. I clenched my teeth, my jaw tightening.

"It was just hair, Emerson. It grew back."

Everything in me wanted to push the switch on the Taser. Believing they would do to me what other boys had done to my mother, knowing the anguish her rape had put Grandfather through, I had decided on suicide as I walked from the bus up Easterbrook that day. I did not even want Grandfather to see my horribly shorn head. He found me at my desk writing my last note, and he homeschooled me from that day on. But they were just threats. It was just hair.

I hardly recognized my own voice when I growled, "You had best say nothing else."

After a few minutes, Joey tested the water. "Emerson, I'm not responsible for you hiding out. You do know, don't you, that you were the one that felt like you didn't belong because you thought you had a white father?"

I tried to bore a hole through him with my eyes.

"Really. I didn't do that to you. You did it to yourself. Standing Bear must have thought so too. That's why she gave you a white name."

"Mr. Horseshoe, Ralph Waldo Emerson was a white man who stood up to the government against the taking of Native lands. My mother knew that I would stand up to protect these mountains as well, no matter what my DNA might be. And I have. I always will."

"Okay. I get it, Emerson. I wouldn't blame you if you called and turned me in. I deserve it. I wouldn't even blame you for using that Taser on me."

I turned toward him. "So, then tell me why I should not?"

He looked at me strangely then, half smiling even, as if the power had somehow just shifted between us.

"Because we're kin."

I shook my head. "If any kinship exists between us at all, I cannot imagine how distant it must be."

"No, Emerson, no." He shook his head and laughed. "You *really* never figured it out?

Heat rose in me, warming my cheeks, colliding with the chill in the air. I did not know what game he played, but it was just like him to try.

"You don't know, do you, Emerson? I'm your half-brother."

CHAPTER EIGHTEEN

Joey spat the words, then sat back on the swing with a look of satisfaction. My thoughts raced with his accusation. He had intended to shame me; I could hear it in his tone. I kept my eyes forward. I would not allow Joey Horseshoe the joy of seeing my surprise. Still, the realization that we did indeed look a lot alike clawed at the edges of my mind. Nausea swirled in my stomach.

Vultures circled at a distance over Crawl. Vultures can digest the most horrible things. God was telling me I could digest this, whatever it might turn out to be.

Finally, Joey caved, and the quiet standoff between us ended.

"So, when did your grandfather tell you?"

He was baiting me.

"Did he tell you that Johnny Whitefeather was in on the rapes? You and I both look like him. You know that, right? Our father was probably Johnny Whitefeather?"

I turned my head to my tormentor. "If you believed that a Native fathered me, why did you call me Half Breed?"

"I just did that to get your goat. If you remember, I also called you Native Princess." Filled with a new power of control, he draped both arms over the back of the swing. "My mom got raped just like yours. Just about the same time, in fact. But *you* end up with these mountains, spoiled rotten by Two Eagles, and I end up with nothing. Guess you could say I carried a chip."

I swallowed hard despite my effort not to. Dancing Fawn had been raped? I had not heard this before. Still, the audacity of him thinking that losing my mother and grandmother created a win for me made my stomach churn. And the thought that I might have had a half sibling all these years . . . surely Grandfather would have told me if that were true, even if only a possibility. Wouldn't he?

The fact was, Joey's tribe had always assumed dominance. They expected us to give up our mountains to expand their tribal lands enough that they could be granted casino rights. Not because we were blood kin, but because we were Native. In the name of Native unity. But Grandfather never believed that alcohol and gambling would profit any Native people and would not budge. Joey's people knew our matrilineal tribe meant the land was mine, but Grandfather stood in the gap between us, assuring them that I believed the same thing. I still did.

"Are you really going to turn a brother in to the law? Or worse yet, turn me out to let Portia's family get me. They aim to kill me, you know."

I looked over at Joey.

He took his arms from the swing and leaned forward, lowering his voice. "I'm just asking to stay for a little while."

I leaned over the side of the rocker in his direction. "I will tell you what I will do. I will grant you a favor since you apologized. But not the one you asked. I will let you leave without a police escort. If you give me any trouble, I will call the police before you can get down Easterbrook."

"Come on, Emerson."

I stood, placed his knives in my coat pocket, and walked down the veranda steps. Never had I felt so strong. So unbeatable. When I heard the swing squeak, I turned and pointed the Taser at his chest. "Do not move."

He watched as I walked to his truck and opened the door. Under the driver's seat, amongst the empty beer cans and chewing tobacco pouches, I found a small caliber handgun, which I put in my pocket with the knives. A search of the passenger side and glove compartment yielded no further weapons. I shut the door and stopped to stare at him. He was staring back, but not moving. I opened the metal toolbox that ran the length of the cab behind the back window and pulled out his shotgun then hoisted it over my shoulder with my free hand. Moving to the front of the pickup, I unloaded the handgun, knives, and rifle onto the blue hood of his truck, then pulled out my phone. I took close-up pictures of the stampings on the guns. If they were registered, it would come back to him; if not, Rick would still take my word for it. And they could be stolen. I stepped back far enough to get the arsenal, his license plate, and blue hood in the next shot. Joey said nothing. When I finished, I loaded his weapons into his toolbox.

"Leave," I said loudly, stepping back from his truck. "Never come up Easterbrook, Crawl, or Crow. Not ever again."

He sat still for a moment, then finally stood and walked across the veranda and down the steps. When he passed me, his voice was low. "You'll be sorry for this, Emerson."

I motioned with my head for him to get in his truck. "I believe in the sanctity of the mountains, Joey. Your family are good people, so I hope they can find a way to get a casino without my inheritance. But you, Joey Horseshoe, are not a good person. You can be grateful that I have not called the police and did not keep your weapons. I have now done you two favors."

Joey opened the driver's side door and stood glaring over the hood at me. I took another picture. "If you contact me, the pictures go to the sheriff and your parole officer." I blinked slowly.

Joey Horseshoe got in his truck and slammed the door. The engine roared to life, then he slammed the truck into reverse, sped backward to turn the truck around, then stomped the gas down the driveway. I climbed the steps and sat down hard in the closest rocker. My heart pounded from the adrenaline rush and the feeling of success that made me want to shout out to the mountains that I was victorious.

Because dates on phones could be altered, I would email the pictures to Madeline in case I ever needed to revoke his bail. And then it hit me . . . time stamps. That was it. Joey was using the newspapers in the cemetery next door to Agnes Mindell as time stamps to prove my negligence. Long ago, ancestors from both our tribes were buried there, and the graves were respectfully maintained in common. But for many years since then, Joey's tribe had used other sites to bury their dead. However, according to a centuries-old document that my great-grandfather's great-grandfather had signed, failure to maintain the common graves would move ownership of our private land to the tribal mother. Because I had no tribe to claim as my own, the new "tribal mother" would be in Joey's clan.

The last thing on my mind since Grandfather died nine months ago had been pulling weeds, and he may not have kept up with maintenance while he was ill. I swallowed hard to force the bitter taste of bile back down. How long had it been now? And how much longer would they wait to stake their claim? After today, surely it would not be long. And cleaning the cemetery now might be just the kind of activity that would get me killed.

CHAPTER NINETEEN

As the rumble of Joey's old pickup moved steadily down the mountain, my energy drained along with it. Lack of sleep, the continuous threat of Enaldo, the idea that Joey could be my half-brother, my rage, and the subversive plot to take my mountains were having a cumulative effect. Everything seemed like responsibility, and the idea of cleaning the cemetery overwhelmed me. I knew that if I left just one grave untouched it would become the focus of their photos. I had days of work ahead of me, and I was exhausted, hopeless, and incompetent to know where to begin.

I was drained. An empty shell. In trying to save myself, I had lost myself. I no longer knew who I was. Nothing stirred me. Not even the idea of a walk in the mountains. Surely in my current state I would trip over a root or tromp on a habitat. I had no footing to climb out of the deep hole I had fallen into. So, I sat motionless on the veranda as though I were waiting for a strong wind to blow me where I needed to be.

My eyes scanned the rolling view of blue mountains without the usual connection to joy or peace, just my eyes moving over the landscape. Hollow and hopeless, I felt as though I had fallen through a hatch into an unknown world I could not navigate. I asked my Creator for help. I had no idea what I needed.

I considered more coffee, a nap, visiting Aunt Hattie. These ideas did not stir me either. I watched to my right as clouds moved over Crow Mountain, leaving shadows across the ridges. From the corner of my eye, I noted movement in the driveway ahead of me and shifted my gaze to see the ochre-and-brown shell of a woodland box turtle moving across the blue stone in the driveway. He was highly visible because he was out of place. Was this my Creator's answer to my call for help?

Turtle medicine: home on earth, longevity, perseverance, and protection.

I thought about the message. In the environment of the driveway, the turtle was exposed and unprotected, other than its limited shell. As it moved toward the edge of the woods, within seconds of entering the forest floor, it blended and disappeared.

Energy bubbled within me. I did not blend in the world that had tormented me, but the earth was the home that offered me protection and the best chance of longevity. I felt depleted when I knew I was exposed. Even the smallest walk in the wood would resolve that, just as it did for the turtle.

With just enough energy and motivation to accomplish it, I strapped on the backpack designed to carry firewood and walked to the edge of the driveway where I had watched the turtle disappear. No trace of him. I continued my walk, awake and aware now with renewed energy to observe my surroundings. My eyes were drawn to the base of Crawl. Something out of the ordinary. An area of disturbed rocks darker in color than the surrounding rocks. An hour's hike down Easterbrook and another hour across the valley would take me there. I had no other plans that required me, and my Designer had called me to walk in the woods.

After the fiery start to daybreak, the morning was perfect. Low humidity and clear skies. The earth was cold from freezing night temperatures, the dense woods of the forest colder than my mountaintop. My breath came out in clouds as I walked through dips in the terrain.

When I drew within two hundred yards of the site, I saw that the huge rocks had been flipped. Their undersides, now exposed, were a deeper color from moisture. Near the rocks was a dark crevice. Possibly a cave. Energy poured through me and my scalp tingled.

Bears. Bears flip rocks looking for worms, ants, and other insects. Bear medicine: strength, courage.

Perfect. The gift I needed.

Listening intently for animal sounds, I drew within a hundred feet. Nearby trees bore long scrape marks from sharp nails, five or six feet high on the tree bark. Signs of a large adult bear marking territory. The leaves scattered beneath the trees had been tramped down as though a steam roller had been through—the pattern of a female bear stomping over and over to mark her spot, making a home for bearing young. The signs were fresh. She would prepare the site, wait a few days keeping an eye on it, then return to hibernate.

I stood and listened, watching, waiting for at least a half hour. She was not near. I approached the large rocks that had been overturned and peered into the dark crevice. My heart sang. It was a cave. I wondered if the sow had instinctually known that if she turned over the large rocks, she would unearth an opening to a cave. The perfect place for her to shelter safely while she was in torpor with decreased heart rate, breathing, and lowered body temperature. In January she would give birth to cubs. Perhaps the customary two, but possibly up to five.

I squatted near the flipped rocks and wet my finger, then stirred it in the dirt. When I pulled my hand back up, several long, dark hairs were stuck to my finger. Joy flew through me. I would watch for her as she released her cubs into our world. A world we both understood and thrived in.

I hiked back to the spot at the edge of the woods two hundred feet away where I had spotted her new home, so well hidden. I smiled, realizing that Lenore Lee shared a commonality with her bear sister. If Grandfather had been with me, I would have turned to him and said, "I had lost my way. I have no footing with Enaldo, Joey pulled the rug out from under me, and the tribe's threat on the mountains is relentless. But God gave me signs to follow so that I could reconnect. Here, with the turtle and bear medicine, I remember who I am. Who you taught me to be. I am putting pieces together again. Here, I fit. Connected to God, my ancestors, and the earth."

I imagined him beside me. His long, gray hair floating freely about, the sun warming his head as it did mine. He closed his eyes, smiled, and nodded twice, then spoke words I had heard him say many times: "You asked and then you listened, Little Bit."

Hair on my arms stood in anointing. Energy soared through me. I was connected. The polar opposite of the desolation I had experienced as Joey sped down the mountain.

In the Bible, Joshua and Moses were told to take off their shoes for they were standing on holy ground. Bending over, I took off my moccasins and socks and stood barefoot, taking in the goodness of God to hear and answer, the warmth of the sun that gave life to everything, the fresh mountain air I breathed in and that circulated through my body. I had been led to this place. As my feet registered the cold uneven earth beneath me, I turned in all four directions, memorizing what I saw, anchoring it in my being. If I lost my way again, I would recall it all.

My warm breath formed puffs of vapor in the cold air as I walked back to the cabin, thick socks and moccasins returning my feet to normal. My thighs felt powerful making long strides in the steeper stretches as I moved through the woods. At times I stopped to note the location of wildlife nests; squirrels, owls, and smaller birds whose habitats were exposed by bare trees, as well as wood burls protruding on tree trunks. I had been the age of the little girls when Grandfather taught me to mind map the mountains, memorizing water sources, downed trees, burls, and nesting sites.

Near the top of Easterbrook, a rabbit dashed out and disappeared under some brambles. I had watched them from the veranda moving about at this location.

Rabbit medicine: fear.

Fitting because leaving the deep woods to return to the cabin would once again elevate my concerns for safety. In the next day or two I would invite the girls up the mountain, teach them how to find rabbit runs and tunnels, then bring them to this spot so they could point out his burrow. Bunny, being the most observant of the three, would likely figure it out first. I anticipated how her nose would crinkle when she smiled as the bouncing rabbit with the white tail bounded away and dove into another blind.

Often over the past weeks I had lain in bed at night and gone back over my mind maps like a student preparing for exam. Isolation, the cold, and the shortened daylight of December stretched the nights like warmed taffy. Blackout shades protected me from detection, but the heavy fabric also created a thick shroud, hemming me in, burying me blindly to the world that was once open and free. Each night, as though my pillow held my fears, my worries returned. Was I putting Aunt Hattie, Madeline, and the little girls at risk with my presence? Perhaps even the artists-in-residence? When I voiced that concern to my elders, they disagreed. But in the deep quiet of the cabin at night, the fear that I was a magnet for violence kept sleep from coming. I had grown to truly love the companionship of my mothers and the children. Was I denying my intuition to serve my own selfish needs?

• • •

The day after Joey's bombshell and finding the bear's den was unusually warm for the first of December, so I set out for more downed ash branches. With low humidity, my vista seemed to stretch hundreds of miles farther. In an autumn world of brown, my eyes were drawn to the blue of a jay feather atop an orange leaf. I stooped to pick it up, thanking God for the medicine of the blue jay: fearlessness, protection, and determination. I embodied those attributes in the woods. I hoped for the same in the outside world.

I fingered the soft vanes of the feather, admiring touches of brilliant blue, and stuck the shaft of its quill down into the hard twist of hair at the top of my braid. All three girls were eager to learn about wildlife. I suspected learning about the meaning of finding feathers would delight them. "Each one, teach one," Grandfather often said. He would have approved of my having three students. He seemed to have always known that I would share what he taught me.

But he had also been convinced I would be a Spirit Warrior Woman, and I wondered if he would still see those characteristics in me, were he here now. Ever since the four-eagle bone token slid from its paper sleeve, I had continuously lost all faith that I would one day own the qualities it would take to rightfully call it mine. I could not fathom earning that token. I could not foresee being the person he believed would embody that call.

In my life, every venture with others had caused me regret. I was riddled with distrust of people, besides my mothers and the three children. Perhaps Grandfather thought he had seen that kind of courage when I was willing to take my life to save him hurt and shame. But I had not felt brave at the time, only my love for him. Would Grandfather's prophecy of me ever become reality? I touched the blue jay feather over my ear as I walked back toward my cabin and considered these things.

When I approached the crest of the last hill before the cabin, I paused behind a huge oak to listen before coming into view. Hearing nothing, I peeked around. The coast was clear.

Along the driveway, staggered stacks of rocks were exactly where I had placed them. A driver would not have noticed, and a vehicle would have knocked them over.

I crossed the driveway and walked toward the veranda steps. Something reflected in the gravel. A small piece of silver foil. My heart pounding, I stooped to pick it up.

A chewing gum wrapper. It could not have blown up the mountain. This was dropped.

Moving swiftly to the closest side of the cabin, I released my backpack from my shoulders and quietly laid it down, flattening my back against the stone wall that faced east. Pulling the Taser from my right pocket, I uncapped it and turned it on. With my free hand, I pulled my phone from my back pocket and hit the home button to call Rick.

My screen was blank.

I hit the button again, and the red outline of a dead battery illuminated the center. My walk had created too much roaming to hold a charge.

I was on my own.

For what seemed like hours, I stood listening, jumping at every noise, waiting for Enaldo or his associates to make a move. I finally determined to creep around to the north side behind the cabin. If I detected anything unusual, I could quickly go down the ancestors' trail.

Cautiously, I peeked into my windows, grateful that I had left the blinds and curtains open. Nothing inside appeared changed. When I reached the back door, I rose on tiptoes to peer through the small panes at the top where I could see straight to the front door. Grandfather's shotgun still hung over the door frame; his antique Native blowgun above it.

The soft moss on the north side of the cabin accepted my weight like memory foam and absorbed any sound as I crept around to the west side near the ancestors' trail. Maybe I should take it. Disappear. Make sure I was safe. Yet, nothing had moved. There were no unnatural sounds. Surely if someone were here they would have rushed me by now. My spider senses were not telling me that someone was on the mountain with me or anywhere nearby. Someone had been in my driveway though. Perhaps they had come, found the cabin empty, and left to return later. I would have to be certain. I needed to proceed with caution, but I could not just continue to stand outside.

My eyes searched every quadrant of the east side. Seeing no disturbance, I moved around the cabin where I could peek at the driveway. Patiently I waited, but saw nothing. Eventually I accepted that there were no signs of anyone or anything that should not have been there. I crept around the veranda and up the steps, trying to avoid the squeaks, but a floorboard sounded under my weight, causing my heart rate to go nuclear. I froze like a flamingo, one foot in the air. Hearing nothing and with my leg starting to shake, I eased my right foot back onto the veranda floor.

I reached the east bank of windows and could see that the locks were still engaged and secure. The door was a few more steps away. The jamb was intact, the locks engaged.

The flutelike "ee-oh-lay" call of a wood thrush startled me. I quickly turned and put my back to the cabin wall. *Only a bird, Emerson.*

I took a breath, but I could not discount the medicine of the bird that had startled me.

Wood thrush: a symbol of solid, healthy relationship that will not change.

I shook my head to clear my thoughts. I would have to consider that some other time, it seemed contradictory and unrealistic. I first needed to know if I was alone on the mountain.

I looked down to pick my next step and noticed a piece of folded notebook paper lying on the threshold between the screen and front door. I clinched my teeth, tightening the muscles in my jaw. I looked around. Still no one.

Moments seemed like hours. I barely breathed for fear that whoever had left the note was on the other side of the door, waiting for me to open it. Finally, I squatted, and using my fingernails pried the screen door open in a glacially slow movement, just enough to pinch the edges of the wrinkled paper. I took a deep breath and pulled it from between the doors, hoping there was no string attached to something under the oak door that would fall and alert intruders that I had retrieved it.

I eased the screen door shut.

Looking closely at the paper, it seemed as though it had been folded and refolded several times, as though someone had tried to make the blue lines on the white paper line up. I opened the folds.

At the top of the page, written in red crayon, were several X's and O's. At the bottom, in purple crayon, Bunny had written her name. Deetsy and Miah had written their names in blue. I looked at the note pinched in my hands as though it were a mirror reflecting the coward I had become.

Here, on my veranda, amidst the mountains of my heritage, where Grandfather reared me to be masterful in my environment, I could no longer recognize myself.

CHAPTER TWENTY

My hands trembled as I refolded the note. The shaking paper mocked the brave person I wanted to be. Maybe it was for the best that Grandfather had not lived to see this version of me. From skilled huntress to the hunted. I had become the prey. Hiding from and behind everything. Creeping around the cabin. Hiding behind trees. Sliding around the chimney. Panicking over a plastic rat, a gum wrapper, and now, a love note. The shame was a heavy weight that forced my chin to my chest as tears welled and then spilled down my cheeks, leaving their telltale marks on my jacket.

I clutched the note so tightly, my fingers began to burn, my thumb and forefinger yellow from my grasp. A love note. A simple love note that should have brought me great joy had brought me instead to this place of devastation. Bile rose in my throat, a reminder of the fear that rolled in my belly and threatened to be expelled. I re-opened the note and ran my fingertip over the crayon's waxy texture, taking in every stroke of the X's and O's. A hot rush of guilt flushed inside me, heating my face like a fire within. I had wanted them to love me and I wanted to love them. I had spent so many years avoiding others and ignoring the growing need inside me that I had not recognized it even as it influenced my choices. I had refused to calculate the risk to them.

In a moment, I recalled that in this very spot, Grandfather had predicted all of this.

Like a hologram, a vision appeared before me on the veranda

steps. I saw me, at Bunny's age, sitting beside Grandfather as he shared stories of our people. "One day, Little Bit, you will be the one to pass down these stories. And you will be the one to buy moccasins for little feet."

At this, I had stretched my legs out in front of me, twisting my ankles so that the fringe of soft cowhide danced with my movement. Grandfather smiled, then put a finger to his ear. "You will teach little ears to hear the will of God through nature. Every bird call, the weather, animal sounds"—he pointed to his eye—"and they will learn from you how to look for His presence."

He put his hand on his heart and urged me, by a motion of his head, to do the same. "Can you feel it?" he asked, when I had done so.

I nodded.

"We are the heartbeat of the earth, Little Bit. Just as a bird connects the earth and sky, while we are here, we connect everything to God."

In an instant, the image in front of me shifted. Now it was me on the veranda steps with the girls. Bunny, holding the baby Jesus in a pink sweater with a doll bottle, looking up at me and smiling so hard her nose crinkled. Miah, stretching out her tiny legs, marveling that her soft moccasins felt like ballet shoes. Deetsy, looking up and smiling. I had never seen Deetsy smile, yet the image was so real, I gasped.

My heart was full. I wanted to believe this vision. But as soon as I tried to accept it, the image suddenly changed. I saw all three girls bound and gagged in the darkened back seat of a car. I could smell the automobile leather and the suffocating sensation of stale air in the confined space. I heard them whimpering. I saw their huge eyes pleading with me.

I gasped, and the vision disappeared.

My heart pounded, my breathing froze. I dropped to the floor of the veranda, drew my knees to my chest, and dropped my forehead on them. Everything in me wanted to deny the vision. Chills ran over my body again and again.

I had seen many visions before. Grandfather with wings had been a prophecy of what was to come. I had denied that vision, yet my disbelief had not kept it from being so. I could not deny this one. It looked and felt as real as the hard porch floor beneath me. In a single moment, all uncertainty was gone and my decision was made. No more hiding. I could no longer wait out Enaldo.

I looked up to the sky and cried out to God for a divine plan. Not a plan made on the run, behind mountain laurel or from the top of the roof. The plan of a warrior.

My mind surged through ideas. For what seemed an eternity, I searched, knowing a vision would come. And when it did, I would know it in my heart. I would feel its power and all doubt would clear.

The sun moved in the sky, casting shadows from the tree line on the driveway toward the veranda. Evening was approaching. I tried to imagine what Grandfather would say. Memories of his wisdom came to me. "The opposite of fear is faith. The two cannot exist together."

That was it. Fear had been pushing away my answer. I had to center myself in faith and not allow fear to rule my thoughts.

I must wait with perfect assurance that it would come.

I breathed deeply for many minutes. I could not push for the vision, for as Grandfather taught, the door to the soul opens inward. If we push against that door, we guarantee it will never open.

The sound of birds overhead drew my attention. A blue jay chasing a hawk.

Blue jays were fierce defenders. The hawk had gotten too close to the jay's nest. Although the jay was a tenth of the hawk's size, the jay was relentless in mobbing its predator, staying close to the bigger bird's tail. I watched as the two flew in circles, the hawk trying to avoid the smaller bird. The jay would defend his young, no matter the odds.

The hair on my arms and neck stood in anointing. My fingers found the blue jay feather in my braid as I drew in a deep breath.

I was the jay.

• • •

Madeline led me to the smallest dining room in Maple Grove, where lunch was set for the two of us in front of the picture window that overlooked her stables, riding ring, and pond.

"Have a seat. There's coffee on the credenza. Want some, sweetie?"

I nodded, and Madeline motioned for me to sit as she approached the antique cherry table and returned with a silver pot. She poured the dark brew into Wedgwood china cups.

Our first "tea party" had occurred in the same room before my legs were long enough to reach the oriental carpet beneath her Queen Anne dining room chairs. Our shared delight in enjoying her finery had resulted in every occasion thereafter being festive, with Sarah Kate, Madeline's long-time cook and housekeeper, loving the tradition as well, always making sure my favorites were served on the finest of place settings.

Madeline sat down to my right, at the head of the table, and smiled as she busied herself with shaking out her linen napkin, placing it on her lap, and picking up a silver spoon. I had always loved the contrast of being at home in the deep woods and the opulence of Maple Grove with Madeline. But the news I was about to share made me a threat to her peace and serenity, a dark cloud moving in to block the sunshine of her joy.

Madeline stirred cream and two cubes of sugar into her coffee as she spoke.

"I'm getting the barn and riding ring ready, and I've bought three Tennessee Walkers. I'm so excited. I think these girls need to know how to ride, and it will be good for them to learn how to take care of horses."

I could not recall seeing her so happy. Using her natural maternal instincts had created such joy.

She placed her fingers on her cup handle and paused, looking at me, then rested her hands in her lap. "Something is different. Maybe I shouldn't have started with my good news. What's going on with you, hun?"

I hesitated. This could be our last tea party. I had not intended to dampen the spirit of our meeting until after lunch. But just as Madeline always validated my instincts, I would confirm hers. "You are correct, Madeline. Yesterday, the three girls climbed Easterbrook."

Madeline looked at me without blinking. "I'm stunned. All the way up the mountain?"

I nodded.

"That is a long hike for little legs. I was talking to the gardener near the front gate yesterday morning around ten and I noticed they were at Stopping Place. I thought it was odd that Deetsy had on her backpack, but I thought they were getting ready to poke around in the creek. I've seen them scout around a lot lately. They're building a playhouse in the woods behind your Aunt Hattie's, you know. I had no clue they would walk all the way up Easterbrook."

I nodded.

She took a sip of her coffee and set the cup back on the saucer. "Well, you must have at least enjoyed the visit. Did they stay long?"

"I was out on the mountain." I looked down at my lap and unfolded the linen napkin, fingered the finely crocheted lace around the edges, then flattening it against my legs. I looked back at my mother. She had not grasped the gravity of their actions. "They left me a love note."

"I'm not at all surprised. There's no doubt they love you."

I took a sip of coffee while considering the best way to approach my concern. "Madeline, if they come up the mountain at the wrong time . . ."

Madeline drew in a quick breath. "I hadn't thought of that." She looked down the length of the table as though her thoughts needed the space, then turned her eyes to me. "Hun, what would be the odds of that?"

I swallowed hard. "I believe they are far greater than the odds of encountering and then being hunted by an executioner."

Madeline's hand went to her mouth and then moved slowly down to her chest. She sat silently for long moments before speaking. "You are probably right. They are coming this afternoon to bake cupcakes with Sarah Kate. I'll tell them not to walk up there again." Her voice was filled with urgency.

I shook my head. "I do not want them to think they have done anything wrong. I will talk to them and tell them I am going away for a little while and when I get back they can come up and visit me anytime."

"You're going away? I hope that means you're going on some sort of vacation until the police or FBI can resolve all of this."

"I have never lied to you, and I will not start now. I am not going on a vacation."

"Where are you headed, hun?" She dropped her hands in her lap, concern now etched in deep lines on her face.

"I need you to trust me, Madeline. It is not a good idea for me to tell you where I am going. Or for how long. Leena Rose has agreed to allow me to call her on a burner phone to get updates from Colony Row. She will then call you and let you know that I am all right."

Madeline's face seemed to melt, her voice lowered and slowed. "Why wouldn't you just call me or your Aunt Hattie?"

"The mob could trace or tap your phones. I do not think they will bother with Leena Rose."

Madeline shook her head. "I would have never in a million years thought you'd leave Easterbrook again. Especially since the marshals couldn't muster it." Madeline shook her head slowly, the silken rose colors of her head scarf reflecting the light. She reached over to where my forearm rested on the table and placed her hand on it, her eyes pleading. "Emerson, please tell me what this is about."

"Madeline, I cannot."

She squeezed my arm slightly and nodded. "At first it made me anxious thinking of you staying here and now it makes me more anxious to think of you leaving. I suppose I just need time to adjust to all these changes. But I trust you. You are wise beyond your years. You always have been." She pulled her arm back and again rested both hands in her lap. "And I've been worried about those children ever since you told me about Deetsy and Bunny hiding out in the lean-to. I knew it was only a start to have them memorize the code to the walker's gate in case they needed me quickly. But they shouldn't have to live in any situation that causes them to leave home in the night. So yesterday I reported my concerns to the Department of Social Services. I'm ready to be an emergency foster placement if the agency ever needs me."

No sooner did my spirit lighten at the win-win of the situation than hot shame replaced it. My selfishness became apparent to me. I had been so caught up in my own worries that I had not considered solutions for the children while I was away.

Madeline was silent, and when I met her eyes, she added, "And I might come clean and let Jons know I'm the owner and CEO of the trust. He has to be more responsible about Miah being outside at all hours of the night. Hattie May said that his studio lights were bright enough to light up the backyard at midnight last night and she saw Miah out there catching snowflakes with her tongue. On a school night. On top of it all, she is starving herself, and everyone but him can see it. None of these girls are in good hands."

"Madeline, God put the girls in exactly the right place to get the care they need. From you and Aunt Hattie."

"Well, I haven't stopped caring for you, Emerson. If I knew your plan I might know how to help, hun." She stirred her coffee and looked up at me. "Is there *anything* I can do?"

"Yes. Keep Aunt Hattie calm."

She set down her spoon and rested her hand near her cup. "This scares me." Madeline's eyes filled with tears.

"And please let Leena Rose know if anyone spots Enaldo."

"Are you telling Rick what you're up to?"

"No. I need to do this alone. Leena Rose will have a sealed envelope with a note from me about what I have planned. I asked her not to open it unless no one hears from me for a week. Just in case."

"Oh my. Now I'm really scared. But you have my word . . . unless we don't hear from you. Then I think I will have to call out the cavalry."

"That is fine."

Madeline leaned forward toward me, her chin tucked. "Hun, please tell me that you are sure you know what you are doing."

"Madeline, I am only sure that I am called to do this. When I come back, this will be over."

She paused. "And if you don't come back?"

I ran my fingers along the embroidered edge of the napkin in my lap, then followed the ironed creases to the edge and folded it back into the original rectangle. Taking a deep breath, I smoothed it out against my leg and looked to Madeline. "Then this will be over."

CHAPTER TWENTY-ONE

Leena Rose buckled her seat belt and looked over to me. The light from the dashboard outlined her face in the early morning darkness. "All set?"

I nodded.

Steering her car out of her driveway, she turned left on Colony Row so as not to pass Maple Grove or Aunt Hattie's. Morning was risky. Both women were early risers.

"Have you heard from the abbess?" I asked.

"Yes, late last night. Communication in a convent is sporadic. I talked with the mother superior and she confirmed everything the sister told us yesterday. She said to text her with your destination, then she will text you back with the address of the nearest domestic violence shelter. That way she is the only one who knows where you are. When you arrive at the shelter, tell them you're seeking asylum from domestic violence. After that, they cannot confirm or deny that you are in residence."

"Thank you, Leena Rose. That is a good plan."

As we passed the trailer where the little sisters lived, I looked up the steep drive to their home. Total darkness.

"I've packed you a bag of snacks," Leena Rose said as she maneuvered a tight curve, her headlights catching a red fox at the edge of the road before he deftly disappeared into the thick woodlands. The fox validated my plan—a symbol of stealth and cunning. I was grateful for its message.

"Thank you. For the snacks. And most especially for agreeing to this."

"You're welcome. I'm thinking you are probably safe to sleep on the train. I doubt anyone would bother you dressed as you are."

"Good." But I knew I would not sleep. I would use the train's Wi-Fi to research Giovanni. I hoped to hit pay dirt with information on his favorite barbershop, restaurants, and other haunts.

"It's a brilliant disguise. Around here a sister would draw attention, but you'll be almost invisible in a big city."

"And I am hoping for invisibility."

"The internet has truly changed the world. It amazes me that you could have a habit shipped overnight. That isn't how it used to be."

"Leena Rose, thank you again for helping me. And for allowing me to use your computer and credit card."

"I'm glad to help."

I smoothed the long, apron-like scapular over my knees and adjusted my veil. Had I known the stiff pieces would take getting used to, I may have chosen to practice wearing them at the cabin. "I know you do not think you are taking a risk, but I still believe you could be. You are not a nun anymore. You have no need to buy a habit."

"I can always say I bought it as a gift for a sister. Anyway, I don't think there's much of a chance anyone is tracking my purchases." Leena Rose braked at a stop sign, then turned onto the highway.

I nodded.

As the car's headlights illuminated the yellow lines in the road, taking me closer to my first destination, my stomach tightened. Because preparation tended to calm me, I began a mental review of my plan: get off the train in New Jersey to avoid the terminal in New York where Giovanni's men were surely on watch; take buses to Little Italy to scope out Giovanni's restaurant and brownstone from the bus windows as I pass . . .

"You'll find a few extra dollars in your lunch bag."

"You did not need to do that. The rosary was gift enough."

"It is not uncommon for Catholics to give rosaries." She glanced toward me briefly, "Or for good friends to give one another a little money for a trip."

"Thank you. I worried that you would find my disguise blasphemous."

"I don't know your mission, but I don't believe for one moment you are wearing a habit to defile. Wearing a habit announces a relationship with God. You're a walking billboard for that."

A walking billboard traveling lightly. My small carry-on suitcase in the back seat held only toiletries, electrical chargers, pajamas, moccasins, and an extra habit.

I twisted the silver wedding band on my left hand, a symbol of the final vows of a nun, the Bride of Christ. The ring, ordered separately, was a bit tight, but at least I would not have to worry about losing it. Putting my hands in the pockets of my tunic, I made a final check: burner phone, tickets, and wallet. A pocket inside my black, down coat held my computer tablet.

"Have you decided on a name, sister?" Leena Rose asked, her voice cheerful as she flashed me a quick smile.

"My name is Sister Rita, after Saint Rita of Cascia."

"Good choice. The patron saint of impossible causes. I might have known you would research the saints."

"I tried to memorize the answers to the most frequently asked questions on Catholicism, and saints are number one."

Leena Rose pulled into the parking lot of the Amtrak station and slid the gearshift into park. "Well, here we are." She shut off the engine.

The lights from the train station highlighted her soft face and brown eyes. I could imagine her in a habit. Her face radiated care. Just an hour ago, she had helped me dress, explaining each piece as I put it on, marveling aloud that I had put such a huge plan into place in less than forty-eight hours.

"Does this make you miss being a sister?" I asked.

She paused, then nodded her agreement. "Every day. I miss the life. But I had choices to make for my parents. Now I feel called to revelation art. But yes, helping you has reminded me of my own solemn vows and the novices I helped to prepare." She sighed. "So many sacred moments."

We sat in silence and watched as others pulled into the parking lot and removed their luggage from their vehicles.

Leena Rose touched my hand. "Go with God, Emerson. If you need me, let me know."

I looked around the platform and the building. Several people were waiting, but I saw no one that I knew.

I opened the back door and retrieved my suitcase. "Thank you again, Leena Rose."

"God bless you, Sister Rita."

Chapter Twenty-two

The total darkness of pre-dawn created a reflection in the thick train glass. Me in a nun's habit. I studied my image. A look of stern contemplation peered back at me. I practiced relaxing my expression, but within seconds my scowl appeared again. My mission seemed as opaque as the scenery outside. Where would I find safety? Would I survive my mission?

As the mystical transition of disappearing darkness revealed the world on the other side of the train car, my own image was no longer reflected back. Sunlight awakened the world, allowing the most minute details to come into focus. First sky, then clouds; trees, then leaves; buildings, then streets and cars.

A sudden vibration beneath my apron-like scapular signaled a received message. Reaching beneath it, I pulled my cell from the pocket in my tunic. My home screen bore a message from the abbess. A deep breath came naturally. I had an address for a safe house.

With my phone plugged in near my seat, I used the train's WiFi to research, quickly adjusting to the motion of the train and clatter of the rails. A simple search on an internet map revealed how perfect the location of the safe house would be. Walking distance from Giovanni's brownstone and restaurant.

At one p.m., the train stopped in Trenton. I grabbed my suitcase and headed for the exit. The platform below me was crowded with people waiting to board. I hesitated at the top of the steps, and a gentleman behind me said, "Let me get that for you, sister." Before I could stop him, he carried my rolling suitcase down the train stairs to the platform, making a path through the boarders for me to follow. I thanked him. He nodded and moved on. He never once looked at my face.

The climate control of the train car had spoiled me. The temperature outside was near freezing. People bundled up in thick scarves, hats, and gloves scurried past me, much surer of their destination than I was. Only a few paused at the Trenton Station message boards, which gave directions on where to board a commuter bus. After finding the proper terminal for Port Authority, I welcomed the walk after the five-hour train ride.

When my bus arrived, a woman behind me instructed her teenage son to lift my bag to the top step. During the year of my residency in New York, I was never acknowledged by strangers in public. Wearing a habit forced me into a limelight I had not anticipated. In fact, I had thought the full head covering and ankle-length skirt would create a turtle-like shell I could retreat into. Respect for the vocation made me stand out instead.

As I climbed the steps and paid my fare, a man on the first seat of the bus stood. "Here you go, sister." I hesitated, but to refuse his gesture would have seemed ungrateful. I only nodded my thanks in case my Southern accent were as strong as my New York coworkers had teased it was. Hopefully he would believe I had taken a vow of silence.

The bus stopped almost every two minutes. My stomach tightened at the thought of how long the ride might take, but it was out of my control. I had a front row seat to the tall skyline, congested traffic, bold taxi drivers, and mix of people on crowded sidewalks. A complete contrast to the quiet and isolation of my mountains. When I arrived at Port Authority on 42nd Street, my anxiety took on a mind of its own.

The noise in the massive bus station was deafening, and as I had hoped, the crowd was enormous. But just as Giovanni's men would be searching for me, I was on the lookout for them, and the number of people moving about made my task difficult. My shaking hands sought to betray me, but the weight of the suitcase as I rolled it through the crowds controlled the trembling somewhat. I tried to stay in the middle or close behind groups of fast walkers.

During my residency, I had grown to tolerate the city, and once outside the station, familiar smells greeted me. Oddly, I felt almost at home. The diesel fuel and bus fumes and the pungent smell of trash dumpsters all contrasted with the pleasant aroma of a hot nut cart or the smell of a passerby's heavy cologne. But perhaps my relentless search for pictures of Giovanni's mob family had created paranoia—I kept thinking I recognized one of them in my periphery, and it took all my restraint to keep myself from constantly turning my head to look. Eventually, concern became too great, and I paused at a newsstand and pretended to look at headlines until I could give myself the all-clear.

I joined other riders waiting at the bus shelter. Standing next to me, a teenager dressed from head to toe in black and wearing ear buds bobbed her auburn head to the beat of music I could hear clearly over the taxi horns, traffic, and pedestrians. When the familiar white transit bus with blue trim arrived, well-seasoned travelers stood waiting for the bus to kneel and for exiting travelers to disembark before boarding. This would be the first in a short series of buses to reach my destination and allow me to scope out Giovanni's restaurant and home on the way. As I moved along the streets of Manhattan, exiting and entering buses periodically along my pre-determined route, the variety of activity and scenery clearly indicated which area of the city I passed through.

Maneuvering up the steps of the final bus on my journey, I glanced furtively down the aisle for a window seat that would give me a good view in Little Italy. I paid my fare and made my way past the front seats to the middle of the bus, the stale smells of lotions, hairsprays, and perfumes changing with every breath. I took my seat and just managed to squeeze my knees and the layers of fabric I wore between my suitcase and the bus wall. Before long, a green-white-and-red banner stretched over the street between two poles came into view, announcing "Welcome to Little Italy."

The streets here were packed with pedestrians swarming like bees from a busy hive. People stopped in front of restaurants to read menus taped to the glass. Folks milling about engaged in conversation with others. Vendors, their tables set up to sell hats, scarves, mittens, gloves, and socks, were everywhere, and pedestrians carried purchases in white plastic bags bearing the "I heart NY" logo. Small wayside shrines with statues of Catholic saints or the Virgin Mary, surrounded by colorful flowers and votive candles, were scattered on corners or tucked into alcoves along the busy streets.

I kept my eyes peeled for the building I had seen in pictures on the internet. Giovanni's restaurant had a distinctive red awning and several outdoor tables. My heart rate increased as the numbers on the buildings came closer. Then, the red awning.

My hands were sweaty, and it seemed as though a weight pressed on my chest. I had to take in everything I could as quickly as possible. Outside of the building, four men sat around one of the tables near the street. Outdoor heaters were stationed near their feet, a NYC fixture in the winter designed to blow warmth to those enjoying the outdoor seating. Standing beside the door, sentry like, was a tall muscular man with dark Mediterranean coloring. He appeared well-groomed, his dark black hair gray at the temples with the sharp lines of a fresh haircut. He wore a knee-length black leather coat that looked buttery soft. His posture was arrow straight and only his head moved back and forth, in the same way I had seen the Secret Service do on television. A long scar sliced down the middle of his forehead from his hairline to the bridge of his nose. His face was pocked with scars. Acne maybe.

The bus stopped for passengers about forty feet before we reached De Alessandro's. My seat height on the bus afforded me a good look over the heads of pedestrians at the men seated out front. They were so well groomed, any of them could have just stepped away from a stylist. Their suits impeccable, sharply cut, fitting perfectly, and even from a distance the overall look of big money was unmistakable.

The bus edged closer in the heavy traffic, and I examined the faces at the table.

For a moment, I went blank, and then startled when I recognized the man in the bluish-gray trench coat at the head of the table facing the street. Ginnova Giovanni. My arms tingled with gooseflesh.

I had researched multiple pictures of Giovanni. His haircut had not changed over the years, but his hair color had, the chestnut brown now whitened on the sides with silver. His appearance at the table was no different from the image on the internet taken just weeks before as he was leaving a courthouse. The charges had been conspiracy to commit murder. The case was still pending. His attorneys asked for another continuance, meaning that while they stalled, Giovanni walked free. Just like Enaldo.

Giovanni's eyes appeared cold, distant, and unmoving. The man across the table leaned forward to speak to him, and Giovanni looked at him dispassionately. Then, without turning his head, his eyes moved to the man on his right-hand side as that man began to speak. Other than shifting his eyes to the speaker and a blink or two, Giovanni could have been one of the mannequins in the Garment District.

His body language gave me a clear sense of him. The other men leaned in to speak to him, yet Giovanni never moved and hardly acknowledged them. It was clear he was in control.

I looked at the other men quickly. I recognized two of them from internet pictures as "made men," kings in the organization. No Enaldo. But then, I had not expected to see him. My idea of hit men was that they stayed out of sight. Besides, Enaldo had a history of changing his appearance. It was possible I could see him and not know it.

As the bus inched past the restaurant, I shifted my focus to memorize the guard. I would likely encounter him first. He was well over six feet. Every part of his face appeared to have acne or some other type of scar. Perhaps a fire? As I mapped the scars, his eyes landed squarely on me and widened slightly. The surprise caused my stomach to flip. I quickly averted my eyes as though I was looking around and moved my head slowly to avoid giving myself away.

I waited a few seconds, then pretending to adjust my veil, I looked back with my peripheral vision. His head was pointed toward my bus. Ice water ran through my veins. My plan had been to get off the bus, walk across the street, and board a bus going in the opposite direction to get another look. No way could I do that now. I could not risk him spotting me twice.

After a time, I realized with a jolt that I was no longer aware of how many stops we had made, nor had I paid attention to riders boarding since we passed De Alessandro's. I had been so rattled, Giovanni himself could have gotten on the bus without me noticing. And I had lost count of the blocks. I searched for numbers on the buildings. Giovanni's would be the distinctive "mars violet" coloring of New York city brownstones with a twelve-foot-high black iron fence running the length of the front yard. Finally, against a cream multi-storied townhome, large gray numbers assured me I had not missed it. His home would be on the next block.

I looked for the distinctive gate I had seen on the internet that led to his fortress. As the black ornate metal came into view, I bent forward to get a better look. At that moment, a male voice with a thick Bronx accent came from behind.

"Looking for something, sister?"

As though he had yanked a cord running through me top to bottom, every muscle tightened. Had Scarface gotten on the bus when the back doors had opened at one of the stops? No. He would have stayed beside Giovanni and sent another soldier to board. I turned to face the man belonging to the voice as we came to a stop in front of the next bus shelter. He stood in the aisle a step behind me, with the body type of a defensive lineman and dressed in a dark, knee-length wool coat. He stared at my suitcase, raising a single eyebrow. My heart plummeted. He was checking out the details. Thank goodness I had had the foresight to remove the Virginia Amtrak tag the minute I got off the train in Trenton.

"No. Thank you," I said, then settled back into the seat. He nodded slightly, then sauntered to the front of the bus, where he turned to the side and held onto the pole near the exit stairs.

I tried to look casually out of the window as we went by Giovanni's brownstone, but I could see that the man at the front of the bus still watched me. The only thing I was able to observe without being obvious was the massive iron entryway. When the bus stopped, I looked forward, and the man glanced toward me once again. Then, without expression, he exited, turned right, and walked in the direction of Giovanni's brownstone.

Had Giovanni just surveilled me?

CHAPTER TWENTY-THREE

I exited the bus at my final stop, my head still spinning from my brush with Scarface and the man he may have sent after me. I was like a bird flown headlong into a window, dazed and out of my league, and I was having difficulty remembering the directions to the shelter. My mind kept going back to the question: Had Scarface recognized me? This, of course, only raised more questions. If he had, he would now be looking for a nun. Would I be safer abandoning the habit? I could not fathom another plan. Best to find the shelter, get food and rest, then consider what my next move should be.

Daylight was fading. I counted down the building numbers as I walked and exhaled audibly when I finally saw the correct house number on the black wrought iron fence outside a brownstone and crossed the street toward it. The abbess had warned the shelter would have no other identification. The mars-violet brownstone was encased by what I now came to think of as the standard black wrought-iron fence. Nothing about the shelter would draw attention.

As though my body had awaited a chance to complain, the aches and discomforts of the trip seemed to take hold of me all at once. Likely the prospect of relief inside the shelter had lowered my defenses enough for me to recognize physical pain. My body ached from the long day, the tension, and the added weight of hauling the suitcase over what by now felt like miles of urban terrain. When was the last time I had really slept? And other than a bite or two, I had not been able to eat since I found the love note. But sanctuary was steps away.

The iron gate held no lock. I walked through, then continued down the walkway and onto the stoop. I pressed the doorbell. The chime rang inside the building. I drew a breath of relief and waited.

No one came.

I rang again, then again, pressing the button twice this time. Still, no one came.

I pressed the doorbell three more times. The minutes waiting dragged like hours. I reached for my phone and searched through my messages and missed calls. Nothing. I checked the house number on the mother superior's text. The addresses matched.

Streetlights had come on since I first stepped on the stoop. Early evening temperatures were taking hold, and dampness settled in. Now the air seemed to cut through me, and my body yearned for the door to open, to be welcomed inside for warmth and respite. I rang the doorbell one last time. The disappointment that followed seemed to sap me of all remaining energy.

I checked my watch. Five after six. I looked around the neighborhood for an idea. The shelter was sandwiched between other brownstones, small businesses, a bakery, and a Korean deli on the corner. Most of the block was residential. The air was filled with the smells of their homes. I detected Mexican, Indian, and Italian food. My stomach growled. I checked my watch again. Eleven after. I decided to go for broke.

I rang the doorbell repeatedly and pounded hard with my fist, at least ten times. Having never been a person who would do such a thing, I looked around self-consciously as I did.

They must have a reason. Perhaps there had been some sort of incident or emergency. A threat. A lockdown. An evacuation. Did the abbess change her mind and decide that I was too risky? Where would I go now?

I could board a bus and go to Penn Station and catch a train. But which train, and leading where?

I picked up my suitcase. Soreness shot through my shoulder. I descended the steps, then stopped before exiting the gate, realizing yet another obstacle. I could not walk back the same way to the bus. Too many chances of running into Scarface or one of Giovanni's henchmen. I hoped I could find a seat long enough to pour over bus routes. But again, a bus to where? I only had enough cash to pay for a couple of nights in a hotel, and Leena Rose and I had both agreed that a nun alone in a hotel for any length of time would be unusual.

What was I to do now? I was an animal cornered with nowhere to run, and now, nowhere to hide. I felt hopelessness and the sureness of death in the marrow of my bones. With each breath I took, they closed in around me. My insides shook from sleep deprivation and lack of food, not to mention the cold. Never had I felt so lost and alone.

CHAPTER TWENTY-FOUR

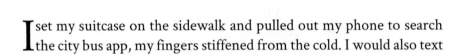

I set my suitcase on the sidewalk and pulled out my phone to search the city bus app, my fingers stiffened from the cold. I would also text the abbess and see if there was another shelter close by.

Behind me, a door squeaked.

"Sister?"

I turned to look, and relief worked its way over me, reviving my energy. A twenty-something nun with a peaches-and-cream complexion stood in the doorway. "Are you . . ."

"I am Rita," I said, my name part of the passcode. I stepped close to her so that I would not have to say the rest of the code loudly. "I have come seeking asylum from domestic violence."

"Please come in," the sister said. She smiled widely, revealing a perfect row of teeth. Her large brown eyes matched her brown scapular.

As she opened the door, I picked up my suitcase and ascended the steps. The warmth of steam heat greeted me inside the foyer. The aroma of chili created a homey ambiance. The sister closed the door behind us.

"Sister Rita, I am so sorry we didn't hear you. It's an old house. The bell doesn't work on the other floors and most of us were in the back. There are ten children in residence right now and they tend to be, shall I say . . . loud."

"I understand."

"I'm Veronica. We have been looking for you most of the day. The abbess said you might arrive by afternoon."

"I am sorry if I caused you any concern."

"Here, let me take that suitcase for you. You can hang your coat right there on the upper hooks."

Before I could say no, Sister Veronica put her hand assuredly on my bag's handle, and I released it gratefully.

"Would you like something to eat or drink before I show you to your room?"

"No, thank you." I removed my tablet from my pocket before taking my coat off, then hung it on a hook near the door. As hungry as I was, I would not trouble the sisters for food after sundown. There was still a granola bar in my tunic pocket.

"I will show you to your room and the bathroom. Then after you freshen up, I will show you around and introduce you if you'd like. This is a good time. You came after dinner and before evening prayers. If you get hungry, there is always something to eat here. If nothing else, having children in residence means there is always peanut butter and jelly."

Sister Veronica moved swiftly up the worn pink marble stairs ahead of me, and I followed behind. Without pause, we rounded the landing from the first floor and continued up to the second.

"This building is too old for an elevator," she said over her shoulder. "I hope you are okay with stairs. Your room is on the third floor with the rest of the sisters."

At the top of the stairs, a long hallway greeted us. At one end, a window looked out onto the street; on the opposite end, a picture of the Sacred Heart of Jesus adorned the wall. Along the hallway there were several crucifixes and crosses that I recognized by name from my research, as well as a picture of Our Lady of Guadalupe. The aged, wide-plank hardwood floors accompanied us vocally, groaning and squeaking with our footfall.

Every door we passed was closed. When we got two doors away from the end of the hall, Sister Veronica reached out and opened the next to the last one, the antique crystal knob making a scratching sound of metal against metal. She looked back at me and smiled. "Everything here makes noise." She flipped the light switch on as she entered.

Sister Veronica lifted my suitcase up onto a vanity. There were five pieces of furniture in the beige-walled room—the vanity, a small desk, wooden chair, single bed with a white chenille bedspread, and a nightstand. Atop the nightstand sat a small lamp and an alarm clock. A three-foot San Damiano Cross hung over the bed, its colorful background making the crucifix the only piece of artwork beneath the overhead bulbs.

She pointed to the wall behind me, opposite the window. "Your closet." It was small but more than I would need. Towels and washcloths were stacked on the shelf along with an extra blanket and pillow. "Your window," she said, walking to the opposite side of the room and shoving aside maroon velvet drapes. "The steam on this radiator is very hot, so be careful. We have heavy drapes to maintain the heat, but it's unnecessary. You will probably need to open the window to cool off. We all get hot up here. But your view of the alley is nice." She moved aside, inviting me to look.

Accepting her invitation, I moved forward and looked down into an alley separating the shelter from another brownstone thirty or so feet away. Trash cans lined the dark walkway. The solitude, quiet, and sparse furnishings were an oasis after the sensory overload of the trip.

"Come. I'll show you the bathroom and where we keep supplies."

We stepped out into the hall and she opened the door across from mine. "The good news, as they say, is that you are close to the bathroom. The bad news is that you are close to the bathroom." She turned to me with a smile. "There are five sisters in residence most of the time, and being this close, you will hear all of us go in and out, plus the banging noise when the hot water comes up the pipes."

"I am grateful to be here. You will not hear me complain."

She nodded.

She motioned for me to go back into my room, then followed behind and shut the door. "I am the sister in charge tonight. We have four families in residence now. Four mothers with children and one single woman. They are all victims of domestic abuse, here to hide from their partners. Sadly, they may decide to return home. On average, an abused woman will leave her partner seven times before she leaves for good. We provide counseling and do the best we can to make sure the children have a cheerful place to grow until we can help them relocate. No one is required to attend our church services, but many come for our nighttime prayers and when the Monsignor comes to deliver Mass on Sundays at three. They help prepare all the meals and are expected to help clean. The sisters run all the errands so that the residents are not seen in public, and we homeschool the children while they are here and provide activities in the afternoons for them as well."

I nodded, determining that in order to keep everyone safe, I would stay to myself, besides doing my part to help out.

"You are here as our guest. The Mother Superior told us to ask you no questions." Her youthful face showed no concern for why I might need such sanctuary. Would she see feel differently if she knew I was only pretending to be who I said I was?

"Should someone come asking for you, we've never heard of you. If they are insistent, we will notify the police, who have been known to respond quickly when we call." She clasped her hands in front of her and smiled. "Well, that's enough for now. You rest. Freshen up. If you want to attend evening prayers, they are at eight o'clock, and I will introduce you to the rest of the sisters and families if they are not putting small ones to bed."

"Thank you, sister."

Sister Veronica turned to leave, her habit making a soft swishing sound as she moved. At the doorway, she turned. "You are safe here," she said in a confident voice.

"Thank you, sister," I managed. Here, yes. But would she say the same thing if she knew who was hunting me just a few blocks away?

CHAPTER TWENTY-FIVE

———— ••• ————— ❋ ——— ••• ————

Despite my deep desire to stay in my safe room and enjoy the solitude, rather than arouse suspicion, and following the lessons Grandfather intended for me with the hunt, I forced myself to join the sisters for evening prayers. I waited until after they had started, then stole in and found a seat in the back of the large front room lined with chairs of all sorts, from comfortable wingbacks to folding metal.

Sister Veronica stood with her back to a window that looked out on the street. She was leading the small gathering of twelve, sisters and residents. She asked for prayer concerns, read a short devotion, prayed, then dismissed us. When I stood, I caught her eye, nodded, and made a quick escape from the room, climbing the stairs as fast as I might without appearing to rush. I was too tired for any small talk, despite my resolution to honor Grandfather's object lessons.

Back in my room, I sat in my chair, pulled out my phone, and called Leena Rose. The familiarity of her soft voice was like a warm hug.

"I am so glad you are safe, Emerson."

"I am. But aside from that I really have nothing to tell."

"You need sleep. Rest. I will call Madeline and tell her that I have heard from you."

After a warm shower, with no hair dryer in sight, I returned to my room. My eyes burned with lack of sleep. My body was tired. But my brain was wide awake. I plugged in my access point and hooked up my tablet, then began shuffling through page after page of sites that might include more information about Giovanni. Focusing on research soon stabilized me, as I became engrossed in my internet searches until noises in the alley below drew my attention. A metal crashing sound.

My body tensed. The clock beside me read 1:20. Moving to the window, I pulled the heavy curtain aside. Across the alley, many of the window shades in the brownstone were up and the lights on. I watched as silhouettes moved past a drawn blind on a third-floor window. On the second floor, a light switched off. I focused my attention downward when the noise sounded again. A streetlight at the end of the alley offered some illumination. An empty tin can was rolling near trashcans. A cat ran out from behind a bin. Then another. And another.

I closed the heavy curtains and returned to my chair. Cats. They are aloof. Their medicine could be urging me to be the same. To distance myself. Fiercely independent, they also land on their feet. I hoped this medicine would prevail.

The room spun when I finally laid my head on the crisp pillowcase. I closed my eyes, and they burned and watered from fatigue. When I awakened, the room was bright, although the drapes were still closed. My clock read 9:30, and I sat up with a jolt. I had never slept so late. Especially in a strange place. But the safety and security of the shelter had apparently registered at a deep level. Below me, there was already movement on the other floors. So much for my spider skills.

I made my way to the bathroom to ready myself for the day, then returned to my room to dress. It was surreal that less than thirty-two hours before, Leena Rose had talked me through the parts of the habit. Without her approval and with no mirror in the room—because sisters saw this as a representation of vanity—I hoped for the best.

Despite having searched late into the night for the haunts frequented by Giovanni, my efforts had been fruitless. With no idea of where to begin, I would have to wait for God to reveal a plan. I certainly did not have one.

Coffee might help.

The second floor where the residents lived was quiet. When I reached the main floor, the door to the right of the foyer stood open. Glancing in, I saw children sitting in rows of school desks. Those near the door immediately turned their attention to me, as if on cue. An adult female I could not see was giving them instructions about using their time wisely. A little boy around eight years old waved from behind his book. His blond hair and bright blue eyes matched that of the older girl sitting next to him. She looked my way when she saw him greet me, but she did not wave. She placed one elbow on her desk and rested her chin in her palm. The boy smiled and waved again. A moment of sadness filled me, with the realization that these children looked cleaner and more well cared for in a domestic violence shelter than Deetsy and Bunny did. I returned the boy's greeting and stepped into the hall that led to the back of the house.

Before I reached the kitchen, the sounds of Brooklyn and Latino accents drifted into the hallway to meet me. The other sisters and resident women I had seen at the prayer meeting the night before were there, most of them seated around a long, wooden table for twelve, with a few more women leaning against the counters. A resident at the counter had her back turned to me and was freshening a cup of coffee.

One of the sisters caught sight of me when I entered, and stopped talking. She sat at the head of the table, coffee cup in hand. "Welcome, Sister Rita. Ten a.m. is our coffee and cake club. I'm Sister Charlotte. We're so glad you're joining us."

The others looked at me.

"Can I pour you a cup, Sister Rita?" The resident who stood at the coffeemaker turned in my direction. Her pale face was marked with blueberry-colored bruises. Black stitches showed through an angry patch of swollen skin above one eyebrow. "I'm Tonya," she said.

I nodded.

A bright-eyed sister wearing a black-and-white habit stood and pulled out the empty chair next to her. "And I am Sister Josephine." She waited for me to come forward. I had noticed during evening prayers that she was my height. Six feet. "Sit here. This is our seat of honor. Well, today anyway."

I slid into the plain wooden chair. "Thank you."

Tonya placed a steaming mug in front of me. As I sipped, the conversations around the table were as varied as the selection of baked goods—scones, sticky buns, donuts, and cheese blintzes. In order to look like a part of things, I slid a sticky bun onto a saucer and tried to eat. But as always, anxiety added extra turns and twists to my intestines and made food unappealing. The more I chewed, the bigger the bite seemed to get.

A small, dark-complexioned woman shared that her children were grateful last night for the new underwear and pajamas. They had slept well for the first time in weeks. I could relate.

She opened a lively discussion about what to tell her children when they asked why they were staying and for how long. Experienced mothers joined in while the sisters remained silent.

In a rare moment of quiet, Jessie, an African-American mother, leaned across the table toward me and asked, "What are you going to do here, Sister Rita? You gonna teach, patch up the bruises, cook, what?"

I was stunned. I had not considered the question. Sister Veronica quickly intervened.

"Sister Rita may need to take a few days off before she joins the community."

"I will do whatever anyone needs me to do," I said, looking down the table. Although I knew I would evaluate any task for risk first.

Sister Charlotte spoke up. "You could be a big help today if you would like to stretch your legs. We always try to send the sisters out in teams. Sister Rosa was supposed to go with Sister Josephine to pick up the donated baked goods, but she twisted her ankle, so now she's teaching. That way she can keep her foot propped. Maybe you could go with Sister Josephine?"

My stomach tightened. I considered for a moment. Walking with another nun on a routine mission sounded safe. It would give me a chance to scout the area. "Of course," I said.

Sister Josephine smiled. "With two of us, it'll be easy to carry the bags. We take reusable ones. I'll show you where we keep them. There's one bakery just down the street. The other two are a bit farther, but it's a nice walk."

I nodded. It should be fine. The neighborhood was used to seeing these sisters on the streets.

"The bakeries like us to collect before noon, so the walkers usually go while the others clean up after coffee break." Sister Josephine paused for effect. "And that also gets us out of major clean-up detail from the children's breakfast," she said with a wink.

Once we had helped by taking the coffee cups and saucers to the sink, Sister Josephine motioned with her head for me to follow her into the hallway. She opened a door to a closet beneath the stairs and pulled out four well-used shopping bags with various company logos and one that stated, "I Heart New York."

Following her to the end of the hall and into the foyer, we stopped at the coat hooks, both of us preparing for the cold. Brightly colored children's coats lined the hallway on waist-height wooden knobs. Glancing into the classroom, I saw that this time both the blond boy and little girl had propped their books on their desktops. They waved from behind them. I waved my fingers from thigh height so as not to look like a full participant in their distraction. I couldn't help but smile.

The morning was chilly, our breaths visible. We left the shelter and turned right. I was grateful for the silence during our walk, even though it allowed my mind freedom to wrestle, alternating between anxiety and reassurance. I finally reminded myself that this was the reason I had come to New York. My mission would likely require more courage than did a walk to the bakery.

With our matching pairs of long legs and quick strides, we moved quickly down the sidewalk. While we waited for a pedestrian sign to change, Sister Josephine turned to me.

"Have you been to St. Patrick's yet?"

"No."

"You can go with us Sunday if you like."

The light blinked green, and I followed her as we crossed. I tried breathing through an open mouth to release the clenching of my teeth and give my jawline a rest. At the next crosswalk, Sister Josephine turned right, in the direction of Giovanni's street. I went numb. We were headed into ground zero.

I willed myself to keep moving, act normal, breathe deep. I walked with my head down so that my veil covered most of my face. We walked briskly, three more blocks. I was grateful Sister Josephine did not engage in small talk. In the next block, on the opposite side of the street, was De Alessandro's.

My legs urged me to outrun the threat. But moving faster would be a dead giveaway. I paced myself with Sister Josephine's steps.

As we approached the restaurant, I glanced over. No one was outside the restaurant. The tables did not yet have the red-and-white checkered tablecloths on them. We stopped at the last crosswalk before De Alessandro's and waited for the light to change. Just then, waiters in black pants and crisp white shirts began bringing out the heaters. I snuck glimpses of the second and third stories, where Giovanni's offices were reported to be. The blinds were drawn.

The fragrances of fresh dough from the bakery up ahead drifted through the air, tempting me, despite the half a sticky bun I had just eaten. A young man, wearing white baker's clothing in contrast with his jet-black hair, ascended concrete steps from a lower level and turned toward us. He balanced an oversized tray of long loaves of Italian bread on his shoulder and walked briskly in our direction, his white apron flapping in the breeze. He nodded as he walked by us.

Sister Josephine turned to the storefront just past where the young man had exited. FEDERICO'S BAKERY was emblazed in a large sign above the door. We were now directly across the street from De Alessandro's.

She held the door open for me, and we stepped just inside the shop, where lines of patrons were being helped at countertops set up in the shape of a U. Some were peering through glass cases and pointing toward exquisite pastries. The rich scents of bread, donuts, and spices were delightful. Two steps from the entrance, Sister Josephine opened a door on the left marked EMPLOYEES ONLY. She led the way, and I closed the door behind us.

Shelves lined both sides of a hallway on our right that led to open doors and a view of a white and chrome kitchen in the back. The sounds of metal trays clanging and cheerful chatter sounded toward us. Sister Josephine stopped halfway down the hall and pulled out a wire basket with DONATIONS on its front. She motioned to the bags looped over my arm. I opened one, and she filled it with wrapped baked goods.

When she was done, she placed the basket back on its shelf and turned toward the door we had come through. "That's all there is to it. We don't even bother them to say thank you. They've asked us not to."

I turned and led the way back out of the bakery and onto the sidewalk, then stopped, unsure of which direction we would take next. While I waited for Josephine to lead the way, I pretended to adjust the filled bag and sneaked peeks at De Alessandro's.

Sister Josephine exited, turned left, and began walking. "This way."

My heart skipped beats. I hoped she would walk straight through the next intersection. If she turned in the restaurant's direction, I could fake an ankle injury on the curbing. It would earn me a ticket back to the shelter. I would tell her I needed a cab. But there were no longer waiters in front of the restaurant, and we were fast walkers. Surely I could risk it if I walked on the street side and kept my head turned in the direction of the bakery.

The walker light turned green and Sister Josephine turned toward De Alessandro's.

Imagining Scarface glowering at me from the other side of the restaurant windows caused my scalp to crawl. I made sure to stay on the side closest to the street and decided I would pretend to struggle with my coat pocket as we passed. That would keep my head down and pointed away.

Just as we reached the front of the restaurant, the front door opened and the wait staff filed out one by one carrying stacks of red-checked linen. We stopped to let them by, and they began spreading the cloths over the outdoor tables. I bent my neck to fidget with my coat pocket.

"Good morning," Sister Josephine said, and I sensed her moving away from me. Before I realized what I was doing, I looked up at her.

"Follow me," she said over her shoulder and walked straight for the restaurant door.

Blood rushed to my temples causing them instantly to pound. Sister Josephine placed her hand on the bar to push, then looked back at me. "This way," she said, and moved inside, holding the door open for me to follow. This was not a bakery.

A couple of the employees paused from their tasks and looked at me as if awaiting my response. Nothing she had said could have forewarned me of this. But I could not afford to attract attention. I would have to follow. And immediately, since she was holding the door open.

I lowered my head and moved inside.

I stepped into a hallway. Toward the back of the hall, two lighted signs announced the restrooms and a door at the end had a red employees-only sign blazoned across the front. Immediately, a deep voice greeted us.

"Morning, sisters." A tall, gray-haired man with a receding hairline entered the hallway from an archway to our left, wiping his hands on a white towel. Smears of tomato sauce created a line across his white apron at the hip.

"Good morning," Sister Josephine answered. "I stopped by last week. I had inquired about the possibility of collecting leftover food that you don't sell to help us feed the homeless. The chef said to check back today."

"Sure. Follow me."

The man led us through the archway into a large dining area. As my eyes adjusted to the low lighting, I noticed that even this early, each indoor table was lit with a small, red-globed lamp. To our left, the blinds on the windows that lined the front of the building were open so that patrons could enjoy the street view. The room was awash with the aroma of Italian spices, baking bread, garlic, and onions.

The man motioned to the bar on our right. "Have a seat at the bar if you'd like."

Sister Josephine moved to the bar but remained standing. I followed. Behind the bar, which ran the full length of the restaurant, a mirrored wall lined by a row of red bulbs provided a backdrop for tiered shelves holding hundreds of bottles of various liquors. The slab of oak that formed the bar, at least a foot thick and thirty feet long, glistened with polyurethane in the dim light. Plush black leather bar stools were lined up in front like waiting servants.

Above the mirror were tiny lenses, barely visible. Cameras. I lowered my head and counted in my mind's eye how many I had seen in a second's glance. Six. And there were probably more. I admonished myself not to make any sudden or suspicious moves, and instead looked to my feet, hoping to project an air of humility or shyness.

"Thank you," Sister Josephine called to the gentleman as he stepped past the bar and through a set of swinging service doors at its side. I could see the bottom of Sister Josephine's tunic and feet as she turned slowly in my direction. "Are you okay?" she asked.

I nodded and turned away from the bar, looking up slightly. Gleaming cherry-wood booths with high backs formed an L against the front and right walls, offering some privacy to diners. The large center of the room was filled with tables covered with checkered cloths, each encircled by four chairs with plush red seat cushions pulled close underneath. Without trying, I spotted security cameras in each corner and over a couple of picture frames.

My chest tightened. Were they surveilling the room right now? If cameras were rolling, they could review them later. Multiple times. I imagined Scarface, after hearing that nuns had visited, rewinding the tape over and over to watch me. Would I be recognizable even with my head down? I clenched my fist with the realization that perhaps I had been careless in looking around the restaurant.

I dropped my head even lower and worked at the zipper of my

coat. There was commotion in the kitchen behind us. Every sound made me want to turn and look. I expected to see Scarface staring at me from somewhere. I envisioned him upstairs, pointing a finger at a monitor and saying, "That's her. She's the one from the video." After what seemed like too long, I let go of my zipper and pretended to concentrate on my nails.

"I almost forgot I needed to check back in here," Sister Josephine said. "If they hadn't come outside to set up, I think I would have." She laughed at herself as she looked around.

We stood for what felt like hours. I tried to focus on slow and steady breathing to avoid panic, but the longer we waited, the harder it seemed to keep my vivid imaginings at bay. I tried to take in the details peripherally while scrambling for reasons why I might leave Sister Josephine in the restaurant alone without arousing suspicion.

Sister Josephine coughed to get my attention. When I looked up at her, she smiled and nodded her head behind us. I hunched my shoulders and furrowed my eyebrows as if to ask "What?" I hoped I could get by without speaking in case there was also voice recording. I did not dare give away my accent.

"Wouldn't it be funny to take a picture of our reflection in that mirror behind the liquor bottles and send it to the abbess? Believe it or not, she has a great sense of humor." She offered a smile. "But of course, I won't."

I forced a smile and nodded.

After a few minutes more, she spoke again. "This is beginning to feel odd. Last week I was in and out. We'll leave if they don't come in a minute."

I was developing a headache. Something *was* wrong. Sister Josephine sensed it too.

Voices and the sounds of pots and pans escaped the kitchen as a short man pushed through the swinging doors near the bar. He wiped his hands on his soiled white apron as he walked toward us.

Sister Josephine's voice sounded upbeat. "Hello. We were wondering if you ever have leftover food that you can't sell and would like to donate to the homeless?"

"What?" he asked, as though she had asked the absurd.

My head pounded as though my brain had outgrown its own skull.

"We are wondering if you are able to help us feed the homeless." She reached over and pulled up the fabric handles of the loaded shopping bag I was holding. "We collect baked goods every day across the street. Last week someone here told me to check back today. I'm sorry but I've forgotten his name."

The man looked at the bag, then at Sister Josephine. Then me. I looked down.

"We don't have many leftovers. We run a tight kitchen. But I tell you what—we see you out there and we have something, we'll let you know."

"Thank you," Sister Josephine said and turned to leave, walking back across the dining room floor. I followed her cue, walking closely behind.

"Or . . ." he said, causing Sister Josephine to stop suddenly and turn in his direction. I stopped as well but did not turn. I instead busied myself with rearranging the baked goods in the bag.

"You give us your number or tell us where to bring it and we'll deliver, how about that?" I noted pressure in his voice. The hair on my neck stood.

Sister Josephine smiled. "Thank you just the same, but we rotate who does our pickups, so a phone number wouldn't help. Thank you again for considering."

Sister Josephine continued toward the door.

"How 'bout you, sister?" he said, obviously addressing me. "Tell me your name, and if we see you out there, we'll yell if we've got something."

Sister Josephine interjected. "We are not allowed to give out personal information. But thank you." She made her way to the archway that led to the hall and outside door, three or four steps ahead of me. When she passed through the arch, she looked briefly down the hall to her left, then turned right toward the exit door and continued.

When I entered the hall, I looked left as well. The hall was darkened near the end, but someone stood in the shadows. The outline of a tall man in a knee-length coat.

Everything in me went weak.

Chapter Twenty-six

Scarface bored holes in me with his eyes. I nodded in greeting, casting my eyes downward, and followed Sister Josephine, willing my legs to walk on shaking knees.

Once outside, Sister Josephine turned to the sidewalk, then walked at a fast clip. I listened with my heart in my throat for the sound of the door closing behind us and exhaled when it did. I stayed hyperalert for the sound of footsteps following. My blood pressure made a swoosh, swoosh sound in my ears, pushing the pain in my head.

Sister Josephine increased her walking speed significantly. I stuck close to her heels.

A half block from the restaurant, she stopped. She turned toward me, then looked behind us. I watched her eyes dart from side to side down the street, her breathing labored. She spoke in a near whisper, still searching the sidewalk behind us. "Okay, that was strange. Very strange. Did that just feel like we walked into a mob movie?"

"Yes," I answered.

"Seriously," she said, making eye contact with me. "That frightened me. I think they were watching us on those cameras. That's why they kept us waiting so long."

At her validation of what I already believed, I could no longer swallow over the knot in my throat.

"I don't know why anyone would want to watch two sisters, but that chef was up to something. I wasn't about to give him our information. Not that we ever do."

I nodded. Seeing her fear caused a new form of panic in me. My chest burned like it was on fire. This was real. It was not my imagination. Where would we be if she had not been so alert?

"Did you see the man in the hallway as we were leaving?" she asked. "Oh my goodness, he scared me."

My knees melted again.

"And the way he looked at you . . ." She pressed her lips together and looked again into my eyes, her eyebrows knit together sympathetically. "Let's just get out of here."

Every nerve cell in my body sent an electric signal, like a swarm of spiders with ice-coated legs running up my spine and over my scalp.

Sister Josephine turned and walked again, almost as fast as before. I kept up with her. She continued to talk without looking at me.

"Let's skip the other bakeries today. We have enough. And we aren't walking down that side of the street ever again. I'm going to tell the other sisters if they get called to come over there to say they're in a hurry and can't make it."

I nodded.

The brisk walk in the cold air used enough adrenaline to lower my panic. When we entered the safe house, I told Sister Josephine I needed to run to the restroom, placed the bags of baked goods on the table, and quickly went up the stairs.

In my room, I closed the door behind me and leaned against the door, breathing hard. Not from the stairs, not from the walk, and not from the cold. Scarface had seen my face twice in a habit now. Had possibly watched me for all that time on camera. It was likely that he would intercept and keep me from approaching Giovanni. How would I get past him?

I needed to know my enemy. Who was Scarface? Without taking the time to remove my coat, I sat heavily in my chair and swiped through page after page of internet images. Anxiety gripped my heart and squeezed each time a face similar to his appeared on the screen. I held my breath at every one, then released it with a silent sigh of disappointment when I realized it was not him. Over and over, the search continued like a new driver hitting breaks, then gas.

In the quiet of my room, the abrupt clanging sound of the heat in the pipes caused me to jump out of my skin. The room suddenly seemed unbearably hot. I rose to remove my coat, veil, and wimple, laid it on the dresser, and opened the window. I pulled aside the heavy curtains and looked out the window.

My hands pressed against the window frame, I noticed movement in the alley below near the door to the street entrance. The moment to see with great clarity was gone, but I got a glimpse of the back of a tall man with dark hair and a black leather coat leaving the alley by the front route. I slammed the heavy curtains together.

The coat had been knee-length.

Same color hair. About the same height. But I had not been able to see the sides of his head to detect any gray at his temples. Was it my anxiety or my logic telling me that it was Scarface?

Had he followed us? Would he waste his time or send a henchman? Didn't he have to stay and protect Giovanni?

I had imagined all of Giovanni's security watching the tape of me with Sasha over and over. Because I had looked toward the parking dispute, the bank camera had captured a head-on shot of my face. His men would have memorized it. I imagined a grainy photo from the video tacked up in Giovanni's offices like a wanted poster.

A sense of urgency enveloped me. I needed to figure this out. Now. If Scarface was onto me, I was endangering everyone in the safe house.

Grandfather always said that the source of the river does not know the destination of its streams. Once we create something, good or bad, we have no idea who, what, or where it will have influence. Or for how long. This was not my paranoia. I was truly a source of trouble. There was no way I could predict how widespread that trouble might be.

I peeked through the open slit between the curtains and, seeing nothing, opened the window to allow fresh winter air inside my stuffy room. Breathing deeply, I stood lost in thought until shivers brought me back to the present.

I walked across my room and sat back in my chair, opened my tablet, and pulled up previous searches. The reality was sinking in. I had no plan. The restaurant could no longer be a portal to meeting Giovanni. And his house was a fortress. Scarface was also likely to be security for Giovanni wherever he went. He would be on the alert for me.

I would need to leave my window open whenever possible to listen for noises from the alleyway. I would train my mind to listen for footsteps. I would allow myself to awaken to noise in my sleep, like a mother trains herself to listen for her baby. And if I saw the mob in the alley, I would have to leave the shelter. It could no longer be a safe house for others if they identified me here.

Search after search on the tablet for Scarface revealed nothing. I tried every possible combination with "scars" under image searches: Italian with acne scars, mob hitman with scars, mob security, La Cosa Nostra, mafiosi, mafia. Every combination involved wading through thirty or more pages of images, hitting the option of going to webpages and continuing searches there.

I tried the same phrases with multiple search engines. Still no Scarface. It was time to give up. I was lightheaded. My eyes stung from the strain. I stood to stretch and suddenly the world started to spin. I sat back down. I had missed lunch. It was midafternoon and I had nothing to show for it. Taking a deep breath, I started to close the leather top on the tablet, then thought of one more search, like a "Hail Mary," pass and typed it in.

Scarface Italian mob.

Images filled the page. Although many of them were the same from other searches, there were new ones as well. On page seven, I hit pay dirt. No doubt, it was Scarface. And the picture was recent. I hit "go to web page," and the engine took me to a site where someone had downloaded mafia photos from all over the world—Italy, Russia, Chicago, Cuba, Miami, and more.

His face popped up, and I sucked in a breath. Scarface had a name—

Luciano Devino. Subsequent searches using his name revealed more pictures and biographical information. Devino had a long RAP sheet of violence. He was twice listed as Giovanni's consigliere, or advisor to the mob boss and underboss.

Something in me settled. Just a bit. I had his name now. If he had not already, he must have been close to identifying me as well. First on the bus. Then I had the nerve to show up in the restaurant. He must have been unsure, or something would have happened to me at De Alessandro's. And maybe to Sister Josephine too. But three times would be too many. He would be sure then. So now what?

With lack of direction, I had nothing to lose by sorting through the advice the artists had given. The first had been Madeline's. In talking about her disease, she had said that everyone has a tender spot. She said she had come to trust those who did not focus on her worst traits, but accepted her as she was.

I filed the advice away. I would need to accept the worst of Giovanni. That would be quite a reach.

I searched tirelessly again. I learned a lot. He loved pizza and mint chocolate chip ice cream. Perhaps the family had a dreaded disease like Huntington's Chorea, a chromosomal disorder, or some other affliction. I searched through genealogy sites. Nothing.

His children were grown, all of them had had lavish weddings, all of them lived in different boroughs of New York. He had grandchildren that played team sports. There were pictures of little girls in tutus at recitals. Because so many people were fascinated with him, there were lots of candid pictures to sort through. But none of the pictures gave me pause.

The sounds in the house were changing. I heard footsteps in the hallway and my back ached from sitting in the chair too long. I glanced at my clock. It was six thirty. I had been at this all day. Now I had missed dinner as well.

I stood slowly to avoid dizziness, went to the window, and peeked through the drapes. The lights in the brownstone across the alley were on in the same pattern as the night before.

I could make peanut butter and jelly if I got hungry. But I could not stop my search.

I tried to relieve the tension, gently moving my neck from side to side. A room without a mirror was turning out to be a true blessing. I had to look frazzled.

I reviewed the advice of the artists again, one by one. Hair on my arms stood when I recalled grumpy Agnes saying, "Never underestimate people. Everyone has a heart. You just have to find it. It's usually a soft spot." I needed to find Giovanni's soft spot.

I thought about how I felt when I looked at pictures of my relatives. The idea of my grandmother, Pale Whispering Moon, caused a soft sense of longing.

I typed in *Ginnova Giovanni's grandmother* and got a few images.

Then I tried *Ginnova Giovanni's mother.*

I hit the lottery. Mariana Giovanni was figural in recent articles suggesting she had either fallen or had some serious illness that could not be confirmed. She was reported to be in a private rehabilitation and nursing center. Energy soared through me.

I continued my search, typing the name of the nursing center, my vigor renewed. *Saint Anthony of Padua's Center.* Saint Anthony, the patron saint of the elderly, and of lost items.

When I clicked on the center's website, my mouth hung open. Mariana Giovanni was only five blocks from the shelter. Eight blocks from Giovanni's brownstone.

I sat back as chills ran up and down my neck and arms. I understood now why people did fist pumps or stood and shouted at sporting events. Internally I was celebrating in that same way, despite not knowing how I would use this new information.

I searched for images of Giovanni with his mother. I found a few. It appeared that her son adored her. One was of him looking lovingly at her over her birthday cake. Another of him helping her into a limousine.

The hair on my arms stood in anointing. My body was confirming. This was his tender spot. Surely an Italian son visits his ailing mother.

Most especially when she is only eight blocks away. This was my next plan. I was joyous.

Now I would eat.

I downed the last granola bar, then refilled my last water bottle at the bathroom faucet. I drank some and winced. The taste of chlorine was strong.

Back in my room, I noted the clock. Nine p.m. I needed to check in with Leena Rose.

Her voice was higher pitched than usual when she answered.

"I'm so glad it's you, Emerson. Are you okay?"

"Yes. I would have called a little earlier, but I was tracing some information and lost track of time."

"Did you find what you needed?"

"Yes. But of course, it creates more questions."

"Are there any I can help you with?"

"Yes. Would it be unusual for a nun to visit strangers in a hospital if the nun was not a nurse?"

There was a moment of silence. "If a sister had a calling to visit the ill, her purpose could be to give comfort, not aid."

"Okay. Thank you. How are things on Colony Row?"

"Tense. Your Aunt Hattie has talked with Madeline and she now knows you are not on top of Easterbrook. She's . . . well, let's just say she is very upset. She contacted Rick to see if he knew, and of course now he's looking into your whereabouts as well. He's been here to talk to me."

My shoulders tensed. "Do they know anything else?"

"No. But Rick asked me why you visited. Someone must have seen you when you were here."

I could think of nothing to say.

"Emerson?"

"Yes?"

"He looked really worried. And maybe angry. I suppose it's a reflection on him since he's your liaison with the marshals."

I swallowed hard. "Do you think he has contacted the marshals?"

After a pause, Leena Rose sighed. "I don't know. But if they come and talk with me, I know nothing."

"I will have a new burner phone tomorrow. I will call you from that. I will get a new one every day from now on in case they try to ping me from your phone. I think I have a plan, but I have no idea how long it will take."

"Emerson, are you sure you want to continue this? When I saw how concerned Rick was, it scared me. I hope I haven't helped put you in harm's way."

"You have done everything you can to keep us all *out* of danger. Please call Madeline and ask her to tell Aunt Hattie that I have talked with you today and that I am well and safe. I do not dare risk calling her. And, Leena Rose . . . I am so sorry to put you in the middle of this."

"It's okay. I will call Madeline for you. Oh, and Rick said to tell you that wherever you are, he hopes you are hiding."

Chapter Twenty-seven

The next morning, the smell of coffee on the first floor surprised me as I sneaked down the last flight of steps. I did not expect anyone else to be up at six a.m. I walked into the kitchen to find Sister Josephine sitting alone at the table with a mug of steaming brew.

"Good morning, Sister Rita."

"Good morning. I wondered who would be up so early making coffee. You mentioned you were not going to be here today." I moved to the cabinet, pulled out a fire engine red mug, poured a cup from the pot nearby, and sat down across the table from her.

"My replacement has a virus. None of us want to see something like that spread through the house so I told her I would stay." She took a sip of coffee, cleared her throat and lowered her voice, although we were obviously alone. "I can't stop thinking about yesterday. I noticed you looked down the whole time we were there. Like maybe you knew something all along. I assure you that whatever is happening, you are safe with me. After all, this *is* a safe house."

"Thank you."

"I wondered if somehow you are concerned about . . . the mafia? It would not be the first time we had someone with that worry. Keep in mind that everyone here puts us at risk in some way. Currently we have two mothers with gang members looking for them. Gang members that have been responsible for drive-by shootings. And worse."

I looked down at the vapor coming off the mug, its coils mirroring the twisting of my stomach. A part of me believed I should warn her so she could help protect the innocents. But the cat medicine had given me a very firm sense of intuition: Stay aloof to land on my feet.

Sister Josephine leaned forward. "Please think about it. You don't have to tell me anything. But I can tell you if I see that man anywhere else."

I nodded. "Sister Josephine, I especially want to know if you see that man with the scars anywhere near the shelter . . . or the alleyway."

She gave me a long look. "You can be sure I will let you know. And I will describe him to the sisters so they can be on lookout too. I will leave you out of it. I will only tell them that I saw him and he alarmed me."

I knew I could print off pictures, give her his full name and a copy of facts from his RAP sheet. But his scars would suffice.

Fueled with caffeine, I wrapped my scarf around my neck tightly, veil under my coat, pulled on my gloves, and braced myself for the bitter cold that had been forecast. According to the internet, the current wind chill temperature in New York City was seven degrees.

The air stung my face as I stepped out onto the porch. Hearing the locks on the doors tumble into place behind me created a deep thud that registered as "no turning back" in the pit of my stomach, although now I had the numeric code to reenter.

The bitter cold had everyone on the streets bundled up with only their eyes showing, bent against the wind, walking at a brisk pace. Even with the frigid temperatures the sidewalks were busy.

I followed the early morning workers. Some of them branched off to rush down steps to the subway. Even at six thirty, people moved in all directions. Taxis left ghostly exhaust trails behind, and the familiar New York smells of diesel fuel, bus exhaust, and the occasional coffee cart and bakery hung as though frozen in the icy air.

Having memorized my route, I walked with purpose to each corner. Only five blocks. I hoped that if there were any issue with not having clearance into the hospital facility, the icy cold would prevent someone from sending me back outside.

I was encouraged after researching social media, where Mariana's grandchildren posted pictures, some of them with Giovanni. His eyes were a bit more alive in pictures with his mother, unlike the other candid shots or professional journalist pictures that showed a well-dressed Italian man with dead eyes.

Before sleeping the night before, I had researched footage of the hospital from every angle. Personal blogs by patients or their loved ones had afforded multiple views of the rooms and hallways. Shift changes occurred at seven a.m., and I had every intention of walking through the doors at exactly that time, when confusion was already at its highest.

My pulse quickened when the six-story, red-brick building, taking up a quarter of the block, came into view. Above the main doorway, ST. ANTHONY OF PADUA was engraved on a slab of marble the size of a minivan. I climbed the wide marble steps, opened the door, and was greeted by warmth and the smell of antiseptic cleaning supplies. Crisp and clean. One of the wealthiest men in the city would not have his mother anywhere less.

I stepped to the side of the doors. A long rectangular reception desk with five-foot counters all around, sat within yards of the entrance. Three hallways dispersed from the desk, forming a T; one to each side and another running at least sixty feet to the back of the building. On the reception desk's countertop, next to a silver bell and an arrangement of fresh red roses and baby's breath, sat a sign that read, "No one on duty. Please ring the bell. We will be with you shortly." There was no one in sight.

I removed my gloves and tucked them in my coat pocket then unwrapped my scarf and stepped forward to the front of the desk. Inside the boxlike reception area were two rolling desk chairs, one facing a computer and the other a phone. Both chairs faced the street. There were shelves and ledges holding various folders, brochures, maps of the building, and a bobblehead nurse paperweight.

At the end of the hall running behind the desk, nurses moved about at their station on a shiny, gray-tiled floor. The hallway to my right led to administrative offices. Brown signs hung over the doors with names like ADMISSIONS and ADMINISTRATION. Near the end, a sign marked LOCKER ROOM was visible just before electronic signs reading STAIRS and EXIT. At the end of the hall, glass doors led outside. The hall on my left held signs that read CHAPEL and QUIET ROOM, and a matching set of electronic signs to denote stairs and exit before another set of glass exit doors.

The clock on the desk read 7:03. As I draped my coat over my arm, a woman dressed in black sweater and slacks with a bright blue scarf around her neck came out of an office on the right side and walked toward me. "Sister? Are you waiting for someone?"

"I am stationed here to serve." My prepared answer.

She nodded. "Good timing, then. Susan, our volunteer, called. She's running late. The cold. Who sent you?"

"The abbess." I held my breath, my heart pounding, and waited for another question.

"Okay. Usually someone lets me know ahead of time. Or at least they call to set things up. Anyway, we can always use the help. We're grateful for all of you."

She walked past me and opened the gate into the reception desk. "Well, the front desk is as good a spot as any, I suppose. Let's put you here until Susan arrives. I'm Natalie Grosswood. You can call me Natalie. I'm the administrator on duty today."

A stunned numbness filled me. The front desk? If Giovanni arrived, would I ask him to call off my murder over the reception desk?

Natalie motioned for me to come around behind the tall counter through the gated entrance on its left side. "Let's see here. Let me give you the tour. These are the phones, of course. You will not have to bother with them. We'll continue to pick them up in my office. But if someone has a visitor, you will need to ask who they are here to see. You will ask for their ID. Approved visitors get a laminated visitor ID with their photo. Type the name of the patient here . . ." Natalie used the mouse to point to a search field on the computer monitor. ". . . and then click here." She moved her hand and clicked, showing me a drop-down menu that read "Approved Visitors."

"Look for the visitor's name. If they are not on the list but they have an ID, that means they are denied access. If that happens, you say you are not sure what is happening and send them to the admissions office." She pointed down the hallway. "First door on the left. We handle it from there. If they do not have an ID, send them to admissions to start the process to get one. If for any reason they give you a hard time, act as though you are perplexed with the system, pick up the phone, and dial the number that is on the top of the handset." Written in red marker and taped securely to the receiver was the extension number 211.

"You can say something like you are having difficulty accessing information and that you need the IT department. But in reality, it doesn't matter what you say; that is a direct line to security and sends an alert. They have you on monitor." She pointed to a camera above the front door and to each corner of the hall. "Security is only steps away and will be here in an instant. If for any reason you feel they are going to try and sidestep security, call the police. Dial 9 for an outside line, then 911. Does all of that make sense?"

I nodded.

"If the person *is* on the list, you check the box beside their name and you will see that an automatic date and timestamp comes up. You don't have to type it in. Ask them to stop back by when they leave, and then you go through the same motions, only this time you will stamp them out. You have to ask for their ID when they leave even if you remember them. We have a scan system where they scan their ID, but there was a glitch so it's not working right now."

I nodded, and she smiled at me. "Most visitors are used to this and aren't disagreeable. We are known for our strict security. It's part of our appeal."

I nodded again.

"You won't be able to give directions inside the hospital, of course, until Susan orients you, but you can point to the elevators right down there and you can give them a map." She pointed to a stack. "And let them know that they can stop anyone that works here—doctor, nurse or aide—and everyone will be willing to help them if they need directions." She pointed down the hall to our left. "I'll be right there if you need me."

"Thank you."

Natalie rose to leave, then stopped. "And when the doctors come in, they rarely use the front doors." She pointed to where I had entered. "Instead, they come through that side door near the chapel." She pointed to our right. "It's locked, but they have a passkey, so you won't have to check ID. But we do ask that you greet them."

I nodded.

"You can sit here and put your things on the other chair. Susan will show you the locker room when she gets here." Natalie looked at me and then brightened for a moment. "Pardon my manners, sister, in my rush I didn't ask your name."

"Rita. I am Sister Rita."

"Thank you for coming, Sister Rita."

I watched as she walked down the hall to her office and shut the door. My hands were clammy and shaking. It was hard to comprehend that I had just walked in off the street and breeched their security system. It was surreal. A miracle.

Aware of the cameras, I was mindful of needing to move slowly, as though I were orienting myself to my surroundings. I turned to check behind me to make sure the coast was clear. The nurses at the end of the long hallway, sixty-foot or so away, seemed occupied. I was alone with computer access.

When I told her my plan to come to New York posing as a nun, Leena Rose insisted I had chosen the perfect disguise, since it would not only change my appearance but also give me access denied to others. I believed her now. My heart raced. I would have to work fast to find Mariana in the computer and memorize her room and her visitor list before Susan arrived.

My fingers shook as I typed causing me to make errors. I eventually succeeded in typing Mariana's name in the search section, and her screen popped up. Fifth floor. Room 512. Pretending to adjust my long veil, I twisted to glance back over my shoulder, then readjusted myself in front of the computer and clicked "Approved Visitors." A long list of names appeared.

Footsteps sounded behind me, headed my way. Soft shoes.

I clicked out of the screen and tried to appear casual as I busied myself with pencils in a cup. When a woman spoke behind me, I jumped, pretending to be startled.

"Sister?"

I turned to face the woman and smiled. She was so short I could not see her neck below the top of the counter. It appeared her head, with curly gray hair and round face, sat atop it.

"I'm sorry, sister. I didn't mean to startle you."

"That is fine."

"I'm Marjorie. Natalie said you were here. Welcome."

"Thank you."

"I'm making your name tag. I want to make sure I have the spelling: R-I-T-A. Is that correct?"

I nodded.

"I'll be right back."

Marjorie walked back down the hall and disappeared into a room between the front desk and the nurse's station.

How long would it take to make and laminate a name tag? Susan could be here any moment. There may not be another chance.

Scanning the halls, I saw no one. I entered the system, again clicking Mariana's name and visitors. There were thirty or more names. Ginnova Giovanni was the third listed. The first two were the names of his sisters and three more sisters after him. I recognized they were listed in birth order. The next names were grandchildren.

A printer sat at my feet, and the print button at the top of the screen was tempting. But what if there was a digital log somewhere that showed what and when activity on a patient's confidential information was printed? Better to use my memory. I looked through the list. About twenty or so names down, my breath caught. Luciano Devino. Scarface. No telling how many more of the names would have panicked me had I known them.

I clicked out of the screen and picked up an ink pen with a flower taped to the top. I applied another layer of tape, waiting for Marjorie to return. When she did, she smiled and held the name tag over the counter. I rose from my seat and took it.

"Thank you, Marjorie."

"You're welcome, sister." She turned and walked back down the hall.

I unhooked the chain and put the name tag around my neck so that I would not have to worry with pulling up my veil. My hair was braided and looped so that it didn't hang below. I pulled out a map of the building and sat back in the seat to study it.

By eight o'clock, no one had entered through the front doors. Several doctors swiped into the side doors and a few nodded toward me. Many did not. Two more times I pulled up the list of Mariana's visitors to memorize them while keeping an eye on the pedestrians who were now streaming in heavier numbers outside on the sidewalks.

Two men turned from the sidewalk and walked up the steps to the front door in single file. The one in front wore a knee-length black leather coat. He was tall, built like Devino. His hat was pulled down over his forehead and a scarf was wrapped tightly over his nose, mouth, and chin. I quickly bent my neck as though I were focused on the paperwork in front of me.

My stomach knotted. My thoughts raced a million miles an hour. They would have to stop at the reception desk. In seconds they would be inches away from me. Would I have the chance to call security if I needed them?

Slightly shorter than the man in the lead, the second man coming up the steps could easily be Giovanni. With the layers of clothing and how quickly I had looked away, it was difficult to tell if these were the two men I had spent hours researching.

I began to pray. As much as I wanted to run or find some way to avoid them, this was why I was here. Perhaps God knew that meeting Giovanni at the front desk was the most fortuitous outcome. All those cameras gave me a level of security. I would have to trust that this was His will.

The outside doors opened, and the lobby was flooded with a rush of frigid air. A friendly female voice said, "Thank you." I glanced up without moving my head. The two men had held open the door for a woman who must have followed them up the steps. She walked toward me. The two men turned a hard right and headed to the administrative offices. The woman, wearing an ankle-length, zebra-print faux fur coat, a black rabbit fur scarf rounding her neck, walked to the desk, biting the index finger of her black leather glove, held it taut while she pulled her hand from its grip, exposing long red fingernails. Once she had removed both gloves, she addressed me in a Bronx accent as thick as her eye makeup.

"Oh my gosh," she said, uncurling her scarf. "I can't believe how late I am. What a disaster this weather is. I had to wait to get my grandchildren on the bus, which, of course, was delayed. Sorry about that, ah . . ." Her eyes scanned my nametag. ". . . Sister Rita."

"It has been quiet." I took a deep breath. Perhaps the first since the two men left the sidewalk to climb the steps.

"Good. Good. Yeah, it's like that when the weather's bad. Okay, let's see." She rounded the counter and entered through the reception desk gate and moved behind me to the other end of the rectangle. "I've got this now. I'm sure there is somewhere else you're supposed to be. I'm Susan, by the way."

It was obvious she wanted to dismiss me. She bent and began stuffing her coat, hat, scarf, gloves, and purse under the cabinet. Underneath the layers of outerwear, she wore a leopard print cardigan and black pencil skirt.

I stood, and she turned to face me. "Was I supposed to check those gentlemen in?" I asked, looking down the hall.

"Oh no. They come by for the deposit every morning. The night auditor has it ready for them. So where have they stationed you?" She bent over the counter and began rearranging the pencil cups and sticky pads.

I froze for a moment, even though I had prepared the answer in advance. "I am not stationed. I am to visit and offer comfort where I am needed." I spoke the words as though my orders had come down from on high.

"Oh . . . okay, then. That's good. This is a one-person shop here at the desk anyway."

I was unsure what to do next, so I reached behind her and grabbed my coat and scarf from the chair and exited out of the gate, shutting it behind me.

Talking to herself more so than me, Susan lowered herself into the chair where I had been sitting and said, "I have some names of new patients to type in so I'm going to get busy before the morning rush. We always get a lot of visitors around breakfast time." She turned and looked up at me with a frown, as though my standing just outside the gate was annoying. "Do you know where to go for patient rooms?" She reminded me of an animal marking her turf.

"Do you have a suggestion?" She was not volunteering to give me a tour. That was clear.

She spun around in her chair to face me, crossed her legs at the knee, and talked in a fast clip. "Well, we have hospice on this floor so that folks can visit their loved ones often with as little effort as possible. Second floor is physical rehab, broken bones and the like. Third is cancer, fourth is cardio, and fifth is pulmonary and stroke. We are pretty much all Catholic here so anyone that doesn't have someone in the room with them will likely be open to a visitor. I'd say explore around a little. If you get down here around ten and again around three, that's when the florists have usually delivered for the day, and you could take patients their arrangements. Don't offer food. Oh, my goodness, whatever you do don't offer food. We've had volunteers that knuckled under and gave candy to diabetics. Just because there is candy in their room doesn't mean it's okay. Sometimes the sitters bring it for themselves. Other than that, I think you'll do fine. Thank you, sister." She uncrossed her legs, spun back around to face the front doors, pulled a manila folder toward her, then leaned into the computer screen with a squint, making it clear that was the extent of my orientation.

"I hate to bother you, but where should I put my coat?"

"Oh . . . sure." She didn't look up. She raised her left hand and pointed a long red fingernail down the hall to her left, while her right hand directed the computer mouse. "You can put it in the locker room. Your name tag will swipe you in. If you have something to lock up, you have to bring your own lock." She never took her eyes off of her screen. I hoped I could continue to meet preoccupied people like Susan. If I had to meet people at all.

I walked down the hall to the swinging sign marked LOCKER ROOM. I turned my name tag over to the bar code and swiped it in the slot on the black lock. A light turned green. How simple. Astounded by the ease of it all, gratitude filled me. A morning of miracles.

The locker room was lined with small metal cabinets like a gym. Restrooms were labeled by gender on each side of the back wall. I went to the back wall and found an open locker. From there, a square of lockers in the middle of the room shielded me from view of the door. I hung my coat on the interior peg and put my scarf and gloves on the shelf. As I prepared to close the metal door, I heard two women enter, engaged in a conversation about the cold. They stopped at lockers close to the door.

"I can't stand this cold. A person could freeze to death walking to the subway," one woman said.

"I know, right?" the other answered.

Locker doors shut, almost at the same time, combination locks clicked, and I heard the sound of their heels tapping to the door. The door shut. Silence.

My body relaxed. I took a deep breath and sat down on the bench behind me. The bank of lockers in the middle of the room gave me a sense of security for a few moments. I pulled out my hospital map and studied it.

The door sounded again, and I rose and put my arms into my locker so that it would appear I was going through my own coat pockets if someone came to the back of the locker room. The heavy sound of a man's shoes walking toward the back made my heart pound. I did not turn. I followed his movement with his footfall, and when he rounded the square bank of lockers, I detected the faint smell of aftershave.

"Sister?" he said, and I turned to greet him.

A tall dark-haired man in his forties stood looking at me. He was well over six feet tall, had thick dark hair, brown eyes, and a wholesome complexion. He smiled, and wrinkles showed around his eyes. "I wasn't expecting a sister."

He held an expensive looking hat in his left hand and black leather gloves in his right. His pale gray trench coat was brightened by a beige Burberry scarf with gray plaid that matched his coat. I stood motionless, my mind a blank. There was really nothing to say, and ever cautious of exposing my southern accent, I remained silent.

"You're new here, aren't you?"

I nodded. He drew closer to look at my name tag. He smiled, and his eyes sparkled. "Sister Rita," he read. "Are you from around here?"

I shook my head no. "California." My heart beat faster. Though he was not likely a threat, I was a bad liar.

"Well, then, you must be . . ." An electronic sound went off and he excused himself to dig beneath his coat and into his suit pocket, pulling out his pager. "Sorry, sister, I have to get this. I'm Dr. Donetta, by the way. I'm sure I'll be seeing you around."

He turned and walked out.

I sat back down on the bench, giving my heart a chance to return to a normal rhythm. Although I had mentally rehearsed conversations, they were all theory until put to use.

Grandfather had been correct. I lacked communication skills with anyone other than him and my mothers. I hated being with strangers. Never saw the need or value in small talk. But if I had listened, perhaps I would be adept at setting others at ease, not making myself seem so suspicious. Perhaps I'd be better able to cover false identity.

CHAPTER TWENTY-EIGHT

———— ••• —— ✳ —— ••• ————

W hen I exited the locker room, I looked down the hall. Susan was on the phone, her left hand flying in animation while she talked.

First floor, hospice. It seemed insincere and dishonest to give them comfort. I had no right to deceive someone in such need about my religious affiliation. For now, I would stick to my plan. Avoid elevators. Each floor had two flights of stairs. On the front side of the building the stairs were on the right-hand corner. On the backside, the left. Going up, I would enter a floor on one side, walk half of the large rectangle of each floor and use the other set to go up to the next floor. On the way back down, I would circle the other way.

I was steps from the first-floor stairwell to my right. I opened the door and shut it behind me. Stale, cool air greeted me. And silence.

Stairwells could be sanctuaries if needed.

As I climbed the two sets of stairs, I was the only person on them. When I pushed open the door to the second-floor rehab, there were people in the halls. A man encouraged an elderly gentleman as they moved past me. "Lean on your walker, Dad."

I stood beside the stairwell door and waited. To buy time, I adjusted my scapular. A man pushing a pole with his IV attached ambled toward me. He stopped, leaned against the wall for a moment, and motioned for me to go ahead.

As I walked through the hall, conversations drifted from some of the rooms. One room door was open, and bright light streamed from its outside window. I passed and then paused. Had I heard a weak voice call "Sister"? A female voice. Perhaps I could handle this.

I backed up and peeked in. A tiny elderly woman smiled from beneath a lavender silk comforter brightened by embroidered purple African violets. Every level spot in the room was covered by framed pictures of what were likely her children and grandchildren. An African violet in a lavender pot sat on the window ledge along with a bouquet of freshly cut assorted flowers that created a riot of mixed color. A huge balloon bouquet of purple and lavender mylar was tied to the foot of her bed.

Her tiny gray eyebrows went up as I entered the room, as though she were the one surprised. "You heard me?" she managed in a frail voice.

I nodded and went over to her bedside. Her thin hand, speckled with brown age spots and lined with blue veins, slid out from under the lush coverlet, and she offered it to me. Her eyes were large and brown, reminding me of Aunt Hattie's and the pictures of my mother and grandmother. I took the tiny hand she presented into both of mine. It seemed natural to lightly rub the top of her thin skin with my thumbs. She smiled weakly.

"Sister . . . what is that . . .? Rita?" She raised her small head up from the pillow, straining to see my name tag.

I nodded.

"I prayed to St. Rita when my boys were growing up. I was sure they were headed for trouble. She must have heard me and prayed for them too." Her thin pale lips spread into a smile. "One is a lawyer. The other one owns a manufacturing plant. And they both have families. It seemed like an impossible cause at the time."

I nodded. I kept my voice low to match hers. "Is there anything I can do for you?"

She shook her head no. "I have a broken hip. I've been told at my age a broken hip can mean the end. I'm ready to die, but my family isn't ready for that. They want me in here doing exercises so I can get out of bed and go home."

I nodded again.

"You sisters," she said with a smile. "I can always tell when you've been cloistered. You have so little to say."

"Conversation has never been my long suit," I admitted and smiled back at her. "But I would be glad to do something for you if I could."

She nodded weakly. "Thank you. Would you mind taking that African violet on the windowsill out of the sun? It faces south and that's far too hot for its little face. I didn't say anything when my granddaughter Kaitlyn put it there yesterday. I didn't want to hurt her feelings. You can set it over here." She pointed to her nightstand.

I released her hand and walked to the window, glanced at the street view for reference, and moved the plant as she had asked.

"Thank you, sister."

I returned and stood by her bed. "Is there anything else?"

She shook her head no. It looked as though she were almost asleep; her thin pale eyelids stayed shut longer when she blinked. With her eyes shut, in a voice I could barely hear, she asked, "Will you come back, sister?"

I looked above her bed at her whiteboard. "I will, Mrs. Garbino."

"Bessie to you, sister."

"Bessie." I reached down, patted her hand, and placed it under her exquisite comforter. "Your room is beautiful, Bessie. I can tell you are loved."

"My family. So how can I leave them?" She said, her eyes still closed. I waited until her breathing became regular with sleep. I had never expected it to be so easy to give comfort to a stranger.

Leaving her room, I kept my head down and walked to the second set of steps at the back of the floor, hoping to avoid conversations. The third floor would have the cancer patients.

I took the stairs and paused at the door. Two nurses stood on the other side talking. I started to turn and sit on the steps, not wanting to disturb their conversation or bring attention to myself, but the hair on my neck stood when I heard the name "Giovanni." Every cell in my body alerted. I put my ear near the door crack to hear.

"That's his *mother*, of all people." The voice was female and angry with a thick New York accent. "I told my husband. I told him. I says, I'm not working the fifth floor, I don't care what they tell me. People around *her* son disappear. They don't call him the Whacker for nuttin'. So, he tells me, he says, 'you gotta work where they say you gotta work.' So I says, 'you want I should swim with the fishes and leave you with three kids to raise?' I don't think so."

Both women chuckled.

She continued, "I told him, I says, 'we both know you ain't exactly fatha of the year, and you would be raisin' them on your own. That man whacks people if they sneeze wrong." Her voice dropped. "You know what I'm sayin'? Am I right? You've lived in this city as long as I have. You know. Giovanni is a monsta."

"I know," the other nurse answered. "And it's like he's some sort of protected species or something the way he gets off in court."

The sound of their feet told me they had moved down the hall.

I took a step away from the door and braced my back against the cool wall. Even the hospital staff was concerned. Worry over a simple mistake was enough to scare them away. What would they do if, like me, they were a threat?

One good thing to come of hearing the conversation, the knowledge that Giovanni and Devino were not nearby. That made this one of the safest floors in the hospital for now. After several deep breaths, I pushed open the door. Ahead, a gaunt man in a wheelchair was parked in his doorway. He looked up at me and with a deep, bold voice said, "Morning, sister."

I nodded and smiled.

He inched his chair out farther as though asking me to stop. "If you aren't in a hurry, I'd love a little company. I'm trying to distract myself from thinking this morning."

I nodded again, and he used his hands to move his chair backward into his room. I followed.

Instead of a window, he had a wall where a striking quilt hung as artwork. The pattern was like stained glass, tiny pieces of brightly colored cloth sewn together to create the likeness of a brilliant sunrise, a multicolored sky with the red rubber ball emerging over the ocean. The quilt on his bed used the same stained-glass effect to depict a deep woodland walk.

I glanced at his whiteboard. "Mr. McKenzie, your quilts are outstanding. Just beautiful."

He smiled. "The one on my bed was my mother's. The one hanging"—he motioned weakly to the wall—"was my grandmother's. God rest their souls. They used to wrap me up in those quilts if I was sick as a kid. My daughters figured that's what they would do if they were still alive, so they brought them to decorate my room."

I nodded. "How thoughtful."

There was a long pause. He thought I should carry the conversation.

My mouth was dry. My head empty of ideas. I reached out and touched the quilt on the bed and fingered the fine stitching. Then I moved to the wall and did the same. "They are lovely. Hand stitched." I looked over my shoulder. He nodded.

He was no better at small talk than I was.

"Is there anything I can do for you?"

He shook his head no and looked at his hands lying limply in his lap.

We were silent again.

"Maybe grab that remote for me if you will, sister. There might be something on TV."

I handed him the remote.

He looked at me weakly. "Thank you, sister. Say a prayer for me. I have two more rounds of chemo. I think the cure is worse than the disease. I've never felt this bad in my life."

I nodded. "I am sorry. I will pray for you. I know that you need a distraction, and I am not good at conversation, but perhaps I could read to you."

"That's okay, sister. I'll watch TV. I don't really feel like talking anyway. I'm not much company, I'm afraid."

"Neither am I."

He smiled.

As he flipped channels, I left the room. I had another place I could step into if I needed to get out of view. Bessie on the second floor and Mr. McKenzie on the third. Inadequacy and regret bubbled up inside of me. He had asked for my help in distracting him and I was incapable. My elders had been correct, I was sorely lacking in social skills.

A few steps from the stairwell sign, the door of the last room on the hall was open. An extremely thin man sat in a wheelchair, his legs and feet sticking out into the hall. A multicolored crocheted lap robe created in a granny square pattern covered him. He looked up and scowled. But it seemed obvious by where he was sitting that he wanted interaction.

I stopped in front of his chair. "Good morning."

He frowned. A young man. Perhaps in his early forties. His face gaunt. A skull with thin skin pulled tight. No hair. An anatomy lesson in blue veins that almost matched the blue of his bulging eyes.

"What?" he growled as though I had interrupted him.

My heart skipped beats. Was he so on edge that even a hello would cause him to ring for nurses or security?

"Is there . . . anything I can do for you?" I asked.

His voice dripping with disgust, he snapped back, "I don't know what you think *you* can do unless you got a miracle under that veil."

I was unsure how to reply for a moment. "We could ask for one." I used my right hand to hold the silver cross dangling from beneath my wimple. I smiled so that he would see I was offering the suggestion with some humor.

He scoffed. "Fat lotta good that's done. Lots of people have prayed for me. Look where I am. Am I at the track smoking cigars with my buds or stuck in here with poison running through my veins?"

I nodded my understanding.

"Well. Go on, then. If you don't have a miracle, I don't need you." He waved his hand to the side, his wrist thin and frail, but strong enough to make a motion to shoo me away.

"But . . ." I searched his face. Something inside would not let me walk away. Perhaps my success with Mrs. Garbino or my failure with Mr. McKenzie challenged me. "I do not believe that prayer can *hurt.*"

"False hope, sister. False hope. I knew when they told me stage four there was no reason to go through all this. And I haven't been to confession in twenty years, so I don't deserve a miracle. The only reason I'm in *this* place is my mother. She's at Mass right now praying for another miracle. Thinks getting me in here was the first miracle since I'm not the right age. Now she's praying for a cure."

"You must love your mother a lot if you are willing to receive treatment to give her hope."

He scoffed. But he did not wave me away again.

"My name is Sister Rita."

He sighed as though an answer would exhaust him. "Dominic."

"Dominic, does your mother visit often?"

"Every. Day." He said this as though he were annoyed by the visits. "Every day I get to see that pained look on her face knowing I did that to her. I wish she would save herself the worry and the false hope. I'm not getting better. It's all just dragging *her* down." He looked like a small child that felt guilt for a terrible deed. He pulled the lap robe up around his waist and stared at me, as if daring me to have a comeback.

My feet were riveted to the spot.

In a move that surprised me, I squatted beside his wheelchair, much as I had done with the frightened girls on Easterbrook. He looked at me with surprise and then focused on his knees.

"I was not with him when Grandfather died. If I had known he was dying, I would never have walked away. I would have known that just being there was being of service to him. I would have treasured each moment with him, no matter how bad his condition. And I was just a granddaughter. A good mother *never* leaves her child if her child is in need. Dominic, it sounds like your mother is being a good mother. She is doing for you what you would have done for her if the roles were reversed. What I would have done for Grandfather."

I saw small tremors in his body as his lips pursed hard into a straight line. He blinked hard to suppress tears. After a moment, he raised his head and eyes to meet mine. They were softer now.

"Okay. I hear you." He busied himself with the top of the lap robe. "You can go now." His voice held no hostility.

"Peace be with you, Dominic." I rose, turned, and walked toward the stairway.

"And also with you." The proper Catholic response.

On the fourth floor, I walked my planned half circle, but few doors were open, and the ones that were had staff inside with the patients.

Next, the fifth floor. Mariana's.

In the stairwell, I stopped halfway up to gather my thoughts and ready myself. There had been nothing much to fear so far. No one had thrown a vase of flowers at me or expected me to recite church dogma. So far so good. But I was entering ground zero. Behind the next stairwell door was the floor where I would likely meet Giovanni. On this floor, where even the staff was afraid to work, I would be an unsolicited visitor and might arouse suspicion. Even with my nametag.

So far, each floor had a seating area by a large window at the end of the hall. My goal: walk the hall, pass Mariana's room, sit by the window, and wait. After all, this was why I was here. I climbed the rest of the stairs, took a deep breath, said a silent prayer, and pushed the bar on the stairwell door.

A few people were walking the hall. Some used crutches or had walkers. I saw my destination, the waiting area at the end of the corridor. As I walked down the stretch of rooms, I kept an eye on the room numbers, though every floor had been the same. Assuming this floor was no different, I would pass Mariana's room on my left and head to the chairs by the window. I would not look into her room. Once seated, I could finger my rosary if someone approached. People would likely not disturb a praying sister. From that position I could keep an eye on the hallway. And wait for Giovanni.

As I neared Mariana's door, the sound of a female voice came through the partially opened door. My shoulder muscles tightened, stiffening my arms and pushing them down. Focusing my eyes on the window, I concentrated on making my arms swing normally.

As I passed her room, I heard an energetic female voice calling, "Sister. Sister."

I froze. My heart pounded in my throat.

She was not supposed to have visitors right now. I had checked her name at reception. I looked at my watch. Eight thirty. That had been an hour ago.

I had disguised myself to get this far. To meet her son. This was the next step. My stomach twisting into a knot, I turned and walked back to the door at Room 512, fearing who I would find inside.

CHAPTER TWENTY-NINE

I had not considered I might be called into Mariana's room. I took a deep breath and straightened, tried to walk confidently to her door.

An immaculately dressed middle-aged woman sat between the patient's bed and the outside wall, facing the hallway. I recognized the small woman in the bed from her pictures. Mariana Giovanni. Another look at the visitor told me it was Ginnova Giovanni's wife, Venecia.

I paused in the doorway. "Did you call me?"

"Yes. Come in, sister," Venecia said.

I scanned the room as unceremoniously as I could. When I realized the two women were alone, the muscles in my shoulders relaxed enough that my arms no longer felt glued to my sides. On the opposite side of the room from her headboard, exquisite arrangements of mixed flowers, at least four feet tall, stood like bookends on either side of a large mirror hung over the middle of a cherry dresser. Their blown glass vases were variations of light blue that matched the silken comforter on the bed. A large window ledge was lined with a variety of other flower arrangements. Most still held floral picks with small greeting cards in their clusters. I walked to Mariana's right side and stood by one of two nightstands that flanked her bed, each holding matching blue vases with flowers about half the size of the ones on the dresser. I leaned in slightly to peer at the whiteboard above her bed, as though I did not know her name. "Hello, Mrs. Giovanni. I am

Sister Rita."

The tiny silver-haired lady with large brown eyes watched me. She nodded.

"She can't talk," Venecia said. "Well, she talks, but we have a hard time understanding, don't we, MiMi?" Venecia stood and bent over her mother-in-law. Her movement caused a soft whiff of perfume to waft toward me.

Reaching to adjust the covers around Mariana's shoulders, Venecia grasped the silk comforter with fingers extended by long, manicured burgundy nails that matched her lipstick. A jingle came from each wrist, adorned with diamond tennis bracelets and gold bangles. Even in the low light of the room, diamonds in her rings reflected boldly from each finger. After seeing pictures of her eight-carat wedding ring on the internet, it was surreal to be so close to it.

Mariana looked up at Venecia, her eyes bore a pleading quality. She made a whimpering sound. Without shifting her gaze from her mother-in-law's eyes, Venecia said, "She's getting better, sister, that's all that matters. Right, MiMi?"

Mariana's eyebrows moved up and down.

Venecia straightened and looked at me. "I'm Venecia, MiMi's daughter-in-law." She flashed a formal smile, one that involved lips, perfectly lined and colored, separating to expose even, white teeth. I returned her smile, although I worried my lips quivered with anxiety.

Venecia's hands smoothed her shoulder-length, dark hair. "MiMi had a stroke on her left side. It caused paralysis on the right and affected her speech. But you are getting better and better aren't you, MiMi?" Venecia looked down and smiled at Mariana who nodded slightly, "I called to you when I saw you walk by because MiMi loves the sisters." She looked at Mariana again. "Don't you, MiMi?"

Mariana nodded to Venecia, then turned her head to look at me.

"Is there anything I can do for you, Mrs. Giovanni?"

Both women were silent.

"I see on your nightstand over there that you have a Bible." I motioned to the nightstand on her left. "I could read for you." Her granddaughter had mentioned on her blog that Mariana loved the book of Luke, and her grandchildren read it to her when they visited.

Venecia looked down and touched her mother-in-law's shoulder. "MiMi, wouldn't you like the sister to read to you? Or maybe just sit with you?"

Mariana nodded.

Venecia pulled the sleeve of her left wrist up and glanced at her Rolex. "This is perfect timing, MiMi. Lido is in front of the hospital with the car idling right now." She laughed. "You know how he is, he's the most punctual driver in the world. It's only 8:33, but even just three minutes late I can see him drumming his fingers on the steering wheel, wondering where I am."

Marianna smiled faintly.

"I'll be back after four. After Lido picks Ashlynn and Jacob up from school he's taking them to an art studio, then he will pick me up. They're making a surprise for you. They can't wait to bring it. Would that be good, a little surprise?" She moved her hand and laid her fingertips on Mariana's left cheek. Her voice was soft and kind like that of a kindergarten teacher comforting a homesick child. Mariana nodded again, but there was no light in her eyes.

Venecia bent to give her mother-in-law a kiss on the cheek and told her how pretty she was. She straightened and turned. A black Louis Vuitton coat was draped over the chair behind her, its brown label contrasted against its black silk lining. Venecia put on the ankle-length coat and wound the matching scarf that had been beneath it around her neck. She picked up a purse with the same trademark, placing the straps over her small shoulder. The petite woman walked to the end of the bed and paused, reached into her coat pocket and pulled out black leather gloves, then blew Mariana a kiss. "Bye, MiMi. You know I'll be back."

I watched her leave, then busied myself straightening the comforter on Mariana's right side as I listened to Venecia's heels tap down the corridor. Her departure brought me relief. But like a kaleidoscope of anxiety, my next thought brought it back. I was with Giovanni's mother. Another thought turned the fickle dial down again: She could not talk. Could not expose me. Even better, she could not ask questions.

I looked at Mariana. Her eyebrows were lightly furrowed.

"Should I call you . . ." I looked up at her whiteboard again. "Ma-re-ah-nah?" I said, as though struggling to get the pronunciation correct.

She nodded.

I walked around the foot of the bed to the chair on the other side, where Venecia had been. There, I would be afforded a view of the door and the hallway. I sat, bringing me eye level with Mariana, not towering over her.

"I love the book of Luke. Would you like me to read from Luke?" It seemed dishonest because of my prior knowledge, even though I had stated truth. I did love Luke. Mariana's eyebrows raised as she nodded.

She looked as though she were concentrating as she tried to speak. "Maaaa aah wit." Her words sounded more like moans. "Maaaa aah wit," she said again, and perhaps because I knew it was her favorite, I realized what she meant.

"Are you saying, 'my favorite'?"

She smiled and nodded her head, her soft, perfectly coifed, silver hair reflecting in the light.

I smiled in return. "You said that really well."

Her smile grew larger, then vanished quickly as she frowned and concentrated on making another sound. "Ooooood," while shaking her head. Then "oood ooohm oooot."

I thought for a moment. Three words. This was like playing charades. The look in her eyes was one of inability. She frowned. She was trying to tell me what she could not do. Talk. I considered what she might be trying to say, and not what it sounded like. "Are you saying . . . words . . . won't come out?"

She nodded. Tears filled her eyes. After a moment she smiled.

"I understand. But you *are* communicating, and it will get better with time."

She frowned and shook her head, her eyebrows pinching and her chin going sideways as though she were in disbelief. Then she nodded toward me.

She did not understand something. And it had to do with me.

"Oh." I smiled. "How did I understand you?"

She nodded.

"It is because your heart speaks. I hear your heart."

She closed her eyes as though to savor my sentiment. I was astounded at my speaking out without taking time to edit. But perhaps I felt free to talk because she could not. "It must be very frustrating."

She opened her eyes and nodded.

I smoothed the silken comforter near the edge of her bed. She was relaxed. She looked at me as though she knew me, not as one she should perhaps not trust.

Her eyes were large and expressive, and I had an instant connection with her. She had the eyes of my grandmother, Pale Whispering Moon. Eyes I knew only from pictures. Grandfather's perpetual advice resounded in my head: *There are no accidents. Everything is part of a greater plan.*

I reached for the Bible on her nightstand. Her name was printed in gold on the front. I took my index finger and ran it over the gold indentations. "It is beautiful."

Tears came to her eyes, collected in pools, and ran down her face.

I rose and retrieved a tissue from a sterling silver box on the nightstand. She did not move, so I dabbed at her cheeks as though touching a baby's skin.

"This box is beautiful too." I turned to throw the tissue in the trash. She made a motion with her left hand for me to turn the box over. I did, then looked at her. She nodded yes. Under the box was an inscription. "For the most beautiful face on earth. May all your tears be tears of joy. Ernesto."

I placed my hand over my heart. "That is so beautiful, Mariana. Is Ernesto your husband?"

Although I knew.

She nodded yes, and the tears sprang up. Then she moved her

head side to side as if to say no.

I paused as though I was thinking. "Ernesto is no longer with us?"

She shook her head yes.

She weakly pointed with her left hand to the Bible.

"He had the Bible inscribed for you as well?"

She nodded yes.

"He truly loved you." I placed the box back on her nightstand.

Mariana listened as I read. When I got to the fourth chapter of Luke, I noticed that her eyes stayed shut longer and longer. "Mariana, I will read until you fall asleep. Then I will tiptoe out and let you rest. But I promise you I will come back and pick up where you drift off."

She looked at me without expression and nodded yes. She opened her mouth, but no sound escaped. She tried again to make a word. The tip of her tongue was touching her bottom teeth. Having watched her closely, I realized that most of the words that I had recognized had begun with her tongue in that position. She was unable to command her tongue to move farther than the inside of her bottom teeth.

She was tired, I was leaving. What would she say?

"Mariana, are you saying thank you?" I asked.

She bobbed her head yes.

It seemed like light years ago that I made the plan to sit at the end of the hall. Now I had a seat by the matriarch. Not only that, in such a short time, I cared about her.

A sound in the hall brought me back. The weighty advance of men's shoes toward Mariana's door.

Chapter Thirty

Mariana must have noticed the alarm register on my face. She frowned.

The purposeful steps drew closer. I looked toward the door. If it were Giovanni, I would hope that his mother's presence would offer me the safety to speak.

The steps slowed at her door.

I held my breath; my heart beat so hard I worried my scapular shook. I was alone in the room with Giovanni's mother. Would her son see me as a threat?

Before I could deliberate on the possibility, two men in white lab coats entered and stepped to Mariana's bedside. I felt an urge to exhale my relief.

"Mrs. Giovanni, I'm Dr. Alvan. This is my associate. We've been asked to do a consult."

Mariana nodded agreement. She had been expecting them.

"I will leave, Mariana. But I will be back," I said, and patted her arm.

She smiled up at me.

As I moved back through the hospital taking the opposite route, it felt as though I were a different person. When I understood Mariana, a secret doorway opened, and I had entered a magical relationship. Just as Madeline had said, if I accepted her at her worst, she would trust me. And she did.

Mariana must have understood her sounds were unintelligible. Her expression when she realized her garbled fragments communicated to me was priceless. The way the light filled her eyes. As Leena Rose advised, I had become the instrument, the greatest gift of all.

How easy it would be to get derailed from my original mission. How comfortable to go back into hiding. Even on Giovanni's turf, to remain in denial. No, I was here to meet a monster. I had to make the mountains safe for the girls. For all of us.

As I walked down the last flight of steps to the first floor, a thought stopped me on the fourth step. I had allowed myself to ignore my internal warning system that told me not to get close to the children. If I got close to Mariana, would it end the same? I swallowed hard to push down the mounting fear, imagining the rage Devino would feel if he knew I had infiltrated his boss's inner circle. A known witness to a mob killing, dressed in disguise. Connecting with the girls had put them in peril. Would it be the same with Mariana? With her fragile health, any stressful situation might potentially be her last.

I returned to the locker room and used my name tag, scanning in. I was glad for a break and looked forward to having only a single stressor, disguised as a sister in the city. People would be heading to work or out for breakfast and errands. I donned my coat, scarf, and gloves, and set out to find breakfast, a lock, and a thrift store.

The wind had lain down, the day was warming. The sidewalks swarmed with people, their faces not completely wrapped in scarves now. Some ate breakfast, bagels, or pastries as they walked. The air was filled with the smell of street vendor wares. Already the hot dog cart had wieners and sausages turning. The scent of hot grease lifted from the kabob wagon in a fragrant steam. My stomach growled, reminding me I had not eaten well in a long time.

Stretching my legs to walk in the hurried New Yorker pace felt good. A digital sign on a bank read 9:10, the temperature, as predicted, had warmed with the passing of the bitter cold front to thirty-nine degrees. Almost balmy compared to the frigid air at daybreak.

I found a diner nearby where I could sit with less worry of being seen by one of Giovanni's soldiers. Four blocks from the hospital I opened the doors of Café New York and entered, the busy sounds of street traffic growing instantly dimmer as it shut behind me. A young woman with spiky jet-black hair, a nose ring, and tattoos peeking out from her collar, greeted me with a smile.

Within fifteen minutes of eating eggs, bacon, and toast, and downing a heavy, white mug of rich coffee, my mind raced energetically with ideas, motivating me to take my next steps. Reviewing the morning, a sense of relief and pleasure gave me some degree of satisfaction. There had been no way to predict how things at the hospital would go and it had worked out much better than I could have dared dream. The morning's synchronicities gave me assurance that divine guidance directed my steps. I found it hard to place my encounters with Devino in the same category, but my faith urged that they were orchestrated as well.

As I stepped out of the diner and onto the busy sidewalk, I heard a man call to me from behind.

"Sister Rita."

Surrounded by millions of strangers, who would know my name? I turned to see Dr. Donnetta in layers of workout clothes, moving toward me.

"Wait, sister." He maneuvered through the crowd to get to me. When he caught up he took an exaggerated deep breath. "Can I steal a minute of your time for a special favor?"

I nodded. My chest tightened.

"Can we stand over here against the wall?" he asked, and before I could answer, he held my left elbow, steering me away from the heavy foot traffic.

"I need a favor. I have a patient at St. Anthony's that gets almost no visitors. Well, other than his mother. I was wondering if you would be willing to see him?"

I nodded.

He smiled. "You're the quiet type. That's just what he needs. He's not a talker. He's gruff. Angry, really. Hates cheerful nurses. Kicks them out of his room. Honestly, he doesn't want to live."

"Dominic?"

Dr. Donnetta's eyes widened and brow rose in an expression of "well, will you look at that?" His eyes lit up with his smile. Gleaming white teeth.

"He was sitting in his doorway this morning. I spoke to him."

Dr. Donnetta bobbed his head. "That's him. Did you make some headway?"

I shrugged. "He told me it distresses him that he causes so much worry to his mother."

"Yes. He isn't concerned about himself. There's still a chance to prolong his life for a good while or possibly even cure him, but I'm afraid his attitude is so negative he might defeat the best of treatment."

I nodded. I liked his holistic view. "It seemed he is only getting treatment because his mother wants him to."

The doctor nodded. "That's the way I see it."

"I will stop by as often as he will allow."

"Thank you, sister. I'll see you around." He tipped his head, then turned and burst into a trot.

I found a drugstore where I would daily purchase a new burner phone. While there, I also bought a combination lock. Internet maps helped me find a thrift store. It was fifteen blocks away, fifteen back, but I had the time and needed the exercise. I mind mapped many of the storefronts and businesses as I walked. I would probably not need any of them, but I had been taught to study my surroundings no matter where I was.

The thrift store was easily spotted from a block away. A large pink flamingo stood out front wearing a winter hat and scarf. Mannequins dressed in formal wear, sequins glistening in the sun, beckoned to people who might be considering a Christmas party in December or New Year's less than a month away. Inside, the overwhelming number of things for sale gave me a choking sensation. As an established minimalist, the sight of such a wide variety of consumer items packed onto shelves, hanging from hooks and ceiling tiles overwhelmed me.

There was almost no aisle room because the clothing racks were so jammed with hangers that it was impossible to walk through without pushing against them. I concentrated on why I had come. My street disguise. Surely, I would find it amid all of the chaos of used things.

My luck for the day continued. I found a cheap blonde page boy wig and an oversized floppy pink crocheted hat. A set of large black rimmed ultra-dark sunglasses with rhinestones liberally glued all over the frame, a pink synthetic puffer jacket, leggings that looked like they had been created with multicolored paint splatters, and a gray sweatshirt. All of it fit into a bright orange tote bag with SOHO emblazed on it. Once purchased, I crammed the items into a large brown paper bag with handles in order to keep them from being seen. My street disguise if I needed it in a hurry at the hospital. The polar opposite of a sister in habit.

There was a spring in my steps during my long walk back to the hospital. Some of my stress had lifted. Dominic provided me with a small safety net. If I were stopped, I could say that Dr. Donnetta had asked me to check in on him. Venecia had asked me to comfort Mariana. Both would back me up.

I re-entered St. Anthony's. Susan looked up and waved but didn't speak. The locker room was empty, and I moved to the back wall, found an empty locker, stashed my brown bag with my disguise inside, my coat, hat, and gloves, then secured it with my new combination lock.

My watch said two thirty. To minimize risk, I would spend time with Mariana and leave before Venecia returned at four. The trip using alternate stairs up to the fifth floor was far less stressful than it had been in the early morning. Although still cautious and looking for Giovanni and his associates, having a mission calmed me.

When I reached the fifth floor, I peeked into Room 512. Mariana saw me and smiled. Pausing at the door, I scanned the room as casually as I could to be sure she was alone, then entered and walked to her right side. I would not spend much time in that position as it kept my back to the door. But it did not seem natural to walk around her bed and assume the same position as before. I wanted her permission.

"I am glad to see you awake. Is there anything I can do for you before I read?"

Marianna smiled slightly, then looked at her bedside table and with a trembling right hand tried to point to a large box of chocolates.

"Would you like some candy?"

She nodded agreement.

I looked up to the white board over her bed. In the patient goals section, her meal times were listed along with "regular diet, no restrictions." I reached for the candy, took the top off the box, and held it at an angle so that Mariana could see. With her left hand she pointed to a yellow Jordan almond. She looked up at me and said the sounds I now knew to mean "my favorite." I picked out the paper cup with the candy and placed it in my palm, smiling. "Let's practice."

Mariana's eyes widened in surprise. Then she nodded. She raised her right hand; it trembled and shook. Her fingers neared my palm but missed the mark. Her arm collapsed to the comforter.

"You almost had it. Rest a moment and try again."

She inhaled and her arm shook as she reached up again, her fingers moving with a mind of their own. Her brows were furrowed in concentration. I was tempted to move the paper cup to catch her fingers, but it would defeat the purpose. After several swirling moves, her finger and thumb lit on the candy and she pulled it out. She looked up at me, her hand rested lightly on the edge of my palm.

"Now, one more step." I motioned with my eyes as if to say, "you can do it."

She frowned again, her finger and thumb holding the almond. Her hand detoured several times but she opened her mouth and managed to feed herself the yellow candy. A smile lit her face.

"Well done." I watched with joy as she chewed.

High heels clicked down the hall. I recognized their sound. They were alone; only one set of feet. I glanced at my watch. Three fifteen. I had hoped to leave before Venecia arrived. Why was she early? Did it have anything to do with me?

Venecia breezed in, her bracelets jangling. "Hello, MiMi. And hello, Sister Rita. I'm glad you are here." As she walked to Mariana's bedside, she filled us in. "They dismissed school early today because of a broken heat pipe. I thought I'd just come and spend a little extra time today." She went back to her spot between the window and Mariana's left side, leaned in, and planted a soft kiss on her mother-in-law's cheek. Taking off her gloves, coat, and scarf, she laid them on the same chair as before, next to the one she had sat in.

She turned around and jumped slightly in surprise when she noticed Mariana using her right hand to shakingly point to the box of candy I held. Venecia looked at the open box of candy. "MiMi, look, you haven't eaten your raspberry-filled. Do you want one?"

Mariana shook her head no, smiled, and looked at me.

"Before you came, she asked for a Jordan almond and told me it was her favorite. I got it out of the box, then she took it from my hand and put it in her mouth."

"With her right hand?"

"Yes."

We both looked at Mariana, who was grinning.

"MiMi! You are amazing. You said it was your favorite and fed yourself?"

"We knew you would be pleased. Mariana, can you say it for Venecia so that she knows what it sounds like?"

"Maaaa aah wit," Mariana said, looking at Venecia and smiling.

Tears sprang instantly to Venecia' s eyes. "Oh, my goodness, MiMi, this is wonderful. I understand it now. Sister, what else can she say?" Venecia looked at me, her mouth hanging open slightly in expectation.

"When she opens her mouth and puts her tongue to the back of her bottom teeth she is saying thank you," I looked toward Mariana who demonstrated without my asking.

"Oh my gosh. I can't get over it. Is there more?" she asked, looking from Mariana to me.

"No. Not yet." My scalp tingled anticipating Venecia' s answer to my next question. "But I would like to spend more time with your mother-in-law, if that is not a problem."

"Of course, sister. Of course," Venecia said. She reached down and patted Mariana's hand. "And more Jordan almonds. Lots and lots of Jordan almonds," she said, smiling at Mariana.

"I will leave to let you two visit now, but I will be back."

"Thank you, sister. Thank you so much." Venecia touched my sleeve with her jeweled hand. "I am so grateful. I can't wait to tell everyone."

Walking down to Dominic's room, I wondered if Venecia's "everyone" included Devino. But there was nothing I could do. My spending too much time in Mariana's room without permission would be suspicious.

When I reached the third floor, Dominic was sitting in his doorway. His feet were protruding into the hall, and I walked to stand in front of them.

"What?" he said gruffly, although I had not spoken.

"I am stopping by to say hello."

"Well, now you have."

"Is there anything I can do for you?"

"Did you find a cure for cancer?"

"I am sorry, no." I stood still, unsure of my next move.

"So, you just gonna stand there?"

"They also serve who only stand and wait," I said spontaneously, surprising myself with my answer.

"What the heck does that mean?"

"It is from a sonnet by John Milton. It means that while I do not have a clear job now, by waiting until I do, I am also serving."

Silence.

"You are a person of few words also," I said.

He grunted.

"May I sit quietly with you?"

"What good would that do?" he asked, but his tone implied a bit of interest. Using his upper arms, he pushed his wheelchair back into his room and to the side of his door. I entered, and pulled up a visitor chair from the corner of the room, moved it to within feet of him at the doorway and sat. "You would not be alone. You may find it tolerable."

"Tolerable. Who says tolerable? That's a word you never hear."

It was indeed one of Grandfather's often used expressions.

We sat in silence, watching people walk by, catching snippets of their conversations. I noticed that if visitors were walking together, their tones were usually matter of fact. "She's looking better today" or "He isn't eating as well as he should." If the patient was with the visitor, the tone was different. Cheery. The voices higher. Some of them sounded like preschool teachers.

A middle-aged couple walked by steering a wheelchair. The elderly woman in the chair had deadened eyes, staring straight ahead. Her head was covered with a bright turban that contrasted her disposition. Her color was gray and ashen. Both the man and the woman talked to her as though her eyes were bright and she was full of energy. "You need to get out more often like this, Mama, even if it's just to roll around and see the sights." They offered convincing arguments in a pressured, upbeat tone. Their suggestions contradicted the reality of the woman in the chair.

Dominic cleared his throat. I looked at him.

"Well?" he said. "I see you concentrating. What is it?"

"I understand."

"You understand what?"

"They all sound like cheerleaders on steroids. They are not in sync with the patient."

He nodded.

"Is that what I sound like?" I asked.

He looked at me for a moment and shook his head. "I started to mess with your head and say yes. But, no. Actually, you don't."

We both attuned to the next group strolling by, two men clearly related, the older a vision of the younger's future self.

"Dad, you need to make sure and tell them if you can't eat what they've brought." The younger man guided his father by the elbow with one hand and pushed an IV pole with his other. "They will bring you whatever you want. We keep telling you that. You have to eat."

His voice trailed as they passed by.

I leaned toward Dominic. "And perhaps although they mean to be supportive, they speak as though their loved ones have become incompetent in their illness."

Dominic looked over and nodded. "Yep. That too. Like it shouldn't matter that a poison drip takes your appetite."

"Is your mother like this when she comes?"

He shook his head. "No. She just fights back tears."

I nodded. He had insight. He had compassion. More than anything else, more than his own misery, he hated seeing his mother suffer. The true hallmark of an unselfish person.

After a pause, he asked, "So is it because you're a nun? Why you're quiet?"

I knew I could simply nod. But the wisdom of Grandfather sprang from my mouth: "I was taught to listen, or your tongue will make you deaf."

He considered the words.

After a few more minutes, the metallic sound of squeaky wheels rolled toward us, and Dominic moved forward toward the door. He rolled out looking left in the direction of the sound, then rolled back. "Time for you to go."

I stood and put my chair back in the corner. Dominic backed his chair up near the foot of his bed. Two orderlies came through the door wheeling a tall complex apparatus. A standing wheelchair. "Dom, you ready to stand up?" one of them asked. They did not see me at first, then followed Dominic's eyes toward me. "Oh. Hello, sister. Can we have Dominic for about a half hour?"

I nodded good-bye.

• • •

Five blocks to the shelter seemed like a short hop now compared to that of my hike to the thrift store. When I entered the shelter, I placed my coat on a hook behind the door and walked through the foyer, glancing into the open door of the classroom where the children were being led in afternoon crafts. The blond boy and girl looked at me. They waved as I walked by, and I returned the gesture, then scurried up the steps to my room. A place that now felt like a small sanctuary. I was eager to check in with Leena Rose.

After programming my new phone, I opened the drapes on my window and looked out. It was nice to have someone I could tell, without going into details, that it had been such a good day it seemed miraculous. I dialed Leena Rose's number.

"Emerson, I'm so glad you called. A lot has been popping around here. Are you ready for the updates?"

Her voice sounded heavy. My stomach sank. "Yes. Please."

"Well, first, your Aunt Hattie has been to visit me. I told her if I heard from you that I would tell you that she wants you to call her."

"Thank you, Leena Rose." I held my breath. I knew that was not the source of Leena Rose's worry.

"Then Madeline called and told me to tell you, in her words, 'the marshals are crawling all over Easterbrook looking for you . . . and for Enaldo.'"

I gasped, then covered my mouth, hoping she had not heard it. Was it good or bad that I was not there? I would not want to run into the marshals, but it was bad news to hear they were looking for Enaldo there. Was everyone safe? Did that mean I was safe from Enaldo in New York? Maybe. But I was certainly not safe from Giovanni or Devino.

Lost in thought, I did not reply, so Leena Rose continued. "Rick has come back again. He asked me the same questions as before. I think he believes I know more than I'm saying."

"Was there anything to tell him?"

"I told him I was as concerned as everyone else. That is the truth."

"You have been busy. I am so sorry for all of the intrusions."

"It's quite all right. Word spreads fast here. But there's one more thing."

She paused. I waited.

"Agnes Mendell called me about something going on at the cemetery. She told me she had already talked to your Aunt Hattie about it. She said she saw you leaving my house the day before you disappeared so she wanted me to give you a message if you contacted me."

"Okay."

Agnes was on the right track. How long before someone else figured out I was in contact with Leena Rose. My mothers would never tell anyone. Would Agnes?

But the cemetery. Joey Horseshoe. That meant trouble.

"Agnes told me to tell you that the guys in the truck with the blue hood were back with their newspapers. She stepped out to ask them to take the papers with them and they told her it was sacred burial ground and she was trespassing. They threatened to file a warrant for her arrest. She is not sure if they can or not. She doesn't know what to do."

Anger tightened the muscles in my jaw. "Would you like me to call Agnes?"

"No. Agnes is no problem. What would you like me to tell her?"

"Tell her that I own the land. It is sacred burial ground, but she is not trespassing. But for her safety, she should not approach them. Explain that they are using the newspaper timestamps to prove that I am not fulfilling my duties to care for the land. They want to lay claim to it and take it from me."

"I will do that. And how are things going there?"

After hearing how my problems had overflowed into her life, sharing my small victories seemed selfish. "Good."

"Are you closer to achieving your goal?"

"I do not know. But I believe I am walking in the right direction."

CHAPTER THIRTY-ONE

Susan greeted me like an old acquaintance after a few days. I was beginning to recognize familiar faces. Nurses as well as aides on different floors waved like they knew me.

It had been a week of visiting Mariana twice a day, early morning and after lunch. When I thought I was ready to approach Giovanni, I started going by sometimes after dinner in case he made an appearance. Despite trying to find clever ways to ask, I got no firm answers from Mariana on when he could be expected.

Each day I saw the light in Mariana's eyes grow brighter when I walked into her room. We practiced picking up things with her right hand. A lot of time was spent with her repeating sounds or allowing me to guess short phrases she spoke. It was a game that held no frustration for either of us. We had established a routine. When I guessed what she was trying to say, she affirmed with a smile and nod of her head. On one occasion I winked when she smiled. When she winked in return, we laughed together with delight.

Over the course of my visits, we developed a small vocabulary. I realized she was saying "thirsty" when she put the tip of her tongue against her bottom teeth and moved her jaw twice. When I looked at her and said, "Two syllables. Starts with T," she giggled. Our game of charades blessed us both.

Four days after meeting her, when she had tired of my reading from the Bible, she opened her mouth like a baby bird and moved her head forward a tiny bit. It appeared she wanted to get something out of her mouth. "Out?" I asked. She winked. "Now I must understand what you want out."

She nodded.

"Outside?" I guessed. She shook her head no. I thought for a moment. "Words out?" She nodded her head toward me hard while pointing, her hand trembling far less than it had in days prior. She winked. Oh. She wanted *me* to talk. It seemed safe enough. Every nun has a story before entering the convent.

I told her about my heritage. I shared that I was taught how to listen in many ways so that I could hear what everything had to say. She smiled and slow tears slid down her cheeks. She pointed to her chest, motioning that she was grateful I had stopped to listen to *her*.

The story of why I was reared by Grandfather filled her face with compassion. I could tell her the story of my mother and grandmother without distress, explaining that they were both in heaven with Grandfather, and I would join them when it was my turn. She nodded her understanding and shared belief.

Her eyes brightened when I told stories of the mystery hunts and danced eagerly as I described the legends of the caves and the legacy of Crow Mountain. They narrowed and her eyebrows pulled down in concentration as I told her Lenore Lee's story, and worry lines wrinkled her forehead. I asked if I should spare telling her sad stories, but she shook her head no. Our conversations were a slice of something different, of real life for her.

Was I letting my guard down too much? She would not be able to repeat my stories for quite a while, and they seemed therapeutic for her. Talking with her seemed logical. And if Giovanni ever showed up, I would ask to talk with him in the hall where she would not hear.

I always left before lunch, when the priest was in the building, and again before four when Venecia and the children visited. During afternoon visiting hours, women from her parish and others came to visit. I usually returned at six o'clock and sat with Mariana after her dinner.

Twice a day, upon leaving her room, I would go and sit with Dominic. There was a new balance in my life. Of course, it was temporary. But at least until Giovanni showed up, I had purpose. Still, I felt coiled inside, ready to spring and run. The constant ticking of a doomsday clock kept me on edge. And more time meant more risk for the girls back home. Often enough, my vision re-emerged—images of them bound and gagged—and filled me with a sense of urgency.

Mariana was making rapid improvement. When a week had passed, she moved from the bed to sitting in a chair most of the time, and she was much more adept at using her right hand. She had moved from finger foods to slowly feeding herself with a fork or spoon.

Over the first weekend, I anticipated her son would visit. He did not come on Saturday. Surely on Sunday, I thought. I sat with her, watching the minutes tick by. My anxiety rose with expectation, my hypervigilance fatigued me. But he did not come on Sunday. Mariana's other children and grandchildren streamed in, though, and I always left quickly to allow her time with them.

On Monday, I entered Mariana's room for the third time that day, my now usual after-dinner visit. But this time she was not alone. She sat in a chair, her back to the window, wearing an exquisite pink silk, flower-embroidered bed jacket with a matching lap robe and slippers. Venecia sat next to her. I knocked on the door jamb so as not to alarm them. Both women looked up and smiled.

"You are beautiful, my friend," I said as I came into the room, taking in the fact that they were alone. Mariana lit up, her head bobbing in greeting.

"She is," Venecia agreed.

I walked around the hospital bed, past Venecia' s chair, and knelt beside Mariana. "You are radiant." I smiled, and she returned it. I was about to ask why she was so dressed up when I heard footsteps quickly approach and enter the open door behind me. Mariana looked up, and her eyes began to twinkle as she smiled. I turned toward the door and raised my head above the mattress to see.

My blood ran cold.

Giovanni stood in the doorway. Behind him, a man in a long leather coat turned his back to the door. He was standing guard. I did not have to guess who the man was.

Devino.

"Gino," Venecia said, smiling broadly looking at her husband. "We are so glad you are here. We have a surprise for you, Gino. Don't we, MiMi?"

Giovanni shut the door behind him. In his presence, all the air was sucked out of me. My scalp crawled again and again. I had mentally prepared for this in so many ways—what I would do, what I would say—but now that it had finally happened, I only wanted to run. I gathered the strength to act normal, hoped my knees would support me when I stood, but they wobbled still. I stepped toward the nightstand to make room for Giovanni and leaned back against the hard wood. I slipped my hands behind my back between my hips and the hard surface to steady myself in what I hoped looked like a natural pose.

Giovanni stood silently and did not blink. He wore an exquisite black wool coat. A red scarf beneath his collar draped down both sides of his chest. Peeping through the top buttons of his coat, a white dress shirt contrasted sharply with his olive skin. The silver at his temples looked painted on for effect. He looked just like his pictures, impeccably groomed, a perfect picture of wealth.

He turned his eyes to me. The same look on his face I had seen at the restaurant tables.

"Gino, this is Sister Rita. She's been helping MiMi." There was a lilt of excitement in Venecia' s voice.

I acknowledged Giovanni with a nod. His eyes moved slowly from me to his wife.

"A lot has happened since you left town. I know you don't normally like surprises, but you'll love this one. I'm sure of it," Venecia said. "Won't he, MiMi?"

I turned to look at Mariana in time to see her nod. I stayed focused on her, not wanting to turn back in Giovanni's direction. I knew he could identify me if he looked at me long enough.

Venecia stood and walked to her husband. Her tiny size was even more apparent against his six-foot-plus frame. As she took his arm and started to explain, Giovanni looked from her, to me, then to his mother.

"We've been so anxious to surprise you. Sister Rita has been working with your mother and helping me understand what MiMi is saying. She can say some things now." She turned with enthusiasm to Mariana. "Can't you, MiMi?"

Mariana nodded and smiled. Giovanni came around the bed toward us, Venecia following. I pressed tighter against the nightstand.

He knelt in front of Mariana and took her small hand in his. "Mama."

I had read about his voice, rich and smooth, like a professional singer. One tabloid had remarked, "Giovanni, the Grim Reaper, proves the voice of death is deeper than the ocean he commands to swallow his victims."

He was only two steps away. I could smell his aftershave. I felt a forcefield radiating from him, pushing me to step back as far as I could. But there was nowhere to go. Was this the time that God had ordained? How would I get him alone? Devino was in the hallway.

Mariana moaned a little, her smile melting into tears.

"Mama, don't cry," Giovanni said as he took her other hand, squeezed them both.

"Remember, honey, the doctor said that crying was connected to the stroke. She's okay," Venecia returned to the chair next to Mariana. "Aren't you, MiMi?"

Mariana nodded through her tears. Giovanni hugged his mother, maintaining contact for a moment before releasing her. Mariana whimpered. He let go and straightened, looking at her closely. His voice was soft. "Try not to cry, Mama."

"She'll stop," Venecia offered. "Gino, the sister," she said, nodding in my direction. "She's like a . . . like a person-whisperer or something. She understands MiMi better than anyone."

Giovanni stood and faced me. My heart rate went nuclear, but I held his laser-beam gaze. He extended a well-manicured hand. I leaned forward to accept. His grip was firm. His hands warm.

I looked at Mariana, who watched with great interest. Her eyebrows furrowed. Giovanni looked down at his mother. "Is it true, Mama? You've been talking to the sister here?" He motioned toward me.

Mariana smiled and shook her head yes. She looked at me and opened her mouth.

I stepped forward slightly and hoped my voice would not forsake me. "She is saying she wants to talk," I said. "The open mouth means she wants to get words out."

"Is that right, Mama?"

Mariana nodded yes and smiled. Giovanni turned again to me. His features went cold, his voice now firm and business-like. "This was not the best time for this surprise. I only popped in to say hello. I'm afraid I'm already late." He turned to Venecia. "I have to go."

Mariana tensed.

"See though? MiMi is communicating. Didn't I say? And every time I'm here, the sister teaches me how to understand her a little bit more."

Mariana moaned and we all looked her way. She looked at Giovanni and pointed her head toward him. She made her sounds for "my favorite," then looked up at me.

"Sir, your mother just said that you are her favorite."

"That's what she said, honey. I know how she says it too."

Giovanni squatted again at his mother's feet and held her hands, his long fingers engulfing them. "I know, Mama. I know I am."

Venecia leaned around Giovanni and addressed me, "It's been a running joke in the family for a long time. Gino is the only son. That's why he's her favorite."

Tears threatened to spill from Mariana's eyes. I turned around and retrieved a tissue from the silver box on the nightstand behind me. When Giovanni stood and pulled back, I moved toward Mariana. I offered her the tissue as tears slid down her cheeks. But instead of taking it, she tilted her head back, allowing me to gently pat her face. She looked into my eyes and then up to her son. She wanted him to see me care for her in that way. She had been wiping her own cheeks for the last few days.

She made the sound for "thank you." I interpreted, and she smiled. "You are welcome."

But there was something more. She shook her head no and said "thank you" louder, with her tongue behind her teeth, and nodded toward her son.

I looked at Giovanni. "She is thanking me for interpreting for her."

Mariana nodded her head.

"I have to go for now, Mama. But I'm so glad you're doing better."

"I told MiMi it might only be a minute, but I knew you'd come when you got back into town, even if it was for just for a little bit. Didn't I say that, MiMi?"

Mariana nodded.

Venecia stood and rubbed Giovanni's shoulder. Mariana looked up at Venecia and said her version of "thank you."

"You're welcome," Venecia said, then looked over at me and smiled proudly.

"Mama, when I come back, make sure the sister is here so we can talk." Giovanni turned and looked at me. This was a demand. A violent chill began to work its way from my center core and outward through my body. I would not be able to hide its effects much longer. Today would not be my day to beg for mercy.

• • •

With Giovanni and Venecia gone, I turned to Mariana. Though everything in me wanted to bolt, I could not leave yet. I needed to buy time in the safety of the hospital room. I could not risk running into Giovanni and Devino on my way out.

"I have an idea. Let's practice saying something you can surprise your son with on his next visit. How does that sound?"

Mariana nodded.

I walked toward her and sat on the chair beside her. I put my hands under my thighs to still the shaking that had made its way to my extremities. "What would be special?"

"Blah . . . yur."

I thought for a moment. "One syllable?"

She shook her head.

"Two?"

She nodded. "Blah-yur," she repeated.

I tried mimicking the sounds, then went through the alphabet in my head like I used to do as a child, when I tried to rhyme a word using each letter in succession. Not until I got to "P" did I understand.

"Prayer?"

Mariana smiled and winked.

"I think that's a wonderful idea. Do you know which prayer you'd like to recite?"

She nodded.

"Let's see . . . the Lord's Prayer?"

She shook her head.

"Is this a Catholic prayer?"

She nodded.

It was for her son. "Is it a child's prayer?"

More nodding.

"'Now I Lay Me Down to Sleep'?" Even though I doubted that was a Catholic prayer.

Another shake of her head.

The muscles in my stomach tightened. My mind was wired after my encounter with Giovanni and Devino, and I needed time to research. I wanted to pull out my phone and search the web, but Mariana was watching me.

She frowned. I had to think quickly.

"My mind is cloudy today. Sometimes I need coffee after dinner." I forced a smile. "Would you mind if I went down to the cafeteria to get a cup of coffee?"

She nodded and gave me the "gaaah" sound for "go," then waved her hand.

"Can I bring you a cup?" I asked.

A headshake.

I walked to the door and opened it as slowly as I could without looking suspicious. When I glanced back, Mariana was frowning, her face pinched. I wanted to ignore the nagging thoughts that something was wrong. Perhaps she was just upset her son had left so abruptly. But my intuition poked me.

The hall was clear, so I moved quickly to the stairwell, opening the door a crack and listening. Quiet. As soon as the door shut, leaving me alone in the tomb-like stairwell, I stood at the top guard rail and pulled out my phone. I quickly typed "Catholic children's prayers" into the search bar. The results seemed to take forever to load. When it did, the majority of hits were connected to the Guardian Angel prayer. I memorized the first line. "Angel of God, my guardian." This was a long prayer. If this were it, we may be weeks waiting to surprise Giovanni. I had already been at the safe house for over a week. No one on Colony Row knew where I was. Devino was on my heels. My internal clock was ticking louder than ever.

I ran down the steps to the cafeteria in the basement, got coffee, and hurried back up the steps, five flights. I paused at the fifth-floor stairwell door and listened. Nothing. I opened the door, saw no one, and began my return. Within moments, I heard feet closing in fast behind me. At Mariana's door, I stopped and turned slightly to see who was approaching. Lauren, Mariana's evening nurse. Her eyes were wide, and she did not wear her customary smile. She was headed my way.

I pushed Mariana's door open. The tiny woman was sitting on the edge of her chair, her eyes frantic, her hand over her mouth.

She was the image of sheer panic.

CHAPTER THIRTY-TWO

Iheld the door open for the nurse, who followed me in, and allowed it to close behind us, then moved to the closest nightstand and set down my coffee. I did not trust myself to hold it steady through whatever was coming next. I turned to the nurse, who spoke to me in spats between breaths, her voice octaves higher than usual.

"Sister . . . Mr. Devino . . . Mr. Giovanni's assistant. He was looking for you. And . . . and I told him you had left for the day. I thought you had." She looked at Mariana, whose face was still awash with fear. "He came in here first, didn't he, Mrs. Giovanni?"

Mariana's eyes looked to each of us as if her lids were frozen open. Without moving her hand from her mouth, she nodded yes.

"Didn't you think she was gone for the day too?" Lauren asked, begging for backup.

Mariana dropped her hand to her lap. She hesitated, then nodded slightly.

My vision blurred with each beat of my heart. Mariana had known I was coming back. Had she lied to Devino? She lied to her nurse. My body went weak. I leaned my left hip against Mariana's bed for support and caught sight of myself in the mirror across the room. I looked as frightened as the two women did. Somehow, we were all in this together.

I swallowed hard before speaking, petrified at what I was about to ask.

"Mariana, did you tell him I had gone for the day?"

Tears spilled over and ran down her cheeks. She looked down, took a deep breath, and nodded.

I looked at Lauren. "I went for coffee before leaving the hospital but then changed my mind and decided to come back for a minute or two."

"Well, I . . . I-I'm supposed to call and let Mr. Devino or Mr. Giovanni know if you come back."

Mariana began to moan. When Lauren and I looked at her, she was shaking her head no.

"Mariana is probably too tired for more company. Is that it, Mariana?"

She looked at me and nodded.

"I will call Mr. Giovanni myself and find out what he needs. You don't have to worry with this, Lauren." I looked at the nurse, and when she did not appear convinced, I pulled my phone from beneath my scapular. "I will only be a minute here, so they will not have time to get back anyway. I can stop at the restaurant or his brownstone if they need me. You are okay."

"Okay . . ." Lauren paused. "I'll chart that. Is all of that okay with you, Mrs. Giovanni?" she asked, looking furtively at her patient.

Mariana managed a weak nod.

"Anything I can do for you before I go?"

Mariana shook her head.

As the nurse turned to leave, I realized there was one more gap to close.

"Lauren?"

She turned.

"I am leaving in just a moment, so if he should call, you can tell him I have already left. By the time you get back to the nurse's station, that will likely be true."

Lauren glanced from me to Mariana, who nodded agreement. "Okay," she said, hesitantly. She stood a moment more, as though her feet were superglued to the floor, her eyes darting about the room.

"You are my patient, Mrs. Giovanni. So, you want me to tell him that Sister Rita is not here?" She looked at Mariana.

Mariana nodded.

"That would be correct because I am leaving right behind you."

Lauren turned and left the room, and instead of letting the door shut behind her, she brought it to a quiet close.

How much time had I just bought? Devino had heard about Venecia' s surprise, a sister in Mariana's room. If I had known the Guardian Angel prayer, I would have been in her room when he got here. My stomach flipped with the thought. Synchronicity. The miraculous presence of God. In this case, the absence of knowledge had been a miracle.

I walked over to get a tissue for Mariana but did not try to hand it to her. Instead, I patted her tears and she allowed it. She looked up at me. Her eyes pleaded with me.

"You are worried for me?" My voice shook.

Tears welled again.

"Please do not be. I will make everything okay."

Mariana's brows pulled tighter. She shook her head.

"You do not think I can?"

Mariana frowned, looked down at her hands, then shrugged.

"I can try. We promised him a surprise. Let's work on it."

Mariana shook her head and sounded "gaaah," motioning for me to go.

"Mariana . . . I do not know what Mr. Devino told you, but I am no threat to anyone. I would like the opportunity to talk with your son and ask for his help. I am afraid Mr. Devino might misunderstand that and not allow me near him. For now, the only place Mr. Devino will not be looking for me is in your room. So, we can work on our surprise for your son. That will give me some time to sort this out."

Mariana did not respond right away. She appeared to be in thought. I wanted something positive to say to Giovanni about his mother when I saw him next. I wanted in some small way to prove to him that I keep my promises. Even if Devino was on my heels.

"For just a few minutes?"

Mariana finally nodded yes.

"First. Touch your heart."

She placed her right hand on her chest.

"Good. Now can you make a fist and touch your heart twice?"

She made a fist and touched her heart twice. Her face was tight with worry.

"Very good," I said. "We can make that the sign for 'I love you.'"

Mariana nodded. She pointed to me, made a fist, and touched her heart twice.

"I love you too, Mariana," I said sincerely.

"Gaaah." Mariana moved her hand to wave me away, her eyes widening. She was clearly frightened for me.

"Okay. I will go. I am so sorry this worries you. I will be okay."

I walked to her door and this time peeked out to make sure the coast was clear. I looked back. Mariana was watching me. I nodded my head in good-bye and scooted to the steps.

Once in the stairwell, I shut the heavy door behind me and leaned against the rail, looking down the flights. What had Devino said to affect Mariana so deeply? Did he tell her I was an imposter? Did he say I was a threat? If he had told her I was not who I pretended to be, it had not affected her in the way he likely expected. She was trying to protect me now. She had told me that she loved me.

Nausea swirled, and I clutched the rail harder.

As much as I wanted to take my chance and run, my equilibrium was impaired. I felt I could fall or throw up with any movement. I sat on the first step and put my head between my knees. After a few minutes, my stomach stopped churning and my legs felt less like jelly. I stood and went down the first flights of steps between the two floors. I continued this way, pausing at the halfway point on every floor. If Devino came from either direction, I could attempt to outrun him and go to a nurse's station and scream for help.

I decided I would try the third floor. I knew that even if Devino were gone, he could have called in collaterals to be on lookout for a tall nun. Perhaps one on every floor.

Cautiously, I opened the door and looked. The hall was clear. With long strides I made my way to Dominic's room. His door was shut.

I tapped and opened the door a few inches.

Darkness.

I eased into the room and shut his door behind me. The blinds and draperies were shut, and my eyes struggled to adjust from the well-lit corridor to his darkened room.

"Dominic?" I whispered.

"Come in."

In the muted light, I walked to the foot of his bed. He was covered, with the comforter pulled up to his chin.

"Are you feeling poorly, Dominic?"

"I have cancer. What the heck do you think?" He spoke with his typical gruffness, but the former volume and gusto were gone.

"Is there anything I can do for you?"

He grunted.

"May I sit with you for a little while?"

"They also serve who only *sit* and wait?" he managed weakly, in a diminished yet surly tone.

"Yes," I said and pulled a chair up near his bed. He did not protest. I had not seen him like this. Had he taken a turn for the worse?

I sat down and put my hands under my thighs. Perhaps now I could recover from the fright. Formulate my next moves.

After a few minutes of silence, Dominic cleared his throat. I looked up.

"Are you praying?"

"No," I answered. "But I can."

"Well, if you've been praying for me to change my mind, it worked. I had another treatment today. That's why I feel so awful."

I could not help but smile. "I am so glad, Dominic. Thank you for telling me."

"Anything to keep you and my mother off my back. And keep Dr. Donnetta from quoting statistics to me."

"Is there anything I can do to make you more comfortable?"

"No. Just shut the door when you leave." He closed his eyes.

"Dominic, I will sit here for a little bit if you are all right with that."

"Whatever. That's tolerable."

I smiled again, despite myself.

Within minutes, Dominic was snoring softly. I looked at my watch. I would wait forty-five minutes. That would give me time to make my way through the halls during the start of the seven p.m. visiting hour, when lots of people would be moving about. If my instincts directed, I would check in with Mrs. Garbino on the second floor and ask how her African violets were doing. Hopefully I could move through the halls with the visitors. There would be safety in numbers. Even if I were caught.

But the quiet wait gave me time to worry. I thought about Mariana. She had looked so stressed. I could not rid my mind of the image of her with her hand over her mouth, sitting on the edge of her chair. I had not known she could move to the edge of the chair alone. Clearly fear had propelled her.

If something happened to me and I never returned, she would guess that Devino or her son had a part in it. What would that do to her? No. I had to survive. I had to complete my mission. Now it wasn't just the girls; Mariana could be deeply affected by this as well. I just needed to get as far as the locker room so I could get to the tote with my stashed street disguise.

When forty-five minutes was up, I stood and moved my chair back against the wall under the window. Easing the door open, I saw that the hallway was clear and moved as fast as I could to the stairwell. Stairwells had become a refuge, and the stale, cool air was a welcome relief.

I paused between the third and second floors. Did I need to take another break at Mrs. Garbino's? I decided against it.

The first floor door was only feet away from the locker room. I peeked out, saw no one suspicious, and made a dash. I swiped my ID to get in. Two women stood by their lockers near the door. They had their backs turned to me and were in a discussion about what sort of carryout they should take home. I rounded the block of lockers in the middle of the room, found mine, and fumbled with the combination. It took two tries to finally hit the three numbers, 10-10-24, correctly. I opened my locker, got out the brown bag, and pulled out the SOHO tote, then went into the restroom, and changed. I placed my habit in the empty tote. When I listened at the door I could still hear the women talking. I would have to wait. I could not enter a nun and exit a blonde in a floppy pink hat.

Their conversation turned to weekend plans. Minutes dragged on. I reminded myself that often the very piece of the puzzle I disliked the most turned out to be the most important. This piece was timing. God's timing. I had to believe that. I waited until I heard their feet and the door shutting behind them.

CHAPTER THIRTY-THREE

After walking to the shelter as fast as I could without arousing suspicion, I arrived as a blonde in a pink jacket and multicolored leggings. I entered the code on the numeric lock. I could not get off the street fast enough. It seemed everyone in New York looked like one of Giovanni's soldiers.

Inside, I was relieved that no one was in the front room, although I heard voices coming from the back. Relief flooded me; no one would see me in disguise. I took the stairs two at a time.

Once in my room, I threw the tote on the bed and moved to the window. I used my fingers to create a sliver of opening in the heavy drapes to check the alleyway. Clear. Curling into a fetal position on the bed, I lay there fully clothed, trying to process what had happened and what my next steps should be.

I sat up to call Leena Rose. I was determined I would not let my conversation betray my worry. But her voice at "hello" stood my hairs on end.

"Oh, Emerson. Thank goodness you called."

"Oh no. What is it?"

"Well first of all, everyone is safe. Madeline has Bunny and Deetsy. She went to Social Services and got temporary custody of them this morning. They are in her care until things can be resolved in court."

I stood without realizing what I was doing, then sat down heavily in the chair near my bed so I could better listen to what Leena Rose had to say. The children were safe. Madeline would not let them wander. And Miah would not likely wander alone.

"What happened?"

"There's no easy way to tell you this, Emerson. Last night, Bunny and Deetsy were out late, and . . ."

"What, Leena Rose? Tell me."

She drew a deep, audible breath. "They were out around eleven. They told Madeline they were headed to the church for some reason. I'm not clear about that part. But before they got there, they heard a car moving slowly down Colony Row. They said the car had no lights on. They hid behind some trees and were going to wait for it to pass. Deetsy said she was able to see four men in the car. They had all of the windows down, despite it being so cold out. They were using flashlights to look for house numbers and mailboxes. Then the car pulled up in front of the trees the girls were hiding behind and stopped. Deetsy heard one of them say, 'What was that?' and another one said, 'I heard it too.' She said she could see the flashlight beams all around her on either side of the tree she was hiding behind. Then she heard one of them say, 'It's just a cat,' and the car moved on. A second or two later, Maestro came up and rubbed himself against her legs. The girls said they were scared to death, Emerson. They still are."

Dizziness overcame me for the second time in a day. I lowered my head toward my knees, but could not get a deep breath so I straightened back up.

"When the car finally got far enough away, the girls ran to Madeline's house. They knew the code to her gate, so they used it and rang her doorbell over and over. She instantly took them in, of course."

"Of course."

"Madeline called Rick. When Madeline told him what the girls said, Deetsy spoke up and gave them the license plate number. She had seen it in the moonlight and memorized it. She said she knew it was important from TV."

"Those poor children." The visual of the sisters hiding behind trees with Enaldo's men that close created waves of nausea from the pit of my stomach. I saw a flashback of my vision, the little girls held hostage in a car. Acid burned a hole in my throat like molten lava. I swallowed to keep it down.

"Deetsy said they knew the men were bad because she smelled men's perfume and not alcohol. Isn't that remarkable how they put those pieces together?"

"Yes, it is."

"Rick called Madeline later to say that when he ran the plates, they came back associated with the mob, so he put out an APB. Rick told Madeline she had to let you know, if she had any way of getting in touch with you. He wants you to stay clear of Colony Row."

I was numb. This was real. It was happening now. My mothers, the little girls, maybe even the artists, were all in trouble. And Rick . . . he was clearly in the crosshairs.

Devino in New York.

Enaldo on Colony Row.

Nowhere was safe now.

The girls might be with Madeline, but Enaldo would also know where Aunt Hattie and Madeline lived. He and Devino would likely work as a team. If they put two and two together, they might think I had plans to harm Mariana.

"Emerson? Are you still there?"

"Yes." My voice came out a whisper. I was still having trouble breathing. "Is there anything else?"

"Well. Nothing as big as that. But I will tell you that Megan called Rick as well. She had been sitting out on her porch waiting for Agnes to come out for their moonlight walk, and when Megan saw the car, she knew something was suspicious, so she hid and watched. Megan told Rick that they stayed parked at Stopping Place for quite a while, waving their flashlights everywhere like they were looking for your driveway before they finally moved on. She doesn't think they found it."

This time. But they would come back. They would figure it out.

And when they found the cabin empty, they would go back to Colony Row. They would take a hostage, stop at nothing to drive me out of hiding.

"Leena Rose, please make sure everyone knows not to go out if they can avoid it and never at night. And will you please ask Aunt Hattie to move in with Madeline for the time being? She will be safer at Maple Grove."

"That's already come up. I suggested it. She said no. She said she has Bill's old shotgun and she's not afraid to use it. Her exact words were that if she's the first one to catch up with Enaldo, she's going to knock him into next week and have him looking both ways for Sunday. And she told Madeline that none of us have to worry about her because she can still shoot the ears off a gnat if she has a mind to."

In the past, her turn of phrase might have made me smile. But not now. Aunt Hattie spoke colorfully, but she always meant what she said. She was stubborn. And that might put her at great risk.

"She also told me to tell you to keep your hind end right where it is. Said you're about as safe here as a long-tailed cat in a room full of rocking chairs."

"I agree."

I could not tell Leena Rose I was no safer in New York.

"She also told me she's going to give you a good talking to when you get back."

I hoped to live long enough to be scolded.

CHAPTER THIRTY-FOUR

There was a deadly drumbeat in my brain, as though I were watching a heartbeat monitor after the removal of life support. How many blips would there be before it was too late?

There was no sleep to be had. I could barely lie down for five minutes before my muscles had to move. I went over and over possibilities. But after a long, sleepless night, I had only one plan: Get to Giovanni as soon as possible.

The next morning, I trudged through pouring snow toward St. Anthony's, counting on Venecia to brave the elements since she told me she never missed a day of visiting. But it was likely that Devino and Giovanni had alerted her. After all, she had set up Giovanni's visit during a time she knew I would be there. There had been suspicion in Giovanni's eyes when I appeared from behind the bed. I wondered if Venecia was scolded for surprising him. I could only imagine the scene when Devino heard there was a nun in the room and he had not gone in the room first to clear it for his boss.

If I could just get to Venecia first, I could explain the situation to her. That I meant no one harm, that I just needed to talk with Giovanni and ask for mercy. I would beg Venecia to make sure I could talk with him today. I hoped she would help. She might, if I asked in front of Mariana.

Although the taxis could still manipulate the roads, the sidewalks were not completely clear. Large banks of snow were piled at intersections, making crossing the street tricky. In some places, the passage between the piles was only wide enough for one person at a time to step up on what should have been the curbing. People were still on the streets though. It was Tuesday, a workday. But the heavy snowfall had quieted the city more than usual.

I had to talk with Giovanni. There was risk to everyone around me now. Even Mariana. My head calculated multiple scenarios, but I could not fathom how things might work any more than I could have predicted Venecia calling me into Mariana's room that first day. I had to trust God's divine plan.

Trust is an exercise, not a feeling.

Grandfathers words came back every time my mind confronted me with a possible disastrous outcome. Every time I struggled to mentally overcome the rising fear in my mind. I could not afford to fail. I had been led this far. My warrior spirit pushed me, despite my insecurities. If Giovanni did not come to see his mother today, I would find him, even if I had to go to the restaurant to do it.

But I had deceived him and those closest to him. Giovanni might want me out of the picture before I could ever explain why. He was known to eliminate obstacles without blinking. And no one in New York knew my real identity. It would be easy to make me disappear.

If I were threatened and had the chance, I would say that I had mailed the whole story to the commonwealth attorney. I had not, but I had indeed left such a letter on my bed at the shelter with a dated note that read, "If I do not return in two days, please mail this." He would either believe me or have me murdered. Either way, everyone would be safe. Enaldo would no longer circle Colony Row.

The sleepless night had left me with an exaggerated startle response. Taxi horns made me jump. I gasped when another pedestrian accidently brushed my arm. The line, "Never take a knife to a gun fight," repeated in my head. All I had to battle Giovanni with was words. These were the arrows in my quiver. He had soldiers. Soldiers with an arsenal.

Although I arrived at St. Anthony's at my usual time, 8:30 a.m., the atmosphere inside was subdued. Susan was not in her place at the reception desk. There was the eerie quiet of a snow day. No one was in the halls as I walked to the locker room. I put the SOHO tote with my disguise back into my locker, although I could not fathom needing it again.

There were a few nurses at their stations, but no patients in the halls on the first floor. On the second floor, two patients pushed walkers. I thought about stopping by and saying good morning to Mrs. Garbino, but her door was shut, and I realized then that my anxiety was prompting me to procrastinate.

On the third floor, Dominic's door was shut as well. The snow had created too much of an obstacle for early morning visitors, and the unusual quiet gave me a sense of foreboding that I wished I could ignore. I climbed the last flight of stairs to the fifth floor. With all my contingency plans, I was sure of one thing: Despite the weather and the quiet, today was the day.

I had to make something happen.

CHAPTER THIRTY-FIVE

———— ••• —— ✳ —— ••• ————

I pushed open the stairwell door on the fifth floor, and it seemed all the activity of the other floors had repositioned itself in front of Mariana's room.

Nurses and doctors huddled outside of her room. Two of her favorite interns, both with stern faces, shook their heads as they listened intently to the doctors and nurses. The bevy of medical professionals blocked my view of at least ten of Mariana's family hovered in a second cluster behind them. There was no one left at the nurse's station. Everyone was attending to the mob boss's mother.

"Sister," I heard Venecia's voice pleading as she made her way around the medical professionals toward me where I stood frozen in the doorway. Tearstains of melted mascara spoke her distress. She looked years older than she had just the day before. And behind her, a man followed.

Devino.

I worked hard to keep my hand from flying to my mouth and my feet from flying through the door. What now? I could ask Venecia to wait just a moment, I must have dropped something on the steps. I could run through the building, out onto the street, fast as I could to the police station. I had practiced the escape route many times in my head. But Devino would follow. I could outrun him. I was sure of that. Unless he had men planted and waiting outside the building.

But was this not the chance I had waited for? If Devino was here, then Giovanni was too. If I ran now, I would never again be allowed this close to him. I would be running for the rest of my life, however long that might be. They would search twice as hard now that I had infiltrated the family, and they would surely take hostages from Colony Row.

The scene played out in slow motion, my thoughts in warp speed. My energy surged, then drained. Devino turned his head to look behind him. I followed the direction and saw Giovanni emerging from the cluster near his mother's door. Giovanni nodded, and both men moved toward me, their eyes cold as steel. Devino slipped his right hand inside his jacket and kept it there. He was gripping a pistol. I knew he was. He was two steps behind Venecia, who was wiping at her tears. His hulking frame loomed over her petite one.

They had no idea what to expect of me. The slightest movement, and I was sure Devino would pull that gun. He would likely shoot me, even with witnesses present. Perhaps he had an extra gun, a clean one to plant. For all they knew, I was already armed.

Synchronicity. This too had to be divine timing. I had to trust it.

I would not run.

I had come to speak to Giovanni. My date with destiny was now.

Grandfather's words flew into my head: *God within me is more powerful than everything around me.* And as though a coin had been flipped, a steely faith steadied me.

"Sister," Venecia cried as she reached me. Her cool, thin hand reached out, the cluster of diamond rings contrasting against the black of my tunic as she grasped my forearm. "It's MiMi." She spoke the words without falter and then, as though it had taken all her strength, she appeared to crumble into herself. I reached out to support her, and she collapsed on my shoulder.

Devino took a giant step and came behind her, his hand still firmly planted inside his left jacket pocket. Behind him, Giovanni closed in. Both men watched my hands, which I placed on Venecia' s shoulders where they could be seen.

Venecia shuddered, her shoulders heaving with quiet sadness.

Was my precious friend dying? I held Mariana's daughter-in-law and prayed it was not so.

Venecia pulled away and looked me in the eyes. Her face was filled with sorrow. I carefully let my arms fall to my sides. Giovanni moved forward and put his arm around his petite wife, enveloping her. She turned toward him. "I will be okay. I'm just so glad Sister Rita is here. She can help us pray."

"I need a word with the sister," he said, his eyes never leaving mine. Venecia nodded her approval. "You were headed to the restroom when the sister came. And you could be a love, stretch your legs and get me a cup of coffee."

Venecia looked at him and nodded. Then she turned her eyes to me. "Sister Rita, would you like a cup?"

I shook my head.

Once Venecia was out of sight, Giovanni looked to Devino and nodded toward the door behind me, then grasped my arm and forcefully turned me around, herding me into the stairwell. Immediately, my mind conjured an image of my long skirts, the two killers at my back, and their ability to pitch me over the railing. Did a tragic "accident" await me inside?

CHAPTER THIRTY-SIX

My legs wobbled, but the grip Giovanni had on my arm assured me I would make it. Giovanni pushed me by the arm ahead of him. Devino followed.

I could think of no way out. I would likely die here. I could not get my breath. Let alone plead for mercy. I was paralyzed in their presence.

Giovanni shoved me roughly against the stair rail. The hard metal rod pressed deeply into my stomach. As I opened my mouth to speak, to beg for a moment to explain, someone called loudly from the other side of the door.

"Sister Rita? Mr. Giovanni?"

I was afraid to turn around, but Giovanni quickly grabbed me again and twisted my arm in the direction of the door. My arm burned with his grip.

When Devino opened the door, Dr. Donnetta pushed it farther, his face appearing around its corner. "Sir, I need to speak with Sister Rita for a few minutes. I hope you don't mind, Mr. Giovanni, but the sister has been visiting quite a few of my patients, and I urgently need to catch her up. I only have a few moments before I start my rounds." His face was serious. He looked from Devino to Giovanni, never once at me.

"Is Dominic okay?" I asked. "His door was shut when I came up this morning." I made my eyebrows frown in fake concern for Dominic, yet I was fully aware that all four of us knew the conversation was phony and contrived. What a chance Dr. Donnetta had taken interrupting

Giovanni.

Dr. Donnetta opened the door wider and stepped partway inside. "Yes. He is okay, but we need to talk. And we need to talk about Mrs. Giovanni as well." With this, Dr. Donnetta looked at the two men. "Mr. Giovanni, as I'm sure you know, Sister Rita is here twice a day with your mother. She's performed invaluable services for her. Everyone on this floor believes she is the reason your mother has made such a rapid recovery."

Giovanni's grip on my arm tightened. I tried not to flinch.

Two male interns approached from behind Dr. Donnetta. One of them spoke loudly over his shoulder. "Hi, Sister Rita. I'm glad you are here. We're going to need you."

Giovanni's grip loosened. Slightly.

"Mr. Giovanni, I wonder if I might accompany you and Sister Rita into your mother's room. I need to show her a few things she should keep an eye on. I hate to interrupt, but if all of you could just follow me."

Giovanni looked briefly at Devino and then nodded his approval and released my arm. I stifled the urge to rub it with my other hand.

We followed Dr. Donnetta through the hallway. The family and group of medical professionals surrounding Mariana's door parted like the Red Sea.

Dr. Donnetta entered the darkened room first and addressed the head nurse standing by her bed. "Wanda, all of you can step out for a minute." He stood aside and she and the other nurses left. Dr. Donnetta went to Mariana's bedside and bent over his patient. Giovanni moved around the bed to the other side and stationed himself facing the door, where Devino stood. Both watched keenly my every move.

When Dr. Donnetta straightened, I could finally see my friend. She looked frailer than ever in the soft glow of the headwall luminaire, and as pale as the bed linens around her. She was hooked up to numerous monitors. Her breathing was so shallow I could barely detect any movement. Oxygen ran through a cannula under her nose, cables and leads came from beneath her blue silk comforter to the heart monitor over her head. I could hear her heartbeat and see it register on the screen with her blood pressure and pulse rate. The sight of her left me dizzy. It was my presence in her life that had created this. It had to have been. She had been fine before. I grasped her bedrails with both hands.

Dr. Donnetta leaned over her again to adjust some tubing and began instructing me.

"Sister Rita, Mrs. Giovanni had a heart attack yesterday evening. We sedated her. She has not yet regained consciousness. The sooner she does, the better. Since Mrs. Giovanni values your presence so highly, I assume you'll be spending quite a bit of time with her until then. She will need it, now more than ever. And goodness knows you would be better for her than a hired sitter.

"Don't let the tubing get crimped or coiled." He pointed to the digital equipment circling her bed at the top. "If the monitors begin to hum with crisis, we'll be alerted in the nurse's station. But we need you to press her call button, right here, still." He pointed to the white button with the red tip that had been on Mariana's bed since I had been visiting. Nothing new. I looked from the tubing to Giovanni. His icy stare signaled he knew this as well.

"Her family has been here all night. I have gone over all this with them." He looked at Giovanni. "What's most important is that we don't allow her to become upset or stressed for any reason. She needs rest and peace. I believe Sister Rita is the perfect prescription. Our charts show dramatic drops in her blood pressure after each of her visits, not to mention how motivated she has been during therapy since Sister Rita began spending time with her."

The doctor's voice had begun to strain. Like every other staff member in the hospital, he knew who he was dealing with, and he knew he was endangering his own life now, in trying to protect mine. I lowered my head and squeezed the rail for strength and began to pray.

Dr. Donnetta touched my hand. "Are you all right, Sister Rita?"

"I will be. I can be here for her. I will not leave. This has all just taken me by surprise." I raised my eyes to meet the doctor's. "Thank you for briefing me. I want to help."

Dr. Donnetta looked at Giovanni. "Your mother is a strong woman. But still, with the positive change in your mother's health and attitude toward recovery since Sister Rita began working with her, I would suggest you make her presence mandatory."

Giovanni gave a small nod, though his expression remained unmoved, his eyes locked to mine.

A buzz from Dr. Donnetta's waistband drew his attention. He pulled out his pager, read it, and hit a button. He fastened it back to his belt and allowed his white lab coat to fall back over it. Just as he opened his mouth to speak, a red light on the intercom above Mariana's bed lit up and a voice emanated from it. "Dr. Donnetta, you are needed immediately at the nurse's station on the third floor."

Dr. Donnetta looked at Giovanni, then me. He spoke in the direction of the intercom. "I'll be right there." He adjusted a tube next to the bed and turned to me. "I still need to speak with you about the other patients. I'll return as soon as I'm able."

I nodded.

The doctor left, and I moved to stand in the spot he had occupied. Alone with the mob again. The predators in reach of their prey. The thought of Devino at my back petrified me. I imagined how quickly he might end my life with a silenced weapon, then plant a gun on me. It was not as if Mariana could be a witness.

I looked down at my friend, her face so tiny, haloed in soft gray curls against her pillow. Although I knew her strength, I could only see how powerless she was, and I realized for the first time how alike we were. We both had only God to save us now.

Giovanni reached out and took his mother's hand, and for the first time took his eyes off of me. I took her other hand into mine and rubbed it gently, fighting tears.

"We have a problem," Giovanni said at a low volume, making his Grim Reaper voice more ominous. I looked up at him. He glanced at his sleeping mother, then back at me. "My staff tells me they were unable to vet you as a nun. You are clearly not who you say you are, and you have shown up in too many places too many times." He paused and blinked. "I'll give you one chance to explain."

My thoughts returned to the night of the potluck. Megan had said I should listen to my heart and be bold. "Mr. Giovanni, I love your mother." I looked over at the sleeping Mariana, then back at him. I had spoken my truth, and it resonated deeply in my being.

Giovanni's dark eyes did not waver.

"It is true that I am not who I have said." I spoke with such confidence it surprised even me. I was finding that truth was easy to speak. Unconsciously I rubbed Mariana's hand. She stirred slightly so I stopped. Glancing at her, I noticed that her eyes fluttered. I looked up to see if Giovanni had noticed, but his eyes were again locked onto mine. I straightened and prepared to release my final quiver.

"Mr. Giovanni, my name is Emerson Grace Coffee. I came to New York . . . I came to New York to find you. To speak with you, that is. To ask you for your help."

A glint in his eyes. The first change since he shoved me into the stairwell, though I could not tell what it meant.

"Sir, one of your employees thinks that I saw something I did not see. I needed to find you and tell you I am no threat to anyone. I had faith that when you heard me, you would understand . . . and that you would help me. After getting to know your mother, I am assured you come from good people. I am asking for your help." I swallowed hard and worked to maintain eye contact with Giovanni. To show him my confidence in my story. He did not respond, so I continued.

"Just before I moved from New York back to Virginia, I was out with a friend. I understand that . . ." Why was it so hard to say his name? I took a deep breath for courage. "I understand that Anthony Enaldo bumped into me . . . But I did not notice him. In fact, I hardly remember the incident at all. Still, US marshals arrived at my cabin and told me a video of the encounter had put me in Enaldo's crosshairs. So I came to ask you . . . I came to ask you to make it clear to Enaldo that I saw nothing, that I know nothing, that I cannot testify to anything. This is what I told the marshals when I refused witness protection. I am no threat to Enaldo or to anyone else. Sir, you are the only person that can help me.

"Mr. Giovanni, I believe that everyone has a place in their heart that hears truth and honors it. My story is truth. Please, Mr. Giovanni, will you help me?"

Suddenly, Mariana squeezed my hand. I jumped and turned to look at her.

She was looking back at me.

"Mama!"

Giovanni leaned over and held his mother's face in both hands. He kissed her forehead, then smoothed her hair back while she looked into his eyes. After a moment, she raised her right hand and made a loose fist. It trembled as she laid it on her chest then raised it slightly and allowed it to collapse against her chest again.

My voice came out a whisper. "That is a sign we practiced. She is saying she loves you."

"I love you too, Mama." He continued to stroke her hair.

Just as Agnes said, I was seeing the human behind the malevolence.

Giovanni tenderly hugged his mother's shoulders, then stood and looked at her for a long moment before turning his eyes to me. In his silence, I could see his struggle. A fork in the road. As Dr. Goff had advised, I needed to allow time for the chemicals to work.

Mariana moved, drawing our attention. She made a fist again, and with great effort, tapped her heart twice, this time looking at me.

I leaned close to her. "I love you too," I whispered, then swiped my tears with the back of my hand.

Tears made their way down her pale cheeks toward the cannula.

Tissues and other medical supplies filled her two nightstands now. Everything else had been moved to the dresser. I reached for a tissue and patted her cheeks. "You are so loved. Do you know that?"

Mariana nodded gently, then looked at her son. He rubbed her hand, and her eyebrows knitted together in concern. She made a sound. She wanted to talk.

Giovanni leaned closer and spoke gently to his mother. "Mama, don't try and talk. The nurses gave you some medicine to help you rest, but you are going to be okay now. You need to rest, though, Mama."

Mariana blinked in recognition. She looked at him, and then moved her eyes to me and made the sound again.

"Do you know what she's saying?" Giovanni asked.

I leaned over Mariana and listened to her make the sound again, watching closely the movements of her mouth.

"Are you saying please?"

Mariana blinked acknowledgment, then moved her head slightly to nod yes. She looked from him to me again.

Understanding dawned over Giovanni's face. "Mama, did you hear us talking? Me and the sister?"

Mariana nodded and blinked yes. Her face contorted in concern. She made the sound for "please" again.

The muscles in Giovanni's jaw tightened and released. He rubbed his mother's hand gently in both of his. This was his vulnerable spot, as Madeline would have said. My best opportunity to secure my safety and the safety of everyone else on Colony Row. It was now or never.

"Mariana, I came to New York to speak to your son." She looked to me. "I only planned on meeting with him in the hallway and asking him to talk with me. But Venecia called me into your room the first day I was here. So, I met you instead. I could not know I would come to love you, and you me. But I am grateful for it, and I understand why God put the two of us together."

Mariana nodded gently while her son and I stood in silence. The chemicals were working.

Giovanni stroked the side of his mother's face. "Don't worry, Mama. I won't let anything happen to your sister. I promise you. You rest. You've got nothing to worry about. Just rest."

I patted Mariana's hand and waited as Giovanni kissed her forehead, then walked around the foot of her bed. His back was rigid, and his anger appeared only sheathed. He nodded to Devino, who turned to exit, then motioned for me to step between them.

He had said the words I wanted to hear, but could I trust them?

CHAPTER THIRTY-SEVEN

——— ••• —— ✳ —— ••• ———

When he reached the window at the end of the corridor, we were alone. He did not sit in the chairs or tell me to sit.

He turned to look at me, his face stern. His voice was a low growl. "I am troubled by how easily you got near my family. My sick mother, of all people. Had you meant her harm . . ." Giovanni turned to look out the window, his broad back to me. "It won't happen again."

I waited in silence. No words seemed appropriate.

"No one finds out my security was breached." He turned sharply to face me. "Are we clear?"

I nodded. "Of course."

He looked me in the eyes without waver. "I made a promise to my mother. I will keep that promise. No harm of any sort will ever come to you or to your people . . . Or your mountains." He turned back around and again stood with his back to me, looking out of the window.

My people? My mountains? So he knew about me, and he knew Enaldo was there.

"Thank you."

"You have managed quite a feat."

His voice was tinged with something other than rage. After a moment he turned to look at me as though he was seeing me for the first time. "Are you even Catholic?"

"No, sir. I am not. I *am* Christian, however."

"Why a nun?" he asked.

"I thought it would be a good disguise."

Giovanni frowned. "My mother has good instincts. You've spent a lot of time with her. I expected her to be angry with you. You deceived her too."

"I think she was beginning to doubt me. She seemed suspicious when she wanted to say the Guardian Angel prayer for you, and I did not know it."

I saw a glint of recognition in his eyes. Giovanni turned back to the window.

I stood in silence for what seemed like forever.

"She obviously cares about you," he said without turning.

"Sir, I care about her as well."

Giovanni turned to me. The light moved in his eyes. I could see his mother's spirit in them.

"You outwitted a lot of smart people. Some of the best."

I held his gaze.

"I will keep the promise I made to my mother. But only if you guarantee me your silence."

I nodded. "I will tell no one, sir. I assure you."

"Does anyone else know?" he asked.

I shook my head. "No one would have approved."

"Then go home. Give me an hour to contact my people. There are four of us that know. Mama isn't talking, and my guard won't. So, if this gets out, it's on you. Then all bets are off."

I nodded.

With that he turned and walked past me.

"Sir," I said.

He stopped, turned and looked at me, his face bare.

"Thank you. But . . . I would like to stay. I would like to be here with your mother. She needs me now more than ever."

"She doesn't know you."

"Actually, she knows a lot. I told her much about my childhood and the ways of my people. I would like to stay until she is stronger."

Giovanni bored holes in me with his eyes. The chemicals were working.

"She needs me," I added confidently.

He blinked. Taking a deep breath, Giovanni looked down the hall to Devino and gave a signal. He looked back at me. "Okay, you stay. But you do not talk to my mother about my business. Even if she asks. And you remain undercover. When you are ready to leave, let her down easy and tell my wife a story she will believe. I feel certain you can come up with something."

I nodded. I imagined humor in his last statement, although he had not smiled.

Giovanni started to walk off and then turned to add, "You don't look like one in that habit, but you are a warrior. And a smart one."

CHAPTER THIRTY-EIGHT

The aroma of rich foods filled the fellowship hall at potluck Tuesday, giving me a sense of home I had not expected. After a month away from Colony Row, everything about being back, even the small talk with the artists, created connection on a deeper level than I could have guessed.

Grandfather would have been proud. I had stayed in New York three weeks after meeting with Giovanni to help care for Mariana. She was recovering quickly, and out of what seemed like love for me, she had let me know she thought I should go home, assuring me she would be okay. Later, when I told Venecia that I had been reassigned, Venecia looked disappointed but said she understood. Mariana gave me a conspiratorial wink.

Aunt Hattie had been more than happy to attend the potluck as a celebration of my return, and was granted the honor of starting the meeting. After Madeline called the meeting to order and recognized her, Aunt Hattie looked left and right down the long dining table from her position at its center as she spoke.

"Folks, I got more to be grateful for than I can say grace over. We've got our girl back safe and sound, and she says no New York City hooligans are gon' come near us now. Madeline says y'all been asking how that happened. Well, I can't tell how she knows. I asked her my own self seven ways to Sunday and come up emptier than a rain barrel in a drought. And if she was gon' tell anybody, it woulda be me."

Aunt Hattie's voice was stern. The artists glanced at each other as though to compare reactions.

"Now Emerson ain't one to do a lotta talking, so there ain't no way she's gon' waste her breath telling no lie. Never has. Never will. It's over 'cause she says it's over." Having said her piece, Aunt Hattie sat back, smoothing her apron over her knees, then crossed her arms over her midsection. My breath came easier. She had at least silenced everyone's curiosity.

Aunt Hattie had said many of the same things when she invited Rick and Madeline and me to dinner the night before. Rick had argued that I had been home for two days, and the marshals, the FBI, and Virginia police had not had any word that could confirm what I had told them, so he would remain hyperalert until they did. Aunt Hattie patted his hand and leaned in close to him to say, "Won't be long before you know your bets is safer placed on Emerson than anyone else."

Rick was quiet as he took in her words. When he looked at Madeline, she was nodding her agreement. He shook his head, the side of his mouth creeping up in a half smile. "Okay, fine. I would like to know, but I accept that I never will." He looked over at me and my stomach tightened. "I think you might be more respected than anyone I've ever known."

"That's just 'cause you didn't know her granddaddy," Aunt Hattie offered. "But Emerson is just like him. They were two peas in a pod."

I could understand why my news was difficult to accept. No one else had all the pieces.

And they never would.

The artists at the potluck, however, did not seem nearly as concerned about how I had secured safety. After Aunt Hattie spoke, Madeline asked the artists if anyone had anything else to say. After a moment, Gideon summed it up: "All's well that ends well."

"All right then," Madeline said. "Well, the business part of our potluck this week is going to be short." She sat directly across from Aunt Hattie, and took care to bend over her plate and look up and down the table as she had done. "Just a few items. Both artists we discussed the past few weeks have accepted residences. We have the cartoonist who calls himself Barney Spice moving into the Pierce Place. As you know since he sent each of us some of his past collections, he is a humorist and wants to write about an art colony.

"Stewie will be leaving soon, and the first of the month we have a choreographer, Elleane Avante-A'light, coming to live in Pleasant Grove. She creates human art with outdoor paint, music, and dance. She wants to create what she calls a mountain palette, so we'll see what that's all about. And the last thing is that Jons and Miah arrived safely in New York yesterday for Miah's audition for a summer internship at the Met."

The artists looked from one to another again and nodded. Perhaps they were beginning to jell.

"And if you'll indulge me . . ." Madeline placed her arm around Deetsy, seated to her right, and Bunny to her left. "The girls were able to join us tonight thanks to their new foster and soon-to-be-adoptive parents. And since I'm their unofficial grandmother, I have to add that I am so proud of them. They have been visiting Maple Grove twice a week with their new sisters for riding lessons, and they are becoming wonderful equestrians."

Deetsy looked up at Madeline, and as if it were the most natural thing in the world for her to do, she smiled. I felt bubbles of delight. Her smile was just as I had imagined it would be.

"I'm a 'questrian?" Bunny asked, frowning.

Deetsy leaned forward to look past Madeline. "That means a horse rider."

Bunny smiled, her nose crinkling. "I'm a 'questrian, sure nuff, 'cause I love ridin' Queenie."

Madeline squeezed the girls' shoulders. Both had changed so radically in the month since I left for my mission. They were now impeccably dressed, their hair, no longer dull and unkempt, was shining with health and beautifully styled, and Madeline said they had been joyous from the moment they learned that their school nurse, Doris Wade, and her husband had petitioned to adopt them. Their new sisters, Kimberly in Deetsy's class and Linda in Bunny's, had apparently pled with their mother to pack the girls a lunch each day, resulting in them visiting the nurse's office for daily hugs, support, and enough food to take home for snacks. As Madeline said, it was a match made in heaven.

Dr. Goff cleared his throat, and we all looked his way. "I truly hoped to have incorporated this adventure into a script for my serial murder movies, but without a proper ending, writing this story would be pointless." His voice resonated his disappointment. He continued, "Emerson, it would make your character the star of a movie."

"Does that mean she would act in the movie?" Megan asked.

Dr. Goff looked my way. "Do you have acting skills?"

When I laughed and said an emphatic, "Noooo," the group lightened. It was true that I could imitate a nun. But only if lives depended on it. "But I am curious about something myself."

Everyone looked my way.

"I heard that Agnes and Megan reported seeing Enaldo's car—"

"I'll explain." Agnes scowled. She straightened in her seat and laid her pen firmly on her writing pad.

"Agnes, you don't have—" Megan began.

"No. It's time. I want to."

Megan sat back.

"We have been walking late at night for more than a month."

Gideon frowned, looking at his wife. "So you have a secret life now?"

Megan drew in her breath to respond, but Agnes spoke first.

"Give her a break, will you? You of all people should know what a jewel you're married to, but you're too busy being intimidated by her." Agnes turned and looked at me. "Before we started walking, I kept finding things at my door. Comic books, funny movies, joke books. Little gifts, as if I had a secret pal or something. But I don't like secrets, and I don't need a *pal*." She said the last word with a sneer. "Then organic food started showing up. An apple, kale chips, some sort of Brussels sprout salad, DHA, cod-liver oil. Things like that."

The artists looked at one another as if they might pinpoint the culprit, and eventually all landed on Stewie.

"Don't look at me. Even I'm not that odd." Stewie said, looking toward Agnes. "And I'm pretty odd."

"It isn't odd at all," Agnes insisted. "Not if you have cancer. And somebody in this close-knit group of ours was observant enough to realize I do." Everyone now turned to look at Megan. The self-professed attention-deficit queen had picked up on it when no one else had.

Agnes cleared her throat and continued. "With all the healthy things, I figured it had to be Megan. So I walked across the street when she was outside and told her I'd figured it out." Agnes looked at Megan. "I may not have been so nice about it."

A few of the artists looked down at their plates. No argument there.

"I told her I wasn't anybody's pity case. And I wanted to know how she knew. So . . . you tell them, Megan," Agnes said and with a sweep of her hand moved the focus to Megan, who sat erect and motionless, as though she were in trouble.

"Well, my mom had cancer a few years before we . . . before I got married. I helped her with her macrobiotic diet. My mom . . . she stopped laughing when she got treatment. She needed humor. You know, there are studies that show laughter helps cancer patients. Even though Agnes writes humor, I thought she could use a laugh that she didn't have to write."

Megan looked at Agnes, and Agnes motioned for her to continue.

"Anyways, I also noticed that Agnes didn't have the right color. She looked . . . well, she looked like a person looks when they're going through chemo."

Stewie asked, "How in the world did you figure that out? We only see each other at potlucks on Tuesdays."

"Well, I'm an artist. I notice things like color." Megan was forgetting she was in a room with others who would notice color.

"Anyway, my mom had a hard time sleeping at night when she

was going through chemo. One night I was sitting on the porch steps, looking up at all the stars, because out here in the boonies you see a zillion of them, and I noticed Agnes was still up. So, I just decided to go over and see if she wanted to go for a walk." Megan raised and dropped her shoulders and then sat back.

"Who are you? Do I even know you?" Gideon asked incredulously. "You've been sitting outside at night? And walking?"

Megan looked at him, hurt registering across her features.

"Correct, Gideon, you do *not* know her," Agnes barked. "This one has a heart of gold. But it's wasted on you."

"Agnes, hun, I am so sorry," Madeline said. "With everything that's been going on, I didn't realize. How are you now, and is there anything CAT can do for you?"

"I'm in remission. Megan went with me to the last PET scan and I'm all clear." Agnes picked up her pen. "So now you all know. Change of subject, puh-lease."

Aunt Hattie leaned forward. "Well, you're lookin' right as rain now. I wish I woulda known, but I'm gon' make it up to you. And I ain't takin' no for an answer."

Agnes looked up with a frown, then her face relaxed. "You don't need to do that, but I'll go easy on you if you do."

"Well then, where were we?" Madeline asked.

I leaned forward from where I sat across from Bunny. "I have something to say. I want to thank all of you. Every single one. Deetsy and Bunny are here tonight because they had a huge part when they reported the car and the license plates. They also helped the rest of you as you cleaned up my ancestors' cemetery. When you did that, you saved my mountains. There is no way I can ever thank you enough."

They all shot furtive looks, one to the other.

"I think there is something you all are not telling me."

Bunny piped up. "I know what it is."

Deetsy leaned forward to scowl at her.

"Please, tell me, Bunny," I asked.

"You ain't even gon' believe it, 'cause I didn't think she liked none of us. Except Megan maybe."

This time, Deetsy scowled harder.

"Well, she don't," Bunny said in protest, then looked back at me. "It was Miss Agnes."

Agnes spoke up from the end of the table. "That's all right, Bunny. I love honesty, and you are the most honest person I know. You go ahead and tell your story."

"Okay. Well, what I was fixin' to say was that it was Miss Agnes that got us all to workin'. She even paid for somebody to bring us all a picnic. We had ice cream and everything. And Miss Agnes even gave Deetsy a hug when she fell and hurt her knee." Bunny spoke as though they had all witnessed a miracle. In fact, they might have. And when Deetsy smiled for the second time that night, I knew I had as well.

"I only did it to keep the newspapers from flying all over my yard," Agnes insisted.

All around the table, everyone smiled now.

"What?" Agnes demanded.

"Agnes, hun, I don't think you can play that mean card anymore. We all have your number now," Madeline said with a note of humor in her voice.

Agnes sneered. "Whatever," she said, then returned to her pen and notebook.

I did not plan to say what I said next. But when I did, an unexpected joy filled me, and I sensed once again that if I turned, I would see Grandfather's spirit standing behind me. I felt his presence so strongly, in fact, that I nearly did turn. But I did not. Now I understood that even if I could not see him, he was there. He was with me in everything I did. And his eyes were closed, and he was smiling and nodding twice.

"Everyone, I would like to have next Tuesday's potluck on top of Easterbrook. We can have a cookout. And I would love it if you all came early to take in the view."

Agnes cleared her throat and lifted her focus from her notepad. "This time I'll be the first to speak." She looked me in the eyes. "I accept your invitation, Emerson, and I look forward to it."

CHAPTER THIRTY-NINE

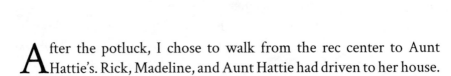

After the potluck, I chose to walk from the rec center to Aunt Hattie's. Rick, Madeline, and Aunt Hattie had driven to her house. Though the night had been busy, we all decided it was the perfect date. The anniversary of the day Aunt Hattie met Lenore Lee and saved her life. We would gather and open her jar from the cave.

As I crested the hill past Maple Grove, the moonlight reflected dully off of a vehicle parked at Stopping Place. Joey Horseshoe sat on the pickup's blue hood, leaning back on the windshield, looking up at the stars . . . or perhaps in an alcohol-induced sleep.

My moccasins allowed me to walk undetected. When I was within yards of his truck, I stood, feet shoulder-width apart, and cleared my throat.

He bolted upright. "Geesh, Emerson. You gotta sneak up on a person like that?"

"Are you waiting for me?"

"What do you think?"

I did not reply.

"I heard you were back in town, and since you told me I can't come up Easterbrook again, I had to wait here." He swung his legs to the side, slid off the hood, and came to stand in front of me, three feet away. He hoisted himself up much straighter than his normal posture. I wanted to laugh. The fact that I had stood up to a mob boss and his soldiers with nothing but a nun's habit to protect me made standing up to Joey Horseshoe no challenge at all.

There was silence between us in the moonlight. I could not smell alcohol. That was a plus.

"We got business, sister." His tone was low and threatening.

I wanted to caution him not to call me sister, but that was a conversation for another time. Another time, and another battleground of my own choosing.

I waited.

"You cleaned up the cemetery to save yourself. Don't think we don't know."

I said nothing.

"So when I heard you were back, I figured it was only right of family to give you a warning. You're not as smart as you think." He bobbed his head, sneering. "Two years ago, we got a firm commitment from the people who are going to fund the casino. They have money coming out their ears, and they told us that cemetery or not, they have attorneys that can take you down. They can find loopholes in that ancient deed of your great-great-granddaddy's, now that you have no tribe. They said they'll make sure you deed the mountains to our tribe so that we can build that casino. And they. Don't. Play."

But as long as I was alive, there was still one more member of my tribe. Me. The Endling.

"That deed was written when small tribes got along, Joey. We buried our dead together and watched over their graves together. We were part of a bigger community back then. The Native community. It is perhaps a good thing they did not see what was to come. If they could, they would have been so ashamed."

"Well, that deed won't hold water, Emerson. And these guys are gonna come after you if you try."

I tried to sound nonchalant, even though my heart betrayed me. Still, his words did not concern me as much as they would have just a month before.

"You sound very sure of yourself, Mr. Horseshoe. Like this is a good plan for you. But it must be a better plan for them. The odds are always with the house."

Joey straightened, his back stiff. "They fund it, build it, and run it. We get a percentage, per cap, and don't have to do anything."

It was just like Joey to honor a plan where he would not have to do anything.

"Now that you're back, I'm gonna turn 'em loose on you. Just thought I'd warn you. You may as well play nice and be done with it." He put his hands on his hips and widened his stance.

I reached up and unbuttoned the top button on my coat, dug with my fingers around my collarbone and pulled out a gold chain. The bear bone totem with four eagles dangled at my fingertips. "Joey," I began, strength and peace increasing in exponential proportion as I spoke. "I left here Emerson Grace Coffee. I returned Emerson Grace Four Eagles. I am a warrior woman. Now *you* are the one that has been warned."

Joey's shoulders slumped just a bit. He pulled his hair behind his shoulders with one hand. "And who named you Four Eagles?"

"Grandfather," I answered without pause.

He frowned, then after a moment, he challenged. "You may think you're better than me, Emerson. You might even think you're smarter than me. But you aren't smarter than the man who wants these mountains."

"Who is this man you are so proud of? Are you afraid to say his name?"

"I'm not afraid. He's on *my* side. You're the one that needs to be afraid. He's the mob, and he *owns* New York City. You'll see. Look up Ginnova Giovanni."

The urge to laugh was so intense that one nearly slipped out. I waited a moment before speaking to ensure that my voice would hold no trace of humor. But before I could, a barred owl sounded above our heads, and Joey jumped. I smiled in the moonlight as I reflected on the medicine and a poem I would teach the girls:

Something ends when owl appears,
but endings do not all bring tears.

The struggle to save my mountains had ended. Now another sensation I had never known overcame me. But it was not as if I had acquired a new emotion. It was more like a fire had been extinguished. A fire I had struggled to control for as long as I could recall. Perhaps I had never quite recognized its challenge against my serenity until it had dissipated. My worry was gone. Peace filled the void. There was only one soul I wished to bear witness to such a triumph, and I felt again as though that soul and all our ancestors were with me at Stopping Place. In my heart I could hear him saying, "Remember you are loved, Little Bit."

"Good night, Joey," I said, then turned to walk across Colony Row to Aunt Hattie's driveway.

CHAPTER FORTY

———— ••• — ❀ — ••• ————

"I know it wasn't the best'a plans to open Lenore Lee's jar tonight since we had the potluck, but it's the closest thing I have to some sort of anniversary date," Aunt Hattie said, "and I'd like to get this done before I go visit her grave up Easterbrook tomorrow." She looked at Madeline, then Rick. A huge smile swept across her face when her eyes found me. "Emerson, you gon' love this. That granddaddy of yours wanted me to tell you something after you solved Lenore Lee's mystery. I'm thinking this here is the last step." Her eyes twinkled as she leaned forward. "He said to tell you that your mountains is full of mystery, and one a them mysteries is another hunt."

I gasped, and energy poured through me.

Aunt Hattie lowered her chin. "And he was mighty particular that I tell you this next part in these here words . . . that 'on that day, you will know where to look on your lonesome.'" She sat back with a satisfied smile.

Adrenaline cleared my head like a pot of strong coffee. Another mystery. Grandfather had been thinking of me. I hoped his last months were filled with the distraction and knowing how joyous I would be when Aunt Hattie shared his message.

"On your lonesome" was not a phrase Grandfather used, though. He was referencing Lonesome Chimney Trail, so named because the only thing left standing from a long-ago homestead was the chimney.

The three of them must have been waiting patiently while I

thought, because when I looked at them, they were all watching me.

"That is really good news, Aunt Hattie."

"I knew it was gon' make you happy. Okay. Well, now. This here is Lenore Lee's night. So, let's get to it."

Aunt Hattie moved her hand to the galvanized top of the colbalt-blue half-gallon mason jar. She tried to twist, but it did not budge. She handed the jar to Rick. "Mama always said can't never could do nothing. But these old hands can't open that jar."

With one hand, Rick held the jar firm against his chest and used the other to unscrew the inch-thick top. He placed it back in front of Aunt Hattie.

"Thank you kindly, Rick," Aunt Hattie said.

"Well, we know Hattie Mae didn't peek," Madeline said.

"Nah. These old hands done got weak as kittens. Besides, this here needs witnessing."

She pulled off the top of the jar and laid it to the side. Tilting the jar toward her, she reached in and pulled out a folded piece of pale flowered cloth and held it against her cheek. "You done found her treasure all right. This here's the apron I let her make on that old treadle sewing machine. She was so proud." She laid the apron on the table and unfolded it to reveal a 5-inch plastic kewpie doll, the red heart on its chest still clear with the words "Kewpie, Germany," written inside of it. When she looked up at us, tears were forming in her eyes. "I knew she loved it 'cause she kept it up under her pillow." She set the doll down on the placemat and touched its face with her index finger. "I'm proud as a possum that she thought that much of it."

Rick and I shared a look and a smile.

As Aunt Hattie reached into the pockets sewn into the bottom edge of Lenore Lee's apron, she retrieved two large pieces of topaz and amethyst and laid them on the placemat. "She found these at Mineral Springs on Easterbrook, I'll warrant you," she said knowingly. "And these here is big pieces. Real treasures."

She reached into another pocket and pulled out three arrowheads and a palm-sized stone, thick on one side and flat on the other. She turned the stone over and held it up.

"Scraping tool for hides," I offered. "She was smart to recognize it as a treasure."

"Now don't that just take the cake? I wouldn'ta known." Aunt Hattie nodded and placed the rocks on the placemat. She turned the jar toward her and looked inside. Her hands proved too large to reach whatever it was, and turning the jar upside down did not dislodge it from its place. Aunt Hattie rose from her chair, went into the kitchen, and got a set of tongs. Standing over the jar, she inserted the tongs and pulled out a thick piece of yellowed folded paper, curled upward where it had conformed to the round bottom of the jar.

"Now what have we got here? 'Cause that child could neither read nor write. I don't reckon I ever saw her with a piece of paper. And I know for certain I didn't send her none neither."

Aunt Hattie pulled the folded paper apart as we all unconsciously rose in our chairs to bend and look. Along the top of the page, in uneven script, were the words Crawl, Crow, and Easterbrook.

Aunt Hattie unfolded the paper again, her eyes widening. "Emerson, them bank robbers that was rumored to hide their treasure in a cave up on Crawl Mountain—they musta been real," she said as she turned the paper toward us. We took a collective breath as her finger pointed to a rudimentary map under the inscription for Crawl Mountain. "'Cause looky here. X marks the spot."

The End